SHARP

Bernard Cornwell was b
Essex, and now lives ma
He has sold over five million copies of his books and is
translated in nine languages. As well as the Sharpe series
he is author of the bestselling Warlord trilogy about King
Arthur and the King Alfred series. Bernard Cornwell was
awarded an OBE in 2006.

For more information visit *www.bernardcornwell.net*

For exclusive updates on your favourite HarperCollins
authors visit *www.AuthorTracker.co.uk*

BERNARD CORNWELL

Sharpe's Company

Richard Sharpe and the
Siege of Badajoz,
January to April 1812

HARPER

This novel is entirely a work of fiction. The names,
characters and incidents portrayed in it are the work
of the author's imagination. Any resemblance to actual
persons, living or dead, events or localities
is entirely coincidental.

Harper
An imprint of HarperCollins*Publishers*
77–85 Fulham Palace Road,
Hammersmith, London W6 8JB

www.harpercollins.co.uk

This paperback edition 2008

1

Previously published in paperback by Fontana 1983
Reprinted eleven times

First published in Great Britain
by Collins 1982

A catalogue record for this book
is available from the British Library

ISBN 978 0 00 7276233

Typeset in Postscript Linotype Baskerville by
Rowland Phototypesetting Ltd,
Bury St Edmunds, Suffolk

Printed and bound in Great Britain by
Clays Ltd, St Ives plc

Sharpe's Company
is for the Harper family,
Charlie and Marie,
Patrick, Donna and Terry,
with affection and gratitude

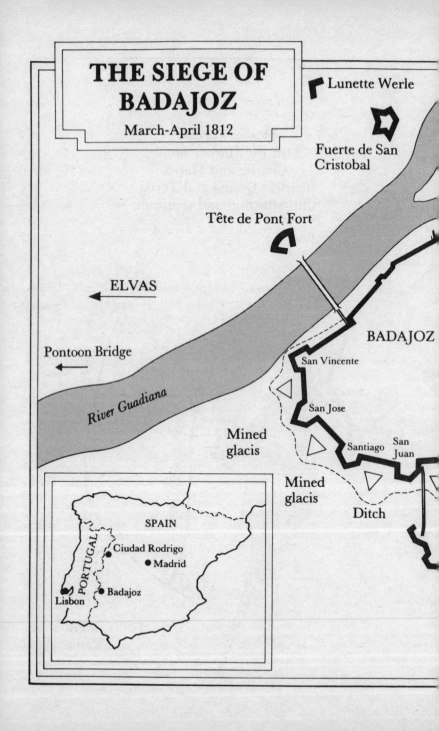

THE SIEGE OF BADAJOZ

March-April 1812

Lunette Werle

Fuerte de San Cristobal

Tête de Pont Fort

ELVAS

Pontoon Bridge

River Guadiana

BADAJOZ

San Vincente

San Jose

Mined glacis

Santiago

San Juan

Mined glacis

Ditch

SPAIN

PORTUGAL

Ciudad Rodrigo

Madrid

Lisbon

Badajoz

Half mile

N

Rivillas Stream

Castle

Dam Fort
(San Roque)

San Pedro

Dam

Trinidad

Santa
Maria

San
Roque

Ditch

Pardaleras

*Flood
water*

Picurina

⑫

⑥

⑤

④

Batteries,
numbered in
order dug

⑩

FIRST PARALLEL

⑪

⑨

⑧

③

SECOND PARALLEL

⑦

②

①

British
Camp

'Now thou art come unto a feast of death'

William Shakespeare
Henry VI, Part I, Act 4, Scene 5.

Part One

January
1812

CHAPTER 1

A pale horse seen a mile away at sunrise means the night is over. Sentries can relax, battalions stand down, because the moment for a surprise dawn attack has passed.

But not on this day. A grey horse would hardly have been visible at a hundred paces, let alone a mile, and the dawn was shredded with dirty cannon smoke that melded with the snow-clouds. Only one living thing moved in the grey space between the British and French lines; a small, dark bird that hopped busily in the snow. Captain Richard Sharpe, huddled in his greatcoat, watched the bird and willed it to fly away. Move, you bastard! Fly! He hated the superstition in himself. He had spotted the tiny bird and, quite suddenly and unbidden, the thought had come to him that unless the bird took wing within thirty seconds, then the day would end in disaster.

He counted. Nineteen, twenty, and still the damned bird hopped in the snow. He could not tell what kind of bird it was. Sergeant Harper would know, of course, the huge Irish sergeant knew all the birds, but knowing what kind of bird it was would not help. Move! Twenty-four, twenty-five, and in desperation he bundled a crude snowball and skittered it down the slope so that the small bird, startled, sprang up into the skeins of

smoke with a couple of seconds to spare. A man must sometimes make his own luck.

God! But it was cold! It was all right for the French. They were behind the vast defences of Ciudad Rodrigo, sheltered in the town's houses and warmed by wide hearths, but the British and Portuguese troops were in the open. They slept by vast fires that died in the night and yesterday, at dawn, four Portuguese sentries had been discovered frozen, their greatcoats iced to the ground, dead by the river. Someone had tipped them in, breaking the Agueda's thin ice, because no one wanted to dig graves. The army had taken its fill of digging; for twelve days they had done nothing else; batteries, parallels, saps and trenches, and they never wanted to dig again. They wanted to fight. They wanted to carry their long bayonets up the glacis of Ciudad Rodrigo, to go into the breach, to kill the French, and take those fires and houses for themselves. They wanted to be warm.

Sharpe, Captain of the South Essex's Light Company, lay in the snow and stared through his telescope at the largest breach. He could not see much. Even from the hillside, five hundred yards from the town, the snow-covered slope of the glacis hid all but the top few feet of Ciudad Rodrigo's main wall. He could see that the British guns had done damage and knew that the stones and rubble must have cascaded into the hidden ditch to make a crude ramp, perhaps a hundred feet wide, up which the attackers must climb to get into the heart of the fortress town. He wished he could see beyond the breach to the alleyways at the foot of the shot-scarred church tower that was so close to the walls. The French would be busy there, building new defences, siting fresh cannon, so that when the attack burst over the rubbled mound of the breach it would be met with

14

precisely planned horror, flame and grapeshot, death in the night.

Sharpe was afraid.

It was a strange knowledge, known to him alone, and he was ashamed of it. It was not certain that the attack would be on this day, but the army, with the instinct of men who know that the time has come, were confident that Wellington would order the assault this night. No one knew which battalions would be chosen, but which-ever units were to brave the assault they would not be the first attackers to climb the breach. That was a job only for volunteers, the 'Forlorn Hope', whose suicidal task was to draw the defenders' fire, force them to spring their carefully prepared traps, and clear a bloody path for the battalions that followed. Not many of the Forlorn Hope would live. The Lieutenant who com-manded, if he was still alive, would receive his Captaincy on the spot and his two Sergeants would be made Ensigns. The promises of promotion were easily given because they rarely had to be kept, yet there was never a shortage of volunteers.

The Forlorn Hope was for the brave. It may have been a courage born of desperation, or foolhardiness, but it was courage just the same. Men who survived a Hope were marked for life, famous among their com-rades, envied by lesser men. Only the Rifle Regiments gave a badge to the survivors, a laurel-wreath that was sewn to the sleeve, but Sharpe did not hanker after medals. He simply wanted to survive a test, the supreme test of almost certain death because he had never been in a Forlorn Hope. It was a foolish desire, and he knew it, but it was there.

It was not just a test. Richard Sharpe wanted the promotion. He had joined the army at sixteen, as a Private, and worked his way through the ranks until he

was a Sergeant. On the battlefield of Assaye he had saved the life of Sir Arthur Wellesley and had been rewarded with the telescope and a commission. Ensign Sharpe risen from the gutter, but still ambitious, still needed to prove, day after day, that he was a better soldier than the privileged sons who purchased their promotions and climbed the officers' ladder with monied ease. Ensign Sharpe became Lieutenant Sharpe and, wearing a new uniform, the dark green of the 95th Rifles, he fought his way through Northern Spain and Portugal; the Corunna retreat, Rolica, Vimiero, the Douro crossing, and Talavera. He had taken the French Eagle at Talavera when he and Sergeant Harper had hacked their way into an enemy battalion, cut down the standard bearer, and brought the trophy back to Wellesley. He became the Viscount Wellington of Tala-vera. And Sharpe had been gazetted, just before the battle, as a Captain. It was the promotion he most wanted; the chance to lead his own Company, but the gazette was now two and a half years old and it was still unapproved.

He could hardly believe it. In July he had gone back to England and spent the last six months of 1811 recruiting in London and the Shires for the shrinking South Essex Regiment. He had been feted in London, dined by the Patriotic Fund, and presented with a fifty-guinea sword for the capture of the French Eagle. The *Morning Chronicle* had dubbed him 'the scarred Hero of the Field of Talavera' and suddenly, for a few days at least, everyone had wanted to meet the tall, dark-haired Rifleman with the scar that gave his face an unnatural, mocking expression. He had felt out of place in the draped softness of London's drawing rooms and had covered his discomfort by shrinking into silent watchful-ness. The reticence had been thought dangerously

attractive by his hostesses who had kept their daughters upstairs and the Rifle Captain to themselves.

But the Hero of the Field of Talavera was nothing but a nuisance to the Army Headquarters in the Horse Guards. It had been a mistake, a stupid mistake, but he had visited Whitehall and been shown to a bare waiting room. The autumn rain had spattered through a high, broken window as he sat, his huge sword across his knees, while a clerk with smallpox scars tried to find what had happened to the gazette. Sharpe simply wanted to know whether he was a real Captain, sanctioned as such by the Horse Guards' approval, or merely a Lieutenant in borrowed and temporary rank. The clerk had kept him waiting three hours, but at last returned to the room. 'Sharpe? With an "e"?'

Sharpe nodded. Around him a group of half-pay officers, sick, lame or half-blind, listened curiously. They were all seeking appointments and hoping Sharpe would be disappointed. The clerk blew dust off the papers in his hand.

'It's irregular.' He peered at Sharpe's dark green jacket. 'You said the South Essex Regiment?'

'Yes.'

'But that, if I'm not mistaken, and I rarely am, is the uniform of the 95th?' The clerk gave a small, self-satisfied laugh, as if in celebration of a small victory. Sharpe said nothing. He wore the uniform of the Rifles because he was proud of his old Regiment, because the job with the South Essex was only ever intended as a temporary attachment, and how was he to tell this pinched bureaucrat about leading his small band of Riflemen from the horrors of the Corunna retreat down to join the army in Portugal where they had been arbitrarily joined to the redcoats of the South Essex. The clerk twitched his nose and sniffed. 'Irregular, Mr

Sharpe, very irregular.' He selected the top piece of paper with ink-stained fingers. 'This is the document.'

He held Sharpe's gazette as if the document might reinfect him with smallpox. 'You were given a Captaincy in 1809?'

'By Lord Wellington.'

The name cut no ice in Whitehall. 'Who should have known better. Dear me, Mr Sharpe, he should have known better! It's irregular.'

'But not unknown, surely?' Sharpe had suppressed his urge to vent his irritation on the clerk. 'I thought it was your job to approve these documents.'

'Or disapprove them!' The clerk laughed again and the half-pay officers grinned. 'Disapprove, Mr Sharpe, or disapprove!' Rain fell down the chimney and hissed on the meagre coal fire. The clerk, his thin shoulders heaving with silent laughter, tugged a pair of spectacles from the recesses of his clothing and clipped them on to his nose as if the gazette, seen through smeared glass, might reveal new cause for merriment. 'We disapprove them, sir, most of the time. You allow one and you allow all. It upsets the system, you know. There are rules, regulations, standing orders!' And the clerk shook his head because it was obvious Sharpe understood nothing of the army.

Sharpe waited for the head-shaking to cease. 'It seems to have taken you a long time to make any decision on this gazette.'

'And still not made!' The clerk said it proudly, making it seem that the length of time proved the gravity of the Horse Guards' wisdom. Then he seemed to relent and offered Sharpe a rueful smile. 'The truth is, Mr Sharpe, that there was a mistake. A regrettable mistake and your visit has happily rectified the mistake.'

He peered over his glasses at the tall Rifleman. 'We are really most grateful to you for drawing it to our attention.'

'Mistake?'

'It was filed wrongly.' The clerk plucked another piece of paper from his left hand. 'Under Lieutenant Robert Sharp, no "e", who died of the fever in 1810. His papers were, otherwise, in perfect order.'

'Which mine are not?'

'Indeed, no, but you are still alive.' The clerk looked peevishly at Sharpe. 'We do have a chance of tidying up when an officer is translated to glory.' He took off his glasses and cleaned them with Sharpe's folded gazette. 'It will be attended to, Mr Sharpe, with expedition. I promise you. With expedition!'

'Soon?'

'That's what I said, isn't it? It would be wrong to say more.' The clerk pushed his spectacles back into place. 'Now, if you'll pardon me, there is a war on and I have other duties!'

It had been a mistake, Sharpe realized afterwards, to visit Whitehall, but it was done and he could only go on waiting. Surely, he told himself a dozen times each day, they could not disapprove the gazette. Not after he had taken the Eagle? After he had brought the gold out of the burning Almeida, and after he had savaged the finest French troops in the deathtraps of Fuentes de Oñoro? He stared gloomily across the snow at the scar in Ciudad Rodrigo's defences. He knew he should have volunteered for the Forlorn Hope. If he had led it, and survived, then no one could have denied him the Captaincy. He would have proved himself, captured the rank, and the pox-scarred bureaucrats of Whitehall could scratch themselves into a well-ordered eternity because nothing they could do, nothing, could have

taken the Captaincy away from him. A pox on the bloody lot of them!

'Richard Sharpe!' A quiet voice behind him, full of pleasure, and Sharpe twisted round.

'Sir!'

'I could feel a pricking in my thumbs! I knew you had to be back with the army.' Major Michael Hogan slithered on the snow towards him. 'How are you?'

'I'm well.' Sharpe scrambled to his feet. He beat the snow off his greatcoat and shook Hogan's gloved hand.

The Engineer laughed at him. 'You look like a drowned tinker, so you do, but it's good to see you.' The Irish voice was rich and warm. 'And how was England?'

'Cold and wet.'

'Ah well, it's a Protestant country.' Hogan conveniently ignored the freezing dampness of the Spanish countryside around them. 'And how is Sergeant Harper? Did he enjoy England?'

'He did, and most of what he enjoyed was plump and giggled.'

Hogan laughed. 'A man of sense. You will give him my best wishes?'

'I will.' The two men stared at the town. The British siege guns, long, iron twenty-four-pounders, were still firing, their reports muffled by the snow, and their shots erupting flurries of snow and stone from the walls either side of the main breach. Sharpe glanced at Hogan. 'Is it a secret we're attacking tonight?'

'It is a secret. Everyone knows, of course, they always do. Even before the General. Rumour has it for seven o'clock.'

'And does rumour extend to the South Essex?'

Hogan shook his head; he was attached to Wellington's staff and knew what was being planned. 'No, but

I was hoping I could persuade your Colonel to lend me your Company.'

'Mine?' Sharpe was pleased. 'Why?'

'Not for much. I don't want you lads in the breach, but the Engineers are short-handed, as ever, and there's a heap of stuff to be carried up the glacis. Would you be happy?'

'Of course.' Sharpe wondered whether to tell Hogan of his wish that he had gone with the Forlorn Hope, but he knew that the Irish Engineer would think he was mad, so he said nothing. Instead he lent Hogan his telescope and waited silently as the Engineer stared at the breach. Hogan grunted. 'It's practical.'

'You're sure?' Sharpe took the glass back, his fingers instinctively feeling for the inlet brass plate; 'In Gratitude. AW. 23 September 1803'.

'We're never sure. But I can't see it getting any better.' The Engineers had the job of pronouncing when a breach was 'practical', when, in their judgment, the rubble slope could be climbed by the attacking infantry. Sharpe looked at the small, middle-aged Major.

'You don't sound very happy.'

'Of course not. No one likes a siege.' Hogan was trying, like Sharpe earlier, to imagine what horrors the French had prepared in the breach. A siege, in theory, was the most scientific of all fighting. The attackers battered holes in the defence and both sides knew when the breaches were practical, but the advantage was all with the defenders. They knew where the main attack was coming, when, and roughly how many men could be fed into the breach. There the science stopped. There was great skill needed to site the batteries, in sapping forward, but once the science of the Engineers had opened up the breach, it was left to the infantry

to climb the defences and die on the rubble. The siege guns did what they could. They would fire till the last moment, as they were firing now, but soon the bayonets would take over and only raw anger would take the attackers through the prepared horror. Sharpe felt again the fear of going into a breach.

The Irishman seemed to sense his thoughts. He clapped Sharpe on the shoulder. 'I've a feeling about this one, Richard. It's going to be all right.' He changed the subject. 'Have you heard from your woman?'

'Which one?'

Hogan snorted. 'Which one! Teresa, of course.'

Sharpe shook his head. 'Not for sixteen months. I don't know where she's been.' Or even, he thought, if she was still alive. She fought the French in the 'Guerrilla', the 'little war', and the hills and rocks of her battles were not far from Ciudad Rodrigo. He had not seen her since they parted below Almeida and, thinking of her, he felt a sudden longing inside him. She had the face of a hawk, slim and cruel, with dark hair and eyes. Teresa was beautiful as a fine sword was beautiful; slim and hard.

Then, in England, he had met Jane Gibbons whose brother, Lieutenant Christian Gibbons, had tried to kill him at Talavera. Gibbons had died. Jane Gibbons was beautiful as men dream of beauty; blonde and feminine, slim as Teresa was slim, but there the resemblance ended. The Spanish girl could strip a Baker rifle lock in thirty seconds, could kill a man at two hundred paces, could lay an ambush and knew how to give a captured Frenchman a lingering death as payment for her own mother's rape and murder. Jane Gibbons could play the pianoforte, write a pretty letter, knew how to use a fan at a county dance, and took her delight in spending money at Chelmsford's milliners. They were as different

from each other as steel is from silk, yet Sharpe wanted both, though he knew such dreams were futile.

'She's alive.' Hogan's voice was soft.

'Alive?'

'Teresa.' Hogan would know. Despite the shortage of Engineers, Wellington had put Hogan on his own staff. The Irishman spoke Spanish, Portuguese, and French, could break the enemy's codes, and spent much of his time working with the Guerrilleros or with Wellington's Exploring Officers who rode, alone and in uniform, behind French lines. Hogan collected what Wellington called his 'intelligence' and Sharpe knew that if Teresa were still fighting, then Hogan would have news.

'What have you heard?'

'Not much. She went south for a long time, by herself, but I heard she was back up here. Her brother is leading the band, not herself, but they still call her "La Aguja".'

Sharpe smiled. He had given her the nickname himself; the needle. 'Why did she go south?'

'I don't know.' Hogan smiled at him. 'Cheer yourself up. You'll see her again. Besides, I'd like to meet her!'

Sharpe shook his head. It had been a long time and she had made no effort to find him. 'There must be a last woman, sir, like a last battle.'

Hogan whooped with laughter. 'God in heaven! A last woman. You gloomy bastard! You'll be telling me next that you're training for the Priesthood.' He wiped a tear from his eye. 'A last woman, indeed!' He turned to stare once more at the town. 'Listen, my friend, I must be busy, or I'll be the last Irishman on Wellington's staff. Will you look after yourself now?'

Sharpe grinned and nodded. 'I'll survive.'

'That's a useful delusion. It's good you're back.' He smiled and began trudging through the snow towards

Wellington's headquarters. Sharpe turned back towards Ciudad Rodrigo. Survival. It was a bad time to be fighting. The turn of a year was when men looked ahead, dreamed of far-away pleasures, of a small house and a good woman, and friends of an evening. Winter was a time when armies stayed in their quarters, waiting for the spring sunshine to dry the roads and shrink the rivers, but Wellington had marched in the first days of the New Year, and the French garrison of Ciudad Rodrigo had woken one cold morning to find that war and death had come early in 1812.

Ciudad Rodrigo was just the beginning. There were only two roads from Portugal into Spain that could take the weight of heavy artillery, the endless grinding of supply carts, and the pounding of battalions and squadrons. Ciudad Rodrigo guarded the northern road and tonight, as the church bell sounded seven, Wellington planned to take the fortress. Then, as all the army knew, as all Spain knew, there was the southern road to capture. To be safe, to protect Portugal, to attack into Spain, the British must control both roads, and to control the southern road they must first take Badajoz.

Badajoz. Sharpe had been there, after Talavera and before the Spanish army had feebly surrendered the city to the French. Ciudad Rodrigo was big, but small compared with Badajoz; the walls in this snow looked formidable, but they were puny next to the bastions of Badajoz. Richard Sharpe let his thoughts go south, drifting with the cannon-smoke over Ciudad Rodrigo, south over the mountains, to where the vast fortress cast dark shadows on the cold waters of the Guadiana River. Badajoz. Twice the British had failed to take the city from the French. Soon they must try again.

He turned away, to rejoin his Company at the foot of the hill. There could be a miracle, of course. The

garrison of Badajoz might get the fever, the magazine might blow up, the war might end, but Sharpe knew they were vain hopes in a cold wind. He thought of his Captaincy, of his gazette, and though he knew that Lawford, his Colonel, would never take the Light Company from his command, he still wondered why he had not volunteered for the Forlorn Hope. It would have made his rank secure and he would have passed the test of overcoming the fear that each man had of being first into a defended breach. He had not volunteered and if he could not prove his bravery, that had been proved so many times before, in the breach at Ciudad Rodrigo, then the proof would have to come later.

At Badajoz.

CHAPTER 2

The orders came late in the afternoon, surprising no one, but stirring the battalions into quiet activity. Bayonets were sharpened and oiled, muskets checked and re-checked, and still the siege guns hammered at the French defences, trying to unseat the hidden, waiting cannon. Grey smoke blossomed out of the batteries and drifted up to join the low, bellying clouds that were the colour of wet gunpowder.

Sharpe's Light Company, as Hogan had requested, were to join the Engineers on the approach to the largest breach. They would be carrying huge hay-bags that would be thrown down the steep face of the ditch to make a vast cushion on to which the Forlorn Hope and the attacking battalions could safely jump. Sharpe watched as his men filed into the forward trench, each holding one of the grotesquely stuffed bags. Sergeant Harper dropped his bag, sat on it, pummelled it into comfort, and then lay back. 'Better than a feather bed, sir.'

Nearly one man in three of Wellington's army came, like the Sergeant, from Ireland. Patrick Harper was a huge man, six feet four inches of muscle and contentment, who no longer thought it odd that he fought for an army not his own. He had been recruited by hunger from his native Donegal and kept in his head a memory of his homeland, a love of its religion and language,

and a fierce pride in its ancient warrior heroes. He did not fight for England, less still for the South Essex Regiment, but instead he fought for himself and for Sharpe. Sharpe was his officer, a fellow Rifleman and a friend if it was possible for a Captain and a Sergeant to be friends. Harper was proud to be a soldier, even in his enemy's army, because a man could take pride in doing a job well. One day, perhaps, he would fight for Ireland, but he could not imagine how that could happen because the land was crushed and persecuted, the flames of resistance trampled out, and, in truth, he did not give the prospect much thought or hope. For the moment he was in Spain and his job was to inspire, discipline, humour, and cajole the Light Company of the South Essex. He did it brilliantly.

Sharpe nodded at the hay-bag. 'It's probably full of fleas.'

'Aye, sir, it probably is.' Harper grinned. 'But there's no room on my body for another flea.' The whole army was verminous; lice-ridden, flea-bitten, but so inured to the discomfort that they hardly noticed it. Tomorrow, thought Sharpe, in the comfort of Ciudad Rodrigo, they could all strip off, smoke out the lice and fleas, and crush the uniform seams with a hot iron to break the eggs. But that was tomorrow.

'Where's the Lieutenant?'

'Being sick, sir.'

'Drunk?'

Harper's face flickered in a frown. 'That's not for me to say, sir.' Which meant, Sharpe knew, that Lieutenant Harold Price was drunk.

'Will he be all right?'

'He always is, sir.'

Lieutenant Price was new to the Company. He was a Hampshire man, the son of a ship-builder, and

gambling debts and unwanted pregnancies among the local girls had persuaded his sober, church-loving father that the best place for young Price was in the army. The ship-builder had purchased his son an Ensign's commission and, four years later, had been happy to pay the five hundred and fifty pounds that had secured Master Price's promotion to Lieutenant. The father had been happy because the vacant Lieutenancy was in the South Essex, a Regiment that was safely abroad, and he was glad to see as great a distance as possible between himself and his youngest son.

Robert Knowles, Sharpe's previous Lieutenant, had gone. He had bought himself a Captaincy in a Fusilier Battalion, making the vacancy Price had purchased, and Sharpe, at first, had not liked the change. He had asked Price why, as the son of a ship-builder, he had not joined the navy.

'Seasick, sir. Could never stand up straight.'

'You can't do that on land.'

Price had taken a few moments to understand, then his round, friendly, misleadingly innocent face had grinned. 'Very good, sir. Droll. But still, sir, on land, if you follow me, there's always something solid underneath. I mean if you fall over, then at least you know it's the drink and not the bloody ship.'

The dislike had not lasted. It was impossible to dislike Lieutenant Price. His life was a single-minded pursuit of the debauchery denied him by his stern, God-fearing family, and he retained enough sense to make sure that when he was supposed to be sober he was, at the very least, upright. The men of Sharpe's Company liked him, were protective towards him because they believed he was not long for this world. They reasoned that if a French bullet did not kill him, then the drink would, or the mercury salts he took for the pox, or a jealous

28

husband, or, as Harper said admiringly, sheer bloody exhaustion. The big Sergeant looked up from his hay-bag, nodded down the trench. 'Here he is now, sir.'

Price grinned weakly at them, winced as twenty-four pounds of roundshot hammered overhead towards the city, then stared agape at Harper. 'What are you sitting on, Sergeant?'

'Hay-bag, sir.'

Price shook his head in admiration. 'Christ! They should issue them every day. Can I borrow it?'

'My pleasure, sir.' Harper stood up and courteously waved the Lieutenant to the bag.

Price collapsed, groaned in satisfaction. 'Wake me when glory calls.'

'Yes, sir. Which one's Glory?'

'Irish wit, oh God, Irish wit.' Price closed his eyes.

The sky was darkening, the grey clouds turning sinister, bringing on the inexorable moment. Sharpe pulled his huge sword a few inches from the scabbard, tested the honed edge, and pushed it back. The sword was one of his symbols, with the rifle, which proclaimed he was a fighter. As a Light Company officer, he should have kept to the tradition that decreed he carried a Light Cavalry sabre. He hated the curved, light blade. Instead he used a Heavy Cavalry sword, straight-bladed and ill-balanced, that he had picked up from a battle-field. It was a brute of a weapon, thirty-five inches of cumbersome steel, but Sharpe was tall and strong enough to wield it easily. Harper saw Sharpe's thumb test the edge. 'Expecting to use it, sir?'

'No. We don't go beyond the glacis.'

Harper grunted. 'There's always hope.' He was loading his seven-barrelled gun, a weapon of extreme unorthodoxy. Each of the barrels was a half inch wide and all seven were fired by a single charge that punched

out a spray of death. Only six hundred had been made by the gunsmith, Henry Nock, and delivered to the Royal Navy, but the massive recoil had smashed men's shoulders and the invention had been quietly discarded. The gunsmith would have been pleased to see the huge Irishman, one of the few men strong enough to handle the weapon, meticulously loading each twenty-inch barrel. Harper liked the weapon, it gave him a distinction similar to Sharpe's sword, and the gun had been a present from his Captain; purchased from a chandler in Lisbon.

Sharpe pulled the greatcoat tight and peered over the parapet towards the city. There was little to see. The snow, glinting with a myriad of metallic sparks, led to the slope of the glacis which was a continuation of the hill on which Ciudad Rodrigo was built. He could see where the breach was hidden behind the glacis because of the dark scars in the snow where the siege artillery had fired short. The glacis was not designed to stop infantry. It was an earthen slope, easily climbed, that was banked in front of the defences to bounce the roundshot screaming over the defenders, and it had forced Wellington to capture the French forts on nearby hills so that the British artillery could be placed high up and fire down, over the glacis, into the walls.

Beyond the glacis was a ditch, hidden from Sharpe, that would be stone-faced and wide and, beyond the ditch, the modern walls that masked, in their turn, the old mediaeval wall. The guns had pierced both walls, old and new, and turned them into a stretch of rubble, but the defenders would have prepared horrid traps to guard the gap.

It was nine years since Sharpe had been part of a besieging force, yet he could remember clearly the fierceness of the fight as the British had climbed the

30

hill to Gawilghur and plunged into the maze of walls and ditches that the Indians had defended with ferocious bravery. Ciudad Rodrigo should, he knew, be more difficult; not because the men who defended this town were better soldiers, but because, like Badajoz, it was defended with the science of modern engineering. There was something horridly precise about the defences, with their false walls and ravelins, their mathematically sited bastions and hidden cannons, and only passion, anger, or screaming desperation would force the science to yield to the bayonets. The desperation would not subside quickly. Sharpe knew that once the attackers broke through the breach, their blood raised to a desperate pitch, the men would be ungovernable in the town's streets. It had always been so. If a fortress did not surrender, if its defenders forced the attackers to shed their blood in an assault, then old custom, soldiers' custom, dictated that all inside the fortress belonged to the attackers' vengeance. Ciudad Rodrigo's only hope lay in a short, easy fight.

Bells rang the Angelus in the town. The Catholics in the Company, all Irish, made sketchy crosses and scrambled to their feet as Lieutenant-Colonel the Honourable William Lawford, the South Essex's Commanding Officer, came into sight. He waved the men down, grinned at the sight of the snoring Price, nodded amicably to Harper, and came and stood beside Sharpe. 'All well?'

'Yes, sir.'

They were the same age, thirty-five, but Lawford had been born to the Officers' Mess. When he had been a Lieutenant, lost and frightened in his first battle, Sergeant Richard Sharpe had been with him, guiding him as Sergeants often guide young officers. Then, when both men had been in the torture chambers of the

Sultan Tippoo, Lawford had taught Sharpe to read and write. The skills had made it possible for Sharpe, once he had performed an act of suicidal bravery, to be made into an officer. Lawford stared over the parapet at the glacis. 'I'll come with you tonight.'

'Yes, sir.' Sharpe knew that Lawford had no need to be there, but also knew he could not dissuade him from coming. He glanced at his Colonel. As usual, Lawford was immaculately uniformed; gold lace glinting above the clean, yellow facings of the scarlet jacket. 'Wear a greatcoat, sir.'

Lawford smiled. 'You want me to disguise myself?'

'No, sir, but you must be bloody cold, and we all like a shot at a fancy Colonel.'

'I'll wear this.' Lawford held up a cavalry cloak, fur trimmed and lavish. The fastening was a gold chain at the neck and Sharpe knew the cloak would billow open and leave the uniform exposed.

'It won't hide the uniform, sir.'

'No, Sergeant.' Lawford smiled. He had spoken softly and the remark was an acknowledgement that their relationship was still the same, despite the promotions. Lawford was a good officer who had turned the South Essex from a frightened Regiment into a hardened, confident unit. But soldiering was not Lawford's life; instead it was a means to his ends, political ends, and he wanted success in Spain to pave the way to power at home. In war he still relied on Sharpe, the natural soldier, and Sharpe was grateful for the trust and the freedom.

Beyond the river, towards Portugal, the fires of the British camp glowed bright in the dusk. In the trenches the battalions waiting for the assault shivered, gratefully drank the rum that was issued, and went through the tiny rituals that always preceded battle. Uniforms were

pulled straight, belts made comfortable, weapons obsessively checked, and men felt in pockets or pouches for the talismans that kept them alive. A lucky rabbit's foot, a bullet that had nearly killed them, a memento of home, or just a plain pebble that had caught their eye as they lay under heavy fire on a battlefield. The clocks moved up from the half hour towards the hour.

Generals fidgeted as they tried to persuade themselves their plans were as near perfect as possible, Brigade Majors fussed over last minute orders, while the men themselves wore that wary, stretched look that soldiers have before an event that demands their deaths to make it memorable. Packs were piled, to be guarded by men who would wait in the trenches, and bayonets were slotted and twisted on to musket barrels. The job, General Picton said, would be done with cold iron; and there would be no time to reload a musket in the breach, just to push on, bayonet out, reaching for the enemy. They waited for night. Made small jokes, fought with the imagination.

At seven it was dark. The big church clock in the tower that had been chipped and scarred by cannon balls, whirred as it geared itself to strike the hour. The sound was clearly audible over the snow. The orders must come soon. The siege guns stopped firing, a sudden silence that seemed unnatural after the days of hammering at the defences. Sharpe could hear men coughing, stamping their feet, and the little noises were terrible reminders of how small and frail men were against the defences of a fortress.

'Go!' The Brigade Majors had the orders. 'Go!'

Lawford touched Sharpe's shoulder. 'Good luck!'

The Rifleman noticed the Colonel was still uncloaked, but it was too late now. There was a stirring in the trenches, a rustle as the hay-bags were pushed

out of the trench, and then Harper was beside him and, beyond the Sergeant, Lieutenant Price, wide-eyed and pale. Sharpe grinned at them. 'Come on.'

They climbed up on the fire-step, over the parapet, and went in silence towards the breach.

1812 had begun.

CHAPTER 3

The snow was brittle, crunching beneath Sharpe's boots, while behind him he could hear the sounds of men slipping in the whiteness, their breath rasping in the cold air, their equipment clinking as they started up the hill towards the glacis.

The crest of the defences were limned by a faint, red haze where the lights in the town, fires and bracketed torches, glowed in the night mist. It seemed unreal, but to Sharpe battles often seemed unreal, especially now as he climbed the snow-slope towards the silent, waiting town and with each step he expected the sudden eruption of cannon and the shriek of grape. Yet the defenders were quiet, as if they were oblivious of the mass of men who churned the snow towards Ciudad Rodrigo. In two hours at the most, Sharpe knew, it would all be over. Talavera had taken a day and a night, Fuentes de Oñoro all of three days, but no man could endure the hell of a breach for more than a couple of hours.

Lawford was beside him, the cloak still held over one arm and the gold lace reflecting the dim, red light ahead. The Colonel grinned at Sharpe; he looked, the Rifleman thought, very young.

'Perhaps we're surprising them, Richard.'

The answer was instant. From ahead, from the left and right, the French gunners put matches to the

priming tubes, the cannons banged back on their trails, and the canisters were spat over the glacis. The crest of the defences seemed to erupt in great, boiling clouds of smoke that were lit by internal lances of flame that reached from the wall, over the ditch, to spear their tongues of light on to the snow-slope. Following the thunder, so close that the sounds were indistinguishable, came the explosions of the canisters. Each was a metal can packed with musket balls which were blown apart by a powder charge. The balls hammered down. The snow was spotted with crimson.

There were shouts far to the left and Sharpe knew that the Light Division, attacking the smaller breach, were pouring over the glacis into the ditch. He slipped on the snow, recovered, and shouted at his men. 'Come on!'

The smoke rolled slowly from the glacis, carried south on the night wind, and was then put back by the gunners' next volley. The canisters cracked apart again, the mass of men hurried as the shouts of officers and Sergeants drove them up the slope to the dubious safety of the ditch. Far back, behind the first parallel, a band played and Sharpe caught a snatch of the tune and then he was at the top of the slope, the ditch black beneath him.

There was a temptation to stay a few feet down the slope and hurl the bags hopefully into the darkness, but Sharpe had long taught himself that the few steps of which a man is afraid are the important steps. He stood on the crest, Lawford beside him, and shouted at his men to hurry. The hay-bags thumped softly down in the blackness.

'This way! This way!' He led them right, away from the breach, their job finished, and the Forlorn Hope were jumping down into the ditch and Sharpe felt a pang of envy.

36

'Down! down!' He pushed them flat on the crest of the glacis and the cannons crashed overhead so close that the Light Company could feel the lick of their hot breath. The battalions were coming behind to follow the Forlorn Hope. 'Watch the wall!' The best help that the Light Company could be now to the attack was to snipe over the ditch as soon as any target could be seen.

All was blackness. Sounds came from the ditch; boots scuffing, the scrape of a bayonet, a muffled curse, and then the scrabbling of feet on rubble that told him the Hope had reached the breach and were climbing the broken stone slope. Musket flashes dazzled from the breach summit, the first opposition to the Forlorn Hope, but the fire did not appear to be heavy and Sharpe could hear the men still climbing.

'So far . . .' Lawford left the sentence unfinished.

There were shouts from behind and Sharpe turned to see the attackers reaching the crest and jumping recklessly into the ditch. There were shouts as men missed the hay-bags, or landed on their comrades, but the leading battalions were in place, and they were going forward in the darkness, and Sharpe heard the growl that he remembered from Gawilghur. It was an eerie sound made by hundreds of men in a small place, steeling themselves to go into the narrow breach, and it was a sound that would last till the battle was decided.

'It's going well!' Lawford's face was nervous. It was going too well. The Hope had to be nearing the end of their long climb, the 45th and 88th were on their heels, and still the only French reaction was the few musket shots and the canister that still exploded far behind over the hurrying reserves. Something more had to be waiting in the breach.

A flame flickered on the walls, spread like fire catching on dry thatch, then heaved itself up into the air

and down into the ditch. Another flame followed, then another, and the breach was lit like daylight as the carcasses, oil-soaked, hardpacked straw that was bound in tarred canvas, were lit and tossed into the ditch so that the defenders could see their targets. There was a cheer from the French, a triumphant, defiant cheer, and the musket balls plucked at the Forlorn Hope, revealed close to the summit of the jumbled stone slope, and the cheer was answered by the 45th and 88th as the battalions ran forward, a dark mass in the tangled maze of the ditch, and the assault began to look easy.

'Rifles!' Sharpe shouted. He had eleven Riflemen left, apart from Harper and himself, of the thirty men he had led away from the horrors of the Corunna retreat three years before. They were the core of his Company, the green-jacketed specialists, whose modern Baker rifles could kill at three hundred paces and more, while the smooth-bore musket, the Brown Bess, was virtually useless at more than fifty yards. He heard the distinctive crack of the weapons, less muffled than the muskets, and saw a Frenchman fall back as he tried to throw another burning carcass down the breach slope. Sharpe wished he had more rifles. He had trained some of his redcoats to use the weapon, but he would have liked more.

He ducked down beside Lawford. The French had switched to grapeshot that left the cannon barrels like duck shot from a fowling piece. He heard the whistle of balls over his head, saw a flame stab down into the ditch towards the crowded battalions, but in the fire-light he could see the redjacketed British were nearing the mid-point of their climb. The Forlorn Hope, still almost intact, were just paces from the top, their bay-onets held out, while behind them the lower half of

the breach was darkened by the mass of the assaulting column.

Lawford touched Sharpe's arm. 'It's too easy!'

Muskets spat at the assault, but not enough to check the attack. The men in the ditch felt victory close, easily gained, and the column moved on to the breach like a beast uncoiling from the ditch. Victory was close, just seconds away, and the growl was a cheer that rose with the column's climb.

The French had let them come. They let the Hope reach the very top of the shattered wall and then they unmasked the defence. There was a twin explosion, horrendous and earshattering, and flames startled across the breach. Sharpe winced. The cheer was laced with screams, spattered by the rattle of grapeshot, and he saw the French had mounted two guns, in hidden casements dug deep into the core of the walls either side of the breach, that could fire across the attack. They were not small guns, not field-guns, but massive pieces whose flames lanced clear across the full hundred feet width of the breach.

The Forlorn Hope disappeared, snatched into oblivion in a maelstrom of flame and grapeshot, and the head of the column was shattered by the gunfire that lacerated the upper half of the breach, clearing it with contemptuous ease. The growl faltered, turned into cries of alarm, and the column retreated, not from the guns, but from a new danger.

Flames appeared in the smoke-shrouded rubble, livid serpents that flickered in the stone, forked lightning that ran quicksilver down the scoured stones to touch the mines that had been hidden in the breach. The explosions tore the lower slope apart, flinging men and masonry into the air, blowing the first attack into failure. The meat-grinder of the breach had begun to turn.

The growl was still audible. The men from Connaught and Nottinghamshire were going back to the breach, over their mangled dead, past the blackened, smoking pits where the mines had been dug, and the French screamed insults at them; called them boy-lovers and weaklings, and followed the insults with more burning carcasses and lumps of timber or stone that avalanched on the slope and hurled men back into the blood-soaked base of the breach. The vast guns in their hidden, flanking casements were being reloaded, ready for their next targets, and they came, clawing their way up the blood-slick ramp till the thunder crashed again, the flames slapped at the breach, and the myriad scraps of grapeshot blasted the stones clear.

The assault had been bloodily repulsed, but there was no thought except to go forward. The foot of the ramp was crowded with the men of the two battalions who climbed again in the mindless, seething bravery of siege warfare.

Lawford clutched Sharpe's arm, leaned close to his ear. 'Those bloody guns!'

'I know!' They fired again, a fraction early, and it was plain that no man could climb past their fire. They were dug into the very heart of the town's thick, low wall and no British siege gun could have hoped to reach them; not unless Wellington had fired at each hidden casement for a week until the whole wall collapsed like the breach itself. In front of each gun, revealed by the burning carcasses, was a trench that defended the gunners from their enemy on the breach, and as long as the two guns were firing, across and slightly ahead of each other, there could be no victory.

The troops were climbing again, slower now, wary of the guns and trying to avoid the burning grenades that the French were tossing on to the slope. The red

explosions punctured the scattered attackers. Sharpe turned to Harper. 'Are you loaded?'

The huge Sergeant nodded, grinned, and held up the seven-barrelled gun. Sharpe grinned back. 'Shall we join in?'

Lawford shouted at them. 'What are you doing?'

Sharpe pointed at the nearest side of the breach. 'Going after the gun. Do you mind?'

Lawford shrugged. 'Be careful!'

There was no time to think, just to jump into the ditch and pray that their ankles would not twist or break. Sharpe fell awkwardly, slipping on the snow, but a huge hand grabbed his greatcoat, hauled him upright, and the two men ran across the floor of the ditch. The jump had been twenty feet and it seemed as if they had fallen into the bottom of a giant cauldron, an alchemist's vessel of fire, and the flames poured in from above. Carcasses rolled down, musket and cannon flame spat from above, and the fire spilt on to the living and dead flesh in the ditch and was reflected red on the underside of the low clouds that rolled southwards to Badajoz. There was only one way to live in the cauldron, and that was to go upwards, and the column was climbing again as Sharpe and Harper skirted the mass of men, and then the guns spoke, and the attack was flung back by the flame-borne grape-shot.

Sharpe had been counting the gaps between the shots and knew that the French gunners were taking about a minute to reload each giant gun. He counted the seconds in his head as the two men struggled past the mass of Irishmen to the left of the breach. They fought their way through the crush, going for the very edge of the slope, and the surge of men carried them forward so that, for an instant, Sharpe thought they would be carried on to the rubble slope itself. Then

the guns fired again and the men ahead recoiled, something wet slapped Sharpe's face, and the attack was broken into small groups. He had a minute. 'Patrick!'

They threw themselves into the trench beside the breach, the trench that protected the gun. It was already filled with men sheltering from the grapeshot. The French gunners, over their heads, would be sponging out and desperately ramming the huge, serge bags of powder into the vast muzzles while other men waited with the lumpy, black bags of grapeshot. Sharpe tried to forget them. He looked up the wall to the casement's lip. It was high up, far higher than a man's height, so he braced his back on the wall, cupped his hands and nodded to the Sergeant. Harper put a massive boot into Sharpe's hands, cocked the seven-barrelled gun, and nodded back. Sharpe heaved and Harper pushed up, the Irishman weighed as much as a small bullock. Sharpe grimaced with the effort and then two of the Connaught Rangers, seeing their intention, joined in and pushed up on Harper's legs. The weight suddenly disappeared. Harper had grasped the casement's edge with one hand, ignoring the musket bullets that flattened themselves on the wall beside him, threw the huge gun over the edge, aimed blindly, and pulled the trigger.

The recoil slammed him back, cruelly throwing him on the opposite lip of the trench, but he scrambled to his feet, screaming in Gaelic. Sharpe knew he was telling his countrymen to climb the wall and attack the gun crew while they were still dazed by the shattering blast. But it was hopeless trying to climb the steep wall, and Sharpe thought of the surviving gunners loading the huge cannon. 'Patrick! Throw me!'

Harper seized Sharpe like a bag of oats, took one breath, and threw him bodily upwards. It was like being

lifted by a mine explosion. Sharpe flailed, his rifle slipping from his shoulder, but he caught it by the barrel, saw the casement's edge and desperately threw out his left hand. It held, he had a leg on the stonework; he knew the French muskets were firing at him, but he had no time to think of that for a man was running at him, a rammer raised to strike down, and Sharpe struck out with his rifle. It was a lucky effort. The brass-hilted butt caught the Frenchman on the temple, he staggered back, and Sharpe had dropped over the casement, found his feet, and the huge sword rasped out of the scabbard and the joy was there.

The gunners had been hit hard by the seven bullets that had ricocheted round the stone emplacement. Sharpe could see bodies lying beneath the huge, iron barrel of what he recognized as a siege gun, but there were still men alive and they were coming at him. He swung the long blade at them, drove them back, hacked down with the sword and felt it shudder as it cleaved a skull. He screamed at them, scaring them, slipped on new blood, tugged the blade free and swung again. The French went back. They outnumbered him six to one, but they were gunners more used to killing at a distance than seeing the face of their enemy wild over a naked sword. They cowered back and Sharpe turned, back to the casement's edge, and found an arm clinging desperately to the stonework. He grabbed the wrist and heaved a Connaught Ranger into the sunken gun-pit. The man's eyes were bright with excitement. Sharpe yelled at him. 'Help the others up! Use your sling!'

A musket ball went past his head, clanging off the barrel of the gun, and Sharpe whirled to see the familiar uniforms of French infantry running down the stone stairs to rescue the gun. He went for them, wild with the madness of battle, and the crazy thought whirled

in his head that he wished the mean-faced bastard clerk in Whitehall could see him now. Perhaps then Whitehall would know what its soldiers did, but there was no time for the thought because the infantry were coming down the narrow space beside the barrel. He leaped at them, shouting and lunging with the point to drive them back and he knew he was outnumbered.

They checked, let him come, and then countered with their long bayonets. The sword was not long enough! He swung at them, smashing bayonets to the side, but another came past his swing and he felt the blade catch in his greatcoat. He seized the barrel with his left hand, pulled the man off balance and brought the great brass hilt of the sword down on his head. He was forced back. Another bayonet flickered at him, making him dodge wildly so that he slipped against the siege gun, his sword was whirling uselessly, flailing for balance, and he saw the bayonets above him. His anger was useless because he could not parry.

The shout was in a language he did not speak, but the voice was Harper's and the massive Irishman was crunching the enemy with the seven-barrelled gun held like a club. He ignored Sharpe, stepped over him, laughed at the French, swung at them and went forward as his ancestors had gone into fine, dawn-misted battles. He chanted the same words that his ancestors had, and the Connaught men were beside him and no troops in the world could have stood against their anger and their attack. Sharpe ducked under the barrel and there were more enemy, fearful now, and he hacked up with the blade, drove them back, stabbed with it, screaming the challenge. The French scrambled for the stone stairs in their rear, and the crazed men in red and green coats came on, stepping over the bodies, hacking and clawing at them. Sharpe felt the blade grate on a

44

rib and he swung it clear, and suddenly the only enemy were the survivors who cowered at the foot of the stairs, shouting their surrender. They had no hope. The men of Connaught had lost friends on the breach, old friends, and the blades were used in short, efficient strokes. The bayonets ignored the French cries, worked swiftly, and the casement was thick with the smell of fresh blood.

'Up!' There were still enemies on the wall, enemies that could fire down into the gun-pit, and Sharpe climbed the stairs, the sword a streak of reflected fire-light ahead of him, and suddenly the night air was cool and clear and he was on the wall. The infantry had fallen back down the ramparts, fearful of the carnage round the gun, and Sharpe stood at the stair's head and watched them. Harper joined him, with a group of red-jacketed 88th, and they panted so that their breath fogged.

Harper laughed. 'They've had enough!'

It was true. The French were pulling back, abandoning the breach, and only one man, an officer, tried to force them back. He shouted at them, beat at them with his sword, and then, seeing that they would not attack, came on himself. He was a slim man with a thin, fair moustache beneath a straight, hooked nose. Sharpe could see the man's fear. The Frenchman did not want to make a solo attack, but he had his pride, and he hoped his men would follow. They did not. Instead they called to him, told him not to be a fool, but he walked on, looking at Sharpe, and his sword was ridiculously slim as he lowered it to the guard. He said something to Sharpe, who shook his head, but the Frenchman insisted and lunged at Sharpe, who was forced to leap back and bring up the huge sword in a clumsy parry. Sharpe's anger had gone in the cool air, the fight was

45

over, and he was irritated by the Frenchman's insistence. 'Go away! *Vamos!*' He tried to remember the words in French, but he could not.

The Irish laughed. 'Put him over your knee, Captain!' The Frenchman was little more than a boy, ridiculously young, but brave. He came forward again, the sword level, and this time Sharpe jumped towards him, growled, and the Frenchman rocked back.

Sharpe dropped his own blade. 'Give up!'

The answer was another lunge that came close to Sharpe's chest. He leaned back and beat the sword aside. He could feel his anger returning. He swore at the man, jerked his head down the ramparts, but still the fool came forward, incensed by the Irish laughter, and again Sharpe had to parry and force him back.

Harper finished the farce. He had worked his way behind the officer and, as the Frenchman looked at Sharpe for another attack, the Sergeant coughed. 'Sir? Monsewer?' The officer looked round. The giant Irishman smiled at him, came forward unarmed and very slowly. 'Monsewer?'

The officer nodded to Harper, frowned, and said something in French. The huge Sergeant nodded seriously. 'Quite right, sir, quite right.' Then a giant fist travelled from some place low down, up, and straight on to the Frenchman's chin. He crumpled, the Connaught men gave an ironic cheer, and Harper laid the senseless body beside the rampart. 'Poor wee fool.' He grinned at Sharpe, immensely pleased with himself, and looked over towards the breach. The fight still went on, but Harper knew his part in the assault was done, and well done, and that nothing could touch him this night. He jerked his thumb at the Connaught Rangers and looked at Sharpe. 'Connaught lads, sir. Good fighters.'

'They are.' Sharpe grinned. 'Where's Connaught? Wales?'

Harper made a joke at Sharpe's expense, but in Gaelic, so that he was forced to listen to the Rangers' good-humoured laughter. They were in good spirits, happy, like the Sergeant from Donegal, that they had played a good part in this night's fight, a part that would make a fine story to weave through the long winter nights in some unimaginable future. Harper knelt to go through the unconscious Frenchman's pockets and Sharpe turned to look at the breach.

The 45th, on the far side, were dealing with the second gun. They had found planks, abandoned in the trench, and thrown them over to the casement lip and Sharpe watched, admiringly, as the Nottinghamshire men charged across the perilous path and took their long bayonets to the gun crew. The growl had become a whoop of victory and the dark beast in the ditch uncoiled across the undefended breach and swarmed past the two silent guns towards the streets of the town. A few shots came from doors and windows, but only a few, and the British horde flooded down the rubble to where the breach had smothered the old mediaeval wall. It was over.

Or nearly. A second mine had been put in the ruins of the old wall. Black powder had been crammed into an old postern and now the French lit the fuse and ran back into the streets. The mine exploded. Flame streaked up from the darkness, old stones shattered outwards, boiling smoke and dust, and with it came the stench of roasted flesh and the head of the victorious column was uselessly decimated. For a second there was a stunned silence, time just to draw breath, and then the shout was not for victory, but for revenge, and the troops took their anger into the defenceless streets.

Harper watched the howling mob flow into the city. 'You think we're invited?'

'Why not?'

The Sergeant grinned. 'God knows, we've deserved it.' He was dangling a gold watch and chain and he started forward towards the ramp that led down towards the houses. Sharpe followed and suddenly stopped. He froze.

Down where the second mine had exploded, lit by a flickering length of old timber, was a mangled body. One side seemed sleek with new blood, a sleekness speckled with the ivory of bone, but the other side was gorgeous in yellow facings and gold lace. A fur-trimmed cavalry cloak covered the legs. 'Oh God!'

Harper heard him and saw where he was looking. Then both men were racing down the ramp, slipping on ice and slushy snow, and running towards Lawford's body.

Ciudad Rodrigo was won; but not at this price, Sharpe thought, dear God, not at this price.

CHAPTER 4

There was a scream from inside the town, shots as men blew open the doors of houses, and over it all the sound of triumphant voices. After the fight, the reward.

Harper reached the body first, plucked the cloak to one side, and bent over the bloodied chest. 'He's alive, sir.'

It seemed to Sharpe like a parody of life. The explosion had sheared Lawford's left arm almost clean from his body, crushed the ribs and flicked them open so they protruded through the remnants of skin and flesh. The blood was flowing beneath the once immaculate uniform. Harper began tearing the cloak into strips, his mouth a tight line of anger and sorrow. Sharpe looked towards the breach where men still clambered towards the houses. 'Bandsmen!'

The bands had played during the assault. He remembered hearing the music and now, idiotically, he could suddenly identify the tune he had heard. 'The Downfall of Paris'. By now the bandsmen should be doing their other job, of caring for the wounded, but he could see none. 'Bandsmen!'

Miraculously Lieutenant Price appeared, pale and unsteady, and with him a small group of the Light Company. 'Sir?'

'A stretcher. Fast! And send someone back to battalion.'

49

Price saluted. He had forgotten the drawn sword in his hand so that the blade, a curved sabre, nearly sliced into Private Peters. 'Sir.' The small group ran back.

Lawford was unconscious. Harper was binding the chest, his huge fingers astonishingly gentle with the tattered flesh. He looked up at Sharpe. 'Take the arm off, sir.'

'What?'

'Better now than later, sir.' The Sergeant pointed at the Colonel's left arm, held by a single, glistening shred of tissue. 'He might live, sir, so he might, but the arm will have to go.'

A splintered piece of bone protruded from the stump. The arm was bent unnaturally upwards, pointing towards the city, and Harper was binding the brief stump to stop the weakly pulsing blood. Sharpe picked his way to Lawford's head, treading carefully for the ground was slick, though whether with blood or ice it was impossible to see. The only light came from the burning timber. He put the point of his sword down into the bloodied mess and Harper moved the blade till it was in the right place. 'Leave the skin, sir. It'll flap over.'

It was no different from butchering a pig or a bullock, but it felt different. He could hear crashes from the city, punctuating the screams. 'Is that right?' He could feel Harper manipulating the blade.

'Now, sir. Straight down.'

Sharpe pushed down, with both hands, almost as if he was driving a stake into mud. Human flesh is resilient, proof against all but the hottest stroke, and Sharpe felt the gorge rise in his throat as the sword met resistance and he heaved down so that Lawford tipped in the scarlet slush and the Colonel's lips grimaced. Then

it was done, the arm free, and Sharpe stooped to the dead fingers and pulled off a gold ring. He would give it to Forrest to be sent home with the Colonel or, God forbid, to be sent to his relatives.

Lieutenant Price was back. 'They're coming, sir.'

'Who?'

'The Major, sir.'

'A stretcher?'

Price nodded, looking sick. 'Will he live, sir?'

'How the hell do I know?' It was not fair to vent his anger on Price. 'What was he doing here anyway?'

Price shrugged miserably. 'He said he was going to find you, sir.'

Sharpe stared down at the handsome Colonel and swore. Lawford had no business in the breach. The same, perhaps, could have been said of Sharpe and Harper, but the tall Rifleman saw a difference. Lawford had a future, hopes, a family to protect, ambitions that were within his grasp, and soldiering was not where those ambitions finally lay. They might all be thrown away for one mad moment in a breach, a moment to prove something. Sharpe and Harper had no such future, no such hopes, only the knowledge that they were soldiers, as good as their last battle, useful as long as they could fight. They were both, Sharpe thought, adventurers, gambling with their lives. He looked at the Colonel. It was such a waste.

Sharpe listened to the great noise coming from the city, a noise of rampage and victory. Once, perhaps, he thought, an adventurer had a future, back when the world was free and a sword was the passport to any hope. Not now. Everything was changing with a suddenness and pace that was bewildering. Three years before, when the army had defeated the French at Vimiero, it had been a small army, almost an intimate army,

51

and the General could inspect all his troops in a single morning and have time to recognize them, remember them. Sharpe had known most officers in the line by face, if not by name, and was welcome at their evening fires. Not now. Now there were generals of this and generals of that, of division and brigade, and provost-marshals and senior chaplains, and the army was far too large to see on a single morning or even march on a single road. Wellington, perforce, had become remote. There were bureaucrats with the army, defenders of files, and soon, Sharpe knew, a man would be less important than the pieces of paper like that folded, forgotten gazette in Whitehall.

'Sharpe!' Major Forrest was shouting at him, waving, hurrying over the rubble. He was leading a small group of men, some of whom carried a door, Lawford's stretcher. 'What happened?'

Sharpe gestured at the ruin about them. 'A mine, sir. He was caught by it.'

Forrest shook his head. 'Oh God! What do we do?' The question was not surprising from the Major. He was a kind man, a good man, but not a decisive man.

Captain Leroy, the loyalist American, leaned down to light his thin, black cigar from the flickering flames of the timber baulk. 'Must be a hospital in town.'

Forrest nodded. 'Into town.' He stared in horror at the Colonel. 'My God! He's lost his arm!'

'Yes, sir.'

'Will he live?'

Sharpe shrugged. 'God knows, sir.'

It was suddenly freezing cold, the wind reaching over the breach to chill the men who rolled the Colonel, still mercifully unconscious, on to the makeshift stretcher. Sharpe wiped the sword blade on a scrap of Lawford's

cloak, sheathed it, and pulled the collar of his greatcoat high up his neck.

It was not the entry into Ciudad Rodrigo that he had imagined. It was one thing to fight through a breach, overcome the last obstacle, and feel the elation of victory, but to follow Lawford in a slow, almost funeral march was destroying the triumph. Inevitably, too, though Sharpe hated himself for thinking of it, there were other questions that hung on this moment.

There would be a new Colonel of the South Essex, a stranger. The Battalion would be changed, maybe for the better, but probably not for the betterment of Sharpe. Lawford, whose own future was seeping into the crude bandages, had learned to trust Sharpe years before; at Seringapatam, Assaye, and Gawilghur, but Sharpe could expect no favours from a new man. Lawford's replacement would bring his own debts to be repaid, his own ideas, and the old ties of loyalty, friendship, and even gratitude that had held the Battalion together would be untied. Sharpe thought of the gazette. If it was refused, and the thought persisted that it might, then Lawford would have ignored the refusal. He would have kept Sharpe as Captain of the Light Company, come what may, but no longer. The new man would make his own dispositions and Sharpe felt the chill of uncertainty.

They pushed deeper into the town, through crowds of men intent on recompense for the night's effort. A group of the 88th had hacked open a wine-shop, splintering the door with bayonets, and now had set up their own business selling the stolen wine. Some officers tried to restore order, but they were outnumbered and ignored. Bolts of cloth cascaded from an upper window, draping the narrow street in a grotesque parody of a holiday as soldiers destroyed what they did not want to

loot. A Spaniard lay beside a door, blood trickling in a dozen spreading streams from his scalp, while in the house behind were screams, shouts, and the sobbing of women.

The main square was like a bedlam let loose. A soldier of the 45th reeled past Sharpe and waved a bottle in the Rifleman's face. The man was hopelessly drunk. 'The store! We opened the store.' He fell down.

The French spirit store had been broken apart. Shouts came from the building's interior, thumps as the casks were stove in, and musket shots as crazed men fought for the contents. A house nearby was in flames and a soldier, his red jacket decorated with the 45th's green facings, staggered in agony, his back burning, and he tried to douse the flames by pouring a bottle over his shoulder. The spirit flared, scorched his hand, and the man fell, writhing, to die on the stones. Across the plaza a second house was burning and men shouted for help from its upper windows. On the pavement outside women screamed, pointing at their trapped men, but the women were scooped up by redcoats and carried shrieking into an alley. Nearby a shop was being looted. Loaves and hams were slung from the door, to be caught on outstretched bayonets, and Sharpe could see the flicker of flame deep inside the building.

Some troops had kept their discipline and followed their officers in futile attempts to stop the riot. One horseman rode at a group of drunks, and flailing down with a scabbarded sword, split the group apart, and rode out with a young girl, screaming, clinging to his saddle. The horseman took the girl to a growing huddle of women, sheltered by sober troops, and turned his horse back into the melee. Shrieks and screams, laughter and tears, the sound of victory.

Watching it all, in silent awe, the survivors of the

French garrison had gathered in the centre of the plaza to surrender. They were mostly still armed, but submitted patiently to the British troops who systematically worked their way down the losers' ranks and pillaged them. Some women clung to their French husbands or lovers, and those women were left alone. No one was taking revenge on the French. The fight had been short and there was little ill will. Sharpe had heard a suggestion, floating as a rumour before the assault, that all surviving Frenchmen were to be massacred, not as revenge, but as a warning to the garrison at Badajoz what to expect if they chose to resist in their larger fortress. It was no more than a rumour. These French, silent in the midst of rampage, would be marched into Portugal, over the winter roads to Oporto, and then back by ships to the foetid prison hulks or even the brand new prison, built for prisoners of war, in the bleakness of Dartmoor.

'Good God.' Major Forrest's eyes widened as he stared at the rioting troops. 'They're animals! Just animals!'

Sharpe said nothing. There were few rewards for a soldier. The pay would make no man rich, and the battlefields that yielded booty were few and far between. A siege was the hardest fighting and soldiers had always regarded victory in a breach as reason for losing all discipline and taking their reward from the conquered fortress. And if the fortress was a city, so much the more loot, and if the inhabitants of the city were your allies, then that was bad luck; they were in the wrong place, at the wrong time. Life had always been like that, and always would, because this was ancient custom, soldiers' custom. In truth Ciudad Rodrigo was not suffering much. There were, to Sharpe's eyes, plenty of sober, disciplined troops who had not joined the riot and who

would, by morning, have swept up the drunks, disposed of the corpses, and the city's ordeal would soon end in alcoholic exhaustion. He looked round, trying to identify a hospital.

'Sir! Sir!' Sharpe turned. It was Robert Knowles, who had been his Lieutenant till the previous year, but was now a Captain himself. The 'sir' was pure habit. 'How are you?' Knowles smiled in delight. He wore the uniform of his new Regiment. Sharpe gestured at Lawford's body and the young Captain's face fell. 'How?'

'A mine.'

'Christ! Will he live?'

'God knows. We need a hospital.'

'This way.' Knowles had entered the town through the smaller breach, attacked by the Light Division, and he led the party north, through the crowds, and into a narrow street. 'I passed it on the way here. A convent. Crauford's there.'

'Wounded?' Sharpe had thought Black Bob Crauford to be indestructible. The General of the Light Division was the toughest man in the army.

Knowles nodded. 'Shot. It's bad. They don't think he'll live. There.' He pointed to a big, stone building which was topped by a cross and fronted by an arched cloister lit by bracketed torches. Wounded men were lying outside, tended by friends, while screams came from the upper windows behind which the surgeons were already at work with their serrated blades.

'Inside!' Sharpe pushed through the men in the doorway, ignored a nun who tried to stop him, and forced a path for the Colonel's stretcher. The tiled floor was gleaming with fresh blood that looked black in the candlelight. A second nun pushed Sharpe aside and looked down at Lawford. Her eyes saw the gold lace,

the torn elegance of the blood-stained uniform, and she rapped orders at her sisters. The Colonel was carried through an arched doorway to whatever horrors the surgeons would inflict.

The small group of men looked at each other, saying nothing, but on each face there were deep lines of tiredness and sorrow. The South Essex, that had achieved so much under Lawford's leadership, was about to change. Soldiers might belong to an army, wear the uniform of a Regiment, but they lived inside a battalion and the commander of the Battalion made or broke their happiness. Their thoughts were all the same.

'What now?' Forrest was weary.

'You get some sleep, sir.' Leroy spoke brutally.

'Parade in the morning, sir?' Sharpe suddenly realized that Forrest was in command until the new man was appointed. 'The Brigade Major will have orders.'

Forrest nodded. He waved a hand towards the doorway where Lawford had disappeared. 'I must report this.'

Knowles put a hand on Forrest's elbow. 'I know where the Headquarters will be, sir. I'll take you.'

'Yes.' Forrest hesitated. He saw a severed hand lying on the checkered tiles and he nearly gagged. Sharpe kicked the hand out of sight beneath a dark wooden chest. 'Go on, sir.'

Forrest, Leroy, and Knowles left. Sharpe turned to Lieutenant Price and Sergeant Harper. 'Find the Company. Make sure they have billets.'

'Yes, sir.' Price seemed shocked. Sharpe tapped him on the chest.

'Stay sober.'

The Lieutenant nodded, then pleaded. 'Half sober?'

'Sober.'

'Come on, sir.' Harper led Price away. There was no doubt about which man was in command.

Sharpe watched the men coming into the convent; the blinded, the lamed, the bleeding, French and British. He tried to blot the screaming from his ears, but it was impossible, the sound penetrated the senses like the acrid smoke that hung in the city's streets this night. An officer of the 95th Rifles came down the main stairway, crying, and saw Sharpe. 'He's bad.' He did not know who he was talking to, except that he saw in Sharpe another Rifleman.

'Crauford?'

'There's a bullet in his spine. They can't get it out. The bastard was standing in the middle of the breach, right in the bloody middle, and telling us to move our arses. They shot him!'

The Rifle officer went out into the cold night. Crauford never asked his men to do anything he would not do himself, and he would be there, cursing and spitting, leading his men on, and now he would die. The army would not be the same. Things were changing.

A clock struck ten o'clock and Sharpe thought it had been just three hours since they slipped over the snow towards the breach. Just three hours! The door through which Lawford had been carried was opened and a soldier dragged out a corpse. It was not the Colonel. The body, pulled by the heels, left a jellied slime of bloodied mud on the tiles. The door was left open and Sharpe crossed to it, leaned on the post, and stared into the candle-bright charnel house. He remembered the soldier's prayer, morning and evening, that God keep him from the surgeon's knife. Lawford was on the table strapped tight, his uniform cut away. An orderly leaned on his chest, obscuring the face, while

a surgeon, his apron stiff with blood the colour of burnt ochre, grunted as he pushed in the knife. Sharpe saw Lawford's feet, still encased in the boots with the swan-neck spurs, jerk in the leather straps. The surgeon was sweating. The candles guttered in the draught and he turned a blood-spattered face. 'Shut the bloody door!'

Sharpe closed it, cutting off the view of severed limbs, the waiting bodies. He wanted a drink. Things were changing. Lawford under the knife, Crauford dying upstairs, the New Year mocking them. He stood in the hallway, in dark shadow, and remembered the gas lighting he had seen in London's Pall Mall just two months ago. A wonder of the world, he had been told, but he did not think so. Gas lighting, steam power, and stupid men in offices with dirty spectacles and neat files, the new denizens of England that would tie up the world in pipes, conduits, paper, and above all order. Neatness above all. England did not want to know about the war. A hero was a week-long wonder, so long as he was not untidily scarred like the beggars in the streets of London. There were men with only half a face, covered in suppurating sores, rodent ulcers, men with empty eye sockets, torn mouths, ragged stumps who had cried out for a penny for an old soldier. He had watched them being moved on so they did not sully the pristine, hissing light in Pall Mall. Sharpe had fought beside some of them, watched them drop on a battle-field, but their country did not care. There were the military hospitals, of course, at Chelsea and Kilmain-ham, but it was the soldiers who paid for those, not the country. The country wanted the soldiers out of the way.

Sharpe wanted a drink.

The door of the surgeon's room banged open and

Sharpe turned to see Lawford being carried on a canvas stretcher to the wide staircase. He hurried to the orderlies. 'How is he?'

'If the rot doesn't get him, sir . . .' The man left the sentence unfinished. His nose was dripping, but he could not wipe it because both hands were on the stretcher. He sniffed. 'Friend of yours, sir?'

'Yes.'

'Nothing you can do tonight, sir. Come back tomorrow. We'll look after him.' He jerked his head upwards. 'Lieutenant Colonels and above are on the second floor, sir. Bleeding luxury. Not like those in the cellar.' Sharpe could imagine it, had seen it often enough, the dank cellars where the wounded were crammed on verminous pallets, one part of the 'ward' always left as a death room where the hopeless could simply rot. He let them go, and turned away.

Ciudad Rodrigo had fallen, the great fortress of the north, and the history books would record the fact and, for years to come, the victory would be remembered with pride. In just twelve days Wellington had surprised, surrounded, assaulted and taken a city. A victory. And no one would remember the names of the men who had died in the breach, who had struggled to silence the great, killing guns sunk in the wide wall. The English would celebrate. They liked victories, especially those far from home that fortified their sense of superiority over the French, but they did not want to know about this; the screams of the wounded, the thump of severed limbs, the slow drip of thick blood from the hallway ceiling.

Sharpe pushed into the cold street and hunched down inside his collar against a sudden flurry of snow. There was no joy for him in this victory; only a sense

of loss, of loneliness, and of some unfinished task he must perform in a breach. It could all wait.

He went in search of drink.

CHAPTER 5

It had begun to snow again, a thin sprinkling that flecked the greatcoats of the collapsed drunks in the street. It was cold. Sharpe knew he should find somewhere warm, somewhere to clean the big sword properly before the rust pits began, somewhere to sleep, but he wanted a drink first.

The city was quieter. There were still shouts echoing down empty alleyways, an odd musket shot, and once, inexplicably, a muffled explosion. Sharpe did not care. He wanted drink to drive away the self-pity, the nagging thought that, without Lawford, he could be a Lieutenant again under the orders of a Captain ten years younger than himself, without experience, and his mood turned savage as he made his way towards the flickering lights of the plaza where the French spirit store had been broken open.

The French prisoners were still in the square's centre, though without their officers who had given their parole and gone off to bed or to drink with their captors. The French soldiers sat shivering and weaponless. Their guards watched them with curious eyes, their hands thrust into pockets, their loaded and bayoneted muskets slung on cold shoulders. Other sentries guarded the houses, stopping the last looters who still staggered, drunk, in the light of the burning buildings. Sharpe

was stopped at the liquor store by a nervous sentry. 'Can't go in there, sir.'

'Why not?'

'General's orders, sir. Orders.'

Sharpe snarled at him. 'The General sent me. He's thirsty.'

The sentry grinned, but still brought his musket down across the doorway. 'I'm sorry, sir. It's orders, sir.'

'What's going on?' A Sergeant appeared, a big man, walking slowly. 'Trouble?'

Sharpe faced the Sergeant. 'I'm going in there for drink. Do you want to stop me?'

The Sergeant shrugged. 'Up to you, sir, but I'd advise against it. Bloody raw alcohol, that is, sir. It's killed a couple of lads.' He looked Sharpe up and down, saw the blood on the uniform. 'In the breach, were you, sir?'

'Yes.'

The Sergeant nodded and unslung a canteen from his neck. 'Here you are, sir. Brandy. Took it off a prisoner. Compliments of the 83rd.'

Sharpe took it, made his thanks, and the Sergeant let out a long, slow breath as he watched the Rifleman walk away. 'You know who that was, lad?'

'No, Sarge.'

'Sharpe. That's who that was. Lucky I was here.'

'Lucky, Sarge?'

'Yes, lad. Otherwise you might have had to shoot a bleedin' hero.' The Sergeant shook his head. 'Well, well, well, so he likes a drop, does he?'

Sharpe walked close to one of the burning houses where the heat of the fire had melted the snow into a glistening sheen on the cobbles. A broken table was tipped on its side and he perched on it, watching the

prisoners in the snow, and wished he could get drunk. He knew he would not. As soon as the first, fierce brandy was in his throat he knew that he was being indulgent. He must find the Company, clean the sword, think of tomorrow, but not yet. It was warm by the burning house, the first warmth he had known in days, and he wanted to be alone for a while. Damn Lawford for walking into a breach where he had no business!

Hooves clattered on stones and a group of horsemen entered the plaza. They wore long, dark cloaks, broad-brimmed hats, and Sharpe could see the outlines of muskets and swords. Partisans. He felt an obscure, unfair anger. The Guerrilleros were the men and women of Spain who fought the 'Guerrilla', the 'little war', and they were achieving what the Spanish armies had failed to achieve; they were pinning down thousands and thousands of Napoleon's troops, troops the British would not have to face, but somehow the presence of the Spanish horsemen in the plaza of Ciudad Rodrigo annoyed Sharpe. These partisans had not fought through a breach, had not faced the cannon, yet here they were, come to pick like vultures at a carcass they had done nothing to kill. The horsemen stopped. They stared at the French prisoners with a silent menace.

Sharpe turned away. He drank again and stared into the white-heat where the house had collapsed into a furnace-like intensity. He thought of Badajoz, waiting to the south, Badajoz the impregnable. Perhaps the pox-scarred Whitehall clerk could write the garrison a letter, telling them their presence was 'irregular', and Sharpe laughed at the thought. Damn the bloody clerk.

There was a shout behind him that made him turn round. A single rider had left the group of horsemen and was walking his horse along the front row of pris-

oners. The French squirmed back, fearing the revenge of the Spanish, and the British sentries tried ineffectually to force the horse away. The rider spurred into a trot, into a canter, and the snow spurted from the hooves that crashed on the cobbles beneath. The rider's face turned towards Sharpe, the heels slammed down, and the horse came towards the lone Rifleman in the light of the burning house.

Sharpe watched the man come. If he wanted drink, then he could find his own. There were sparks from the cobbles as the horse was reined in and Sharpe found himself wishing grimly that the beast would slip and tip its rider into an ignominious heap. So the man was a brilliant horseman, but that did not give him the right to disturb a man who had deserved a quiet drink. Sharpe turned away, ignoring the dismounting Spaniard.

'You've forgotten me?' Sharpe heard the voice and the drink was forgotten. He spun round, standing up, and the rider took off the broad-brimmed hat, shook her head, and the long dark hair fell either side of a face that was like a hawk. Slim, cruel, and very, very beautiful. She smiled at him. 'I came here to find you.'

'Teresa?' The wind snatched snow from a rooftop, whirled it crazily above the sparks of the burning house. 'Teresa?' He reached out for her and she came to him and he held her as he had held her that first time, two years ago, beneath the blades of the French lancers. 'Teresa? It's you?'

She looked up at him, mocking him. 'You forgot me.'

'Christ in heaven! Where have you been?' He began to laugh, his misery banished, and touched her face as if he wanted to prove it was her. 'Teresa?'

She laughed, too, with real pleasure and put a finger to his scarred cheek. 'I thought you might forget me.'

'Forget you? No.' He shook his head, suddenly tongue-tied, though there was so much to say. He had hoped to find her the year before when the army had marched to Fuentes de Oñoro just a few miles from Ciudad Rodrigo. This was Teresa's country. He had thought she might look for him last year, but there had been no sign of her, and then he had gone to England and met Jane Gibbons. He pushed that thought away and looked instead at Teresa and wondered how he could have forgotten this face, the life in it, the sheer force of her presence.

She smiled and jerked her head at the rifle on her shoulder. 'I still have your gun.'

'How many have you killed with it?'

'Nineteen.' She made a grimace. 'Not enough.' She hated the French with a pure, terrifying hatred. She turned in his arms and stared at the prisoners. 'How many did you kill tonight?'

Sharpe thought of the fight in the casement. He shrugged. 'I don't know. Two maybe, three?'

She looked up at him again and grinned. 'Not enough. Did you miss me?'

He had forgotten how she would mock him. He nodded, embarrassed. 'Yes.'

'I missed you.' The statement was said matter-of-factly, almost flatly, that gave it a ring of absolute truth. She pulled away from him. 'Listen.' She jerked her head at the other horsemen. 'They are impatient. Are you going to Badajoz?'

He was confused by her sudden question. 'Badajoz?' He nodded. It was an open secret. Nothing had been said to the army, but every man knew that both fortresses must be taken. 'Yes, I suppose so.'

'Good. Then I'm staying. I must tell my people.' She turned to her horse.

'You're what?'

'You don't want me to?' She was mocking him again, and laughed. 'I will explain, Richard, later. Do we have somewhere to stay?'

'No.'

'We'll find somewhere.' She swung herself on to the horse and nodded again towards the Partisans. 'They want to be on their way. I'll tell them they can go. Will you wait here?'

He saluted her. 'Yes, ma'am.'

'That's better.' She smiled at him, dazzling him with her beauty, with the joy on her face, and then she spurred back across the slush.

He grinned and turned back to the fire, facing its warmth, and felt a vast relief that she had come. He wished she would never go. Then he wondered at her words, hearing, distantly in his mind, the faint alarm at the very mention of the name. Badajoz. Tonight was a victory, but it led only to one place, to the place where the British, the French, the Spanish; to where the gunners and the infantry, the cavalry and the Engineers, all marched.

And now, it seemed, the lovers were marching too. To Badajoz.

CHAPTER 6

They found a house, hard by the walls, that had been used by French gunners. There was food in the kitchen, hard bread and cold tongue, and Sharpe lit a fire and watched Teresa as she stabbed the loaf with her bayonet and ripped the blade downwards. He laughed.

She glared at him. 'What's funny?'

'I don't see you as a housewife.'

She pointed the blade at him. 'Listen, Englishman, I can keep a house, but not for a man who laughs at me.' She shrugged. 'What happens when the war ends?'

He laughed again. 'You go back to your kitchen, woman.'

She nodded, sad at the thought. She carried a gun, as other Spanish women carried guns, because too many men had shirked the role, but when peace came the men would be brave again and push the women back to the stoves. Sharpe saw the wistfulness on her face. 'So what must we talk about?'

'Later.' She brought the plate over to the fire and laughed at the unsavoury lumps of food. 'Eat first.'

They were both ravenous. They washed the food down with watered brandy and then, beneath blankets that had once graced the backs of French cavalry horses, they made love by the fire and Sharpe wished he could trap the moment, make it last for ever. The quietness of a small house in a captured city; the only noises the

calls of sentries on the wall, the barking of a dog, the dying crackle of the small fire. She would not stay, he knew that, to be a camp follower. Teresa wanted to fight the French, to revenge herself on a nation that had raped and murdered her mother. Perhaps, he thought, he could not expect, could never expect this happiness to be for ever. All happiness is fleeting and his mind shied away from the thought of Lawford lying in the Convent. Teresa would go back to the hills, to the ambushes and torture, the harried French in the rock landscape. If he had not been a soldier, Sharpe thought, if he had been a gamekeeper or a coachman, or any one of the other jobs he might have found, then he might have found, too, a settled existence. But not like this, never as a soldier.

Teresa's hand pushed over the skin of his chest, then round to his back, and her fingers were light on the thick, ridged scars. 'Did you find the men who flogged you?'

'Not yet.' He had been flogged, years before, when he was a Private.

'What were their names?'

'Captain Morris and Sergeant Hakeswill.' He said the names tonelessly. They were deep in his mind, waiting vengeance.

'You'll find them.'

'Yes.'

She smiled. 'You'll hurt them?'

'Very much.'

'Good.'

Sharpe grinned. 'I thought Christians were supposed to forgive their enemies.'

She shook her head, the hair tickling him. 'Only when they're dead. Anyway.' She plucked a hair from his chest. 'You're not a Christian.'

'You are.'

She shrugged. 'The priests don't like me. I have been learning English from a priest, Father Pedro. He's nice, but the others . . .' She spat at the fire. 'They do not let me take the Mass. Because I am bad.' She said something in quick, guttural Spanish, something that would have confirmed the opinion of the priests. She sat up and looked round the room. 'Those pigs must have left some wine.'

'I didn't see any.'

'You didn't look. You only wanted me under the blankets.' She stood up and searched the room. Sharpe watched her, loving the straightness of her body, the strength in her slimness. She opened cupboards and pulled their contents violently on to the floor. 'Here.' She tossed him a wooden shelf, loose from a cabinet. 'Put it on the fire.'

Sharpe sprinkled it with powder, to help it light, and when he turned back she had found wine and brandished it to him. 'You see? The pigs always have wine.' She saw him looking at her and her face became serious. 'Am I different?'

'No.'

'You're sure?' She stood facing him, naked, her face worried.

'I'm sure. You're beautiful.' He was puzzled. 'Should there be something different?'

She shrugged, crossed the room and sat beside him. The cork was half out of the bottle and she pulled it free and smelt the wine. 'Awful.' She drank some and handed the bottle to Sharpe.

'What's the matter?'

He knew the moment had come when she would talk.

She was silent for a few seconds, staring into the fire,

70

then she turned abruptly to him, her expression fierce. 'You are going to Badajoz?'

'Yes.'

'You're sure?' She seemed desperate for his certainty.

Sharpe shrugged. 'I can't be sure. The army will go there, but we may be sent to Lisbon, or maybe stay here. I don't know. Why?'

'Because I want you to be there.'

Sharpe waited for her to continue, but she stopped talking and stared, instead, into the fire. The wine was sour, but he drank some, and then pulled the stiff blanket up round her shoulders. She looked sad. 'Why do you want me to be there?' he asked gently.

'Because I will be there.'

'You'll be there.' He spoke the words as if they described the most normal thing on earth, but inside he was grasping for a reason, any reason, that would take Teresa into the largest French fortress in Spain.

She nodded. 'Inside. I've been there, Richard, since April.'

'In Badajoz? Fighting?'

'No. They don't know me as "La Aguja". They think I am Teresa Moreno, niece of Rafael Moreno. That's my father's brother.' She smiled ruefully. 'The French even let me carry a rifle outside the city, can you imagine that? To protect myself against the horrid Guerrilleros.' She laughed. 'We live there, my aunt, uncle, myself, and we trade in furs, leather, and we want peace so the profits can be high.' She made a face.

'I don't understand.'

She leaned away from him, poked at the fire with the bayonet, and then drank more wine. 'Will there be trouble there?'

'Trouble?'

71

'Like tonight? Killings? Thieving? Rape?'

'If the French fight, yes.'

'They will fight.' She looked at him. 'You must find me in the city, you understand?'

He nodded, puzzled. 'I understand.' A dog howled outside at the soft, falling snow. 'But why in Badajoz?'

'You'll be angry.'

'I won't be angry. Why Badajoz?'

Again she was silent, biting her lip and searching his face, and then she took his hand and placed it, beneath the blanket, on her bare stomach. 'Is it different?'

'No.' He stroked her skin, not understanding. She breathed deep.

'I had a baby.' His hand went still on the warm flesh. She shrugged. 'I said you'd be angry.'

'A baby?' His mind seemed to whirl like the snow above the flames.

'Your baby. Our daughter.' Tears came to her eyes, and she buried her head on his shoulder. 'She's ill, Richard, so ill, and she cannot travel. She could die. She is so little.'

'Our daughter? Mine?' He felt the beginnings of joy.

'Yes.'

'What did you call her?'

She looked up at him, her eyes bright with tears. 'Antonia. It was my mother's name. If it had been a boy I would have called him Ricardo.'

'Antonia.' He said the name. 'I like it.'

'You do?'

'Yes.'

'And you're not angry?'

'Why should I be?'

She shrugged. 'Soldiers do not need children.'

He pulled her close, remembering the first kiss, not many miles from here, under the rainstorm as the

72

French Lancers searched the streambed. They had been given so little time together. He remembered the parting in the shadow of Almeida's smoke. 'How old is she?'

'Just over seven months. She's very small.'

He supposed she would be. Tiny, vulnerable, ill, and inside Badajoz, surrounded by the French, ringed with the walls that rose dark above the Guadiana. His daughter.

Teresa shook her head. 'I thought you'd be angry.' She spoke the words as soft as the snow that fell beyond the shuttered windows.

'Angry? No. I'm . . .' But the words could not be found. A daughter? His? And this woman was the mother of his child? It seemed to sink in, with a wonderment and a confusion, and there were no words for him. More than a daughter, a family, and Sharpe thought he had no family, not since his mother died near thirty years before, and he held Teresa tight, crushing her, because he did not want her to see his eyes. He had a family, at last, a family.

In Badajoz.

CHAPTER 7

'Where are we going?'
 'Badajoz!'
The Battalion found the joke endlessly amusing. It took just one man in a company to shout the question and the rest of the men took a deep breath and bawled out the answer. They exaggerated the Spanish pronunciation; the guttural, choking sound of the 'j' drawn out to the final 'th' sound of the Spanish 'z'. The name, shouted by the South Essex, sounded like four hundred men simultaneously vomiting and spitting, and the amusement had carried them far down the familiar Portuguese roads. They marched close to the frontier, going south.
 'Where are we going?'
 'Badajoz!'
It was still cold. The snow had gone, except from the hilltops, and the final ice had melted in the rivers, but the wind stayed in the north and brought daily rain that flogged through the greatcoats, soaked blankets, and made the nightly billets steamy and damp. Most of the army was still in the north, close to Ciudad Rodrigo, attempting to persuade the French that no move was contemplated against the huge southern fortress that guarded the invasion route from Lisbon.
 'Where are we going?'
 'Badajoz!'

Lawford was alive, feverish and weak, but growing stronger in the convent hospital where Crauford had died. In a month or so, as his old battalion faced Bada-joz, the Colonel would be shipped home and, doubtless, taken by carriage from the dockside to the family estate. He had smiled when Sharpe visited him, and struggled to sit up. 'It's only the left arm, Richard.'

'Yes, sir.'

'I can still ride, carry a sword. I'll be back.'

'I hope so, sir.'

Lawford shook his head. 'Bloody foolish thing to do, eh? Still, you were wrong about one thing.'

'What's that?'

'No one shot me, and I didn't wear the cloak.'

'Then you deserved to be shot.'

Lawford smiled. 'I'll take your advice next time.'

If there was a next time, Sharpe thought. Lawford might be back, as he hoped, but not for months, and not with the South Essex. There would be a new Colonel and the rumours had blown through the Regiment like musket smoke over a battlefield. There had been a suggestion, greeted with dismay, that Sir Henry Sim-merson might return to Spain, but Sharpe doubted whether the old Colonel would want to give up his lucrative job with the new-fangled Income Tax. Another thought was that Forrest might be promoted, then that was discounted, and other names came and went. Every Lieutenant Colonel whose path brought him near the South Essex was carefully scrutinized in case he should be the new man, but, as they marched one dawn across the Tagus, into the south, Forrest still commanded and there was no news of Lawford's replacement.

Teresa rode with the Battalion. The Light Company knew her, remembered her from the fighting around Almeida and, somehow, though Sharpe never spoke of

75

it, the men learned of the child's existence. Harper, marching with his effortless stride, grinned at Sharpe. 'Not to worry, sir. The baby'll be all right, so she will. The lads will all look out for her.'

The wives of the Battalion, marching at the rear with their children, brought small presents to Sharpe and Teresa. A blanket, a pair of baby's mittens knitted from an unravelled sock, a carved rattle. Sharpe was surprised, touched and embarrassed by the pleasure the news had caused.

The men themselves were confident, looking forward to Badajoz because the casualties at Ciudad Rodrigo had been blessedly light. The South Essex, like the rest of the army, thought that if they could storm the breaches at Ciudad Rodrigo for only sixty dead, then they would slice through the defences of Badajoz for a similarly light loss. Teresa listened to them and had shaken her head. 'They don't know Badajoz.' Perhaps, Sharpe thought, it was as well that they did not.

'Where are we going?'

'Badajoz!'

They stopped three days in Portalegre, letting a rainstorm hammer overhead that had made the roads treacherous and a river crossing impassable. They were the only battalion in town, living in comfort, but Sharpe could see from the doorposts of the houses how frequently the army had used this road. The Commissary marked the doors with chalk; thus SE/L/6 meant that six men of the South Essex's Light Company were to be billeted in that particular house, but each house had a jumble of such fading marks that spoke of the years of this war. The marks told of English Regiments, Irish, Welsh, Scottish, German, Portuguese, and there were even strange markings left by the French battalions.

Only when Badajoz was taken would the war move again into Spain and leave Portalegre to its customary peace.

Sharpe and Teresa slept in an inn, the Battalion's headquarters, and for Sharpe the three days were a period of contentment, perhaps his last before they would meet again, if they did, inside high, dark fortress walls. Teresa was leaving soon, riding on ahead to Badajoz, to the small, sick baby. She had to leave before the British arrived at the city and its gates were shut.

'Why Badajoz?' Sharpe asked the question again, lying in the Portalegre attic as the afternoon rained itself into a soaking night.

'I had family there. I didn't want her born at home.'

He knew why! Because his daughter was a bastard, with the mark of shame on her. 'But they know, don't they?'

She shrugged. 'They know, but they don't see what they know, so they pretend they do not know.' She shrugged again. 'And my father's brother is a rich man, they're childless, and they look after her well.'

Antonia was ill. Teresa did not know what was the matter, nor indeed did the doctors, but the child was small, did not hold her food, and the sisters in the convent had said that the child would die.

Teresa shook her head. 'She will not.' It was said with grim determination; no child of hers would give up easily its hold on life.

'And she has black hair?' Sharpe was enthralled by any scrap of information.

'You know she has, I have told you a hundred times. Long, black hair, and she was born with it, then it all fell out, and now it is coming back. And she has a little nose. Not like mine, and not bent like yours.'

'Perhaps she isn't mine.'

She hit him, laughing. 'She's yours. She scowls, like

this.' And she screwed up her face in imitation of Sharpe and growled at him so that he pulled her down on to the bed and they lay in silence, the rain slapping at the window, and he wondered what lay ahead on the greasy, stony road.

'Perhaps we should marry?'

She did not reply at first. She lay beside him and listened to the rain, to voices downstairs, and then the clatter of hooves in the stableyard. 'Someone's travelling.'

He said nothing.

She traced the scar on his cheek. 'Would you live in Casatejada?'

He still lay silent. To be a stranger in a strange land? To be Teresa's man, dependant on her for survival? He sighed. 'Maybe. After the war.'

She smiled, knowing the answer to be meaningless. This was the fourth year of fighting the French in Spain, and still the country was occupied by the enemy. No one could remember a time of peace. Before they fought France, the Spanish had fought against the English until their fleet sailed to utter defeat at Trafalgar, sunk or captured with the French fleet. There was no peace beyond the borders. Russia, Austria, Italy, Prussia, Denmark, Egypt, India, war everywhere, until now even the Americans were talking of war as if the young nation wanted to prove it could stand with the old world in a game that had racked the globe for two decades. It was a war fought on three continents, on all the oceans, and some men believed this was the final war, the ending of everything, the withering destruction foretold in the Bible. God only knew when it would end. Perhaps only when the last Frenchman, still dreaming of ruling the world, was hammered and battered into the blood-soaked mud.

Teresa kissed him. 'After the war, Richard.'

Her hand lay over the pocket in his shirt and she pushed in her fingers to draw out the gold locket which contained Jane Gibbons's picture. Sharpe had stolen the locket from her murdered brother. Teresa clicked it open and mocked him with her smile. 'You met her, in England?'

'Yes.'

'She's pretty.'

'I suppose so.'

He tried to take the locket from her, but she closed strong fingers on it.

'You suppose so! She is pretty, isn't she?'

'Yes, very.'

She nodded, satisfied. 'You'll marry her.' He laughed, thinking of the impossibility of the idea, but she shook her head. 'You will, I can tell. Otherwise why do you carry this?'

He shrugged. 'Superstition? It keeps me alive.'

She frowned at him and crossed herself; forehead, belly, nipple to nipple, an extravagant cross to warn off a demon. 'What's she like?'

Sharpe pulled a blanket over Teresa; her only dress was drying by the small fire. 'She's slim, she smiles a lot. She's very rich and she'll marry a very rich man.' He grinned at her. 'She's soft. Comfortable.'

Teresa dismissed the implied criticism; anyone who had the chance to live in soft comfort was a fool to refuse. 'How did you meet her?'

Sharpe was feeling uncomfortable and tried to change the subject, but she insisted. 'Tell me, how?'

'She wanted to know how her brother died.'

Teresa laughed. 'And you told her?'

'Not the truth. I told her he was killed by the French, fighting bravely.'

79

She laughed again. She knew the story; how Lieutenant Gibbons had tried to kill Sharpe and how Patrick Harper had bayoneted the Lieutenant. Sharpe thought back to the small, dark church in Essex, the blonde girl listening to his stumbling story, and the white marble stone that mocked the truth about her vicious, selfish, and sadistic brother.

To the memory of Lieutenant Christian Gibbons, a Native of this Parish, who Volunteered 4 February, 1809, from the Militia of this County into the Regiment of the South Essex, then United with the British Army in the Wars against Tyranny in Spain. He Distinguished Himself on the Field of Talavera where, by Night and by Day, the Attacks of the Enemy were Routed. Such was his Intrepidity that, having Endured the Assault of the Outnumbering Enemy, He and His Company Attacked and Captured a Standard of the French, the First such Glory to be Gained by our Armies in Spain. While thus Confirming his Courage and Spirit, he met a Hero's Death on the 28th Day of July, 1809, in the Twenty-Fifth Year of his Age. This Monument is erected as a Just Tribute to so much Heroism and Worth by Sir Henry Simmerson, Commander of the Victorious Regiment, and by His Fellow Parishioners. AD. 1810.

Sharpe had laughed to himself, not just because Sir Henry had managed to claim a marble credit for the capture of the Eagle, which had happened after Sir Henry had been relieved of command, but because the whole stone was a lie. Gibbons had been nowhere near the Eagle when Sharpe and Harper had fought their way through the enemy battalion, but the marble would still be there, surmounted by its carved pile of weapons,

when the truth had long been forgotten. There was a knock on the door. 'Who is it?'

'Price, sir.'

'What is it?'

'Someone to see you, sir. Downstairs.'

Sharpe swore. 'Who?'

'Major Hogan, sir?' Price made it a question, as if Sharpe might not recognize the name.

'Good God! I'm on my way down!'

Teresa watched as he pulled on long boots and buckled the sword. 'Is this the Hogan we send papers to?'

'Yes. You'll like him.' He felt her dress, it was still damp. 'You'll come down?'

She nodded. 'Soon.'

The main room of the inn was noisy, good natured, and boisterous. Sharpe pushed his way through the officers and saw Hogan, dripping wet, by the serving hatch. The Irish Major held out a hand in welcome, but gestured first at the officers. 'They're in good spirits.'

'They think Badajoz will be easy.'

'Oh.' Hogan raised his eyebrows, then made room for Sharpe on the bench. 'I hear you're a father.'

'Does anybody not know?'

'Don't be ashamed. It's a fine thing, so it is. Wine?'

Sharpe nodded. 'How are you?'

'Cold, wet, busy. Yourself?'

'Dry, warm and lazy. What's the news?'

Hogan poured wine and took out his snuffbox. 'The French are dithering like wet hens. They're not trying to retake Ciudad Rodrigo, and they're not sending troops to the south, instead they're all sending letters to each other, blaming each other.' Hogan raised his glass. 'Your health, Richard, your family's health.'

Sharp blushed self-consciously, but raised his glass. He watched Hogan take a vast pinch of snuff. 'What are you doing here?'

The Major's eyes watered, his mouth opened, and he sneezed fit to extinguish a chandelier. 'Mary, Moses and Martha, but that's powerful muck! Badajoz, Richard, always Badajoz. I'm taking a wee look and then reporting back to the Peer.' He wiped his moustache. 'Mind you, I don't expect it to have changed much from the last year.'

'And?' Sharpe knew Hogan had been present at both failures to take Badajoz in 1811.

Hogan shrugged. 'It's a bastard, Richard, a real bastard. The walls are like the Tower of London, so they are, and you can add Windsor Castle up on that hill over the river. They've got ditches that can swallow an army.' The Irishman shook his head. 'I would not be hopeful.'

'As bad as that?'

'Who knows?' Hogan swallowed wine. 'It's a big place, so it is, and they can't defend every inch of those walls. I suppose the Peer will put in several attacks at once, I don't know.'

Wellington probably would attack the walls in several different places, just as he had put three attacks on to Ciudad Rodrigo in the one night, but several attacks at once did not guarantee success. Old soldiers, men who had fought with Wellington in India, knew that he did not like siege work. The Peer was frugal with his men in battles, fought for their health between campaigns, but would throw them like random grapeshot at the walls of a fortress to shorten a siege. Sharpe shrugged. 'It has to be done.'

'As the virgin said.' Hogan grinned. 'What news of you?'

'Not much.' Sharpe traced the letter 'A' in spilt wine on the table, then scrubbed it out. 'Recruits are joining us at Elvas. Two hundred men and officers, so we're told, but no news of a Colonel. Have you heard?'

Hogan spat out an olive pip. 'Not a word. I'll bet you two cases of wine to one, that you'll get one before the siege.'

'Which starts when?'

Hogan thought about it, juggling an olive in his hand. 'Three weeks? The guns are coming round by sea. Everything's moving.'

Sharpe looked through the small window by the back door at the rain which was pelting down. 'You'll need better weather.'

Hogan shrugged. 'It can't rain for ever.'

'That's what Noah's brother said.'

Hogan smiled. 'Aye, but at least he was spared shovelling elephant dung for forty days.'

Sharpe grinned. The Battalion would soon be shovelling mud, digging forward to the great fortress and, as he thought of Badajoz, his expression changed. Hogan saw the worry.

'What's the problem?'

Sharpe shook his head. 'Nothing.'

'Would it be that gazette, now?'

Sharpe gave a minute shrug. 'I suppose so.'

'They're fool's gold, sure enough, but they can't take it away from you, not now.'

'Would you bet me some wine on that?'

Hogan said nothing. There was no answer. The Horse Guards had promoted officers who were totally blind, others who were only outside of the madhouse because of their money and connections, and they were certainly not in the habit of ratifying gazettes simply because a man was good at his job. Hogan shook his

head, raised his glass again. 'A pox to pen pushers.'

'May they rot in agony.'

There was a heaving of bodies near the serving hatch, a welcoming smile on Hogan's face, and Major Forrest joined them. Sharpe half listened to Hogan repeating his news, but his thoughts drifted away, back to that damned gazette. If only they would ratify it, he could relax. He tried to imagine what would happen if they did not, if he were to find himself a Lieutenant again. He would have to salute Knowles, call him 'sir', and someone else would lead the Company that Sharpe had trained, brought up, and led through two years of war. He remembered his first sight of them; cowed and helpless, but now they were as fine as any soldiers in the army. He could not imagine losing them, losing Harper? Good God! Losing Harper!

'Good God!' For a moment Sharpe thought Hogan had been reading his thoughts, and then he saw the Major staring across the room. Hogan shook his head. 'If ever any beauty I did see which I desired and got, 'twas but a dream of she.' Teresa had come into the room and was crossing towards them. Hogan turned to Forrest. 'Would she be your lady, Major? She can't be Sharpe's. The man has no taste! He hasn't even heard of John Donne, let alone recognize a misquotation. No. Something as beautiful as that would only fall in love with a man of taste, a man like you, Major, or me.' He twitched at his collar as Forrest blushed with pleasure.

Lieutenant Price had gone on his knees to Teresa, blocking her path, and was offering her his undying love in the form of a red pepper held up like a rose. The other Lieutenants encouraged him, shouted at Teresa that Harold Price had prospects, but she just blew him a kiss and stepped past him. Sharpe was so immensely proud of her. In any place in the world, in

any drawing room, in any theatre, in any palace, let alone in a damp, smoky inn at Portalegre, she would be counted beautiful. The mother of his child. His woman. He stood up for her, embarrassed that his pleasure was obvious to so many, and offered her a chair. He introduced Hogan who dropped into his fluent Spanish and made her laugh. She glanced at Sharpe, eyes fond under the long, dark lashes, listened to the Irishman's nonsense, and laughed again. The Engineer toasted her, flirted with her, and looked at Sharpe. 'You're a lucky man, Richard.'

'I know, sir, I know.'

Lieutenant Price was left with the red pepper. He threw it across the room and followed it with a bellowed question. 'Where are we going?'

'Badajoz!' The room roared with laughter.

Part Two

February–March
1812

CHAPTER 8

Halt!' Boots thudded on to the roadway. 'Stand bloody still, you bastards! Still!' The Sergeant cackled, ground his few remaining teeth together, turned away and immediately spun back. 'I said still! If you want your sodding bum scratched, Gutteridge, I'll do it with my bayonet! Still!' He turned to the young officer and snapped an immaculate salute. 'Sir!'

The Ensign, visibly nervous of the tall Sergeant, returned the salute. 'Thank you, Sergeant.'

'Don't thank me, sir. My job, sir.' The Sergeant gave his habitual cackle, a wild, discomfiting sound, and his eyes flicked left and right. The Sergeant's eyes were blue, almost a baby blue, the Ensign decided, while the rest of him was yellow, fever yellow, a sickly cast over his hair, teeth and skin. The baby blue eyes settled on the Ensign. 'Are you going to find the Captain, sir, are you? Tell him we've arrived, sir?'

'Yes, of course.'

'Give him my best, sir. My very best.' The Sergeant cackled again, and the cackle turned into a racking cough, and the head twitched on its long, scrawny neck that had the terrible scar.

The Ensign walked into the courtyard that had SE/LC chalked on the gatepost. He was relieved to be away from the Sergeant, his constant bane on the long journey from the South Essex depot, and relieved that

the other officers of the South Essex Light Company could now share the brunt of the Sergeant's madness. No, that was not right. The Sergeant was not mad, the Ensign decided, but there was something about him that spoke of the possibility of utter horror that lurked just below the yellow surface. The Sergeant was terrifying to the Ensign, as he was to the recruits.

The soldiers in the courtyard were almost as frightening. They had the look that other veterans in Portugal had assumed, a look quite at odds with soldiering in England. Their uniforms had turned from scarlet into either a faded, whitish pink, or else into a dark, virulent purple. The commonest colour was brown where jackets and trousers had been repeatedly patched with coarse, peasant cloth. Their skins, even in winter, were dark brown. Above all, the Ensign noticed, was their air of confidence. They carried themselves casually, at home with their polished and battered weapons, and the Ensign felt ill at ease in his new scarlet jacket with its bright yellow facings. An Ensign was the lowest of all commissioned officers and William Matthews, a sixteen-year-old who pretended to shave, was scared by the first sight of these men he was supposed to command.

A man was bent beneath the yard pump, a second man working the handle so that water pulsed on to his head and naked back. As the man stood up Matthews saw a lattice of thick scars that had been caused by a flogging and the Ensign turned away, sickened by the sight. His father had warned him that the army attracted the filth of society, the troublemakers, and Matthews knew he had just seen such a piece of human flotsam. Another soldier, for some reason dressed in Rifle green, saw his expression and grinned. Matthews knew he was being watched, and judged, but then an officer

appeared, dressed properly, and it was with relief that he crossed to the newcomer, a Lieutenant, and saluted. 'Ensign Matthews, sir. Reporting with the recruits.'

The Lieutenant smiled vaguely, turned away, and vomited. 'Oh, Christ!' The Lieutenant seemed to be having trouble in breathing, but he stood upright again, painfully, and turned back to the Ensign. 'My dear fellow, frightfully sorry. Bloody Portuguese put garlic in everything. I'm Harold Price.' Price took off his shako and rubbed his head. 'I missed your name. Frightfully sorry.'

'Matthews, sir.'

'Matthews. Matthews.' Price said the name as if it might mean something, and then held his breath as his stomach heaved and, when the spasm had passed, breathed out slowly. 'Forgive me, my dear Matthews. I think my stomach's delicate this morning. You wouldn't, I suppose, do me the honour of lending me five pounds? Just for a day or two? Guineas would be better.'

His father had warned him of this, too, but Matthews felt it would be unwise to begin his acquaintance with his new Company by a churlish refusal. He was aware of the soldiers in the yard listening and he wondered if he was an innocent in some kind of private joke, but what else could he do?

'Of course, sir.'

Lieutenant Price looked astonished. 'My dear fellow, how kind! Splendid! I'll give you my note, of course.'

'And hope the Ensign gets killed at Badajoz?'

Matthews spun round. The tall soldier, the one whose back was so horribly scarred, had spoken. The man's face was scarred, too, and it gave him a knowing, even mocking expression, that was belied by his voice. He grinned at Matthews. 'He's doing it to everyone.

91

Borrowing in the hope that they die. He should make a tidy enough profit.'

Matthews did not know what to say. The soldier had spoken in a kindly way, but he had not used the word 'sir', which was disconcerting, and Matthews had the feeling that what little authority his lowly rank endowed was already being dissipated. He hoped the Lieutenant would intervene, but Price's expression was sheepish as he put the shako on his head and grinned at the scarred man. 'This is Ensign Matthews, sir. He's brought the replacements.'

The tall, scarred man nodded at the Ensign. 'Glad you're here, Matthews. I'm Sharpe, Captain Sharpe. What's your name?'

'Matthews, sir.' The Ensign gaped at Sharpe. An officer who had been flogged? He realized his answer had been inadequate. 'William, sir.'

'Good morning and welcome.' Sharpe was making an effort to be pleasant. He hated mornings and this morning, in particular, was unpleasant. Today Teresa was going from Elvas and riding the few miles, across the border, to Badajoz. Another parting. 'Where did you leave the men?'

Matthews had not left them anywhere; the Sergeant had made all the decisions, but he pointed through the gate. 'Outside, sir.'

'Get them in, get them in.' Sharpe rubbed his hair dry with a piece of sacking. 'Sergeant Harper! Sergeant Read!' Harper could settle the recruits into the Company, while Read, the Methodist teetotaller, could fuss over the Company books. It would be a busy day.

Sharpe dressed hurriedly. The rain had stopped, at least for the moment, but the wind still came cold from the north and brought with it high, streaked clouds that promised more bad weather in March. At least,

being the first troops to arrive, the Battalion had the pick of Elvas's billets and the men lived in comparative comfort even as they stared across the border at Badajoz. The two fortresses were just eleven miles apart, either side of a shallow valley, but, despite their closeness, they were vastly different. Badajoz was a city, the capital of a province, while Elvas was a small market town that found itself in the centre of wide, spreading defences. Impressive as were the Portuguese walls, they were small compared with the Spanish fortifications that barred the road to Madrid. Sharpe knew it was fanciful, but there seemed something sinister about the huge fortress to the east and he hated to think of Teresa going behind the towering walls and wide ditches. Yet she had to return to the child, his child, and he would have to find her and protect her when the moment came.

His thoughts of Teresa and Antonia suddenly stopped, wrenched violently away, replaced by a loathing thick as vomit. His past was here, in Elvas, a hated past. The same yellow face, with the same twitch, and the same cackle! My God! Here, in his Company? Their eyes met, and Sharpe saw the insolent grin that seemed to verge on total insanity.

'Halt!' The Sergeant glared at the replacements. 'Left turn! Still, you bastards! Keep your bloody mouth shut, Smithers, or I'll use it to clean out the stables!' The Sergeant turned smartly, marched to Sharpe, and crashed to a halt. 'Sir!'

Ensign Matthews looked between the two tall men. 'Sir? This is Sergeant . . .'

'I know Sergeant Hakeswill.'

The Sergeant cackled, showing his few yellow teeth. Spittle dribbled on to his stubbled chin. Sharpe tried to work out the Sergeant's age. Hakeswill had to be

forty, at least, maybe forty-five, but the eyes were still the eyes of a cunning child. They looked unblinkingly at Sharpe with amusement and scorn. Sharpe was aware that Hakeswill was trying to outstare him so he turned away and saw Harper buckling his belt as he came into the courtyard. He nodded at the Irishman. 'Stand them easy, Sergeant. They need sleeping space and food.'

'Sir.'

Sharpe turned back to Hakeswill 'You're joining this Company?'

'Sir!' He barked the reply, and Sharpe remembered how punctilious Hakeswill had always been in the etiquette of the army. No soldier drilled more exactly, replied more formally, yet every action seemed imbued with a kind of contempt. It was impossible to pin it down, yet it had something to do with the expression in those childlike eyes, as if there was a freak inside the rigorously correct soldier that watched and laughed as it fooled the army. Hakeswill's face twitched into a grin. 'Surprised, sir?'

Sharpe wanted to kill the man on the spot, to blot out those offensive eyes, still for ever the twitch and the teeth-grinding, the cackle and the grin. Many men had tried to kill Obadiah Hakeswill. The scar on his neck with its fiery red folds of skin had been put there when he was just twelve years old. He had been sentenced to death by hanging for stealing a lamb. He had been innocent of the charge. His real offence was that he had forced the vicar's daughter to undress for him by holding a viper at her neck, its tongue flickering, and she had fumbled off her clothes and screamed as the boy attacked her. Her father had rescued the girl and it had been simpler to accuse the boy of stealing a lamb, more certain to end in death, and the deal had been struck with the Justices. No one, even then, had

wanted Obadiah Hakeswill to live except, perhaps, his mother, and the vicar, if he could have thought of a way, would have gladly strung her alongside her foul son.

He had lived somehow. They had strung him up, but he was still alive, with the stretched, scrawny neck and its livid scar to prove he had once been hanged. He had found his way into the army and into a way of life that suited him. He put up a hand and rubbed the scar below his left ear. 'Be all right, sir, now that I'm here.'

Sharpe knew what he meant. There was a legend that Hakeswill the indestructible man, the survivor of a judicial execution, could not be killed and the legend did not diminish with time. Sharpe had seen two files of men blown away by grapeshot, yet Hakeswill, standing immediately to their front, had not been touched.

Hakeswill's face twitched, hiding the laugh that was prompted by Sharpe's unexpressed hatred. The twitch stopped. 'I'm glad I'm here, sir. Proud of you, I am, proud. My best recruit.' He had spoken loudly, letting the courtyard know of their joint history; and there was a challenge, too, as unspoken as their hatred, which announced that Hakeswill would not submit easily to the discipline of a man he had once drilled and tyrannized.

'How's Captain Morris, Hakeswill?'

The Sergeant grinned, then cackled into Sharpe's face so that the officer caught the foul breath. 'Remember him, sir, do you? He's a Major now, sir, so I hear. In Dublin. Mind you, sir, you was a naughty boy, you'll pardon an old soldier for saying so.'

There was silence in the courtyard. Every man was listening to the words, aware of the hostility between the two men. Sharpe dropped his voice, so no one but Hakeswill could hear. 'If you lay a finger on any man in

this Company, Sergeant, I'll bloody kill you.' Hakeswill grinned, was about to reply, but Sharpe was faster. 'Shun!' Hakeswill snapped upright, his face suddenly clouded with anger because he had been denied his reply. 'About turn!'

Sharpe left him there, facing a wall. God damn it! Hakeswill! The scars were on Sharpe's back because of Hakeswill and Morris, and Sharpe had sworn on that far-off day that he would inflict as much pain on them as they had on him. Hakeswill had beaten a Private into bloody insensibility; the man had recovered his consciousness, but never his senses, and Sharpe had been a witness. He had tried to stop the hammering and, for his efforts, was accused by Morris and Hakeswill of the beating. He had been tied to a cart's wheel and flogged.

Now, suddenly face to face with his enemy after all these years, he felt an uneasy sense of helplessness. Hakeswill seemed untouchable. He had the confidence of a man who simply did not care what happened to him, because he knew he was indestructible. The Sergeant went through life with a suppurating hatred of other men, and, from behind his mask of military conformity, spread poison and fear throughout the companies he served. Hakeswill, Sharpe knew, would not have changed, any more than his appearance had changed. The same great belly, perhaps a few inches bigger, a few more lines on the face, another tooth or two missing, yet still the same yellow skin and the mad stare, and Sharpe remembered, uncomfortably, that once Hakeswill had told him they were alike. Both on the run, both without family, and the only way to survive, the Sergeant said, was to hit hard and hit first.

He looked at the recruits. They were wary, as well they might be, cautious of this new Company. Sharpe,

though they could not know it, shared their unease. Hakeswill, of all people, in his Company? Then he remembered the gazette, and knew that the Company might not be his, and he felt his thoughts begin their profitless descent into gloom so he snapped them away. 'Sergeant Harper?'

'Sir?'

'What's happening today?'

'Football, sir. Grenadier Company playing the Portuguese. Heavy casualties expected.'

Sharpe knew that Harper was trying to cheer up the newcomers and so he dutifully smiled. 'A light day, then, for your first day. Enjoy it. Tomorrow we work.' Tomorrow he would be without Teresa, tomorrow would be a day nearer Badajoz and tomorrow he might be a Lieutenant. He realized the recruits, some of whom he had found himself, were waiting for him to continue. He forced another smile. 'Welcome to the South Essex. I'm glad you're here. This is a good Company and I'm sure it will stay that way.' The words sounded incredibly lame, even to himself, as if he knew they were untrue.

He nodded at Harper. 'Carry on, Sergeant.'

The Irishman's eyes flicked towards Hakeswill, still facing the wall, and Sharpe pretended not to see. Damn Hakeswill, he could stay there, but then he relented. 'Sergeant Hakeswill!'

'Sir!'

'Dismiss!'

Sharpe walked into the street, wanting to be alone, but Leroy was leaning on the gatepost and the American lifted an amused eyebrow. 'Is that how the Hero of the Field of Talavera welcomes recruits? No calls to glory? No bugles?'

'They're lucky to get a welcome at all.'

Leroy drew on his cigar and fell into step beside

Sharpe. 'I suppose this unhappiness is caused by your lady leaving us?'

Sharpe shrugged. 'I suppose so.'

'Then shall I share other news?'

Leroy had stopped and his dark eyes seemed to be amused.

'Napoleon's dead?'

'Alas, no. Our Colonel arrives today. You don't seem surprised?'

Sharpe waited for a priest, mounted on a drooping mule, to go past. 'Should I be surprised?'

'No.' Leroy grinned at him. 'But the usual reaction is to say "who, why, what, how do you know?" Then I give you all the answers, and that's called a conversation.'

Sharpe's depression was dissipated by Leroy. 'So tell me.'

The thin, laconic American looked surprised. 'I never thought you would ask. Who is he? His name is Brian Windham. I've never liked the name Brian, it's the sort of name a woman gives to a boy in the hope he will grow up honest.' He tapped ash on to the roadway. 'Why? I think there is no answer to that. What is he? He is a mighty hunter of foxes. Do you hunt, Sharpe?'

'You know I don't.'

'Then your future may be gloomy, as mine may be. And how do I know?'

He paused.

'How do you know?'

'Because our good Colonel, honest Brian Windham, has a forerunner, a messenger, a John the Baptist to his coming, a Paul Revere, no less.'

'Who?'

Leroy sighed; he was being unusually loquacious. 'You've never heard of Paul Revere?'

98

'No.'

'Lucky man, Sharpe. He called my father a traitor, and our family called Revere a traitor, and I rather think we lost the argument. The point is, my dear Sharpe, that he was a forerunner, an agent of warning, and our good Colonel has sent such a warning of his arrival in the shape of a new Major.'

Sharpe looked at Leroy, the American's expression had not changed. 'I'm sorry, Leroy. I'm sorry.'

Leroy shrugged. As the senior Captain he had been hoping for the vacant Majority in the Battalion. 'One should expect nothing in this army. His name is Collett, Jack Collett, another honest name and another fox-hunter.'

'I'm sorry.'

Leroy began walking again. 'There is something else.'

'What?'

Leroy pointed with his cigar into the courtyard of the house where the officers were billeted and Sharpe looked through the archway and, for the second time that morning, he had a sudden, unwelcome shock. A young man, in his middle twenties, stood next to a pile of luggage that his servant was unstrapping. Sharpe had never seen the officer before but the uniform was only too familiar. It was the uniform of the South Essex, complete even to the silver badge of the Eagle that Sharpe had captured, but it was a uniform only one man could wear. It had a curved sabre, slung on chains, and a silver whistle holstered on the crossbelt. The insignias of rank, denoting a Captain, were not epaulettes, but wings made from chains and decorated with a bugle horn. Sharpe was looking at a man dressed as the Captain of the South Essex Light Company. He swore.

Leroy laughed. 'Join the downtrodden.'

No one had the guts to tell him, except Leroy! The

bastards had brought in a new man, over his head, and he had never been told! He felt a huge anger, a depression, and a helplessness in the face of the army's cumbersome machinery. He could not believe it. Hakeswill, Teresa going, and now this?

Major Forrest appeared in the archway, saw Sharpe, and came towards him. 'Sharpe?'

'Sir.'

'Don't jump to conclusions.' The Major sounded miserable.

'Conclusions, sir?'

'About Captain Rymer.' Forrest nodded towards the new Captain who, at that moment, turned and caught Sharpe's eye. He bowed briefly, a polite acknowledgement, and Sharpe forced himself to respond. He looked back to Forrest.

'What happened?'

Forrest shrugged. 'He bought Lennox's commission.'

Lennox? Sharpe's predecessor had died two and a half years before. 'But that was . . .'

'I know, Sharpe. His will was in the courts. The estate has only just released the commission for sale.'

'I didn't even know it was for sale!' Not, Sharpe thought, that he could have afforded the fifteen hundred pounds.

Leroy lit a new cigar from the butt of his old. 'I doubt if anyone knew it was for sale. Right, Major?'

Forrest nodded miserably. An open sale meant that the legal price had to be paid. It was far more likely that Captain Rymer was a friend of one of the lawyers who had cut out the competition, sold it to Rymer, and in return received a higher price. The Major spread his hands. 'I'm sorry, Sharpe.'

'So what happens?' Sharpe's voice was hard.

'Nothing.' Forrest tried to sound hopeful. 'Major

Collett, you haven't met him, Sharpe, agrees with me. It's a mix up. So you stay in command till Colonel Windham arrives.'

'Later today, sir.'

Forrest nodded. 'Everything will be all right, Sharpe. You'll see. Everything.'

Sharpe saw Teresa walk through the courtyard, carrying her saddle, but she did not see him. He turned away and stared over the rooftops of Elvas, pink in the sunlight, and saw that a cloudbank, riding the north wind, had bisected the landscape with its shadow. Spain lay in shadow and Badajoz was a dark citadel far away. He swore again, foully and at length, as if the curses might fight for him against the ill fortune. He knew it was fanciful, stupid even, but it seemed as if the fortress that barred the eastern road, its walls high over the Guadiana, was at the centre of the evil, spreading a baleful fate over all who came near. Hakeswill, Rymer, Teresa going, all things changing, and what else, he wondered, would go wrong before they lanced the evil in Badajoz?

CHAPTER 9

Everything about Obadiah Hakeswill was graceless and repulsive to the point of fascination. The body was huge, but any man who mistook the belly for a sign of weakness would be caught by the arms and legs that had massive strength. He was clumsy, except when performing a drill movement, though even when he was marching there was a hint that, at any moment, he might become some snarling, shambling beast; half wild, half man. His skin was yellowish, a legacy of the Fever Islands. His hair was blond, going grey, and stretched thinly over his scarred scalp, falling lank to the stretched, tensed, obscenely mutilated neck.

Some time in the past, even before the hanging, he had known he would never be liked and so, instead, determined to be feared. He had one advantage. Obadiah Hakeswill was afraid of nothing. When other men complained of hunger or cold, dampness or disease, the Sergeant simply cackled and knew that it would end. He did not care how much he was hurt in a fight; wounds mended, bruises disappeared, and he could not die. He had known that from the moment he had dangled on the rope's end; he could not die because he was protected by a magic, his mother's magic, and he was proud of the foul scar, the symbol of his invulnerability, and knew that it frightened other men. Officers did not cross Obadiah Hakeswill. They feared the conse-

quences of his anger, the foulness of his looks, and so they humoured him, knowing that in return he would stick to the letter of the regulations and would support their authority against the men. Within those limits he was free to take his revenge on a world that had made him ugly, lumpen, and friendless, a world that had tried to kill him and which now, above all, feared him.

He hated Sharpe. To Hakeswill officers were officers, born, like John Morris, to their exalted station and the purveyors of reward and privilege. But Sharpe was an upstart. He came from the same gutters as Hakeswill, and the Sergeant had once tried to break him and failed. He would not fail again. Now, sitting in the stable behind the officers' house, stripping a hambone with his fingernails and cramming the scraps into an open, churning mouth, he took pleasure at remembering their meeting. Hakeswill had recognized the officer's embarrassment and chalked it up as a small victory to be followed and exploited. There was the Sergeant too, the Irishman who would be worth baiting, and he cackled as he stuffed the food into his mouth and scratched the flea-bites in his armpit. There was profit in fear, none in harmony. Hakeswill had made himself comfortable by reducing companies into divided camps; those for him and those against. Those he disliked would be forced to pay money, or services, so that the Sergeant's life would be bearable. Hakeswill had a shrewd idea that Patrick Harper would not allow it to happen easily, nor Sharpe, but he laughed out loud. He had not re-enlisted in an active service battalion, one that would lead to the rich pickings of a war, to be thwarted by those two.

He fished in his ammunition pouch and came up with a handful of coins. It was not much, a few shillings, but all he had managed to steal in the chaos of the

arrival. He had come to the stable to count his gains and to hide them deep in his pack. He preferred services to money. Soon he would discover which soldiers in the Light Company were married, and which had the prettiest wives. Those were the ones to go for, the ones who would be reduced to quaking misery by Hakeswill's battery of weapons till they would offer anything for a release from his torment. Their wives were his usual price. He knew that, on average, two or three would give in; would bring their women in tears to some straw-filled stable like this and, after a while, the women surrendered. Some came drunk, but he never minded that, and one had tried to rip him with a bayonet and he had killed her, and blamed the husband for her death, and he laughed as he remembered the man's execution, hung from a high tree. It would take time to become comfortable in this new battalion, to root around in it like a beast settling in its lair, but he would do it. And, just like an animal slumping into rest, he would first claw out the rocks that would be uncomfortable beneath his yellow hide, rocks like Sharpe and Harper.

He had the stable to himself. A horse moved in the stall behind him, light chinked between the thick, curved roof tiles, and the Sergeant was glad of the time to be alone, to think. Stealing equipment was a good beginning. Pick your men, steal from them, then report the loss and have them charged, hoping that the new Colonel was a flogging man. It was extraordinary what a man would do to avoid a flogging, and what a woman would give to save her man from the lashes! It was so easy, and he laughed again. Two or three savage floggings and the Company would be eating out of his hand! There was even a rumour, that had flashed through the Battalion like wildfire, that Sharpe had

lost the Company. That was good news; it removed an obstacle, and Hakeswill had judged that Price would be no great problem. The new Ensign, Matthews, was a mere boy, and the only problem was Patrick Harper. His fault was probably excessive honesty, and Hakeswill grinned. It was so easy!

The door of the stable opened and Hakeswill froze. He liked to stay unseen; to watch without being watched. One person entered, he could tell by the foot-steps, and walked to the row of stalls behind Hakeswill as the big, wooden door closed under its own ponder-ous weight. The newcomer was hidden from him and he moved, infinitely slowly, timing his movements so that the rustle of straw should seem like the stirrings of a draught and then, thankfully, a horse staled noisily and the splashing covered the sound of him kneeling up to peer through a chink in the boards.

He almost crowed with delight. It was a girl; a girl with the kind of beauty a man might dream of, but know he could never possess. She was a native, too, he could see that by the clothes and by her dark skin and hair, and native girls were always fair game. He tensed himself. He wanted this girl. He forgot everything; Sharpe, Harper, his plans, everything, for he was sud-denly swamped with lust for this girl and he began to edge the bayonet from its scabbard.

Teresa heaved the saddle on to her horse, pulled the blanket straight beneath the leather, and pulled the girth through its thick buckle. She spoke to the horse in Spanish, murmuring to it, and heard nothing strange in the stable. She did not want to leave Sharpe, to return to the *Afrancesados*, the French-lovers, in the city, but Antonia was there, and ill, and Teresa had to go back to protect her child through the siege. After that, pray God, the child would be well enough to be moved.

And marriage? She sighed and looked up to the roof. It was not right that Antonia should be a bastard, yet Teresa could not see herself following this army like a puppy behind a pack, and she knew Richard Sharpe would not leave to live in Casatejada. Marry anyway? At least the baby would have a name, a good name, and there was no shame for a child to carry the name of an unknown, absent father. She sighed again. It would all have to wait until the siege was done, or the child better, and suddenly, like a dark cloud, she wondered what might happen if Sharpe died in the siege. She shrugged. She would tell everyone that he had married her before the siege, and no one would be any the wiser.

Hakeswill waited till her hands were full, bridling the horse, and then he rolled over the partition, the bayonet bright in his hand, and grabbed her hair and pulled her down with his lumbering weight. She lashed at him, hopelessly falling, and then he had the needle-point of the slim bayonet at her throat and was kneeling at her head. 'Hello, missy.' She said nothing. She was flat on her back, beside the horse, and his face was upside down above her. Hakeswill licked his lips. 'Portuguese, are we?'

The Sergeant laughed. This was a gift from the gods, a present on his first day with his new Company. He kept the bayonet at her throat and edged his way round so he could see her properly. The horse stirred, but he was not afraid of horses, and then his knees were beside her waist and he laughed aloud. This one was beautiful, even more beautiful than she had looked through the gap in the stalls. This one he would remember for ever. 'Speak English?' The girl said nothing. He pressed with the bayonet, the slightest fraction, not breaking the skin. 'D'you speak English, missy?'

Probably not, which did not matter much, because there was no chance that she would live to tell any tales,

in any language. The provosts would hang a man for rape so the girl would have to die, unless she liked him, of course, which he conceded was not likely. It was not impossible. There had been that bitch in the Fever Islands, the blind girl, but there was no sign that this little beauty was exactly welcoming his attentions.

She did not seem frightened either, which was puzzling and distressing. He expected them to scream, they usually did, but she was watching him calmly with big, dark, long-lashed eyes. The scream might come later, but he was ready for it. In a moment he would hold her throat and move the bayonet into her mouth. He would force the blade down till she was on the point of gagging, so all she could see was the seventeen inches of edged metal protruding from her mouth, gripped in his fist and, in that position, Hakeswill knew, they neither moved, nor screamed, and it was so easy to kill them at the end with one brief, convulsive plunge. Her body could be pushed under straw at the back of the stable and, even if she was found, no one would know it was him. He cackled. 'Obadiah Hakeswill, missy, at your service.'

She smiled at him, transfixing, unexpected. 'Obber-dyer?'

He paused. He had been about to transfer the bayonet. He was suspicious, but he nodded. 'Sergeant Obadiah Hakeswill, missy, and in a hurry, if you don't mind.'

Her eyes, large already, widened as if impressed. 'Sarj-ent? *Si?*' She smiled again. 'Sarj-ent Obber-dyer Hag-swill? *Si?*' She caressed the words, lingered on them.

Hakeswill was puzzled. It was dark enough in the stable, to be sure, but not so dark that she could not see his face. Yet she seemed to like him. It was not

impossible, he supposed, but even if she did like him that was no reason to linger. Reason, indeed, to make haste. 'That's right, dearie, a Sergeant. Mucha Importante.' He was short of room, the damned horse was too close, but then the girl smiled again and patted the straw on her other side. '*Importante?*'

He grinned at her, glad she was impressed, and eased the bayonet back a trifle. 'Move over, then.'

She nodded, smiled again, and her hands went to the back of her neck, and she licked her lips, and Hakeswill's eyes moved to watch her draw up her long, slim, trousered legs, and he never saw the blade that she took from the sheath that hung at the top of her spine. He was fumbling with his buttons when the knife sliced at his face, sprang blood, and the knees kept coming and slammed him against the horse's rear legs. He bellowed, swung the bayonet, but the knife was faster and cut at his wrist, so he dropped the blade, screaming at her, and she kicked at it as she scrambled, fast as a hare, under the belly of her horse.

'Whore!' He reached for her under the horse, but the bitch had his bayonet and stabbed at him, so he was forced back, and then she swore at him in fast, fluent English, and he wiped blood from his face and spat at her.

She laughed, crouching beyond the horse, and she levelled the blade at him. 'Come and get it, Obadiah.'

He stood up and backed into the passageway between the stalls. He was still between her and the door, and there were more ways than one of skinning a cat. He felt his face. The wound was small enough, and his wrist was usable. He grinned at her. 'I'll have you, missy, then I'll carve you into little pieces.' He cackled, feeling his head twitch. 'Bloody little Portuguese whore!' She was still between the horse and the wooden partition

and he went forward as she stood up, his bayonet still in her hand, and she was smiling.

He checked at the sight of the bayonet. She was holding it low, ready to rip it upwards, and there was no sign of trembling. He thought of rushing her, but the bitch looked as if she might do real damage, so he backed away, keeping himself between her and the door, and looked around for the pitchfork that had to be in a stable. He wanted this girl. She was beautiful, and he wanted her, and he would have her, and his face twitched, and the words hammered in his head. He would have her, have her, have her, and then he saw the pitchfork and went back fast, turned, and grabbed at it.

The girl was nearly on to him. She had guts, for a Portuguese bitch, and he twisted to one side to avoid the lunge of the bayonet. Damn her! She had passed him, was by the door, but instead of opening it she stopped, turned, and taunted him. She spoke to him in Spanish, a language of rich insult, and laughed at her own words.

Hakeswill assumed it was Portuguese, a language of which he was as ignorant as he was of Spanish, but one thing was sure. He was not being complimented. He put the pitchfork out ahead of him and stalked towards her. There was no way she could beat this attack and he grinned at her. 'Make it easy for yourself, missy, drop the spike. Come on, drop it!'

Teresa wanted to kill him, not leave it to Sharpe, and she switched to English so she might provoke an angered, unthinking charge. She had to assemble the sentence carefully, make sure it was right in her head, and then she laughed at him. 'Your mother was a sow, sold to a toad.'

He bellowed, the anger exploding like powder.

'Mother!' He ran at her, swinging the pitchfork, and she would have placed the bayonet with the precision of a Bishop pinning down a mortal sin if the door of the stable had not opened, the wood caught the pitchfork's tines, and the ugly Sergeant was tipped off balance, fell and the bayonet stabbed into empty air.

Hakeswill spun as he fell, momentarily dazzled by the sun streaming through the doorway, and had an impression of a giant shadow. A boot caught him; he was kicked as he had never been kicked before, lifted off the ground, slammed backwards, but he kept hold of the pitchfork and snarled at his assailant. The bloody Irish Sergeant! He picked himself up and lunged at the Irishman, but Harper simply caught the pitchfork by its two tines and bent them outwards and apart. Hakeswill pushed forward, using all his strength, but Harper was rock solid and the fork did not move except for the metal which was bent straight as if it was made from wet willow wands.

'What the hell's happening?' Sharpe stood in the doorway, holding it open.

Teresa smiled at him over the bayonet. 'Sergeant Obadiah wanted to have me, then carve me in little pieces.'

Harper pulled the pitchfork away from Hakeswill and tossed it on the ground. 'Permission to commit murder, sir?'

'Denied.' Sharpe came forward, letting the door swing shut. 'Latch that door.'

Hakeswill watched as Harper looped the string over the peg. So this was Sharpe's bloody woman? It looked like that, from the way she smiled at him, touched his arm, and Hakeswill knew he should have pushed the bayonet through the slut's throat when he had a chance. God, but she was beautiful, and he felt the

desire still there and he would have her, by God, he would have her! Then he looked at Sharpe's face, tight with anger, and Hakeswill shrugged. So he was about to have the hell beaten out of him? He had been beaten before, and a beating meant no rape charges, and anyway the girl was the only witness and she was obviously unharmed. His face twitched violently, and he could not stop it, and then he remembered how the girl had angered him, made him rush his attack, and he decided that the same tactics would work on an angry Sharpe. 'Whores for the officers, does she, Captain? How much? I can pay for her filth.'

Harper growled, Teresa started forward, but Sharpe checked them both. He looked only at Hakeswill, took two paces towards him, and it seemed as if he had not heard what the Sergeant had said. He cleared his throat, spoke mildly. 'Sergeant Hakeswill. You and I, through no choice of mine, find ourselves in the same Company. Do you understand?' Hakeswill nodded. So the jumped-up little bastard was going to do his officer act! Sharpe spoke calmly. 'We have three rules in this Company, Sergeant, are you listening?'

'Yes, sir!' Hakeswill fancied the bitch. He would have her, too, when the time came.

'Those rules are as follows, Sergeant.' Sharpe spoke in sweet reasonableness, as a Captain to a valued non-commissioned officer, though whether he was a Captain or no, he still had no idea. 'First, that you fight well, that you fight to win. I know you can do that, Sergeant, I've watched you.'

'Yes, sir!' Hakeswill barked the response.

'Second, that no man gets drunk without my permission.' Sharpe wondered if his permission would be worth a used musket ball in a few hours, but then let Rymer look after Lieutenant Price. 'Understand?'

'Yessir!'

'Good. And third, Sergeant.' Sharpe was now two paces from Hakeswill, ignoring the muttered Spanish threats from Teresa. 'Third, Sergeant, that you steal nothing, except from the enemy, and except when you're starving. Understand?'

'Sir!' Hakeswill was laughing inside. Sharpe had turned as soft as bloody butter!

'I'm glad you understand, Sergeant. Shun!'

Hakeswill sprang to attention and Sharpe kicked him between the legs. Hakeswill snapped forward and the officer's right hand cracked into his face, too high, but with enough force to send him staggering backwards.

'Shun! I'll tell you when to move, you bastard!'

Habit froze the Sergeant, as Sharpe had known it would. Hakeswill's survival in the army depended on absolute obedience to orders. Beyond that, anything could be done, but to disobey orders was to risk losing his stripes, his privileges, and his position to torment others. Hakeswill was hurting badly, but he stood still. Perhaps, the Sergeant thought, Sharpe had not gone quite as soft as he thought, but no man had got the better of Obadiah Hakeswill and lived to boast of it. Sharpe faced him again. 'I'm glad you understand, Sergeant, because that will make our life easier. Don't you agree?'

'Sir!' It came out as a grunt of pain.

'Good. What were you doing to my woman?'

'Sir?'

'You heard, Sergeant.'

'Getting acquainted, sir.'

Sharpe hit him again, hard in the great belly, and again Hakeswill bent forward and again Sharpe brought up the heel of his hand into the face, this time on the Sergeant's nose so that blood started from it. 'Still!'

Hakeswill was shaking with anger, the years of discipline fighting the desire to hit back, but he stilled himself, stood to attention, and then the involuntary twitching spasm jerked his head and Sharpe bellowed again. 'Still! I didn't give you permission to move!' Sharpe stepped closer, almost inviting Hakeswill to hit him. 'What happens next, Hakeswill? I suppose the Company will begin to lose things. Spare boots, camp kettles, pipeclay, brushes, belts, and good Sergeant Hakeswill will be reporting the losses, am I right?' Hakeswill did not move. 'And then it will be sabotage on weapons. Threads stripped on the flint screws, missing tumblers, wet mud down barrels. I know your tricks. How many floggings do you want before they're all paying you money? Three, four?'

There was silence in the stable. Outside there was the sound of dogs, yelping excitedly, but Sharpe ignored the sound. Teresa came forward. 'Why don't you kill him? Let me.'

'I don't know.' Sharpe stared at the ravaged, malevolent face. 'Because he says he can't be killed, and when I kill him, I want it to be in public. I want his victims to know he died, that someone took revenge for them, and if we do it now it will have to be in secret. I don't want that. I want a thousand eyes watching, and then I'll kill him.' He turned his back on the Sergeant, looked at Harper. 'Open the door.'

Sharpe stood to one side, turned back to Hakeswill. 'Get out, and keep going. Just leave here, Sergeant, and keep walking. Eleven more miles and you can put on a blue uniform. Do something for your country, Hakeswill, desert.'

The blue eyes looked at Sharpe. 'Permission to go, sir!' He was still hurting.

'Go.'

Harper held the door ajar. He was disappointed. He wanted to crush Hakeswill, to obliterate him, and as the Sergeant marched past he spat at him. Hakeswill began to sing, very softly. 'His father was an Irishman, his mother was a pig . . .'

Harper lashed out. Hakeswill blocked the blow and turned on the vast Irishman. They were of a size, but Hakeswill was still hurting. He kicked out, missed, and felt the blows crash on his forearms and head. God! But the Irishman was a strong brute!

'Stop it!' Sharpe bellowed.

They were too far gone. Harper hit and hit again, butted with his head, and then a hand grabbed his shoulder and pulled him off. 'I said stop it!'

Hakeswill could see nothing after the butting. He swung a fist at a vaguely green uniform and Sharpe stepped back, brought up a leg, and pushed it into Hakeswill's belly. The Sergeant fell backwards, out into the sunlight, splashing into a yellow puddle of horse urine. Sharpe looked at Harper. He was unhurt, but staring into the yard, over the fallen Hakeswill's head, and the Irishman's face was astonished, stunned.

Sharpe looked into the sunlight. The yard seemed full of dogs, foxhounds, some of whom, their tails busy in ecstasy, explored the fallen man in the beautiful-smelling puddle. In the centre of the dogs was a horse; a black horse, big and beautifully groomed, and on the horse's back was a Lieutenant Colonel who wore, beneath his bicorne hat, an expression of savage distaste. The Lieutenant Colonel looked down on the Sergeant who was bleeding from wrist, nose, and cheek, and then the flinty eyes came back to Sharpe. The rider's hands gripped a crop, his boots were exquisitely tasselled, while his face, above the crowned epaulette, was the kind of face Sharpe expected to see over the

bench of a county court. It was a knowing face, lined with experience, and Sharpe guessed this man could set a plough blade as handily as he quelled a riot. 'I assume you are Mr Sharpe?'

'Yes, sir.'

'Report to me at half-past twelve, Sharpe.' The eyes flicked round the group, from Sharpe to the Irish Sergeant, then to the girl with the bayonet. The Lieutenant Colonel's crop flicked at the horse, it stepped obediently away and the dogs forsook Hakeswill and followed. The horseman had not introduced himself, nor had he needed to. Across a puddle of urine, in the middle of a brawl over a woman, Sharpe had just met his new Colonel.

CHAPTER 10

'Soon, Richard?'

'Soon.'

'You know where to find me?'

He nodded. 'In the house of Moreno, in a narrow street behind the Cathedral.'

She smiled, bent down to pat her horse's neck. 'And there are two orange trees in the court in front of the house. It's easy to find.'

'Will you be all right?'

'Of course.' She glanced at the Portuguese sentries who held open the main gate. 'I must go, Richard. Be happy.'

'I will. And you.' He found it difficult to smile, and the next words sounded awkward. 'Give the baby my love.'

She smiled down at him. 'I will. You'll see her soon.'

'I know.' And then she was gone, her horse's hooves echoing in the dark, curving tunnel of the gateway, and he watched as the Portuguese soldiers wound down the portcullis and slammed the inner gates. He was alone; no, not really alone, for Harper waited for him up the street, but he felt alone. At least he believed that Teresa would be safe. Merchants were still trading from Badajoz, their convoys still going north, east and south, and Teresa would circle the city, find such a convoy, and ride safely back to the house with the two orange trees.

It was just eleven miles away, an easy walk, but he felt as if it were on the far side of the world.

Harper fell into step beside him, his face long. 'I'm sorry, sir.'

'It doesn't matter.'

The Sergeant sighed. 'I know you wanted to make a good impression on the Colonel. I'm sorry.'

'It's not your fault. I should have killed that bastard in the stable.'

Harper grinned. 'Aye, you should. Do you want me to?'

'No. He's mine, and in public.' They edged past ox carts loaded high with spades, gabions and great timber baulks that would become gun platforms. Elvas was filling with material for the siege; only the guns were missing, still being dragged on the roads from the River Tagus and bringing with them the promise of another breach, another Forlorn Hope.

'Sir?' Harper was embarrassed.

'Yes?'

'Is it true, sir?'

'Is what true?'

The Irishman looked down on Sharpe from his huge height. 'That you're losing the Company? I hear there's a new Captain, some youngster from the 51st?'

'I don't know.'

'The lads won't like it, sir, nor will they.'

'The lads will just have to bloody put up with it.'

'God save Ireland.' They climbed a few paces in silence, up towards the town's centre. 'So it is true?'

'Probably.'

Harper shook his head, massively and slowly. 'God save Ireland. I would never have believed it. Will you talk to the General?'

Sharpe shook his head. He had thought of it, but

instantly dismissed the thought. He had once saved Wellington's life, but the debt had long been repaid and the General had already promoted him Captain once. It was not Wellington's fault that the gazette had been refused, if it had, or that a lawyer had sold a commission illegally. It happened all the time. 'I can't run to him every time there's trouble.' He shrugged. 'Something'll turn up, Patrick, it always does.'

Harper, unappeased, slammed a fist against a wall, startling a sleeping dog. 'I don't believe it! They can't do it!'

'They can.'

'Then they're fools.' Harper thought for a second. 'Would you be thinking of moving on?'

'Where?'

'Back to the Rifles?'

'I don't know. Nothing's certain yet. Anyway, the Rifles have all the officers they need, and then more.'

'So you have thought about it.' Harper nodded to himself. 'Would you promise me something?'

Sharpe smiled. 'I know, and the answer's yes.'

'By God, I'll not stay on here without you. I'll go back to the Rifles with you. You need someone sensible near you.'

They parted at the officers' house, just as the great cloud bank engulfed Elvas in shadow and a promise of rain. Sharpe paused in the archway. 'I'll see you at four.'

'Aye, sir, I hope it's you.' There was to be a parade at four at which Colonel Windham would inspect his new battalion.

Sharpe nodded. 'So do I. Make it a good turn-out.'

He did not know where Windham would be, so he paused in the hallway and saw the array of clean, new shakoes on the table. He could not face the big room, the Mess, the pitying glances of his fellow-officers and

118

the inevitable confrontation with Rymer, so he stayed in the hall and stared at a huge, gloomy painting of a white-cassocked priest who was being burned at a stake. The soldiers who stoked the faggots were mean-faced, weaselly, and obviously intended to be the English, while the suffering priest had an ethereal look of forgiveness and martyrdom. Sharpe hoped the bastard had hurt.

'Captain Sharpe?' He turned. A small Major with a clipped moustache was looking at him from a doorway.

'Sir?'

'Collett. Major Collett. Pleased to make your acquaintance, Sharpe. Heard of you, of course. This way.'

Sharpe was regretting his lack of charity to the long burned priest, wondering if the evil wish would bring him bad luck, so he looked up at the painting and winked at the man. 'Sorry.'

'What's that, Sharpe?'

'Nothing, sir, nothing.' He followed Collett into the parlour of the house; a room hung with more gloomy, religious pictures and with vast, brown curtains that seemed to enclose the room in premature night. Colonel Windham was at a low table, feeding scraps of meat to his dogs, and he did not look up as Collett led Sharpe into the room.

'Sir! This is Sharpe, sir!' Collett could have been Windham's twin; the same bowed, horseman's legs, the same leathery skin, and the same cropped grey hair, but, as the Colonel looked up, Sharpe saw shrewd lines on Windham's face that were lacking on the Major. The Colonel nodded affably. 'You like dogs, Sharpe?'

'Yes, sir.'

'Faithful beasts, Sharpe. Feed 'em regular, kick 'em often, and they'll do anything for you. Just like soldiers, yes?'

'Yes, sir.' He was standing awkwardly, shako in hand, and Windham waved him towards a chair.

'Brought the beasts with me. I hear there's some decent sport to be had. Do you hunt, Sharpe?'

'No, sir.'

'Fine sport! Fine sport!' He was holding a scrap of beef high, teasing a hound with it so that the dog jumped vainly, higher and higher, until Windham dropped the food and the dog snapped it in mid air, and took it, growling, beneath the table. 'Shouldn't spoil 'em, of course. Bad for them. That's Jessica, my wife.' He was pointing to the table.

'Your what, sir?'

'Wife, Sharpe, wife. Wife's called Jessica. Colonel's Lady, and that sort of thing. Mrs Windham.' He offered the various categories of his wife in a rapid voice and Sharpe understood that he was not referring to the dog beneath the table, but to an oval portrait, about six inches high, that stood above the dog. The portrait was mounted in a superb filigree silver frame and it showed a woman with dark, severe hair, a receding chin, and an expression of terrifying disapproval. Sharpe had the distinct feeling that the chewing dog would be a better companion, but the Colonel's face softened as he looked at the painting. 'A good woman, Sharpe, a good woman. A force for the good in society.'

'Yes, sir.' Sharpe was beginning to feel slightly confused. He had come to the meeting expecting to be told about the Company, about Rymer, even to be reprimanded for the fracas at the stable yard, but, instead, the new Colonel of the Battalion was extolling the virtues of a good wife.

'She takes a keen interest, Sharpe, very keen. Knows about you. Wrote to me when I said I was getting the

Battalion and sent me a scrap from a newspaper. She thinks you've done well, Sharpe.'

'Yes, sir.'

'She's eager to see people better themselves. Isn't that true, Jack?'

'Indeed, sir.' Collett rapped the words out with an alacrity that made Sharpe wonder if Collett's role in life was to agree with everything the Colonel said. Windham put the portrait back on the table. He had been holding it, cradling it between his hands.

'What was that business about this morning, Sharpe?'

'A private argument, sir. It's been dealt with.' He felt a stab of satisfaction at the memory of punching Hakeswill.

Windham was not satisfied. 'What was the argument about?'

'The girl was insulted, sir.'

'I see.' The expression was one of profound disapproval. 'Local girl?'

'Spanish, sir.'

'Following the troops, no doubt. I want the women cleared out, Sharpe. Proper wives can stay, of course, but there are too many whores. Looks bad. Clear them out!'

'I'm sorry, sir?'

'The whores, Sharpe. You're to clear them out.' Windham nodded as if, the command being given, the deed was as well as done. Sharpe saw him glance, very quickly, at the portrait of the stern Jessica and the Rifleman suspected that Mrs Windham's keen interest in the Battalion extended, by letter, to its moral welfare.

'Where do I clear them to, sir?'

'What do you mean?'

'The next battalion, sir?'

Collett stiffened, but Windham did not take offence. 'I take your point, Sharpe, but I want them discouraged. Understand? I shall make an example of men caught brawling over women.'

'Yes, sir.' The Colonel obviously intended being busy.

'Number two, Sharpe. Battalion's wives are to parade for inspection each Sunday. Ten of the forenoon. You parade them, I'll inspect them.'

'A wives' inspection, sir. Yes, sir.' Sharpe kept his thoughts to himself. Such a parade was not unusual in England, but it was rare in Spain. Officially the wives were subject to army discipline, though very few of them accepted the fact, and Sharpe suspected that the coming Sundays would be amusing, if nothing else. But why him? Why not one of the Majors, or even the Sergeant Major?

'Ten o'clock, Sharpe. And I don't want any unmarried women on parade. Tell 'em that. I'll demand papers. I want no one like that girl this morning!'

'That was my wife, sir.' Sharpe had no idea why he said it, unless it was to puncture Windham's air of certainty, and it worked. The Colonel's mouth dropped; he looked to Collett for help, received none, and stared back at Sharpe.

'What?'

'My wife, sir. Mrs Sharpe.'

'Good God.' The Colonel leafed through papers that were beside his own wife's portrait. 'There's no note here of your marriage.'

'It was private, sir.'

'When? Who gave permission?'

'Sixteen months ago, sir.' He smiled at the Colonel. 'We have a daughter, nearly eight months old.'

He could see the Colonel adding up the figures, receiving the wrong answer, and the discrepancy effectually stopped any more questioning. Windham was

embarrassed. 'Owe you an apology, Sharpe. No offence, I trust.'

'None, sir.' Sharpe smiled seraphically.

'Lives with the Battalion, does she? Mrs Sharpe?'

'No, sir. In Spain. She has employment there.'

'Employment!' Windham looked suspicious. 'What does she do?'

'Kills Frenchmen, sir. She's a Partisan, known as "La Aguja". The needle.'

'Good God alive!' Windham gave up. He had heard about Sharpe from Lawford and from a dozen other people, and he had construed the information as a kind of warning. Sharpe, he had been told, was an independent man, effective in battle, but liable to use irregular means to succeed. He had come up from the ranks, the Colonel knew, which had to be a liability. Windham had never known a man from the ranks to make a successful officer. Either the power went to their heads, or the drink did, and, whichever it was, the men usually resented them. They were good for one thing though; administration. They knew the system backwards, far better than other officers, and they made the best drill-masters in the army. It was true that Lawford had said Sharpe was an exception, but Windham was fifteen years older than Lawford and reckoned he knew the army better. He conceded that Sharpe's record was magnificent, but it was also undeniably true that the man had been given uncommon freedom, and freedom, Windham knew, was a damned dangerous thing. It could give a man ideas well above his station, but he still found himself reluctant to cut him down, even though that was his duty. Windham liked to jump his fences straight, yet here he was, dithering like an old woman on a tubed nag searching for a gap in the hedge! 'I've been lucky, Sharpe.'

'Lucky, sir?'

'In my establishment.'

'Yes, sir.' Sharpe felt like a man who has known execution was coming, but did not believe it, and now the barrels of the firing squad were being levelled.

'Eleven Captains, it's too much!'

'Yes, sir.'

Windham glanced at Collett, but the Major had his eyes down, being no help at all. Damn it then! Straight at the fence! 'Rymer has to have the Company, Sharpe. He's purchased it, used his own money. You can see his rights, I'm sure.'

Sharpe said nothing. He kept his face expressionless. He had expected this, but it did not lessen the bitterness. So Rymer got the prize because Rymer had the money? The fact that Sharpe had captured an Eagle, had been described by Wellington as the finest leader of Light troops in the army, counted for nothing. Such things were meaningless matched against the purchase system. If Napoleon Bonaparte had joined the British Army, instead of the French, he would count himself lucky if he had achieved a Captaincy by now instead of being Emperor of half the world! Damn Rymer, and damn Windham, and damn the whole army! Sharpe felt like walking away, and shaking the whole unfair system from his back. There was a sudden, harsh rattle of rain on the window. Windham cocked his head, just as the foxhounds at his feet had done. 'Rain!' The Colonel turned to Collett. 'My blankets are airing, Jack. Can I trouble you to rouse my servant?'

Collett obligingly left and Windham leaned back. 'I'm sorry, Sharpe.'

'Yes, sir. And the gazette?'

'Refused.' So there it was. The firing squad pulled their triggers and Lieutenant Richard Sharpe gave a

mocking, sardonic laugh that made Windham frown. A Lieutenant again!

'So what am I to do, sir?' Sharpe let the bitterness edge his voice. 'Am I to report to Captain Rymer?'

'No, Mr Sharpe, you are not. Captain Rymer would find your presence an embarrassment, I'm sure you can understand that. He must be given time to settle in. I'll keep you busy.'

'I forgot, sir. I'm in charge of the women now.'

'Don't be impertinent, Sharpe!' Windham snapped forward, startling the dogs. 'You don't understand, do you? There are rules, orders, regulations, Sharpe, by which our lives are conducted. If we ignore those rules, burdensome though they may be, then we open the gates to anarchy and tyranny; the very things against which we fight! Do you understand?'

'Yes, sir.' Sharpe knew it would be pointless to mention that the rules, orders, and regulations were made by the privileged to protect the privileged. It had always been so, and always would. The only thing for him to do now was to get out with his shreds of dignity intact and then get stinking drunk. Show fellow Lieutenant Price how a real expert fell over.

Windham leaned back. 'We're going to Badajoz.'

'Yes, sir.'

'You're senior Lieutenant.'

'Yes, sir.' Sharpe's replies were listless.

'There'll be vacancies, man! If we attack.' That was true, and Sharpe nodded.

'Yes, sir.'

'You can exchange.' Windham looked expectantly at Sharpe.

'No, sir.' There were always officers who found their Regiments going to unpopular places such as the Fever Islands and who would offer to exchange with another

officer in a battalion closer to the gaming tables and far from weird diseases. Usually they would offer a cash bribe to facilitate the exchange, but Sharpe dared not leave Spain, not while Teresa and Antonia were shut up in Badajoz. He listened to the rain on the window and thought of the girl riding. 'I'll stay, sir.'

'Good!' Windham sounded far from pleased. 'There's plenty of work. The mule train needs tidying up, I've seen that already, and, God knows, we'll be swamped with pick-axes and spades. They all need counting.'

'In charge of mules, pick-axes, and women, sir?'

Windham's eyes met the challenge. 'Yes, Mr Sharpe, if you insist.'

'A suitable job, sir, for an ageing Lieutenant.'

'It might, Lieutenant, engender humility.'

'Yes, sir.' An important quality to a soldier, humility, and Sharpe gave another sardonic laugh. Humility had not captured the gun at Ciudad Rodrigo, nor hacked a path through Fuentes de Oñoro's tight streets, nor fetched the gold from Spain, nor taken an Eagle from the enemy, nor rescued a General, nor brought a group of starving Riflemen out of a rout nor killed the Sultan Tippoo, and Sharpe's sardonic laugh became real. He was being arrogant to himself, and perhaps Windham was right. He needed humility. He would now be parading wives and counting shovels, neither of which activity called for much initiative or leadership, and mules were notoriously chary of quick, confident decisions, and humility was best. He would be humble. 'Sir?'

'Yes?'

'A request.'

'Go on, man.'

'I want to lead a Forlorn Hope at Badajoz, sir. I'd like you to forward my name now. I know it's early, but I would be grateful if you would do so.'

Windham stared at him. 'You're unbalanced, man.'

Sharpe shook his head. He was not going to explain that he wanted a promotion that no man could take from him, and that he wanted to test himself in a breach because he had never done it. And if he died, as he surely would, and never saw his daughter? Then she would know that her father had died trying to reach her, leading an attack, and she could be proud. 'I want it, sir.'

'You don't need it, Sharpe. There will be promotion at Badajoz.'

'Will you forward my name, sir?'

Windham stood up. 'Think about it, Sharpe, think about it.' He gestured towards the door. 'Report to Major Collett in the morning.' The interview had been far worse than he had feared and the Colonel shook his head. 'You don't need it, Sharpe, you don't. Now good day to you.'

Sharpe did not notice the rain. He stood and stared across the valley at the fortress. He thought of Teresa closing on the huge walls, and knew that he must go into the breach, whatever happened. The restitution of his rank, and hopefully the command of his Company, demanded it, but, most of all, because he was a soldier, it was pride.

The meek, he had been told, would inherit the earth, but only when the last soldier left it to them in his will.

CHAPTER 11

'Sergeant Hakeswill, sir! Reporting to Lieutenant Sharpe, sir, as ordered, sir!' The right boot crashed into the attention, the arm quivered at the salute, the face twitched, but was full of amusement.

Sharpe returned the salute. It had been more than three weeks since his demotion, yet it still hurt. The Battalion, embarrassed, called him 'sir' or 'Mr Sharpe'. Only Hakeswill twisted the knife. Sharpe pointed to the mess on the ground. 'That's it. Sort it out.'

'Sir!' Hakeswill turned to the working party from the Light Company. 'You heard the Lieutenant! Sort it out and get a bloody move on! The Captain wants us back.'

Hagman, the old Rifleman, the best shot in the Company, who had served with Sharpe for seven years, gave his old Captain a sad smile. 'Nasty day, sir.'

Sharpe nodded. The rain had stopped, but it looked as if it would start again soon. 'How are things, Dan?'

The Rifleman grinned, shrugged, and looked round to see if Hakeswill was listening. 'Bloody terrible, sir.'

'Hagman!' Hakeswill bellowed. 'Just because you're bloody old doesn't mean you can't work. Get your bloody self here, fast!' The Sergeant grinned at Sharpe. 'Sorry, Lieutenant, sir. Can't stop to chat, can we? Work to do.' The teeth ground together, the blue eyes blinked rapidly. 'How's your lady, sir. Well? I was hoping to renew the acquaintance. In Baddy-joss is she?' He

cackled and turned away, back to the working party that was rescuing the fallen shovels from the broken-axled cart.

Sharpe ignored the gibes because to react was to give Hakeswill the satisfaction of having unsettled him, and he looked away from the cart and stared over the grey, swollen river. Badajoz. Just four miles away; a city built on a corner of land formed by the River Guadiana and the Rivillas stream. The city was dominated by the sprawling castle high on the rock hill which stood where the stream flowed into the river. The army had marched from Elvas that morning and now they waited as the Engineers put the last touches to the pontoon bridge that would take the British to the southern bank on which Badajoz stood. Each tin pontoon, strengthened by wooden braces, weighed two tons, and the clumsy, oblong boats, dragged here by oxen, had been floated in a line across the Guadiana. They were all moored now, anchored against the rain-heightened river, and across their top surfaces the Engineers had laid massive thirteen-inch cables. The water foamed dirty between the tin boats as, on top of the cables, planks were slapped into place with a speed that spoke of the frequent practice the Engineers had made in crossing Spain's rivers. Almost before the last planks were in place the first carts were crossing and men shovelled sand and earth on to the planks to make a crude roadway.

'Forward!' The first troops began to cross, unmounted men of the newly arrived Heavy Cavalry Brigade leading their horses. The animals were nervous on the thrumming bridge, but they crossed, and Badajoz was about to be ringed with troops.

On the far bank the cavalry mounted, sorted themselves into squadrons, and, as the first infantry began

to cross, the horsemen put spurs to their mounts and trotted towards the city. There was little they could do against the massive walls; they were a demonstration, a flaunting of intent, and a discouragement to the handful of French cavalry inside Badajoz who might be tempted to ride against the bridgehead.

It began to rain, pitting the swirling, dark water, and soaking the already damp troops as they crossed the river and turned left towards the city. Once there was a cheer from the infantry as a cannon's shot was heard from Badajoz. A squadron of the Heavy Cavalry had ridden too close to the walls, a French gun had fired, and the British riders galloped ignominiously out of range. The cheer was ironic. The infantry might die soon at the hands of the guns, but it was still good to see the fancy cavalry taught a lesson. No cavalryman would have to go into Badajoz's breaches.

The South Essex had become pack mules. The Engineers had over a hundred carts waiting to cross the river and two had snapped their axles. The South Essex would have to carry the loads across the water. Windham reined in beside Sharpe. 'All ready, Mr Sharpe?'

'Yes, sir.'

'Keep the baggage close when we cross!'

'Yes, sir.' No, sir, three bags full, sir. 'Sir?'

'Mr Sharpe?' Windham was eager to be away.

'Have you forwarded my request, sir?'

'No, Mr Sharpe, much too early. My compliments!' The Colonel touched the tassel on his bicorne and wheeled his horse away.

Sharpe hitched his sword up, useless to him for counting spades and pick-axes, and trudged over the mud towards the Battalion's baggage. Each company kept a mule that carried the books, the endless paper-

work that went with a Captaincy, a few paltry supplies and, quite illegally, some officers' baggage as well. Other mules carried the Battalion supplies; the spare arms chest, uniforms, more paperwork, and the surgeon's grim load. Mixed with the mules were the officers' servants, leading spare horses and packhorses, and, mingled among them all, the children. They shrieked and played round the animals' legs, watched by their mothers who crouched beneath makeshift shelters waiting for the order to march. By regulation there should be just sixty wives with the Battalion, but inevitably, after three years at war, the South Essex had collected far more. There were nearer three hundred women marching with the Battalion, the same number of children, and they were a mixture of English, Irish, Scottish, Welsh, Spanish and Portuguese; there was even a Frenchwoman, left behind in the fighting at Fuentes de Oñoro, who had chosen to stay with her captors and had married a Sergeant in Sterritt's Company. Some were whores, following the army's meagre pennies, some were proper wives with papers to prove it, while some called themselves wives and did not need the ceremony. All were tough. Many had married twice or three times in the war, having lost their husbands to a French bullet or a Spanish fever.

The previous morning Windham had cancelled the wives' parade. In barracks the parade made some sense; it kept a Colonel in touch with the families and gave a good officer a chance to detect brutality, but the women of the South Essex did not like the parade, were not used to it, and had showed their discontent. The very first time that Sharpe had lined them for Windham's inspection Private Clayton's wife, a pretty girl, had been suckling her baby. The Colonel had stopped, glanced down, and frowned at her. 'This is hardly the time, woman!'

She had grinned, lifted her breasts towards him. 'When 'e's 'ungry, 'e's 'ungry, just like 'is father.' There was a chorus of laughter from the wives, jeers from the men, and Windham had strode away. Jessica would have known what to do, but not he.

Now, as Sharpe approached the rain-swept baggage, the women grinned at him from beneath their blankets. Lily Grimes, a tiny woman of irrepressible cheerfulness, and a voice with the piercing quality of a well-honed bayonet, gave him a mock salute. 'Given up parading us, Cap'n?' The women always called him Captain.

'That's right, Lily.'

She sniffed. 'He's mad.'

'Who?'

'Bloody Colonel. What did he want us to parade for, anyway?'

Sharpe grinned. 'He worries about you, Lily. He likes to keep an eye on you.'

She shook her head. 'He wants to look at Sally Clayton's tits more like.' She laughed and peered up at Sharpe. 'You didn't look away either, Cap'n. I watched you.'

'I was just wishing it had been you, Lily.'

She shrieked with laughter. 'Any time, Cap'n, you just ask.'

Sharpe laughed, walked away from her. He admired the wives, and he liked them. They endured all the discomforts of the campaign; the nights under pouring rain, the hard rations, the long marches, yet they never gave up. They watched their men go into battle and afterwards they searched the field for a corpse or a wounded husband, and all the while they brought up their children and looked after their men. Sharpe had seen Lily carrying two of her children up a hard road,

her husband's musket, and the family's few belongings as well. They were tough.

And they were not ladies; three years in the Peninsula had made sure of that. Some dressed in old uniforms, most were garbed in voluminous, filthy skirts with tattered shawls and scarves around their heads. They were tanned dark brown, with calloused hands and feet, and most could strip a corpse bare in ten seconds, a house in thirty. They were foul-mouthed, loud, and utterly immodest. No women could live with a battalion and be anything else. They slept with their men, often enough, in open fields with nothing but a tree or hedge to give an illusion of privacy. The women washed themselves, relieved themselves, made love, gave birth, and all in plain sight of a thousand eyes. To a fastidious observer they were a fearful sight, yet Sharpe liked them. They were tough, loyal, kind and uncomplaining.

Major Collett bawled an order for the Battalion to make ready, and Sharpe turned to his command; the baggage. It was chaos. Two children had succeeded in cutting the pannier from one of the Sutler's mules, and the Sutler, a Spaniard who was a kind of travelling shop-keeper with the Battalion, was screaming at the children, but not daring to let go of the straw halter that tethered his other mules.

Sharpe yelled at them. 'Make ready!' They took no notice. The Sutler's assistants caught the children, snatched back the bottles, but then the mothers, sensing loot, attacked the assistants for beating the children. It was pandemonium, his new command.

'Richard!' Sharpe twisted back. Major Hogan was behind him.

'Sir.'

Hogan grinned down from his horse. 'We're very formal today.'

'We're very responsible. Look.' Sharpe waved at the baggage train. 'My new Company.'

'I heard.' Hogan slipped from his horse, stretched, and then turned as there were sudden shouts from the bridge. An officer's horse had become frightened by the sliding, grey water. It was nervously backing in short, jerking steps towards the infantry company behind. The Captain, panicking, was whipping the beast, increasing its terror, and the horse began to rear fitfully.

'Get off!' Hogan shouted. He had a surprisingly loud voice. 'Fool! Get off! Dismount!'

The officer lashed down at the horse, wrenched the reins, and the horse put all its force into bucking the rider off its back. It succeeded. The horse slammed up, screaming, and the officer tumbled from the saddle, bounced once on the roadway's edge, and disappeared downstream into the river. 'Stupid bastard!' Hogan was angry. A Sergeant threw a length of timber into the water, but it fell short, and Sharpe could see the Captain flailing the river, struggling against the freezing current that took him away from the bridge. 'He's had it.'

No one dived in to save the officer. By the time a man had stripped himself of pack, haversack, ammunition pouch, weapons and boots the Captain would be long gone. The horse, free of its burden, stood shivering on the bridge and a Private soothed it, then led it calmly to the southern bank. The Captain had disappeared.

'There's a vacancy.' Sharpe laughed.

'Bitter?'

'Bitter, sir? No, sir. Being a Lieutenant is very satisfying.'

Hogan gave a sad smile. 'I hear you were drunk.'

'No.' He had been drunk three times since the day

Teresa left, the day he had lost the Company. Sharpe shrugged. 'You know that gazette was refused in January? No one dared tell me. Then the new man arrives so someone has to tell me. So I look after the baggage while some half-cooked youngster destroys my Company.'

'Is he that bad?'

'I don't know. I'm sorry.' Sharpe's anger had taken himself by surprise.

'Do you want me to talk to the General?'

'No!' Pride would stop Sharpe bleating for help, but then he turned back. 'Yes, you can talk to the General. Tell him I'll lead the Forlorn Hope for him at Badajoz.'

Hogan paused with a pinch of snuff half-way to his nostrils. He put it back in the box, carefully, and snapped the lid shut. 'Are you serious?'

'I'm serious.'

Hogan shook his head. 'You don't need it, Richard. God! There'll be promotion by the graveload! Don't you understand? You'll be a Captain within a month.'

Sharpe shook his head. He understood, but his pride was hurt. 'I want the Hope, sir, I want it. Ask for me.'

Hogan took Sharpe's elbow and turned him so they were both looking eastwards along the river towards the city. 'Do you know what it's like, Richard? It's bloody impossible!' He pointed to the great stone bridge that carried the road to the city. 'We can't attack there. Anyone trying to cross that bridge will be shredded. So, try the east wall. They've damned the stream and it's one bloody great lake. We'd need the navy to cross that, unless we can blow up the dam and they've built a fort to stop us doing that. There's the castle, of course.' Hogan's words were urgent, almost bitter. 'If you feel like climbing a hundred feet of rock and then scaling a forty-foot wall, and all the time dodging the grapeshot,

135

you're welcome.' He pointed again. 'So there's the west wall. Looks easy enough, doesn't it?' It did not look easy. Even at four miles Sharpe could see the huge bastions, jutting like miniature castles, that protected the wall. Hogan's accent was becoming more pronounced as it always did when the Engineer spoke with passion. 'It looks too easy! They want us to attack there. Why? My guess is that it's mined. There's more bloody powder under that glacis than Guy Fawkes dreamed of. We attack there and we give St Peter his busiest day since Agincourt!' He was really angry now, seeing with his Engineer's eye the problems, turning the problems into blood. 'That leaves the south wall. We have to take at least one outlying fort, perhaps two, and then get through the walls. Do you know how thick they are? What was the distance from the brink of the ditch to the back of the walls at Ciudad Rodrigo?'

Sharpe thought back. 'Thirty yards? Fifty in some places.'

'Aye.' Hogan pointed back to Badajoz. 'A hundred yards, at least, and more in some places. And that ditch is a bastard, Richard, a real bastard. It'll take a minute to cross it, at least, and they have all the flank fire they'll ever need, and more. That wall, Richard, is big. Big! You could put Ciudad Rodrigo's wall in that ditch and you wouldn't even see it. Don't you understand? It is a killer.' He said the words distinctly, trying to convince Sharpe. Hogan sighed. 'Jesus! We can starve them out. We can hope they die laughing, we can hope they get the plague, but I tell you, Richard, I don't know if we can get through a breach.'

Sharpe stared at the great fortress in the slanting, hissing rain. 'We'll have to.'

'And do you know how? By throwing so many poor

bastards into the fight that the French simply can't kill them all. It's the only way and I don't like it.'

Sharpe turned back. 'The poor bastards will still need a Forlorn Hope.'

'And there has to be a bloody fool to lead it, I suppose, and you're proving a fool! For God's sake, Richard, why do you want the Hope?'

Sharpe's anger flared. 'Because it's better than this humiliation! I'm a soldier, not a bloody clerk! I fetch bloody forage, count bloody shovels, and take punishment drills. It's yes, sir, no, sir, can I dig your latrine, sir, and it's not bloody soldiering!'

Hogan glared at him. 'It is bloody soldiering! What the hell else do you think soldiering is?' The two men were facing each other across the mud. 'Do you think we can win a war without forage? Or without shovels? Or, God help us, without latrines? That is soldiering! Just because you've been allowed to swan about like a bloody pirate for years doesn't mean you shouldn't take your turn at the real work.'

'Listen, sir.' Sharpe was close to shouting. 'When they tell us to climb those bloody walls, you'll be glad there are some bloody pirates in the ditch and not just bloody clerks!'

'And what will you do when there are no more wars to fight?'

'Start another bloody one.' Sharpe began to laugh. 'Sir.'

'If you survive this one.' Hogan shook his head, his anger dying as quickly as it had flared. 'Good God, man! Your woman's inside. And your child.'

'I know.' Sharpe shrugged. 'But I want the Hope.'
'You'll die.'
'Ask Wellington for me.'

137

The Irishman frowned. 'You're just hurting in your pride, that's all. In two months, it will be a bad dream, I promise.'

'Maybe. I still want the Hope.'

'You're a stubborn, bloody fool.'

Sharpe laughed again. 'I know. Colonel Windham says I need humility.'

'He's right. It's a wonder any of us like you at all, but we do.' He shrugged. 'I'll talk to the General for you, but I'm making no promises.' He gathered the reins into his hand. 'Would you give me a leg up? If it's not beneath your dignity.'

Sharpe grinned, heaved the Major on to his horse. 'You'll ask him for me?'

'I said I'd talk to him, didn't I? It's not his decision, you know that. It belongs to the General of the attacking Division.'

'But they listen to Wellington.'

'Aye, that's true.' Hogan pulled on the reins, and then checked himself. 'You know what tomorrow is?'

'No.'

'Tuesday, March the seventeenth.'

'So?' Sharpe shrugged.

Hogan laughed. 'You're a heathen; an unrepentant, doomed heathen, so you are. St Patrick's Day. Ireland's day. Give Sergeant Harper a bottle of rum for being a good Catholic.'

Sharpe grinned. 'I will.'

Hogan watched the South Essex break up step as they marched over the bridge, followed by Sharpe and his raggletaggle of women, children, servants, and mules. Hogan was saddened. He counted the tall Rifleman as a friend. Perhaps Sharpe was arrogant, but Hogan, along with all the engineering in his head, kept more than a little of Shakespeare. *In peace there's nothing*

so becomes a man as modest stillness and humility. But this was not peace, this was a horrid campaign and tomorrow, St Patrick's Day, the army would start digging towards Badajoz. Hogan knew that stillness and humility would not capture the fortress. Time might, but Wellington would not give them time. The General was worried that the French field armies, bigger than the British, might march to the rescue. Badajoz must be taken swiftly, paid for in blood, and the assault would come soon, too soon, perhaps even before Lent was over. Hogan did not relish the prospect. The wall could be closed up with the English dead.

He had promised he would talk to Wellington, and so he would, but not as Sharpe had hoped. Hogan would do a friend's duty. He would ask the General, if it were possible, that Sharpe's request should be refused. He would save Sharpe's life. It was, after all, the very least he could do for a friend.

Part Three

St Patrick's Day, March 17th
to
Easter Sunday, March 29th
1812

CHAPTER 12

If a man could have found a new-fangled hot air balloon and flown it over Badajoz, he would have looked down at a city shaped like the quarter segment of a cogged wheel. The castle, ancient stone on rock, was the giant axle boss. The north and east walls were spokes, leaving the axle at right angles to each other, while the south and west walls joined in a long, rough curve that was studded with seven huge cogs.

It was impossible to attack from the north. The city was built on the bank of the River Guadiana, wider at Badajoz than the Thames at Westminster, and the only approach lay across the long, ancient stone bridge. Every yard of the bridge was covered by the guns mounted on the city's north wall while, across the river, the bridge entrance was guarded by three outlying forts. The largest, San Cristobal, could house more than two regiments. The French were sure that there could be no attack from the north.

The east wall, the other spoke, was more vulnerable. At its northern end was the castle, high and huge, a fortress that had dominated the landscape for centuries, but south of the castle, the city wall was on lower ground and faced towards a hill. The French knew the danger and, just where the castle hill dropped steeply to the lower city, they had dammed the Rivillas stream. Now the vulnerable east wall was protected by a sheet

of flood water, as wide as the river to the north, and running far to the south of the city. As Hogan had said to Sharpe; only the navy could attack across the new lake, unless the dam could be blown up and the lake drained.

Which left the huge curve of the south and west walls, a curve nearly a mile long that had no convenient river or stream to offer protection. Instead there were the cogs on the wheel's rim, the seven vast bastions that jutted out from the city wall, each bastion the size of a small castle. San Vincente was the most northerly, built beside the river at the angle of the north and west walls, and from the San Vincente the bastions ran south and west till they met the flooded Rivillas. San Jose, Santiago, San Juan, San Roque, Santa Maria, and so to the Trinidad. The saints, the mother of Christ, and the Holy Trinity, each with more than a score of guns, to protect a city.

The bastions were not the only protection to the great curve of walls. First came the glacis, the earth slope that deflected the round shot and bounced it high over the defences, and then the huge ditch. The drop from the glacis to the ditch bottom was nowhere less than twenty feet and, once in the ditch, the real problems began. The bastions would flank any attack, pouring in their plunging fire, and there were ravelins in the great dry moat. The ravelins were like great, triangular, fake walls that split an attack and, in darkness, could deceive men into thinking they had reached the real wall. Any man who climbed a ravelin would be swept off by carefully aimed cannon. From the ditch the walls rose fifty feet and on their wide parapets they mounted guns every five yards.

Badajoz was no mediaeval fortress hastily converted for modern warfare. It had once been the pride of

Spain, a brilliantly engineered, massively built death trap, that was now garrisoned by the finest French troops in the Peninsula. Twice the British had failed to take the city and there seemed no reason, a year later, to suppose that a third attempt would meet with success.

The fortress had just one weakness. To the south-east, opposite the Trinidad bastion and across the flood waters, rose the shallow San Miguel hill. From its low, flat top a besieger could fire down on to the south-east corner of the city, and that was the single weakness. The French knew it, and had guarded against it. Two forts had been built to the south and east. One, the Picurina, had been built across the new lake on the lower slopes of the San Miguel hill. The second fort, the huge Pardaleras, was to the south and guarded the approach to any breach that might be carved by the guns on the hill. It was not much of a weakness, but all the British had to work on and so, on St Patrick's Day, they marched to the rear of the San Miguel hill. They knew, and the French knew, that the effort would be against the south-east corner of the city, against the Santa Maria and Trinidad bastions, and the fact that the selfsame plan had failed twice before did not matter. From the top of the hill, where curious men gathered to look at the city, the breach made in the last siege could be clearly seen between the two bastions. It had been repaired, in lighter coloured stone, and the new masonry seemed to mock the coming British efforts.

Sharpe stood next to Patrick Harper and stared at the walls. 'Jesus, they're big!' The Sergeant said nothing. Sharpe pulled the bottle from inside his greatcoat and held it out. 'Here. A present for St Patrick's Day.'

Harper's broad face beamed with pleasure. 'You're a grand man, sir, for an Englishman. Would you be

ordering me to save you half for St George's Day?'

Sharpe stamped his feet against the cold. 'I think I'll take that half now.'

'I thought you might.' Harper was glad to see Sharpe, of whom he had seen little in the past month, but there was also an embarrassment in the meeting. The Irishman knew Sharpe needed reassurance that the Light Company missed him, and Harper thought him a fool for needing the words to be said. Of course they missed him. The Light Company were no different to the rest of the army. They were failures, almost to a man, whose failings had led them to courtrooms and jails. They were thieves, drunks, debtors, and mur-derers, the men Britain wanted out of sight and mind. It was easier to empty a town jail to a recruiting party than go through the tedious business of trial, sentence and punishment.

Not all were criminals. Some had been gulled by the Recruiting Sergeants, offered an escape from village tedium and narrow horizons. Some had failed in love and joined the army in despair, swearing they would rather die in battle than see their sweetheart married to another man. Many were drunkards who were terri-fied of a lonely shivering death in a winter ditch and joined an army that offered them clothes, boots, and a third of a pint of rum each day. Some, a few, a very few, joined for patriotism. Some, like Harper, joined because there was nothing but hunger at home and the army offered food and an escape. They were, almost to a man, the failings and leavings of society and to them all the army was one big Forlorn Hope.

Yet they were the best infantry in the world. They had not always been and, without the right leaders, would not be so again. Harper instinctively knew that this army that faced Badajoz was a superb instrument,

better than anything the great Napoleon could muster, and Harper knew why. Because there were just enough officers like Sharpe who trusted the failures. It started at the top, of course, with Wellington himself, and went right through the ranks to the junior officers and Sergeants, and the trick of it was very simple. Take a man who has failed at everything, give him a final chance, show him trust, lead him to one success, and there is a sudden confidence that will lead to the next success. Soon they will believe they are unbeatable, and become unbeatable, but the trick was still to have officers like Sharpe who kept on offering trust. Of course the Light Company missed him! He had expected great things of them and trusted them to win. Perhaps the new man would one day learn the trick, but until he did, if ever, the men would miss Sharpe. Hell, thought Harper, they even like him. And the fool did not realize it. Harper shook his head to himself and offered the bottle to Sharpe. 'Here's to Ireland, sir, and death to Hakeswill.'

'I'll drink to that. How is the bastard?'

'I'll kill him one day.'

Sharpe gave a humourless laugh. 'You won't. I will.'

'How the hell is he still alive?'

Sharpe shrugged. 'He says he can't be killed.' It was cold on the hill and Sharpe hunched his shoulders beneath the greatcoat. 'And he never turns his back. Watch yours.'

'I'm growing eyes in my burn with that bastard around.'

'What does Captain Rymer think of him?'

Harper paused, took the bottle from Sharpe, drank, and passed it back. 'God knows. I think he's scared of him, but so are most.' He shrugged. 'The Captain's not a bad fellow, but he's not exactly confident.' The Sergeant was feeling awkward. He did not like to sound

critical of one officer in front of another. 'He's young.'

'None of us are old. How's that new Ensign?'

'Matthews? He's fine, sir. Sticks to Lieutenant Price like a kid brother.'

'And Mr Price?'

Harper laughed. 'He keeps us cheerful, sir. Drunk as a cross-eyed stoat, but he'll survive.'

It began raining, small, spitting drops that stung their faces. Behind them, on the Seville road, the bugles called the battalions to the evening lines. Sharpe turned up his collar. 'We'd better be getting back.' He stared at the small, blue-uniformed figures on the city parapets, three-quarters of a mile away. 'Those sods will be warm tonight.' He suddenly thought of Teresa and Antonia inside the walls and looked at the big, square, battlemented Cathedral tower. It was odd to think they were so close to her. The rain became heavier and he turned away, back towards the sprawling, makeshift British camp.

'Sir?'

'Yes?'

The Sergeant seemed embarrassed. 'Major Hogan stopped by the other day.'

'So?'

'He was telling us about Miss Teresa, sir.'

Sharpe frowned. 'What about her?'

'Only, sir, that she'd asked you to look out for her. In the city. In case the lads go a bit wild.'

'So?'

'Well, the men are keen to help, so they are.'

'You mean they don't think I can manage?'

Harper was tempted to tell Sharpe not to be so foolish, but decided it might be one step too many over the subtle boundaries of rank and friendship. He sighed. 'No, sir. Just that they're keen to help. They're

fond of her, sir, so they are.' And of you, he might have added.

Sharpe shook his head ungratefully. Teresa and Antonia were his problem, not the Company's, and he did not want a horde of grinning men to witness his emotion at first seeing his child. 'Tell them no.'

Harper shrugged. 'They may try and help anyway.'

'They'll have a problem finding her in the city.'

The Sergeant grinned. 'It won't be difficult. We'll be trying the house with two orange trees, just behind the Cathedral.'

'Go to hell, Sergeant.'

'Follow you anywhere, sir.'

A few hours later the army seemed in hell, or a watery version of hell. The skies opened. Thunder cracked like the rumbling of field guns over wooden boards in the storm clouds. Lightning slashed, piercing and blue, to an earth soaked by great, slanting volleys of rain. Human noise was drowned by the seething water, a constant, crashing downpour in a darkness splintered by jagged, thundering light. Eighteen hundred men were on the hilltop, digging the first parallel; a trench six hundred yards long that would protect the besiegers and from which they would excavate the first gun batteries. The workers were soaked to the skin, shivering, made weary by the sheer weight of water, and sometimes peering through the deluge at the dark citadel starkly revealed in the lightning strikes.

The wind billowed the rain in huge, scything loops; suspended it, and then smashed it down even harder. It plucked greatcoats into fantastic, batlike shapes and drove the water in unstoppable rivulets that filled up the trench, seeped over the men's boots, and sank their spirits down into the cold, sodden earth that yielded each spadeful with such reluctance.

All night they dug, and all night it rained, and in the cold morning it still rained and the French gunners came out of their warm shelters to see the scar of fresh earth curving over the shallow hill. The gunners opened fire, smashing solid shot across the wide ditch, over the glacis, over the floodwaters, and into the wet earth of the trench parapet. The work stopped. The first parallel was too shallow to give shelter and all day the rain weakened the trench and the guns hammered it. The excavation filled with sopping mud that would all have to be scooped out in the night.

They dug all night. It still rained, a rain like the rain before Noah's flood. Uniforms doubled their weight with water, boots were sucked off in the glutinous slime, and shoulders were chafed raw and bleeding with the effort of sinking the trench. On this night the French gunners kept up a harassing and sporadic fire that turned some parts of the mud scarlet until the unending rain diluted the blood, but slowly, infinitely slowly, the spades hacked deeper and the parapet went higher.

The creeping dawn showed a trench deep enough to be worked by daylight. The exhausted battalions filed back through the zigzag trench that led to safety at the rear of the hill, and new battalions took their place. The South Essex, their packs and weapons discarded, went down the crooked way to the mud, the gunfire, and the spades.

Sharpe was left behind. Two dozen men were with him, the baggage guard, and they made crude shelters out of the piled packs and crouched, muskets between their knees, and stared at a wet, grey, dripping landscape. Sharpe could hear the French guns, muffled by rain and distance, and he hated the thought of not seeing what he could hear. He left an old Sergeant

in charge of the guard and walked the trench to the hillside.

Badajoz was a dark rock in a sea of water and mud. The walls were fringed with cannon smoke that was lanced through by the leaping flames of each shot. The French gunners were concentrating their fire to Sharpe's left where the first two British batteries were being dug. A whole battalion was working on the gun-pits. The roundshot smacked into the parapets, destroyed the earth-filled wicker gabions, and some-times smashed a bloody path through the men. The French even tried their howitzers whose short, squat barrels spat shells high into the air, so that the tiny smoke trail of the burning fuse disappeared into the low clouds before dropping on to the wet hillside. Most of the shells simply fell and lay silent, their fuses ex-tinguished by mud or rain, but a few exploded in black smoke and jagged iron fragments. They did no damage; the range was too great, and after a time the French stopped the shell-fire and saved the howitzers for the digging of the second parallel, lower down the hill and much closer to the walls.

Sharpe walked along the hilltop and searched for the South Essex. He found them at the northern end of the parallel where the hill had dropped away to the soaking plain beside the grey, swollen river. Any bat-teries dug here would be firing up at the castle that seemed vast and inviolable on its rock hill. Sharpe could see, as well, the San Roque Fort, the small fortress that Hogan had mentioned, which defended the dam across the Rivillas stream. If the British could blow up the dam, the lake would drain north into the river and the approach to the breach would be far easier. But to blow up the dam would be difficult. It looked to be no more than fifty yards from the city wall and built just beneath

the San Pedro, the single bastion on the eastern side.

A figure jumped out of the trench in front of Sharpe. It was Sergeant Hakeswill. He stalked along the trench edge and cursed down at the men. 'Dig, you bastards! You syphilitic pigs! Dig!' He whirled round after a few paces to see if anyone was reacting to him and saw Sharpe. He snapped into a salute, his face twitching crazily. 'Sir! Lieutenant, sir! Come to help, sir?' He cackled, and turned back to the Light Company. 'Get on with it, you pregnant sows! Dig!' He was leaning over the trench, screaming at them, spittle flailing from his mouth.

It was an irresistible moment. Sharpe knew he should not do it, knew that it was inconsistent with the so-called dignity of an officer, but Hakeswill was bending by the trench, screaming obscenities, and Sharpe was close behind. The second that the temptation came, Sharpe acted, and pushed the Sergeant. Hakeswill's arms beat at the air, he twisted, bellowed, and collapsed into the sopping mud at the bottom of the trench. The Light Company cheered. The Sergeant turned a furious face at Sharpe as he scrambled to his feet.

Sharpe held up a hand. 'My apologies, Sergeant. I slipped.' He knew it had been a childish thing to do, and unwise, but it was a small gesture that told the men he was still on their side. He walked on, leaving Hakeswill twitching, and saw Captain Rymer climbing from the trench to meet him.

If Rymer had seen the incident he said nothing, instead he nodded civilly. 'Nasty day.'

Sharpe felt his usual paralysis in the face of small talk. He gestured at the men in the trench. 'Digging keeps you warm.' He suddenly realized that it sounded as if he were telling Rymer to pick up a spade and he scrabbled in his head for a sentence to correct the

impression. 'One of the advantages of being in the ranks, eh?' He could hardly bring himself to call Rymer 'sir'. Rymer did not seem to notice.

'They hate digging.'

'Wouldn't you?'

Captain Rymer had never thought about it. Birth into the Rymers of Waltham Cross did not encourage a man to think about manual labour. He was a good-looking man, fair-haired, about twenty-five years old, and desperately nervous with Sharpe. The situation was not of Rymer's making, not to his taste, and he was terrified of the time, that Colonel Windham had said was coming, when Sharpe would be returned to the Company as Lieutenant. The Colonel had told Rymer not to worry. 'Won't happen yet. Give you time to settle in, take charge. But you may want him in a fight, eh, Rymer?' Rymer did not look forward to the event.

He looked up at the tall, scarred Rifleman, took a deep breath. 'Sharpe?'

'Sir?' The word had to be said sooner or later, however much it hurt.

'I wanted to say that . . .' Whatever it was, would have to wait. A French roundshot ploughed into the earth nearby, spumed up soaking mud, and then came a second and a third. Rymer's mouth dropped open in astonishment, he froze, and Sharpe grabbed his elbow and pushed him towards the trench. He followed, jumping down the five feet and skidding on the trench floor.

The air was filled with the rumble of cannon balls, and the men stopped digging and looked at each other as if one of them might have the answer to this sudden cannonade. Sharpe looked over the parapet and saw the armed piquets running back for shelter. Every gun on Badajoz's eastern wall, from the high castle, past the San Pedro, down to the Trinidad bastion at the

south-east corner, seemed to be firing at the northern hundred yards of the parallel.

Rymer stood beside him. 'What's happening?'

A piquet jumped over them, cursing the enemy. Sharpe looked at Rymer. 'Do you have weapons?'

'No! Ordered to leave them behind.'

'There must be a company here.'

Rymer nodded, pointed to the right. 'The Grenadier Company. They're armed. Why?'

Sharpe pointed through the murk and the rain to the dark shadows at the foot of the fortress. Coming from the fort that guarded the Rivillas dam were lines of men, formed into marching blue ranks that melded into the shadows so they were difficult to see. Rymer shook his head. 'What is it?'

'The bloody French!' They were coming in force, marching to attack and destroy the parallel, and suddenly they were visible because they drew their bayonets and the rows of steel glistened through the slanting rain.

The French gunners, fearful of hitting their own men, stopped firing. A bugle sounded and, on its note, the hundreds of steel bayonets dropped into the attack position and the French cheered and charged.

CHAPTER 13

It was unfortunate for Captain Rymer. He had been anticipating, with resolve and trepidation, the first time he would lead his own Company into action. He had not imagined it to be like this. Instead he had seen himself on a wide hillside, under a brilliant sky, with the standards snapping in the wind and himself, sabre drawn, taking a skirmish line against the very centre of the enemy's battle. He sometimes considered a wound, nothing too ghastly, but enough to make him a hero back home and his imagination, leaping vast distances, saw him modestly telling the story to a group of admiring ladies, while other men, untested in battle, could only look on in jealousy.

Instead of which he was at the bottom of a muddy trench, soaked to the skin, in charge of men armed only with spades and facing one thousand fully-armed Frenchmen. Rymer froze. The Company looked to him and past him to Sharpe. The Rifleman hesitated for a second, saw Rymer's indecision, and waved his arm. 'Back!'

There was no point in trying to fight; not yet, not till the armed companies could come together and make a proper counter-attack. The working parties scrambled out of the trench, ran back over the wet grass, then turned to watch the enemy jump into the deserted workings. The French ignored them; they were

interested in just two things. They wanted to capture and destroy as much of the parallel as they could and, more important, take back to the city every spade and pickaxe they could find. For each such mundane trophy, they had been promised a reward of one dollar.

Sharpe began walking to the top of the hill, parallel to the trench, keeping pace with the French who hurled spades and picks to their comrades beyond the parapet. In front of the enemy, like startled rabbits, other working parties leaped from the earth and scampered for safety. No one had been hurt in the attack. Sharpe doubted if any man had tried to fire a musket or lunge with a bayonet. It was almost farcical.

Above the enemy was chaos. The British, mostly unarmed, moved like a herd while the enemy, just yards away, systematically stripped the parallel. Some of the French tried to push the parapet down, but the earth was so sodden that it was impossible. The British, glad of a diversion from the unending digging, jeered at them. One or two Frenchmen levelled their muskets, but the British were fifty yards away, doubtful musket range, and the rain was still pouring down. The French were unwilling to unwrap their locks if there was not to be a real fight.

'Bloody chaos, sir.' Sergeant Harper had caught up with Sharpe, strode easily alongside with a spade gripped in his hand. He grinned cheerfully.

Sergeant Hakeswill, the front of his uniform still smeared with thick mud, ran past them. He gave them one malevolent glance and hurried on towards the rear of the hill. Sharpe wondered what the man was doing and then forgot about it as Captain Rymer caught him. 'Shouldn't we be doing something?'

Sharpe shrugged. 'See if anyone's missing?' There was not much else to be done, not till the guard com-

panies that had been ordered to carry weapons could organize an attack on the busy French.

An Engineer in blue coat and wearing an ornate cocked hat ran towards the French. He was shouting at the working parties that were still scrambling for safety. 'Keep your spades! Keep your spades!' It had taken dozens of ox-carts to bring the precious tools from Lisbon and now they were being casually abandoned to the French. Sharpe recognized the blue-coated man as Colonel Fletcher, the Chief Engineer.

A few men turned back to pick up their discarded spades and the leading French troops tugged the rags off their muskets, aimed, and shot. It was a miracle that any fired, but three were dry enough, the smoke coughed and Colonel Fletcher fell backwards, hands clutching at his groin. There was a French cheer as the Colonel was carried away to safety.

The South Essex Grenadier Company came running past Sharpe, muskets at the trail, with Captain Leroy at their head. He had his inevitable cigar in his mouth, sodden and unlit, and as he ran past he raised an eyebrow to Sharpe in ironic acknowledgement of the chaos. There was another armed Company just ahead and Leroy lined his men up next to them. The American looked back to Sharpe. 'Want to join in?'

The French had captured half the first parallel, three hundred yards of trench, and were still pushing up the hill. The two companies of British infantry, outnumbered ten to one, pulled out their bayonets and twisted the blades on to the muskets. Leroy looked at his men. 'Don't bother pulling your triggers. Just cut the bastards.' He drew his sword and swished the thin blade through the rain. A third company, panting and hurried, attached themselves to the small line. The

Captains nodded to each other and ordered the advance.

Other companies were scrambling into position, but the first danger to the French was from the three companies advancing from the flank. They lined the trench, unwrapped the rags from the musket locks, and waited. Sharpe doubted if one musket in ten would work. He drew his own sword, suddenly happy to feel the weight in his hand after the weeks of boredom, and then the British line began a stumbling run as if they wanted to reach the trench before the French could fire their muskets.

A French officer's sword flashed down. '*Tirez!*' Sharpe saw the men's faces flinch as they pulled the triggers, but the rain had done the work for the British. A few shots banged out, but most of the flints sparked on to wet powder that was like thick putty, and the French cursed and waited with their bayonets.

The British cheered. The frustration of days and nights of rain, of the interminable digging, was suddenly to be vented on the enemy; and men who had nothing but spades, or even bare hands, came in behind the armed companies and screamed defiance at the French. Sharpe swung the sword, slipped, and half fell, half jumped into the trench. A bayonet stabbed at him and he hammered it to one side and kicked the man down. Other Frenchmen were trying to scramble out the far side of the parallel, helped by comrades on the parapet. The British bayonets reached for them and blue-uniformed bodies slumped down.

'Watch right!' Someone shouted. A group of French were working their way up the trench, rescuing the men overwhelmed at the point of the British attack, and then they themselves were suddenly fighting for survival. A motley band of soldiers, mostly armed with spades,

waded into the French and Sharpe could see Harper swinging murderously with his makeshift weapon. The Sergeant leaped into the trench, swept a bayonet to one side, and rammed the blade of his spade into the man's solar plexus. He was shouting his Gaelic challenge, clearing the trench with massive, scything blows, and no Frenchman would stand and fight.

The enemy still possessed the parapet. They clubbed down at the British in the trench, jabbed with long bayonets, and, every once in a while, succeeded in making a musket fire down into the parallel. Sharpe knew they had to be forced away. He hacked at the feet of the men nearest him, clawed at the side, and a boot kicked him back to the trench floor.

The French were recovering, drawing their forces together, and the parallel was an unhealthy place. There was a ragged volley of shots as a rank of the enemy uncovered their flintlocks, men fell into the water that poured like a small stream down the trench. Sharpe swung again at the enemy's legs, dodged a bayonet, and knew that the sensible thing was to retreat. He ran down the trench, the mud fouled and slippery beneath his boots, and then a massive hand checked him and Sergeant Harper grinned at him. 'This is better than digging, sir.' He was holding a captured musket, the bayonet bloodied and bent.

Sharpe turned. The French still held a portion of the trench in the centre of the parallel, but the British were attacking from the hill. Only to the north, where Sharpe and Harper caught their breath in the bloodied trench, were the French undisturbed. They were not planning to stay long. Already their officers were sending back half companies, loaded with captured tools, and the sight made Sharpe climb up on the parapet of the French side of the trench. About half of his old

Company were with Harper, some with captured muskets, most with spades. He grinned at them, glad to be back. 'Come on, lads. Up here.'

One Company of Frenchmen formed a guard facing north and the officer watched nervously as Sharpe's ragged band, their uniforms plastered with wet mud, came towards them. They would not attack. The British were not properly armed, under-strength, but suddenly a sword was raised and the small group burst on him, and it was bayonets against spades, and two tall devils were hacking at his men. No one likes hand-to-hand combat, but Sharpe and Harper hurled themselves at the Company and the South Essex came with them. They snarled at the French, clubbed them with spades, and Harper used his captured musket like a mace. The French went backwards, stumbling on the slick mud, blinded by rain, and still the madmen came at them. Sharpe pushed with the sword, going for faces and throats, once having to parry a Sergeant's efficient bayonet. He knocked the blade aside, the Frenchman slipped, the sword was up and falling like an axe into the man's head. Sharpe tried to stop the blow, the Sergeant was defenceless, and the sword swerved and thudded into the wet earth of the parapet. The French were running, back to their main body, and the half-company of the South Essex were left with a dozen prisoners who had fallen on the slippery ground. The French Sergeant, his single arm-stripe bloodied in the fight, looked round his own dead and then at the sword which had so nearly killed him. He had seen the tall officer change the death-stroke, swerve the blow, and he nodded to him. '*Merci, Monsieur.*'

Harper looked at the dozen men. 'What do we do with them, sir?'

'Let them go.' It was no place to take prisoners. They

took their weapons and hurled them across the parallel, out of reach, and searched each Frenchman for wine or brandy. Ahead of Sharpe the battle still raged. The main body of the French had fought their way to within fifty yards of the first battery, but had been held. Scattered parties of men, some armed, some with nothing more than lengths of timber, were charging the French and starting vicious fights in the mud. Officers on horseback galloped at the fringe of the fight, trying to restore order to chaos, but the British soldiers did not want order. They wanted a break from the tedium of digging and the drowning rain, and they wanted a fight. It was like a street brawl. There was no smoke because the muskets would not fire; the noise of the fight was metal clashing on metal, wood on metal, the screams of the wounded and sobs of the dying. From the side, where Sharpe and his half-company shared brandy with their prisoners, it looked like hundreds of swamp monsters grappling in grotesque slow motions.

Sharpe pointed the French Sergeant towards the city. 'Go!'

The Frenchman grinned, gave Sharpe a friendly salute, and led his small band away. Twenty yards from the trench they stopped, picked up six spades. Harper shouted. 'Bring them back!' The French Sergeant made a rude gesture and began running towards Badajoz.

'Let them go.' Sharpe turned back to the fight. 'Come on.'

They trudged up beside the parapet, the rain sweeping across them and down on to the dead in the trench. Broken spades and shattered muskets littered the slope. The sound of the fight, the sound of men clawing each other to death in the mud, was muffled by the rain. A French officer had organized a small group with spades and was trying to fill in the parallel. Sharpe began to

hurry, the ground treacherous, and he turned to see his men strung out as they followed him, but Harper was beside him and the French turned and saw them coming. It was the turn of the French to use spades. A huge man swung at them, forced them back, parried Harper's thrust and Sharpe flailed his sword at the brute, cutting through the spade-handle, and still the Frenchman came at them. Harper bayoneted him, and still he came on, and Sharpe cut at the back of the man's neck until he finally collapsed. 'Come on!'

There was a stinging pain in his back, he whipped round and the French officer, white-faced, was going back from the sword lunge. 'You bastard!' Sharpe went forward, blade level, and the Frenchman came at him. The blades rattled, Sharpe twisted his wrist so that the heavy sword went from the Frenchman's left to his right, under his guard, and Sharpe stamped his right foot forward, ignored his opponent's blade and caught him in the ribs. The French officer tried to back away, slipped on blood and mud but Sharpe kept on going forward, feeling the steel scrape on ribs. His men swept past him with their bayonets held out, their captured bayonets, and Sharpe watched them drive the enemy back.

Bugles called the French back to the city and, within seconds, the hillside was a mass of retreating enemy carrying their wounded and bundles of captured shovels and picks. They were heading straight for the city as if frightened of cavalry pursuit and Sharpe watched as men waded into the floodwater rather than go the long way round by the dam. For ten, twenty yards it was fine, the water came up to their thighs and then, with horrid suddenness, the bottom dropped away. French officers shouted at their men, ordered them away from the water, shepherded them to the Rivillas dam. The sortie was over.

The French cannon opened fire, the roundshot ploughing into mud-soaked red, and the British leaped for the damaged trench. Harper looked at Sharpe's drawn and gory sword. 'Like old times, sir.'

Sharpe looked round his small group. All his Riflemen were there, grinning at him, and a good number of the rest of the Light Company. He grinned at them, then picked up a piece of wet sacking and wiped the sword blade. 'You'd better get back to the Company.'

'Rather stay here, sir.' Sharpe could not see who had spoken. He looked at Harper.

'Take them back, Sergeant.'

'Sir.' Harper grinned at him. 'And thank you, sir.'

'For nothing.' He was left alone. Small groups wandered the area of fighting and picked up the wounded and stacked the dead. There were a lot of bodies, more, he guessed, than had been in the breach at Ciudad Rodrigo. A spade brought down on a man's head is a vicious instrument and the British troops had been frustrated and ready for a fight, for a savage brawl in the mud. A dead Frenchman was curled at Sharpe's feet and the Rifleman crouched and ran his hands through the corpse's pockets and pouches. There was nothing worth taking. A letter folded into quarters which smeared as soon as Sharpe pulled it into the rain, a copper coin, and a loose musket ball that may have been the dead man's talisman. Round the neck, thick with blood, was a cheap metal crucifix. He had tried to grow a moustache, to look like a veteran, but the hairs were wispy and thin. He was hardly more than a boy. One of his boot soles had come loose, was hanging free and vibrating fitfully as the rain struck it. Had that killed him? Had the sole come loose in the fight and, as his comrades ran, had he limped, or stumbled, and had a British bayonet sliced into his neck? The ink washed

off the letter, ran into the mud, but Sharpe could see the last word on the page that was written larger than the rest. '*Maman.*'

He looked at the city, now fringed again with the long flames as the guns hammered the threnody that would not cease till the siege was over. Teresa was there. He looked at the Cathedral tower, squat and arched with bell windows, and thought how close the bell must sound to her. The Cathedral only seemed to have the one bell, a harsh bell whose note died almost as soon as it was struck on the hour and its quarters. He wondered, quite suddenly, if she ever sang to the child? And what was mother in Spanish? *Maman?* Like the French?

'Sir! Sir!' It was Ensign Matthews, blinking through the rain. 'Sir? Is that you, sir? Captain Sharpe?'

'It's me.' Sharpe did not correct the Captain to Lieutenant.

'You'd better come, sir.'

'What is it?'

'The officers' baggage, sir. It's been rifled.'

'Rifled?' He was scrambling out of the trench.

'The Colonel's lost some silver, sir. Everyone's lost something, sir.'

Sharpe swore. He had been in charge of the baggage and, instead of guarding it, he had been brawling in the mud. He swore again and began to run.

CHAPTER 14

'God damn it!' Colonel Windham paced up and down in the tiny sheepfold. He was carrying a riding crop and he cut with it in his fury, slashing at the pile of baggage. When he bent his head to look at the rifled baggage, water cascaded from his bicorne hat. 'God damn it!'

'When did it happen?' Sharpe asked Major Forrest.

'We don't know.' Forrest smiled nervously at the Rifleman.

Windham swivelled. 'Happen? When? This God-damned afternoon, Sharpe, when you were supposed to be in Goddamned command!' There were another dozen officers crowded back against the walls of the sheepfold and they looked to Sharpe with accusing faces. They were all wary of the Colonel's anger.

'Do we know it was this afternoon?' Sharpe insisted.

Windham looked as if he would like to whip Sharpe with his riding crop. Instead he swore again, and turned away. It was not the officers' day-to-day baggage that had been burgled, but their valuables which had been stored in leather mule-bags. None of the baggage, as far as Sharpe knew, had been touched for three days. It contained the kind of things that a man would only unpack if he were in comfortable quarters for a long period; silverware, crystal, the luxuries that reminded

them of home comforts. Windham growled at Major Collett. 'What's missing?'

It was not a long list. Forrest had lost a money draft, but it had been found screwed up and thrown away in the mud. Whoever had slit the bags had not known what to do with the paper. There was a pair of snuff-boxes gone, a gold chain that Sharpe suspected had been looted from Ciudad Rodrigo; certainly the officer who reported that loss had been voluble about his poverty before the siege and remarkably silent afterwards. There was a set of gold scabbard furniture, too valuable to wear in battle, a pair of silver spurs and a pair of jewelled ear-rings that an embarrassed Lieutenant claimed was a present for his mother. Major Collett had lost a shaving mirror with a silver lid and a watch that he said was worth a small fortune. Most important of all was the Colonel's loss; the silver-filigree-framed portrait of his wife, the chinless, stern Jessica. The Colonel, rumour had it, was particularly fond of his wife; she had brought him a small fortune and the hunting rights for half of Leicestershire, and Colonel Windham was furious at the loss. Sharpe remembered the portrait sitting on the low table in Elvas.

Windham pointed the whip at Sharpe. 'Did you lose anything?'

Sharpe shook his head. 'I've nothing here, sir.' Everything he owned he carried on his back, except for the Patriotic Fund sword and the gold stolen at Almeida which were with his London agents.

'Where's your pack?'

'With the others, sir.'

'Is it marked?'

Sharpe shook his head. 'No, sir.'

'Fetch it, Sharpe.'

It did not make sense. Was the Colonel accusing

166

Sharpe of being the thief? If so, why ask Sharpe to fetch his own pack and, in so doing, have an opportunity of hiding the stolen goods? He found the pack, brought it back to the sheepfold. 'Do you want to search it, sir?'

'Don't be a fool, Sharpe. You're an officer.' And thereby, went the unspoken words, and despite all evidence to the contrary, a gentleman. 'I want to see how far our thief's net was cast. See if anything's missing, man!'

Sharpe unbuckled the straps. The French pack was crammed with spare, dirty clothes; two spare locks for his rifle, and a half bottle of rum. He kept only one valuable in the pack and he did not need to look for it; it was gone. He looked up at Windham. 'I'm missing a telescope.'

'Telescope? Anything special about it?'

Something very special; the inlet brass plate that was inscribed *In Gratitude. AW. 23 September 1803*. It had gone. Sharpe pushed his hand desperately down through the clothes, but it was gone. Damn the thief! The telescope had been a gift from Wellington, a valued gift, and Sharpe cursed himself for leaving the pack with all the others. Yet they had been guarded. As the sheepfold with the officers' valuables had been guarded. Windham listened to Sharpe's description and nodded with satisfaction. 'That proves one thing.'

'Proves? What, sir?'

Windham smiled. 'I think we know where our thief comes from. Only one Company would know that pack!' He pointed at Sharpe's gradually soaking clothes in their French pig-skin pack. He turned to Major Collett. 'Parade the Light Company, Jack. Search every man.'

Sharpe tried to protest. 'Sir?'

Windham whipped round on him, held out the crop

accusingly. 'If you had stayed on guard, Sharpe, instead of gallivanting on the hill, this would not have happened. Stay out of it!'

Hakeswill! It had to be Hakeswill! Sharpe knew it, and knew with an utter certainty that the accusation would never be proved. The theft of the telescope, at least, had to have been done in the afternoon because Sharpe had seen the glass in his pack at midday. The Light Company, or most of them, had been with Sharpe fighting the French, but he suddenly remembered the awkward, lumbering figure of the yellow-faced Sergeant hurrying back towards the baggage. The loot would all be hidden by now. And the guards whom Sharpe had left to watch the baggage would all have wandered to the hilltop to see the fight. He strapped up the buckles of his pack. Major Forrest waited till the other officers had filed out the gate. 'I'm sorry, Sharpe.'

'I don't think it's the Light Company, sir.'

'I meant about the telescope.'

Sharpe grunted. Forrest was a decent man, always wanting others to be content. The Rifleman shrugged. 'It's gone, sir. It won't come back.' Hakeswill was too clever a thief to be discovered.

Forrest shook his head unhappily. 'I don't believe it. And we used to be such a happy battalion!' His face suddenly changed, became curious. 'Sharpe?'

'Sir?'

'Colonel Windham said you were married. I didn't like to contradict him.'

'Did you, sir?'

'Good Lord, no! Are you?'

Sharpe shook his head. 'No, sir.'

'But he said you told him you were.'

Sharpe squatted back on his heels and smiled up at the Major. 'I did.'

'For God's sake, why?'

'Don't know, sir. It just came out.'

'But, Good Lord, Sharpe. It goes on your papers, it . . .' Forrest gave up. 'Why don't you tell him the truth?'

'I quite like the idea, sir.'

Forrest laughed. 'Well I never. I thought it was odd when he mentioned it, but I thought it could be true. You're such a private fellow, Sharpe.'

'The way I'm going, sir, I probably will be soon.'

'Don't be ridiculous.' Forrest frowned. 'There'll be a Captaincy soon. There nearly was this afternoon. Poor Sterritt tripped over and had a bayonet through his jacket.'

Sharpe said nothing. He had shamelessly searched the survivors to see if any Captain was missing, but they all seemed to bear charmed lives and a remarkable freedom from disease in the foul weather. He stood up and slung his pack on one shoulder. Over the hill came the thumps of the French guns, a sound so common that men hardly noticed it any more. As common as the endless hissing of the rain.

Forrest looked over his shoulder, at the parading Light Company. 'This is sad, Sharpe. Very sad.'

Windham paraded them and the Sergeant Major called each man forward in turn to have pouches, haversack and pack emptied on to a groundsheet. Another Sergeant went through the packets. Sharpe turned away. He found it sad, too, and unnecessary. He would have paraded them and given them ten minutes to come up with the thief or face the consequences; if, that is, he really believed that one of the Company was the thief. Forrest shook his head. 'He's very thorough, Sharpe.'

'Not really, sir.'

'What do you mean?'

Sharpe gave a tired smile. 'When I was in the ranks, sir, we had packs with false bottoms. He's not looking inside the shakoes. Anyway, a real thief won't have the stuff anymore.'

'He's hardly had time to get rid of it.'

'Sir. One of the women could have it by now, he could have sold it all to the Sutler for a few shillings and a bottle or two. It could be hidden. It won't be found. We're just wasting our time.'

A horseman pulled up outside the sheepfold and saluted Forrest. 'Sir?'

Major Forrest peered through the rain. 'Good Lord! Young Knowles! You've got a new horse!'

'Yes, sir.' Robert Knowles slid from the saddle and grinned at Sharpe. 'Now I'm not in your Company, I'm allowed to ride a horse. Do you like it?'

Sharpe looked morosely at the beast. 'Very nice, sir.'

Knowles stiffened on the 'sir'. He looked from Sharpe to Forrest. His smile went. 'Your gazette?' He stammered at Sharpe.

'It was refused, sir.'

'Stop it.' Knowles was embarrassed. He had learned his trade from Sharpe, modelled himself on his old Captain, and now he had a Light Company of his own he tried to think, every hour, of how Sharpe would lead them. 'It's ridiculous!'

Forrest nodded. 'The world's gone mad.'

Knowles frowned, shook his head. 'I don't believe it!'

Sharpe shrugged. 'It's true.' He felt sorry for having embarrassed Knowles. 'How's the Company?'

'Wet. They want to get on with the fighting.' He shook his head again. 'So who's got your Company?'

Forrest sighed. 'A man called Rymer.'

Knowles shrugged. 'They're mad.' He looked at

Sharpe. 'It seems crazy! You underneath some Captain?'

Forrest tut-tutted. 'Oh, no. Mr Sharpe has special duties.'

Sharpe grinned. 'I'm the Lieutenant in charge of women, pick-axes, mules, and baggage guard.'

Knowles laughed. 'I don't bloody believe it!' He suddenly noticed the strange parade beyond the circular, small sheepfold. 'What's happening?'

'A thief.' Forrest sounded sad. 'The Colonel thinks it might be someone in the Light Company.'

'He's mad!' Knowles kept a fierce loyalty to his old Company. 'They're much too fly to be caught!'

'I know.' Sharpe watched the search. The men had all been processed, and nothing found, and now the Sergeants came forward. Hakeswill stood ramrod straight, his face twitching, as his pack was turned upside down. Nothing would be found, of course. The Sergeant gave Windham a snapping salute.

Harper came forward, grinning with amusement that anyone should think him capable of such an act. Hakeswill first, then Harper, and Sharpe began running up the hillside because, of course, Hakeswill wanted Harper out of the way. Patrick Harper saw Sharpe coming and raised his eyebrows, taking the insult of the search with the same calm tolerance with which he met most of life's indignities, and then the face registered shock.

'Sir?' The Sergeant Major was straightening up.

Sharpe had realized what was happening, but too late. He should have got to Harper sooner. Before the parade.

'Officer of the Day!' Windham's voice was harsh. 'Put the Sergeant under arrest.'

They only found one thing, but it was enough. On

top of the pack, not even hidden, was the silver frame that had enclosed the picture of Windham's wife. The glass had been smashed and the portrait was missing, razored from the filigree that had itself been bent. Windham held the frame, seemed to quiver with rage, and looked up at the huge Sergeant. 'Where's the picture?'

'I know nothing about it, sir. Nothing. So help me, sir, I did not take it.'

'I'll flog you! By God! I will flog you!' He turned on his heel.

The Light Company stood frozen, the rain dripping from shako peaks, their uniforms soaked. They seemed shocked. The rest of the Battalion, crouched in their inadequate shelters, watched as the Officer of the Day assembled a guard and Harper was taken away. Sharpe did not move.

The Company was dismissed. Fires were lit under the shelters in a vain attempt to drive out the dampness. Bullocks were slaughtered for the evening meal, the musket smoke lingering over the panicked survivors of the herd, and Sharpe let the rain chill his skin as he felt a terrible impotence. Knowles tried to move him. 'Come and eat with us. Be my guest. Please.'

Sharpe shook his head. 'No. I must be here for the Court-Martial.'

Knowles looked worried. 'What's happening to the Battalion, sir?'

'Happening, Robert? Nothing.'

He would kill Hakeswill one day, but now he needed proof or otherwise Harper could never be cleared. Sharpe did not know how to get the truth. Hakeswill was cunning and Sharpe knew that the truth could not be beaten out of him. He would laugh at a beating. But one day Sharpe would bury the sword in that belly and

let the rottenness burst out like putrescent ooze. He would kill the bastard.

The bugles sounded sunset, the end of the regulation day, the fourth day of Badajoz.

CHAPTER 15

It rained all night; Sharpe knew, for he was awake most of it, listening to the ceaseless water, the wind, and the sporadic shot from the French cannon that tried to disturb the digging of the batteries. There was no counter-fire from the British; the siege guns, still wrapped in straw and sacking, were waiting for a break in the weather so that the carts could be dragged over the hill and the massive guns put into their emplacements.

Sharpe sat with Harper at the top of the hill and stared down at the dull lights inside the city. They looked far away, blurred by the weather, and Sharpe tried to distinguish the Cathedral and thought of the sick child nearby.

Harper should not have been with him. He was under guard, sentenced to be flogged and reduced to the ranks, but Sharpe had simply told the sentries to look the other way while he and Harper climbed to the hilltop. Sharpe glanced at the Irishman. 'I'm sorry.'

'Nothing to be sorry for, sir. You did all you could.'

Which had amounted to very little. Sharpe had pleaded, begged almost, but the filigree frame was proof enough for the Regimental Court Martial. Sharpe had testified that Harper had been with him all after-noon, fighting the French attack, and that his own tele-scope had disappeared in that time so the Sergeant could not have been responsible. Windham had been

implacable. The telescope, he said, must have been stolen by another thief. Harper was guilty, broken down to a Private, and sentenced to a flogging.

Harper was thinking of the morning. The Donegal voice was soft. 'A hundred strokes, eh? Could be worse.' Twelve hundred lashes was the maximum sentence.

Sharpe handed a bottle to him. Both men were swathed in lengths of tarred canvas on which the rain drummed. 'I got two hundred.'

'The army's going soft, so it is.' Harper laughed. 'And back to a bloody Private, too! They don't even call me a Rifleman in this bloody Regiment. Private bloody Harper.' He drank. 'And when do they think I stole the bloody things?'

'Tuesday.'

'God save Ireland! St Patrick's Day?'

'You were missing from the lines.'

'Jesus! I was with you. Drinking.'

'I know. I told them.'

There was silence between them, a companionable misery. From the slope below came the chink of pickaxes as the batteries were sunk below the topsoil. At least, Sharpe reflected, the two of them had plenty of drink. The Light Company had pooled their resources, scrounged and stolen more, and beneath the canvas shelters there were at least a dozen canteens of rum or wine. 'I'm sorry, Patrick.'

'Save your breath, sir. It'll not hurt.' He knew he was lying. 'I'll kill that bastard!'

'After me.' They sat and thought about the comforting idea of killing Hakeswill. The Sergeant was taking precautions. He had pitched his shelter just yards from the officers' crude, canvas tents, and Sharpe knew that there was no hope, this night, of their successfully spiriting Hakeswill away to some silent, lonely place.

The Irishman chuckled softly and Sharpe looked at him. 'What?'

'I was thinking of the Colonel. What was on the bloody portrait?'

'His wife.'

'She must be a rare beauty.'

'No.' Sharpe uncorked another canteen. 'She looked a sour bitch, but you can never tell with paintings. Anyway, our Colonel approves of marriage. He thinks it keeps a man out of trouble.'

'It's probably true.' Harper sounded unconvinced. 'I hear a rumour that you and Miss Teresa are married. How the hell did that get started?'

'I told the Colonel.'

'You did!' Harper laughed. 'Mind you, you should marry her. Make an honest woman of her.'

'And what about Jane Gibbons?'

Harper grinned. He had met the blonde girl, the sister of the man he had killed, and he shook his head. 'She'll not have you. You have to be born in a big house to marry that kind; lots of money and all that. You're just a foot soldier, like the rest of us. A fancy red sash won't get you into her bed. At least, not for keeps.'

Sharpe chuckled. 'You think I should marry Teresa?'

'Why not? She's a skinny thing, so she is, but you could put some meat on her bones.' Harper profoundly disapproved of Sharpe's taste for slim women.

They sat silent again, listening to the rain pelt on the canvas, and sharing a friendship that rarely had a chance to be expressed or defined. Sharpe had a reputation, with those who did not know him well, of being a man short on words and it was true, he thought, except with a handful of friends. Harper and Hogan; Lossow, the German cavalryman, and that was about all. Exiles to a man, cut off from their own countries

and fighting with a strange army. Sharpe was an exile, too, a stranger in the Officers' Mess. 'You know what the General says?'

Harper shook his head. 'Tell me what the General says.'

'He says that no one ever promoted from the ranks turns out well.'

'Does he now?'

'He says they turn to drink.'

'In this army, who wouldn't?' Harper pushed a canteen at Sharpe. 'Here, get yourself drunk.'

Some fool opened the door of a lantern in the parallel and the French gunners, ever alert, saw the light and suddenly the ramparts of Badajoz blossomed flame and shot. There were shouts from the workings, the light disappeared, but then there was the sick thud of the shots striking home and the screams from the trench. Harper spat. 'We'll never take this bloody town.'

'We can't stay here for ever.'

'That's what you said when you first went to Ireland.'

Sharpe grinned. 'It's the welcome you give us. We don't want to leave. Anyway, we like the weather.'

'You can keep it.' Harper squinted up into the darkness. 'Christ! I wish the rain would stop!'

'I thought the Irish liked rain.'

'We love rain, so we do, but this isn't rain.'

'What is it?'

'It's the flood, the deluge, the end of the whole sodden world.'

Sharpe leaned back on a wicker gabion, abandoned by a working party, and stared up. 'I haven't seen the stars in a week. Longer.'

'That's true.'

'I like stars.'

'That's nice for them.' Harper was amused; he did not often hear Sharpe's tongue loosened by drink.

'No, really. You like birds, I like stars.'

'Birds do things. They fly, make nests. You can watch them.'

Sharpe said nothing. He remembered the nights lying in fields, head on haversack, body inside the sewn blanket, and legs thrust into the arms of the jacket which was buttoned upside down on his stomach. It was the soldier's way of sleeping, but on some nights he would simply lie there and watch the great smear in the sky that was like the camp fires of an unimaginably huge army. Legion upon incomprehensible legion, up there in the sky, and he knew that they were coming nearer, night by night, and the picture was confused in his head by the strange, drunken preachers who had come to the foundling home when he was a child. The stars were mixed up with the four horsemen of the apocalypse, the last trump, the second coming, the raising of the dead, and the lights in the night were the army of the world's end. 'The world won't end in a flood. It'll be bayonets and battalions. A bloody great battle.'

'As long as we're in the skirmish line, sir, I don't mind.' Harper drank more rum. 'I must save some for the morning.'

Sharpe sat up. 'Hagman's bribing the drummer boys.'

'Never works.' Harper was right. The drummer boys did the flogging and were usually bribed by the victim's friends, but under the gaze of the officers they were forced to lay on with their full strength.

Sharpe stared at the dark bulk of Badajoz, relieved by a few hazed lights. There was a fire burning in one of the castle's many courtyards. The dull, brief bell of

the Cathedral rang the half-hour. 'If only she wasn't there . . .' He stopped.

'What?'

'I don't know.'

'If she wasn't there.' Harper's Ulster accent was slow, as if he was treading very carefully. 'You'd be tempted to bugger off. Is that right? Up to the hills? To fight with the Partisans?'

'I don't know.'

'You do. Do you think no one else has thought of it?' Harper meant himself. 'You're not a fair weather soldier only.'

'We'll get desertions soon.'

'Aye, if Hakeswill isn't buried soon.' No one had deserted from the Battalion for months. Other battalions were losing men, a handful each day who slipped across to Badajoz. There was traffic the other way, too, including, so Hogan had told Sharpe, a French Engineer Sergeant who brought with him the plans of the defences. The plans held few surprises, except confirmation that the western glacis was thickly mined.

Sharpe changed the subject. 'Know how many died today?'

'Was it today?' Harper sounded surprised. 'It seems like last week.'

'A hundred of us. They counted nearly three hundred French. And some of them drowned, too. Poor bastards.'

'They always see double counting the French.' Harper was scornful. 'And the French are probably boasting they killed a thousand of us.'

'They didn't do much damage.'

'No.' The French had hoped to set the siege back by at least a week, by forcing the British to re-dig the whole parallel. A week gained would be an extra week during

which a French field army might march to the garrison's relief. Harper opened another canteen. 'The assault will be rough.'

'Yes.'

The rain hissed down, seething on the soaked ground, thudding monotonously on the canvas. It was bitterly cold. Harper offered Sharpe the new canteen. 'I have an idea.'

'Tell me.' Sharpe yawned.

'Am I keeping you up?'

'What's your idea?'

'I'm volunteering for the Forlorn Hope.'

Sharpe snorted. 'Don't be a bloody fool. You want to live, don't you?'

'I'm not being a fool, and I want to be a Sergeant again. Will you ask for me?'

Sharpe shrugged. 'They don't listen to me any more.'

'I said, will you ask?' Harper's voice was stubborn.

Sharpe could not imagine Harper dead. He shook his head. 'No.'

'You keeping it for yourself?' The words were spoken harshly. Sharpe turned and looked at the huge man. There was no point in denial.

'How did you know?'

Harper laughed. 'How long have I been with you? Mary, Mother of God, do you think I'm a fool? You lose your Captaincy and what will you do? You'll go screaming up some bloody breach with your sword waving because you'd rather be dead than lose your bloody pride.'

Sharpe knew it was true. 'What about you?'

'I'd like the stripes back.'

'Pride?'

'Why not? They keep saying the Irish are fools, but I notice precious few laughing at me.'

'That could be your size, not your stripes.'

'Aye, maybe, but I'll not have them saying I failed. So you've volunteered?'

Sharpe nodded. 'Yes. But they won't choose anyone yet, not till the assault.'

'And if they choose you, will you take me?'

'Yes.' He said the word with reluctance.

The Irishman nodded. 'Let's hope they choose you, then.'

'Pray for a miracle.'

Harper laughed. 'You don't want a miracle. They always turn out bad.' He drank rum. 'St Patrick turns out all the snakes from Ireland and what happens? We get so bored that we let the English in to take their place. The poor man must be turning in his grave. Snakes were better.'

Sharpe shook his head. 'If Ireland were five times bigger, and England five times smaller, then you'd be doing the same to us.'

Harper laughed again. 'Now that would be a miracle worth praying for.'

Guns boomed to their right, across the river, as the cannon in the San Cristobal Fort fired over the Guadiana towards the parallel. The long, spitting fire was reflected in the dark water. The gunners on the city wall, not to be outdone, fired their pieces and the night was filled with the noise.

Harper shivered with the cold. 'I'll pray for another miracle.'

'What?'

'A chance to get Hakeswill.' He nodded towards the city. 'In one of those little alleyways. I'll tear his bloody head off.'

'What makes you think we'll get through the wall?'

181

Harper gave a humourless laugh. 'You don't really think we can fail, do you?'

'No.' But then he had not really thought he could lose his Captaincy, had not thought he could lose the Company, and not in his worst dreams had he ever thought he would have to stand and watch Patrick Harper being flogged. The cold, wet night drummed on, bringing the bad dreams true.

CHAPTER 16

Rain, and more rain, increasing in vehemence, so by dawn it was seen that the river had flooded, was foaming white and high on the stone arches of the old bridge and, far more seriously, had swept the pontoon bridge downstream.

'Company!' The last syllable was drawn out, mingling with the shouts of other Sergeants. 'Shun!'

'Stand still! Eyes front!'

A jingle of bridles and bits brought the Battalion's senior officers into the cleared space at the centre of the paraded Companies. Two sides of the rectangle were each formed by three Companies; four Companies were paraded on one long side and faced the solitary wooden triangle.

'Order arms!' Again and again. Hands slapped on wet wood, the brass hilts slopped into the muck. Rain slanted on the ranks.

Sergeants marched stiffly through the sludge, slammed into attention and saluted. 'Company on parade, sir!' The mounted Captains, miserable in their cloaks, acknowledged.

'Battalion ready for punishment parade, sir!'

'Very good, Major. At ease.'

''Talion!' Collett's voice rode over wind and rain. 'Stand at . . . ease!' There was a convulsive shuffle in the mud.

Sharpe, his head foul from the night's drinking, had paraded with the Light Company. Rymer was embarrassed, but it was Sharpe's place, and Hakeswill's yellow face was expressionless. A pulse throbbed beneath the livid scar on the Sergeant's neck. Daniel Hagman, the old Rifleman, had come to Sharpe before the parade and told him that the Company was mutinous. It was doubtless an exaggeration, but Sharpe could see the men were sullen, angry and, above all, shocked. The only good news was that Windham had cut the punishment to sixty lashes. Major Hogan had paid the Colonel a visit and, although the Engineer had failed to persuade Windham of Harper's innocence, he had impressed him by describing Harper's record. The Battalion waited in the sweeping rain, full of cold misery.

"Talion! Shun!' Another shuffle and Harper appeared between two guards. The Irishman was stripped to the waist, showing the massive muscles of his arms and chest. He walked easily, ignoring the rain and mud, and grinned towards the Light Company. He seemed the least concerned man on the parade.

They lashed his wrists high on the triangle, spread his legs and tied them at the base, and then a Sergeant pushed the folded leather between Harper's teeth so that he would not bite his tongue off in the pain. The Battalion's doctor, a sickly man with a streaming nose, gave Harper's back a cursory inspection. He was obviously healthy. A leather strip was tied round his kidneys, the doctor nodded miserably at Collett, the Major spoke to Windham, and the Colonel nodded. 'Carry on!'

The drumsticks came down on soggy skins. The Sergeant nodded at the two lads. 'One!'

Sharpe remembered it. His own flogging had been in a village square in India. He had been tied to an

ox-cart, not a triangle, but he remembered the first slashing cut with the leather thongs, the involuntary arching of the back, the teeth grinding into the leather, and the surprise that it was not as bad as he had expected. He had almost got used to the blows, was feeling confident, and resented it when the doctor stopped the lashes to check that he was still capable of receiving more punishment. Later, the pain had blurred. It had begun to hurt, really to hurt, as the lashes tore at the skin and the alternate blows, from two sides, ripped and frayed till the watching Battalion saw the glint of bone laid open as the blood dripped on to the village dust.

God! It had hurt!

The South Essex watched in silence. The drums, their skins stretched by the rain, could hardly be heard; they were like the muffled beats of a funeral. The lashes sounded soggy as they drew blood, the Sergeant in charge of the flogging chanted the numbers, and in the background the French guns fired on.

The drummer boys paused. The doctor stepped close to Harper's back, sneezed, and nodded to the Sergeant.

'Twenty-five!'

The rain diluted the blood.

'Twenty-six!'

Sharpe looked at Hakeswill. Was there a glint of triumph in the face? It was impossible to tell. The face twitched in a spasm.

'Twenty-seven!'

Harper turned his head to face the Light Company. He was not moving at all as the blows hit him. He spat out the leather gag, grinned at them.

'Twenty-eight! Harder!'

A drummer boy used all his strength. Harper grinned even wider.

'Stop it!' Collett stepped his horse forward. 'Put the gag in!'

They pushed the leather back in Harper's mouth, but he spat it out again, and grinned through the punishment. There was an appreciative murmur from the Light Company, almost a laugh, and they saw that Harper was chatting to the drummer boys. The bastard had beaten the punishment! Sharpe knew it was hurting him, but knew that Harper's pride would not let it show, would only let him pretend a total unconcern.

The punishment finished, made almost farcical by Harper's unbelievable bravery. 'Cut him down!'

Sharpe had seen men crumple to the ground after just two dozen strokes, but Harper stepped away from the cut thongs, still grinning, and did nothing more than massage his wrists. The doctor asked him a question and the Irishman laughed, refused the offer of a blanket to be draped over his bleeding back, and turned to follow his escort off the parade.

'Private Harper!' Windham had spurred his horse forward.

'Sir?' There was almost a contempt in Harper's voice.

'You're a brave man. Here.' Windham tossed a gold coin towards the Ulsterman. For a brief fraction of a second it seemed as if Harper might ignore the coin, then a huge hand whipped up, snatched it from the air, and he gave the Colonel his big, infectious grin. 'Thank you, sir.'

The Battalion gave a low, collective sigh of relief. Windham must have realized, even as the punishment was happening, that he was flogging the most popular man in the Battalion. There had been hostility in the parade, an unusual hostility. Soldiers did not object to a flogging, why should they? If a man deserved punishment then a battalion would line up and watch

punishment done. But soldiers also had a keen sense of injustice and Sharpe, watching Windham, knew that the Colonel had sensed the Battalion's outrage. A mistake had been made. It could not be admitted or reversed, not without proof, but the gold coin had been a clever touch. Windham, for all his pretence at being a simple country squire, was a clever man.

And Hakeswill a cunning man. The Sergeant kept his face expressionless as the parade was dismissed. Hakeswill was triumphant. Harper had been defeated, demoted, and the Company was at Hakeswill's mercy. He now wanted one thing more, and would get it, Sharpe's misery; and thanks to Company rumour, the Sergeant knew where that misery could be accomplished, at the house behind the Cathedral with its two orange trees.

Sharpe found Harper in a shelter, two of the wives putting grease on his back and bandaging the wounds. 'Well?'

Harper grinned. 'Hurt like hell, sir. I couldn't have taken much more.' He held up the golden guinea. 'What do I do with this?'

'Spend it?'

'No.' The Irishman stared past Sharpe into the sea of mud that was swept by great curtains of grey rain. 'I'll keep it, sir, until I've killed the bastard.'

'Or until I kill him?'

'One of us, sir. But make it soon. Before we leave this place.'

If ever they would leave Badajoz, Sharpe thought. That afternoon he took a working party east, towards the Portuguese border. They found the precious pontoons aground in the flood and stripped naked to manhandle the great boats to where oxen could haul them back. The siege was bogged down, in rain, mud and

misery. Badajoz was like a great castle in mid-ocean. The rain had flooded the fields to the south, the west, and the north, and still the wind shrieked at them, brought more water, and though it was a time for effort, the effort could not be made. The trenches were flooded, the sides collapsed, and when gabions were used to shore the batteries, the water dissolved their earth filling into liquid sludge that flowed out leaving a hollow, useless wicker shell.

Everything was fouled with mud. Carts, supplies, forage, food, uniforms, weapons and men. The camp was foul, the only movement the slow flapping of wet canvas in the wind, and fever killed as many as the ceaseless French guns. The time that the French had hoped to gain by their attack on the parallel was given to them by the weather. Morale slumped. The first Monday of the siege was the worst. It had rained for a week, and it still rained, and darkness fell on an army that could scarce even light a fire any more. Nothing was dry, nothing was warm, and a man from a Welsh Regiment, a fusilier, went mad. There were shouts in the night, a terrifying scream as he carved his wife with a bayonet, and then hundreds of men were fumbling in the darkness, thinking it was a French attack, while the madman ran through the camp, slashing left and right with his weapon. He screamed that the resurrection of the dead was here and now, that he was the new Messiah, and finally his Sergeant cornered him and, sensible that no one wanted a court-martial and execution, killed the man with one neat stab.

Sharpe met Hogan that Sunday night. The Major was busy. Colonel Fletcher's wound was keeping the Chief Engineer in his tent and Hogan had taken much of his work. The Irishman was gloomy. 'We'll be defeated by the rain, Richard.' Sharpe said nothing. The spirit of

the army was crushed by the water; they wanted to strike back, to hear their own guns firing at the French, but the guns, like the army, were bogged down. Hogan stared into the wet, pelting night. 'If only it would stop.'

'And if it doesn't?'

'Then we give up. We've lost.'

Outside, in the cold night, the rain smashed down, dripped heavily from the lip of Hogan's tent, and the slow drops seemed to Sharpe to be the drumbeats of defeat. Unthinkable defeat.

CHAPTER 17

On Tuesday afternoon it stopped raining.

There were suddenly scraps of blue sky between the tattered clouds and, like some beast saved from imminent drowning, the army heaved itself out of the mud and attacked the trenches with renewed energy.

They hauled the guns over the hill that night. The ground was still an almost impenetrable sludge, but they hauled on ropes, thrust wicker beneath reluctant wheels, and with an enthusiasm endowed by the break in the weather, the troops took the vast twenty-four-pounders to the newly-dug batteries.

In the morning, in a miraculously clear dawn, there was a cheer from the British camp. The first shot had been fired and they were hitting back! Twenty-eight siege guns were in place, protected by gabions, and the Engineers directed the artillery officers so that the iron balls hammered at the base of the Trinidad bastion. The French guns tried to destroy the siege guns and the valley above the grey, placid floodwaters of the Rivillas was shrouded with smoke that swirled as the cannon balls pierced through the mist.

At the end of the first day, when an evening breeze drifted the smoke southwards, a hole was visible in the masonry of the bastion. It was not much of a hole, more of a chipped dent, surrounded by smaller shot scars. Sharpe stared at the damage through Major Forrest's

telescope and gave a humourless laugh. 'Another three months, sir, and they might notice us.'

Forrest said nothing. He was afraid of Sharpe's mood, of the depression that had come with idleness. The Rifleman had hardly any duties. Windham seemed to have abandoned the wives' parade, the mules were in pasture, and Sharpe's time hung heavily. Forrest had spoken to Windham, but the Colonel had shaken his head. 'We're all bored, Forrest. The assault will cure all.' Then the Colonel had taken his fox hounds south for a day's hunting, and with him half the Battalion's officers. Forrest had tried, unsuccessfully, to cheer Sharpe up. He looked now at Sharpe's morose profile. 'How's Sergeant Harper?'

'Private Harper's getting better, sir. Another three or four days and he'll be on duty.'

Forrest sighed. 'I can't get used to calling him "Private". It doesn't seem right.' Then he blushed. 'Oh dear. I suppose I've put my foot in it.'

Sharpe laughed. 'No, sir. I'm getting used to being a Lieutenant.' It was not true, but Forrest needed reassurance. 'Are you comfortable, sir?'

'Very. It's a splendid view.' They were watching the valley and the city, waiting for the attack that would be made just after dark. Half the army were on the hilltop, in the trench or the new, half finished batteries, and the French must have known that something was about to happen. It was not difficult to guess what was intended. The British guns were more than half a mile from the Trinidad bastion, too far to be truly effective, and the Engineers needed to cut that range in half. That meant building a second parallel, with new batteries, right on the edge of the floodwaters, just where the French had built the Picurina Fort. Tonight the fort would be attacked. Sharpe had desperately hoped

that the Fourth Division, his own, would be chosen, but instead the Third and Light would go forward in the darkness and Sharpe was merely a spectator. Forrest looked down the slope. 'It shouldn't be difficult.'

'No, sir.' Which was true, Sharpe thought, but only half the battle. The Picurina Fort was almost makeshift; a wedge-shaped obstacle facing the British tide and only intended to slow them down. It had a ditch that protected a low stone wall, and on the wall were palisades, split-trunks loopholed for muskets, and the fort was far enough from the city so that the French guns could not douse the attack with grapeshot. The fort should fall, but that still left the lake formed by the dammed Rivillas. The floodwater blocked the direct approach to the city. Unless the lake could be drained, any attack would have to come from the south, squeezed between the water and the south wall, passing by the huge Pardaleras Fort, and the attacking columns would be under fire from scores of French guns and shredded by grapeshot. Sharpe borrowed Forrest's glass again and trained it on the dam. It was remarkably well-built, for a temporary structure, and Sharpe could see a balustraded stone walkway along the dam top that led to the fort, much stronger than the Picurina, that defended the dam. The fort and dam were hard by the city walls. A man with a musket on the San Pedro bastion could easily fire down on to the stone walkway. Forrest saw where he was looking.

'What are you thinking, Sharpe?'

'I was thinking it wouldn't be easy to attack the dam, sir.'

'You think anyone intends to attack the dam?'

Sharpe knew an attack was intended, Hogan had told him so, but he shrugged his shoulders. 'I wouldn't know, sir.'

Forrest looked round conspiratorially. 'Don't tell any-one, Sharpe, but we're going to!'

'We, sir?' Sharpe had a flicker of excitement in his voice. 'The Battalion, sir?'

'I'm speaking out of turn, Sharpe, out of turn.' Forrest was pleased at the quickening in Sharpe's voice. 'The Colonel's offered our services. The General of Division was talking to him. We may be the lucky ones!'

'When, sir?'

'I don't know, Sharpe! They don't tell me these things. Look! The curtain's going up!'

Forrest pointed to the huge number one battery. A gunner had snatched the last gabion from the embrasure and one of the guns, silent for half an hour, bellowed flame and smoke down the hillside. The ball, under-aimed, struck the ground in front of the Picurina, scarred the earth as it bounced, and then fell with a tall splash into the lake. The jeer of the French inside the small fort was audible four hundred yards away.

The gunners raised the barrel half an inch by turning the huge screw beneath the breech. The barrel hissed as it was sponged out. The embrasure had been plugged again as defence against the inevitable fire from the city walls. The powder bags were thrust deep into the gun's throat, rammed home and the ball trundled into the muzzle. A Sergeant leaned over the touch-hole, thrust down with the spike that punctured the powder bags, and then inserted the tube filled with fine powder that fired the charge. His hand went up, an officer shouted orders and the gabions were pulled from the front of the battery. The men crouched with their hands over their ears as the Sergeant touched the priming tube with a match burning at the end of a long pole, and the gun slammed back on the inclined wooden platform. The ball struck the timber palisade of the

Picurina, splintering the tree-trunks, driving the shards of unseasoned wood in vicious showers on the defenders, and it was the turn of the British to cheer.

Forrest was looking at the fort through his telescope. He tut-tutted. 'Poor lads.' He turned to Sharpe. 'That can't be very nice for them.'

Sharpe wanted to laugh. 'No, sir.'

'I know what you're thinking, Sharpe. That I'm too charitable to the enemy. You're probably right, but I can't help imagining that my son is in there.'

'I thought your son was an engraver, sir.'

'Yes, he is, Sharpe, yes he is, but if he was a French soldier he might be in there and that would be most upsetting.'

Sharpe gave up trying to follow Forrest's charitable imaginings and turned back to the Picurina. The other British guns had got the range and the heavy balls were systematically destroying the flimsy defences. The French inside were trapped. They could not retreat, for the lake was to their rear, and they must have known that the cannonade would end in an infantry attack as soon as dusk gave way to night. Forrest frowned at the sight. 'Why don't they surrender?'

'Would you, sir?'

Forrest was offended. 'Of course not, Sharpe. I'm English!'

'They're French, sir. They don't like surrendering either.'

'I suppose you're right.' Forrest did not really understand why the French, a nation he thought to be basically civilized, should fight so hard in such an evil cause. He could understand the Americans fighting for Republicanism; a young nation could hardly be expected to have enough sense to recognize the dangers of such a foul political code, but the French? Forrest

could not understand that. It was made worse that the French were the most powerful military nation on earth, and thus had harnessed their muskets and horsemen to the spreading Republican evil, and it was Britain's obvious duty to contain the disease. Forrest saw the war as a moral crusade, a fight for decency and order, and victory to the British would mean that the Almighty, who could not possibly be suspected of Republican sentiments, had blessed the British effort.

He had explained his beliefs once to Major Hogan and had been deeply shocked when the Engineer had dismissed his ideas. 'My dear Forrest. You are fighting purely for trade! If Boney hadn't closed Portugal's harbours you'd be snug in your Chelmsford bed.'

Forrest remembered the conversation and looked at Sharpe. 'Sharpe? Why are we fighting?'

'Sir?' For a moment Sharpe wondered if Forrest was proposing a surrender to the Picurina Fort. 'Why are we fighting?'

'Yes, Sharpe. Why do you fight? Are you against Republicanism?'

'Me, sir? I couldn't even spell it.' He grinned at Forrest, saw that the Major was serious. 'Good Lord, sir. We always fight the French. Every twenty years or so. If we didn't they'd invade us. Then we'd all be forced to eat snails and speak French.' He laughed at Forrest. 'I don't know, sir. We fight them because they're meddlesome bastards and someone has to stamp all over them.'

Forrest sighed. He was saved trying to explain the political forces of the world to Sharpe because Colonel Windham and a group of the Battalion's officers spotted them and joined them at the parapet. Windham was in a good mood. He looked at the British shot flailing at the remains of the French parapet and slapped a palm with a clenched fist. 'Well done, lads!

195

Give the bastards hell!' He nodded civilly to Sharpe and grinned at Forrest. 'Excellent day, Forrest, excellent. Two foxes!'

Hogan had once mentioned to Sharpe that nothing cheered up a British officer as much as a dead fox. In addition to this double cause for satisfaction Windham had more good news. He pulled a letter from his pocket and brandished it towards Forrest. 'Letter from Mrs Windham, Forrest. Splendid news!'

'Good, sir.' Forrest, like Sharpe, was wondering whether the chinless Jessica had given birth to another young Windham, but it was not to be. The Colonel opened the letter, hummed and hawed as he glanced down the first few lines, and Sharpe could tell from the expressions of Leroy and the other newcomers that Windham had already been spreading whatever the good news turned out to be.

'Here it is! We've had poacher trouble, Forrest, damned bad trouble. Some rascal's been in among the pheasants. My good lady caught him!'

'Splendid, sir.' Forrest tried to sound enthusiastic.

'More than caught him! She bought a new kind of mantrap. Damned thing did so much damage that he died of the gangrene. Here we are. Mrs Windham writes: "It so inspired the Rector that he incorporated Same into last Sunday's sermon to the undoubted Edification of those in the Parish Unmindful of their Station!" Windham beamed at the assembled officers. Sharpe doubted if anyone in the Colonel's parish was unmindful of their station while Mrs Windham was so mindful of her own, but he judged it not the right moment to say so. Windham looked again at the letter. 'Splendid man, our Rector. Rides like a trooper. Know what his text was?'

Sharpe waited for a gun to fire. 'Numbers. Chapter

thirty-two, verse twenty-three, sir?' He spoke mildly.

The Colonel looked at him. 'How the devil did you know?' He seemed to suspect that the Rifleman might have been reading his post. Leroy was grinning.

Sharpe decided not to say that he had slept in a dormitory in a foundling home that had the text painted in letters three feet high down the wall. 'It seemed appropriate, sir.'

'Quite right, Sharpe, damned appropriate. "Be sure your sin will find you out." It found him out, eh? Died of the gangrene!' Windham laughed and turned to greet Major Collett who was bringing the Colonel's servant laden with bottles of wine. The Colonel smiled at his officers. 'Thought we'd celebrate. We'll drink to tonight's attack.'

The guns fired through dusk, and on till, in the darkness, the bugles brought an overwhelming force of British infantry forward against the small redoubt. The gunners on the city wall, hearing the British cannonade stop, lowered their own muzzle and fired over the Picurina at the hill-slope. The roundshot smashed into file after file of the attackers, but they closed up and walked on, and then there were deeper explosions from the city and the watchers on the hill saw the dark red streaks of the shell-fuses arc over the lake as the howitzers started firing. The shells exploded in scarlet blossoms. Riflemen of the 95th formed a skirmish line, curving round the fort, and Sharpe could see the needle flames flickering round the line, seeking the loopholes. The French in the fort held their fire, hearing the commands in the darkness, listening to the rifle bullets overhead, waiting for the actual assault.

On the hill the watching officers could see little except the flames of guns and explosions. Sharpe was fascinated by the guns on the city's parapets. Each shot

spewed flame that, for a few seconds, was bright and stabbing as the shot sped away, but then, for a brief moment, the flame contracted into a strange, writhing shape that existed independently of the cannon; a fading, twisting beauty, like a fire ghost, like intricate folds of flame-made drapery that swirled and disappeared. The sight had a mesmerizing beauty, nothing to do with war, and he stood and watched, drinking the Colonel's wine, until a cheer from the dark field told him that the attacking battalions had lowered their bayonets for the charge. And stopped.

Something had gone wrong. The cheer died. The ditch, that ran clear round the small fort, was deeper than anyone expected and, unseen from the low hilltop, flooded with rainwater. The attackers had expected to jump into the ditch and, using the short ladders they carried, climb easily on to the fort and carry their bayonets to an outnumbered enemy. Instead they were checked. The French defenders crawled to their splintered ramparts and opened fire. Muskets crackled over the ditch. The British fire hammered uselessly at the fort's stonework and shattered palisades while the French toppled men into the water or drove them back into the ranks behind. The French, sensing victory, rammed and fired, rammed and fired, and then, to light their helpless targets, lit the oil-soaked carcasses they had been keeping for the final assault, and rolled the lights down the face of the fort.

It was a fatal mistake. Sharpe, on the hilltop, saw the attackers milling helplessly at the lip of the ditch. In the sudden flame-light, the British were easy targets for the French gunners on the city walls who fired at the sides of the fort, slicing whole ranks of men into eternity with single shots and forcing the attackers to the shelter of the fort's front edge. But the light also revealed a

strange weakness in the fort. Sharpe borrowed Forrest's glass and, through the dim lens, could see that the defenders had driven wooden spikes into the face of the ditch to stop an attempt to climb its inner face. The spikes effectively reduced the width of the ditch to less than thirty feet and, as the glass was impatiently snatched from him by Major Collett, he saw the first ladders laid like a bridge on to the convenient spikes. It was the 88th, the same Regiment that he had fought beside at Ciudad Rodrigo, the men from Connaught. Three ladders held, despite their green, wet, sagging timbers, and the Irishmen made their precarious crossing, into the eye of a musket storm, and some dropped into the drowning ditch, but others scrambled across and the dark uniforms, lit by fire, climbed the fort's escarpment as others crossed behind them.

The lights of the carcasses died, the battlefield went dark, and only the sounds told the story of the fight to the hilltop. Screams came clearly, but few shots, which told those who understood that the bayonets were at work. Then there were cheers, that spread back among the attackers, and Sharpe knew that the British had won. The Connaught Rangers would be hunting the French survivors in the roundshot-shattered fort, the long, thin blades searching the broken timber and he grinned in the night at the thought of a fight well fought. Patrick Harper would be jealous. The men from Connaught would have a few tales to tell, of how they had walked the precarious bridge, and won. Windham's voice disturbed his thoughts.

'That's it, gentlemen. Our turn next.'

There was a brief silence, then Leroy's voice. 'Our turn?'

'We're going to blow up the dam!' Windham's voice was full of enthusiasm.

There were a dozen questions, all asked at once, and Windham chose one to answer. 'When? I don't know when. Three days' time, probably. Keep it to yourselves, gentlemen, I don't want every Tom, Dick and Harry to know. There should be some surprise in our attack.' Windham laughed, his good mood had lasted.

'Sir?' Sharpe's voice was low.

'Sharpe? That you?' It was difficult to distinguish shapes in the darkness.

'Yes, sir. Permission to rejoin the Company for the attack.'

'You're a bloodthirsty bastard, Sharpe.' Windham's voice was cheerful. 'You ought to be my gamekeeper. I'll think about it!' He moved off down the trench, leaving Sharpe uncertain whether he was being considered as gamekeeper or soldier.

There was a sudden glow in the trench beside him and the smell of pungent tobacco. Leroy's voice, deep and amused, came with the smoke. 'With any luck, Sharpe, one of us will die. You'll get your Captaincy back.'

'It had occurred to me.'

The American laughed. 'Do you think any of us think of anything else? You're a bloody ghost, Sharpe!' He put on a morbid tone. 'You remind us of our mortality. Which one of us will you replace?'

'Any offers?'

Leroy laughed. 'Not me, Mr Sharpe, not me. If you think I left Boston just so you could get my shoes, you're wrong.'

'Why did you leave Boston?'

'I'm an American, with a French name, from a Royalist family, fighting for the English, for a German king, who's mad. There, what does that tell you?'

Sharpe shrugged in the darkness. He could think of nothing to say. 'I don't know.'

'Nor do I, Sharpe, nor do I.' The cigar glowed bright, then faded. Leroy's voice was low and private. 'I sometimes wonder if I chose the wrong side.'

'Did you?'

Leroy was silent for a moment. Sharpe could see his profile staring down at the dark city. 'I suppose so, Sharpe. My Father took an oath to defend the King's Majesty and I kind of inherited the burden.' He laughed. 'Here I am, defending away.' Sharpe had rarely heard Leroy talk so much. The American was a silent man who watched the world with ironic amusement. 'You know America is spoiling for war?'

'I heard.'

'They want to invade Canada. They probably will. I could be a General in that army, Sharpe. I'd have streets named after me. Hell! Even whole towns!' He fell silent again and Sharpe knew that Leroy was thinking about his probable fate; an unmarked Spanish grave. Sharpe knew a score of men like Leroy; men whose families had stayed loyal after the American Revolution and who now fought, as exiles, for King George. Leroy laughed again, a bitter laugh. 'I envy you, Sharpe.'

'Envy me? Why?'

'I'm just a drunk American with a French name fighting for a German lunatic and I don't know why. You know where you're going.'

'Do I?'

'Yes, Mr Sharpe, you do. To the top, wherever that is. And that's why our happy band of Captains are so frightened of you. Which one of us has to die for your next step?' He paused to light another cigar from the butt of the first. 'And I can tell you, Sharpe, in my friendliest possible way, that they would much rather see you dead.'

Sharpe stared at the dark profile. 'Is that a warning?'

'Hell, no! I'm just spreading a little gloom in the night.' There was a trampling of feet in the trench and the two officers had to squeeze in to the side to let stretcher bearers pass, carrying the wounded from the Picurina. The men moaned on the stretchers; one sobbed. Leroy watched them pass and then clapped Sharpe on the shoulder. 'Our turn next, Sharpe, our turn next.'

CHAPTER 18

'What do you think?' Hogan sounded worried.

'It's too complicated.' Sharpe shrugged. 'Fifty men could do it. You don't need a whole battalion.'

Hogan nodded, but whether the nod meant agreement was impossible to tell. He looked up at the thick clouds. 'At least the weather's on our side.'

'If it doesn't rain.'

'It won't rain.' Hogan made the statement as if he controlled the weather. 'But it will be dark.' He looked over the parapet at the fort which protected the dam. 'You're right. It's too complicated, but the Colonel insists. I wish you were going.'

'So do I, but the Colonel insists.' Windham had refused Sharpe's request. The Rifleman was not to go with the Light Company, but, instead, he was to stay with Colonel Windham. Sharpe grinned at Hogan. 'I'm his aide-de-camp.'

'His aide-de-camp?' Hogan laughed. 'I suppose that's a promotion of a sort. What are you supposed to do? Run messages for him?'

'Something like that. He didn't want me with the Light Company. He said my presence would embarrass Captain Rymer.'

Hogan shook his head. 'I just hope your Captain Rymer's up to it. I really do.' He looked at his watch, snapped the lid shut. 'Two hours to darkness.'

The plan sounded simple enough. One Company, the Light Company, was to escort twenty sappers to the dam. The rest of the Battalion was to create a diversion by making a false attack on the fort and, under the cover of the noise, the sappers were to stack their twenty kegs of powder at the dam's base. It sounded simple, but Sharpe did not trust it. Night attacks, as the army had discovered only four nights before, could lead to confusion, and the whole of Windham's plan depended on the Light Company reaching the foot of the dam by precisely eleven o'clock. If they were late, and the Colonel would have no way of knowing their progress, the false attack would merely wake up the garrison and put sentries on the alert. Sharpe had suggested to Windham that the false attack was unnecessary, that the Light Company should go alone, but the Colonel had shaken his head. He wanted to lead the Battalion into action, was looking forward to the night's events, and seemed unworried by Sharpe's doubts. 'Of course they'll make it on time!'

There seemed little reason why not. The Light Company and their sappers did not have far to go. In the darkness they would leave the first parallel and head north for the river. Once on the bank of the Guadiana they would turn to their left and follow a path that led to the Rivillas stream below the castle walls. Their faces would be blackened, their equipment muffled, and they would move silently down into the ravine of the Rivillas and turn left. The most difficult moments would be the approach, upstream, towards the dam. It would be a journey of a hundred and fifty yards, within earshot of Badajoz's walls, till the men were between the San Pedro bastion and the dam's fort. It was not a long journey, they had plenty of time to make it, but it would be slowed by the need for absolute silence. Hogan fidgeted with the

lid of his watch. It was he who had convinced Wellington that the dam could be blown up, but his scheme was at the mercy of Windham's implementation. He exchanged his watch for his snuffbox and forced a smile on his face. 'At least everything else is going well!'

The second parallel was being dug. It was much closer to the walls of Badajoz and, from its cover, new batteries were being made that would bring the siege guns within four hundred yards of the city's south-east corner where, on the Trinidad bastion, the chipped dent had become a hole exposing the rubble at the wall's core. The French were sending out work parties at night to repair the damage, while the British kept firing in the hope of killing the workmen. All day and all night the guns fired.

At dusk, Sharpe watched the Light Company move out. Harper was with them, in the ranks, insisting that his back was mended well enough. Hakeswill paraded them. He was making himself indispensable to Captain Rymer, anticipating his wishes, flattering him, taking the burden of discipline from his shoulders. It was a classic performance; the reliable Sergeant, tireless and efficient, and it disguised Hakeswill's victory over the Company. He had divided them, made them suspicious, and there was nothing Sharpe could do. Colonel Windham inspected the Company before they set off. He stopped in front of Harper and pointed to the massive seven-barrelled gun slung on the Irishman's shoulder.

'What's that?'

'Seven-barrelled gun, sir.'

'Is it regulation issue?'

'No, sir.'

'Then take it off.'

Hakeswill stepped forward, his mouth twisted into a grin. 'Give it to me, Private!'

The gun had been a present from Sharpe to Harper, but there was nothing Harper could do. He took the gun from his shoulder, slowly, and Hakeswill snatched it from him. The Sergeant put it on his own shoulder and looked at the Colonel. 'Punishment, sir?'

Windham looked puzzled. 'Punishment?'

'For carrying a non-issue weapon, sir?'

Windham shook his head. He had punished Harper already. 'No, Sergeant. No.'

'Very good, sir!' Hakeswill scratched at his scar and followed Windham and Rymer down the rank. After the inspection, when the Colonel told the Company to stand easy, Hakeswill took off his shako and stared into its greasy interior. There was a curious smile on his face, and Sharpe was puzzled. He found Lieutenant Price, pale beneath the burnt cork on his skin, and jerked his head towards the Sergeant. 'What's he doing?'

'God knows, sir.' Price still thought of Sharpe as a Captain. 'He's always doing it now. Takes his hat off, stares inside, smiles, then puts it on again. He's mad, sir.'

'He takes his hat off? And stares into it?'

'That's right, sir. He should be in bloody Bedlam, sir, not here.' Price grinned. 'Perhaps the army is a madhouse sir, I don't know.'

Sharpe was about to demand the seven-barrelled gun from Hakeswill when Windham, now mounted on his horse, called the Light Company to attention. Hakeswill put his shako on, snapped his heels together, and stared at the Colonel. Windham wished them luck, told them their job was to protect the sappers in case they were discovered and, if they were not detected, to do nothing. 'Off you go! And good hunting!'

The Light Company filed into the trench, Hakeswill

206

still carrying the seven-barrelled gun, and Sharpe wished he was going with them. He knew how dearly Hogan wanted the dam blown, how much easier the assault on the breach would be if the lake was gone, and it irked him to be absent from the attempt. Instead, as the cathedral clock sounded half-past ten, he was at Windham's side as the nine remaining companies of the Battalion climbed out of the parallel on to the dark grass. Windham was nervous. 'They should be nearly there.'

'Yes, sir.'

The Colonel half drew his sword, thought better of it, and slid the blade back into the scabbard. He looked round for Collett. 'Jack?'

'Sir?'

'Ready?'

'Yes, sir.'

'Off you go! Wait for the clock!'

Collett walked forward into the darkness. He was taking four companies towards the city, towards the fort that protected the dam, and, when the clock struck eleven, he was to open fire on the face of the fort to make the French believe that an attack was coming. The other companies, under Windham, were in reserve. The Colonel, Sharpe knew, was hoping that the false attack might reveal a weakness in the fort and turn itself into a real attack. He had hopes of leading the South Essex across the ditch, up the stone wall, and into the defences. Sharpe wondered how the Light Company were doing. At least there had been no shots from the castle, no shouted challenge from the dam's fort, so presumably they were still undetected. The Rifleman felt uneasy. If all went well, according to Windham's timetable, the dam should be blown a few minutes after eleven, but Sharpe's instincts were gloomy. He thought

of Teresa inside the city, of the child, and wondered whether the explosion, if it ever came, would wake up the baby. His baby! It still seemed miraculous that he had a child.

'The powder should be in place, Sharpe!'

'Yes, sir.' He only half heard the Colonel's words but he knew that Windham was merely talking to cover his nervousness. They had no way of knowing where the powder was. Sharpe tried to imagine the sappers, laden down like south coast brandy smugglers, creeping up the ravine towards the dam, but Windham interrupted his thoughts.

'Count the musket flashes, Sharpe!'

'Yes, sir.' He knew that the Colonel was hoping that the fort, by some miracle, would be thinly defended and that the South Essex could overwhelm it by sheer numbers. It was, Sharpe knew, a vain hope.

Off to their left, a half mile up the hill, the flames stabbed from the siege guns and each flash lit the rolling smoke that filled the air over the floodwaters. The French guns replied, firing at the muzzle flashes, but the enemy fire had slackened in the last two days. They were hoarding their ammunition, saving it for the new batteries of the second parallel.

'Not long now.' The Colonel spoke to himself; then, louder. 'Major Forrest?'

'Sir?' Forrest appeared from the darkness.

'All well, Forrest?'

'Yes, sir.' Forrest, like Sharpe, had nothing to do.

There was a sudden crackle of musketry, muffled by distance, from the north and Windham spun round. 'Not us, I think.' It was much too far away to be concerned with the Light Company's attack; far off to the north, across the river, men of the Fifth Division were

keeping the French forts occupied. Windham relaxed. 'Must be soon, gentlemen.'

A shout came from the darkness in front. The three officers froze, listened, and it came again. '*Qui vive?*' A French sentry had challenged. Sharpe heard Windham suck in breath.

'*Qui vive?*' Louder. '*Gardez-vous!*' A musket stabbed from the fort towards the dark field.

'Damn.' Windham spat the word out. 'Damn, damn, damn!'

There were more shouts from the fort, followed by a glow of light that grew, showed leaping flames, and a carcass was hurled into the darkness, across the ditch, and Sharpe could see Collett's companies outlined by the fire.

'*Tirez!*' The shout carried easily. The loopholes of the small fort sprang musket fire, and the British companies replied.

'Damn!' Windham shouted. 'We're early!'

Collett's companies were firing in platoon fire, the volleys rolling down the faces of the companies, the balls hammering audibly on the fort's stonework. The officers were shouting, trying to sound like a larger force, the muskets firing like clockwork. Sharpe watched the defences. The French musket fire was constant and he guessed that each man at a loophole or embrasure had at least two other men loading spare muskets. 'I don't think they're short of defenders, sir.'

'Damn!' Windham ignored Sharpe.

The Cathedral clock sent its flat notes out to mingle with the sound of the firefight. More carcasses were lit in the fort, thrown out, and Sharpe heard Collett ordering his men to go back, into the darkness. Windham was pacing up and down, his frustration obvious.

'Where's the Light Company? Where's the Light Company?'

The gunners on the city wall heaved on the traces, turned their cannon, and loaded with grapeshot. They fired, the flames pointing down into the dark field, and Sharpe heard the whistle of shot.

'Open order!' Collett's voice carried back to Sharpe. 'Open order!' It was a sensible precaution against grapeshot that would keep casualties low, but it would not help to convince the French that a real attack was in progress. Windham drew his sword.

'Captain Leroy!'

'Sir?' The voice came from the darkness.

'Forward with your company! On Major Collett's right!'

'Yes, sir.' The Grenadier Company was ordered forward, adding to the confusion.

Windham turned to Sharpe. 'Time, Sharpe?'

Sharpe remembered hearing the cathedral bell. 'Two minutes after eleven, sir.'

'Where are they?'

'Give them time, sir.'

Windham ignored him. He stared forward at the fort, at the burning carcasses that lit the whole ditch and the front of the field. Small groups of men were running forward, kneeling, firing and sprinting back into the darkness, and Sharpe saw one man fall in a shower of grape, his body motionless in the light of the flames. Two other men ran forward, grabbed his legs, and tugged the body back to their company. 'Aim! Present! Fire!' The familiar orders rang round the field, the muskets fired towards the fort, and the deadly grapeshot pattered down from the high walls.

'Captain Sterritt?' Windham bellowed.

'Sir?'

'Present yourself to Major Collett! Your company will reinforce him!'

'Yes, sir!' Another company went forward and Sharpe, guiltily, thought that another Captain had been sent into the range of the grapeshot. He wondered what had happened to Rymer. There was no firing from the rear of the fort, but no explosion either. He looked constantly, waiting for the eruption of flame and smoke, but there was only silence from the dam.

'Where are they?' Windham pounded a fist against his thigh, cut at the air with his sword. 'Damn them! Where are they?'

Men were stumbling back from the fight, wounded by the grapeshot, and Collett was pulling the companies further back. There was no point, he reasoned, in losing men in an attack that was only a fake assault. The fire from the fort slackened. Still no explosion.

'Damn! We need to know what's happening!'

'I'll go, sir.' Sharpe could see Windham's careful scheme collapsing. The French must know by now that the attack was not real, and it would not take any great intelligence to reason that the dam was the real target. He tried to imagine the sappers again, laden with their barrels. 'They could have been captured, sir. Maybe they've not even reached the dam.'

Windham hesitated and, as he paused, Major Collett shouted nearby. 'Colonel? Sir?'

'Jack! Here!'

Collett came up, saluted. 'Can't go on much longer, sir. We're losing too many men to that damned grapeshot.'

Windham turned back to Sharpe. 'How long will it take you to get there?'

Sharpe thought fast. He did not need to go softly, or take the long way round. There was enough noise and

chaos in the field to cover his movements and he would go as close as he dared to the fort. 'Five minutes, sir.'

'Then go. Listen!' Windham checked Sharpe's movement. 'I want a report, that's all, d'you understand? See where they are. Have they been discovered? How long till they succeed? Understand?'

'Yes, sir.'

'I want you back here in ten minutes. Ten minutes, Sharpe.' He turned to Major Collett. 'Can you give me ten minutes?'

'Yes, sir.'

'Good. Off you go, Sharpe! Hurry!'

He began running, his dark uniform invisible against the night, towards the fort and the hidden dam. He went right, skirting the light of the carcasses, heading towards the ravine of the Rivillas downstream of the dam. He stumbled on tussocks, slipped on damp earth, but he was free, alone and free. Grapeshot whistled overhead, fired from the castle, but he was well beneath it, hidden in the darkness, and the stabbing musket flames from the fort were to his left. He slowed down, knowing that the stream could not be far, wary in case French patrols were lurking in the ravine. He unslung the rifle from his shoulder and pulled the flint back to full cock. The spring was heavy, satisfying, and he felt the sear fall into place. He was armed, what was it Hogan said? Cap a pie, whatever that meant, but it felt good and he grinned at the night as he went forward, slowly now, his eyes searching for the ravine's edge. He had pulled his shako low over his eyes so that the peak hid the white-centred cannon flames from his sight, preserving his night vision, and then he saw a streak of deeper shadow, fringed with bushes, and he knew he had reached the stream bank. He lay flat, pulled himself forward, and peered over the edge.

The ravine was deeper than he had imagined. The bank fell steeply away from him down to a dull sheen of water some eighteen or twenty feet below. There was no sound from the ravine, except the stream's murmur, and no sign of the Light Company or sappers. He looked left. The dam was a black shape next to the fort, just forty yards from him, and it seemed empty, silent, holding back the huge weight of water.

He slithered over the edge, still on his stomach, and let his weight slide him down between long-spined thorn bushes, the rifle held ahead of him, and suddenly there was a challenge. 'Who goes there?' It was a hoarse, frightened whisper.

'Sharpe! Who's that?'

'Peters, sir. Thank God you're here.'

He saw the man's shape, crouched beneath a bush beside the water. He went close. 'What's happening?'

'Don't know, sir. Captain went forward, sir.' Peters pointed towards the dam. 'That was ten minutes ago, sir. Left me here. Do you think they've gone, sir?'

'No. Stay here.' He patted the man's shoulder. 'They'll come back this way. You'll be all right.'

Rymer and the sappers could not be far away, being remarkably silent, and Sharpe waded up the stream, the water up to his knees, and waited for a challenge. It came twenty yards from the dam, just beneath the fort, where small trees arched up over the Rivillas. 'Who goes there?'

'Sharpe!' He whispered. 'Who's that?'

'Hakeswill.' There was a hint of a chuckle. 'Come to help?'

Sharpe ignored it. 'Where's Captain Rymer?'

'Here!' The voice came from beyond Hakeswill and Sharpe pushed past the Sergeant, smelling the man's

breath, and saw a glint of gold from Rymer's uniform. 'The Colonel sent me. He's nervous.'

'So am I.' Rymer offered no further information.

'What's happening?'

'The powder's laid, the sappers have gone back, and Fitchett's up there. He should be putting in the fuse!' Rymer sounded nervous and Sharpe could understand it. If the dam blew now, by mistake, then the Company would be caught by a wall of water.

There were footsteps from the rampart of the fort, just thirty feet above them, and Sharpe heard Rymer draw in breath. The footsteps sounded casual. Rymer began to breath out. 'Oh, God! No!'

A flicker of flame, the size of a candle, that seemed to waver, go out, then spring up fierce and bright. In its light Sharpe could see two men, blue uniformed, who held the carcass and then tossed it out over the ravine so that it fell, sparks flying up from it, down to the streambed. Pieces of burning straw exploded from the carcass, it rolled on the ravine side, tumbling flame, and plunged into the stream. It hissed. The flames flickered, trying to hold the top edge, and then died. Rymer's breath came out in a long, long sigh. Sharpe put his mouth close to Rymer's ear. 'Where are your men?'

'Some here. Most have gone.'

The answer was not much help. Another flame appeared on the ramparts, grew like the first, and this time the French held it longer so that the fire caught fiercely on the oil-soaked straw so that it blazed like a signal beacon. They rolled it over the edge, it bounced once, spraying sparks, and then caught on a thorn bush. The thorns crackled and flared and in the sudden light Sharpe could see the Engineer Lieutenant, Fitchett, crouching motionless by a stack of barrels. The French must see him!

But the French were not sure what they were looking for. Orders had come to look in the ravine, and so they peered over the edge and saw strange dark shadows, which was what a man expected to see at night, and they saw no movement so they relaxed. Sharpe could see the two men clearly. They seemed glad to be away from the front of the fort, were talking and laughing, and then they jerked upright, disappearing from sight, and there came the bark of an order and he supposed an officer had come to the rampart.

Fitchett moved. He began scrambling towards Rymer and Sharpe, trying to move silently, but he was panicked by the burning carcass and he slipped, falling into the stream. A shout from the rampart, an officer's head leaning over the stone, and Fitchett had the sense to freeze and Sharpe saw the officer turn and shout a command. Flames came again on the rampart, a third carcasss, and Sharpe knew they would have to fight. Rymer stared up at the fort, his mouth open.

Sharpe nudged him. 'Shoot the officer.'

'What?'

'Shoot the bastard! You've got Riflemen, haven't you?'

Rymer still did not move so Sharpe took his own Baker rifle, lifted the frizzen to check with a finger that the powder was still in the pan, and then aimed it up, through the stark thorn branches, towards the rampart. Rymer seemed to wake up. 'Don't fire!'

The third carcass was hurled over the rampart, far across so that it bounced on the far side of the ravine and wedged itself on a rock. Fitchett saw it, apparantly falling towards him, and yelped and sprang towards the hidden Company. The French officer shouted.

'Don't fire!' Rymer hit Sharpe's shoulder, ruining his aim so he kept his finger off the trigger. Fitchett fell

215

into the thorn trees, rubbing his ribs where he had fallen. He had remembered the fuse and was trailing it, but Sharpe wondered if any had fallen with the Lieutenant into the water. Fitchett looked wildly round. 'The lantern!'

There was a dark lantern hidden in the trees. Rymer and Fitchett both started looking, bumping into each other, and the first French musket hammered from the ramparts and the ball struck the trunk of one of the trees and Fitchett swore again. 'Jesus! Hurry!'

The French officer leaned over the ravine, searching the shadows, and Sharpe saw the shot, pulled the trigger, and the man went up and backwards, his face smashed red by the bullet and Rymer stared at Sharpe. 'Why did you do that?'

Sharpe did not bother to answer. Fitchett had found the lantern, unclipped the door, and a beam of light slanted in the thorns. 'Quick! Quick!' Fitchett was talking to himself. He found the fuse, thrust the end into the flame, and waited till it was spluttering. 'Back! Back!'

Rymer did not wait to see the fuse burning. 'Back!' He was shouting. 'Back!'

Sharpe grabbed Fitchett. 'How long?'

'Thirty seconds! Let's go!' A second musket exploded on the ramparts, the ball thudding into the earth, and the group of men stampeded down the streambed, led by Rymer, all imagining the sudden leap of powder flame, the shock wave, and the crashing, killing water.

The French, suddenly bereft of their officer, shouted for help. They could see nothing in the light of the carcasses, hear nothing in the lingering echo of their musket shots. Sharpe waited, watching the flickering light of the fuse, listening to the sudden rush of feet on the ramparts. The fuse was burning well, creeping

towards the dam, and he turned and climbed the ravine wall, hard by the stonework of the fort, and a voice stopped him. 'It was a nice shot.'

'Patrick?'

'Aye.' The Donegal voice was very low. 'I thought I'd see if you needed any help.' A huge hand clasped Sharpe's wrist and he was hauled unceremoniously to the brink of the ravine. 'That lot ran fast enough.'

'Be drowned otherwise.' Sharpe wedged himself against the base of a thorn bush. He tried to guess the number of seconds since Fitchett had lit the fuse; twenty? twenty-five? At least he and Harper should be safe. They were high on the bank, just across from the shallow ditch that left the ravine at a right angle to protect the small fort. The French were shouting excitedly; Sharpe heard the rattle of ramrods in musket barrels and then a crisp voice cutting through the chaos. He looked at Harper's vast bulk crouched in deep shadow. 'How's your back?'

'Bloody hurts, sir.'

Sharpe waited for the explosion, pushing himself down to the earth, imagining the kegs splintering and the wooden shards driven outwards. It must be soon! Perhaps Fitchett had used more fuse than he thought?

The volley from the ramparts startled him. The French fired down the ravine and Sharpe heard the balls crash through the thorn spikes like the ripping of calico. A bird screeched indignantly, flapped up into the darkness, and he could hear the trampling of panicked feet downstream. Harper sneered. 'Like wet bloody hens.'

'What was it like?'

Any reluctance Harper had felt about criticizing Rymer to Sharpe had disappeared with the flogging. He spat down the ravine. 'Can't make his mind up,

sir.' It was one of the worst crimes in a soldier's book; indecision kills.

There was no explosion. Sharpe knew that the fuse had been soaked, or had broken, but whatever the cause, the powder was intact. A minute must have passed. Sharpe heard a French officer shouting for silence. The man must be listening for noises downstream, but there was silence, and Sharpe heard more orders given. Light flared on the rampart and he knew more carcasses had been lit. He raised his head and saw three fiery bundles arc into the ravine and he wondered if the carcasses might inadvertently light the fuse, but seconds passed and there was no explosion, and then there were shouts from the fort. The powder had at last been seen.

Sharpe began sliding back down the slope. 'Come on.'

The French were shouting, making enough noise to cover their movements. There was little time. Sharpe thought what he would do if he was the French officer and imagined fetching water that could be thrown down on to the kegs and whatever fuse remained. He needed to see what was left. He slammed to a stop and looked upstream. The new carcasses brilliantly lit the foot of the dam; the kegs were clearly visible and so was the fuse. One end had fallen from a bung-hole in the lowest row of powder barrels, the other had dropped into the stream which had extinguished the fire. Even without the water, the fuse would have been useless. Harper crouched beside him. 'What do we do?'

'I need ten men.'

'Leave it to me, what then?'

Sharpe jerked his head towards the rampart. 'Six to take care of them and three to push those carcasses into the water.'

'And you?'

'Leave me one carcass.' He began to load the rifle, hurrying in the darkness, not bothering with the leather patch that surrounded the bullet and gripped the seven grooves of the Baker's barrel. He spat on the bullet and rammed it down. 'Are we ready?'

'Yes, sir.' Harper was grinning. 'I think this is a job for the Rifles.'

'Why not, Sergeant?' Sharpe grinned back. Damn Rymer, damn Hakeswill, Windham, Collett, all the new people who had disturbed the Battalion. Sharpe and his Riflemen had fought from the northern coast of Spain down through Portugal, then out again, to the Douro, to Talavera, to Almeida and Fuentes de Oñoro. They understood each other, trusted each other, and Sharpe nodded to Harper.

The Sergeant, as Sharpe thought of him, cupped his hands. 'Rifles! To me! Rifles!'

There were shouts from the ramparts, faces leaned over.

Sharpe cupped his own hands. 'Company! Skirmish order!' That should spread them out, but would they obey the old voices? Muskets fired from the fort, the bullets tearing the thorns, and Harper shouted again.

'Rifles!'

Feet trampled up the ravine. An officer shouted from the rampart and Sharpe heard the sound of steel ramrods in French barrels.

'They're coming, sir.'

Of course they were coming! They were his men. The first shapes came into sight, dark uniformed without the crossbelt of the red coats. 'Tell them what to do, Sergeant.' He thrust his loaded rifle at Harper, grinned at him. It was like the old times, the good times. 'I'm going.'

He could trust Harper to do the rest. He broke from the cover of the trees and ran upstream, into the light. The French saw him and he heard the shouted orders. The ground was wet and slippery, dotted with smooth rocks, and once he skidded wildly, flailed his arms for balance, and sensed the musket balls banging down at him. It was a difficult shot for the French, almost straight downwards, and they were hurrying too much. He heard Harper behind him, shouting the orders, and then the distinctive sound of Baker rifles. He followed the white fuse, and the great, sloping earth dam was above him, holding the tons of water, and bullets flecked the slope as Sharpe threw himself at the base of the barrels. The fuse had fallen free and he pushed it into the bung hole, feeling the gritty resistance of the powder. The bung had gone! He looked round, trying not to hurry. The damn thing had disappeared. He tried to pull one loose from another keg, but it had been hammered tight. Then he thought of a stone and scrabbling with his hand, found one, and rammed it into the hole. A musket ball tore at his sleeve, burning the skin, but behind him the light was disappearing as his Riflemen kicked carcasses into the water. They were still firing, and he was aware of voices shouting, and then he was finished, the fuse tight, and he backed away, pushing the white line up the bank, away from the water. He needed fire! He turned and saw one carcass burning, on the far bank. He leaped over to it and the bullets hammered down from above, one hitting the carcass so that it seemed to jump like a live thing. His Riflemen must be reloading.

'Give him fire!' Harper's voice rang clear. There were redcoats in the ravine, running and kneeling, aiming upwards, and Sharpe saw the new Ensign dancing in excitement, his sword drawn. Then the muskets fired

and the balls scoured the ramparts and Sharpe had a glimpse of his Riflemen coming forward again, their guns reloaded.

He would burn himself; there was no choice. The carcass flamed and he bent down, picked it up by its base, feeling the heat. A rock, thrown from the fort, smashed into the straw and it flared on his face, burning, burning, and he turned with it, scorched by the terrible heat and in the corner of his eye, as he turned, he saw a yellow flame, huge and foreshortened, stab from the ravine towards him. Bullets plucked at him, hit him, and he knew he had been shot, but did not believe it, and hurled the carcass at the white fuse.

He tried to run. Pain lanced his leg, his side, and he stumbled. He had thrown the carcass too far. He was falling. He remembered the flaming mass landing too close to the powder, and he remembered the yellow flame that seemed to come from the ravine side. Nothing made sense and then night turned to day.

Flame and light, noise and heat, the deafening, rolling blast thundered up and out so that the men in the British trenches, digging the new batteries, saw the face of the San Pedro bastion lit with flame. The whole face of Badajoz, from castle to the Trinidad, was seared with the light and the dam's fort was outlined black against the sheet of red that slammed up and belched smoke and fragments into the night. The blast was just a fragment of the explosion that had destroyed Almeida, but few men had seen that and lived, while this one was witnessed by thousands who watched the dark night split by fire, and felt the hot wind buffet the sky.

Sharpe was thrown forward, snatched and hurled into the stream, bruised and deafened by the blast, blinded by the flame-sheet. The stream saved his life and he regretted it, knowing that in a second he would be

crushed by the water, flattened by the falling tons of earth, rock and lake. He had not meant to throw the carcass as far as he did, but he had been scorched by flame, hit by bullets, and it hurt, it hurt. He would not see his child. He thought death came slowly and he tried to move as if he could outcrawl the weight of falling water.

Heat slammed back and forth in the ravine. Burning fragments hissed in the water. No muskets fired from the rampart. The blast had pushed the French away from the parapet, dazed by the noise that echoed off the vast city walls, thundered over the plain, and died in the night.

Harper pulled Sharpe upright. 'Come on, sir.'

Sharpe could not hear. 'What?' He was dazed, senseless.

'Come on!' Harper pulled him downstream, away from the fort, away from the dam that still stood. 'Are you hit?'

Sharpe moved automatically, stumbling on rocks, going away. He tried to turn, to look at the dam. 'It's still there.'

'Yes. It held. Come on!'

Sharpe shook himself free. 'It held.'

'I know! Come on!'

The dam still stood! Burning fragments lit the huge wall, scorched and gouged by the explosion, but intact. 'It held!'

Harper pulled at Sharpe. 'Come on! For God's sake, move!'

A body was at Sharpe's feet and he looked down. The new Ensign. What was his name? He could not remember, and the boy was dead, and for nothing!

Harper pulled him downstream into the cover of the trees, dragging Matthews' body in his other hand.

Sharpe staggered, the pain shooting up his leg, and he felt tears in his eyes. It was failure, miserable and complete, and the boy was dead who should not have died, and all because Sharpe had tried to prove he was more than a messenger boy or baggage minder. Sharpe felt as if there was some malevolent fate that had decided to destroy him, his pride, his life, all his hopes; and, in mockery, to make the failure more complete, the fates had shown him something worth living for. Teresa would have heard the explosion, would even now be rocking his child into a restless sleep, but Sharpe, stumbling through the night, felt that he would never see the child. Never. Badajoz would kill him, as it had killed the boy, as it was killing all he had worked and fought for in nineteen years of soldiering.

'You stupid bastards!' Hakeswill appeared in the darkness, his voice like the croaking of the thousands of frogs that lived upstream. He sneered at them, punched at Harper. 'You pig-brained Irish bastard! Move!' He thrust at them with the squat barrels of the huge gun and Harper, still helping Sharpe, smelt the burnt powder from the seven barrels. The gun had been fired and Harper had a vague memory, no more than an impression, of bullets coming from the ravine that had struck Sharpe down. Harper turned to look for Hakeswill, but the Sergeant had gone into the night and Sharpe, his leg bleeding and hurt, slipped and the Irishman had to hold him and pull him up the slope.

His words were drowned by a sudden clamour of bells. Each bell in Badajoz, from every church, hammered into the darkness and for a second Harper thought they were celebrating the failure of the night's fight. Then he remembered. Midnight had turned and now it was Sunday, Easter Sunday, and the bells rejoiced for the greatest of all miracles. Harper listened to the

cacophony and promised himself a most unChristian promise. He would perform his own miracle. He would kill the man who had tried to kill Sharpe. If it was the last thing he would do on this earth, he would kill the man who could not die. Dead.

CHAPTER 19

'Hold still!' the doctor muttered, not so much to Sharpe who was rigid, but because he always said the words when operating. He twiddled the probe in his fingers, looking at it, then wiped it on his apron before pushing it delicately into the wound in Sharpe's thigh. 'You've been wounded a fair bit, Mr Sharpe.'

'Yes, sir.' Sharpe hissed the words. His leg felt as if a serpent with red hot fangs was tearing at him.

The doctor grunted, pushed down. 'Ah! Splendid! Splendid!' Blood welled from the bullet wound. 'I have it.' He pushed, feeling the bullet grate beneath the probe's tip.

'Jesus!'

'A very present help in trouble.' The doctor said the words automatically. He straightened up, leaving the probe in the wound. 'You're a lucky man, Mr Sharpe.'

'Lucky, sir?' His leg was on fire, streaking pain from ankle to groin.

'Lucky.' The doctor picked up a glass of claret that his orderly kept always full. He stared at the probe. 'To leave or not to leave, that is the question.' He glanced at Sharpe. 'You're a healthy bastard, yes?'

'Yes, sir.' It came out as a groan.

The doctor sniffed. His cold had not improved since Harper's flogging. 'It could stay in there, Mr Sharpe, but I think not. You're lucky. It's not deep. The ball

must have lost most of its force.' He looked behind him and selected a long, thin pair of pincers. He inspected the ridged tips, spotted a piece of dirt, and spat on the instrument, wiping it dry on his sleeve. 'Right! Hold still, think of England!' He pushed the forceps into the wound, following the track of the probe, and Sharpe hissed imprecations at him which the doctor ignored. He felt for the bullet, brought out the probe, pushed down again with the forceps, and then tightened his grip. 'Splendid! A moment more!' He twisted, Sharpe's leg exploded with agony, and the doctor pulled out the forceps and dropped them, the bullet in their jaws, on the table behind him. 'Splendid! Nelson should have known me. Right. Tie him up, Harvey.'

'Yes, sir.' The orderly let go of Sharpe's ankles and rooted around under the table looking for a clean bandage.

The doctor took the bullet, still in the forceps, and shook the blood from it in a pail of discoloured water. 'Ah!' He held the bullet up. 'A pistol bullet! No wonder it didn't penetrate. The range must have been too great. Do you want it?'

Sharpe nodded and held out his hand. It was no musket bullet. The grey ball was just half an inch across and Sharpe remembered the fore-shortened yellow flame. The seven-barrelled gun used half-inch bullets. 'Doctor?'

'Sharpe?'

'The other wound. Is the bullet still in?'

'No.' The doctor was wiping his hands on his apron, already stiff with blood. It was the mark of seniority in his profession. 'Straight through, Sharpe, all it did was break the skin. Here.' He held out a tumbler of brandy.

Sharpe drank it and leaned back on the table while

the orderly washed and bandaged his leg. He felt no particular anger that Hakeswill had tried to kill him, merely a curiosity and a thankfulness that he had survived. He was certainly not shocked. Had he been holding the volley gun, and had he seen Hakeswill, he would have pulled the trigger and sent the Sergeant spinning to the devil, and all without a second thought. He looked at the doctor. 'What's the time, sir?'

'Dawn, Sharpe, dawn. An Easter dawn, when all men should rejoice.' He sneezed violently. 'You should take things gently.'

'Yes, sir.' He swung his legs off the table and pulled on the cavalry overalls. There was a neat hole in the leather reinforcements of the right inner thigh where the bullet had entered. The doctor looked at the hole and laughed.

'Three inches higher and you'd have been the last of your line.'

'Yes, sir.' Very droll. He tested his weight and found his leg could take it. 'Thank you, sir.'

'For nothing, Sharpe, except my small skill and humble duty. Half a bottle of rum and you'll be skipping like a lamb. A credit to the Medical Board and the Apothecary General whose obedient servant I am.' He pulled open the flap of his tent. 'Come and see me if you ever need a limb removed.'

'I shall see no one else, sir.'

The troops had stood down from the morning alert, had piled arms, and were finishing meagre breakfasts. The guns were hard at work, firing now at the Santa Maria bastion as well as the Trinidad, and Sharpe imagined the smoke lying over the lake. Damn the powder! The amount of powder needed had been grossly underestimated otherwise Sharpe, Harper and the Riflemen would be heroes this morning. As it was they were

pariahs. Trouble was brewing, Sharpe could smell it. The night's failure needed scapegoats.

Bells clamoured from the city. Easter. Sharpe limped towards his shelter and, to his right, saw a group of Portuguese or Spanish women, followers of the army, picking small, white flowers from a ditch bank. Spring was softening the landscape. Soon it would open the roads and the rivers to the French armies and Sharpe wondered if it was his imagination or were the guns today firing at a faster tempo? Pounding at a city that the British must take if they were to carry the war into the heart of Spain. The guns of Badajoz could be heard by the troops far to the north, at Alcantara and Caceres, and east at Merida, where British outposts stared down the empty roads waiting for a French relief army and listened to the growl of the distant thunder. The guns. They dominated the Easter service, wrenching the thoughts of the people in the cathedral away from the celebrations. The High Altar was resplendent in a white and gold facing, the Virgin draped in gorgeous, bejewelled robes, but the sound of the guns started dust from the high, gold-painted cornice that circled the Cathedral's interior, sifted it down past the Stations of the Cross, and the women prayed, told their beads, and the guns foretold a bloody assault. Badajoz knew what was to come; the city had a long memory of other sieges when Moors and Christians had taken turns to massacre the inhabitants. Be with us now and in the hour of our need.

'Sharpe!' Major Collett, tired and irascible, gestured from Windham's tent.

'Sir?'

'How's the leg?' The question was grudging.

'It hurts.'

Collett offered no sympathy. 'The Colonel wants you.'

The light was yellowed inside the tent, the canvas giving Windham's face a tint of jaundice. He nodded at Sharpe, not unfriendlily, and gestured at a wooden crate. 'You'd better sit.'

'Thank you, sir.' The leg was shooting pain into his groin. He was hungry.

Collett came in behind Sharpe and pulled the flap shut. The Major was short enough to stand upright beneath the ridgepole. For a few seconds there was silence and it struck Sharpe, suddenly, that Windham was embarrassed. He felt a sympathy for the Colonel. It was not Windham's fault that Rymer had purchased the commission, it was not his choice to follow Lawford, and Windham, in the little Sharpe knew of him, seemed a decent enough man. He looked up at the Colonel. 'Sir?'

The word broke the silence. Windham gestured irritably. 'Last night, Sharpe. A pity.'

'Yes, sir.' Whatever the Colonel meant by a pity. The dam not being broken? Matthews' death?

'The General's disappointed. Not with us. We did our job. We got the powder to the dam, we blew it up, and there wasn't enough damn powder. It's the Engineers to blame, not us.'

'Yes, sir.' Sharpe knew that Windham was beating round a very thorny bush. He had not brought Sharpe into the tent to tell him this. Collett gave a pointed cough and the Colonel cleared his throat.

'It seems there was chaos at the dam, Sharpe, is that right?'

The word must have come from Captain Rymer, Sharpe thought, so he shrugged. 'Night attacks are prone to confusion, sir.'

'I know that, Sharpe, I know that. God damn it, man, I wasn't breeched yesterday!' The Rifleman made

Windham nervous, the Colonel remembered his first meeting, back in Elvas, when he had felt the same reluctance to ride straight at the fence. He glared at Sharpe. 'I sent you to bring me back news, nothing else, is that right?'

'Yes, sir.'

'Instead of which you usurped Rymer's authority, organized an attack, stirred up the French, and had one of my officers killed.'

Sharpe could sense his own anger flaring and he fought it. He ignored the reference to Matthews. 'Stirred up the French, sir?'

'Damn it, man, you fired at them!'

'Captain Rymer told you that, sir?'

'I'm not here to argue with you! Did you or didn't you?'

'I returned their fire, sir.'

Silence. Rymer had obviously told a different story. Windham glanced at Collett, who shrugged. Both men believed Sharpe, but Rymer's authority had to be backed up. Windham changed tack. 'But nevertheless you disobeyed my orders?'

'Yes, sir.'

Silence again. Windham had not expected the answer, or perhaps he had expected excuses, and Sharpe had made a simple admission of disobedience. But to ask the reason why, was to invite a criticism of Rymer that the Colonel did not want to hear. He looked at Sharpe. The Rifleman seemed so damned confident. He sat there, seemingly unworried, the strong, scarred face spoke of a competence and trustworthiness that disarmed the Colonel. Windham shook his head. 'Damn it, Sharpe, Rymer's in an impossible position. He's trying to establish his authority over a company and he's finding it difficult while you're on his heels.'

Collett stirred, perhaps disapprovingly, but Sharpe nodded slowly. 'Yes, sir.'

'The rifles, for instance.'

Sharpe felt a flicker of alarm. 'The rifles, sir?'

Collett broke in, his voice harsh. 'Rymer's opinion is that they led to our casualties last night. They're too slow to load and last night they let us down. Muskets would have been faster, more effective.'

Sharpe nodded. 'True, but that was only last night.'

'And that's only your opinion. Rymer disagrees.' Collett paused. 'And Rymer has the Company.'

'Which he must run as he sees fit.' Windham took up from Collett. 'Which means the rifles must go.'

Sharpe's voice, for the first time, rose. 'We need more rifles, sir, not less.'

'Which is what I am talking about!' Windham's voice rose as well. 'You cannot run the Light Company. One man must do it!'

Which was Rymer. Sharpe's anger subsided. He was being punished not for his own failure, but for Rymer's and all three men knew it. He forced a rueful smile. 'Yes, sir.'

Silence again. Sharpe could feel that there was one more thing to be said, one thing the Colonel was shying from, and he had had enough. He would make it easy, get the damned interview over. 'So what happens now, sir?'

'Happens? We go on, Sharpe, we go on!' Windham was avoiding the answer, but then he plunged in. 'Major Hogan talked to us. He was upset.' The Colonel paused. He had plunged in at the wrong place, but Sharpe could guess at what had happened. Windham wanted rid of Sharpe, at least for the moment, and Hogan had engineered an answer that Windham was hesitant about mentioning.

'Yes, sir?'

'He'd like your assistance, Sharpe. For a few days, anyway. The Engineers are short-handed, always are, damn them, and he asked for your help. I said yes.'

'So I'm to leave the Battalion, sir?'

'For a few days, Sharpe, for a few days.'

Collett stirred by the tent pole. 'Damn it, Sharpe, they'll be handing out Captaincies like pound notes on election day soon.'

Sharpe nodded. 'Yes, sir.' Collett had made the point. Sharpe was an embarrassment, not just to Rymer, but to all the Captains who saw him sniffing at their heels. If he could leave the Battalion now, go to Hogan, then there would be no difficulty in bringing him back, after the assault, into a Captaincy. And the assault would be soon. Wellington was not patient in a siege, the fine weather was bringing the possibility of a French counter-move, and Sharpe sensed that the infantry would be hurled against the city very soon. Too soon, probably. Collett was right; there would be vacancies, too many vacancies, made by the French guns in Badajoz.

Windham seemed relieved by Sharpe's evident acceptance. 'That's it, then, Sharpe. Good luck; good hunting!' He barked an embarrassed laugh. 'We'll see you back!'

'Yes, sir.' But not, Sharpe thought, in the way Windham planned. The Rifleman, as he limped from the tent, did not object to the Colonel's solution, or rather Hogan's solution, but he was damned if he would be nothing more than a pawn to be pushed round a board and sacrificed. He had lost his Company, and now he was pushed out of the Battalion, and he felt an anger inside him. He was superfluous. Then damn them all. He would make the Forlorn Hope. He would live and they would take him back, not as a convenient replace-

ment for a dead Captain, but as a soldier they could not ignore. He would fight back! God damn them, he would fight back, and he knew where he was going to start. He heard a cackle come from the Battalion's supply dump. Hakeswill! Bloody Hakeswill who had emptied the seven-barrelled gun at him in the darkness. Sharpe turned towards the sound, winced as the pain seared his leg, and marched towards the enemy.

CHAPTER 20

Hakeswill cackled. 'You bloody fairies! You're not bloody soldiers. Stand still!'

The twelve Riflemen stood still. Each would have gladly killed the Sergeant, but not here, not in the supply dump that was open to the gaze of the whole camp. The murder would have to be done at night, in secret, but somehow Hakeswill seemed always to be awake, or alert to the smallest sound. Perhaps he was right, he could not be killed.

Hakeswill walked slowly down the rank. Each man was stripped to his shirt, the green jackets lying on the ground in front of them. He stopped by Hagman, the old poacher, and pushed at the jacket with his foot. 'What's this, then?' His toe was pointing at the black stripe sewn on the sleeve.

'Senior Rifleman's badge, Sergeant.'

'Senior Rifleman's badge, Sergeant.' Hakeswill imitated Hagman. The yellow face twitched. 'Bloody decrepit, you are!' He pushed the sleeve into the mud. 'Senior bloody Rifleman! From now on you're a bloody soldier.' He cackled, letting his foetid breath wash over Hagman's face. The Rifleman did not move or react; to do so was to invite punishment. Hakeswill twitched and moved on. He was feeling pleased with himself. The Riflemen had annoyed him because they seemed

to him to form an élite group, a close knit group, and he had wanted to smash them. He had suggested to Rymer as they straggled back from the dam that the rifles were a hindrance; he had hinted that Rymer could begin to establish his ascendency over Sharpe's old Company by disbanding the Riflemen, and it had worked. 'You! About turn! You poxed Irish pig! Turn!' His spittle sprayed Harper.

Harper paused for a fraction of a second, and saw an officer watching. He had no wish to end his days in front of a firing squad. He turned round.

Hakeswill drew his bayonet. 'How's your back, Private?'

'Fine, Sergeant.'

'Fine, fine.' Hakeswill mimicked the Donegal accent. 'That's good, Private.' He put the flat of the bayonet high on Harper's back and drew the blade downwards, over the unhealed cuts, over the scabs, and blood welled out to stain the shirt. 'You've got a dirty shirt, Private, a dirty, Irish shirt.'

'Yes, Sergeant.' Harper kept the pain out of his voice. He had promised he would kill this man, and he would.

'Wash it!' Hakeswill sheathed his bayonet. 'About turn!'

The twelve Riflemen watched the Sergeant. He was mad, there was no doubt about that. In the past few days he had taken to a new habit, of sitting by himself, taking off his hat, and talking into it. He talked to his shako as if it was a friend. He told it his plans and his hopes, how he would find Teresa, and his eyes would flick up to the Company to catch them looking at him as they listened. Then he would cackle. 'I'm going to have her.' His eyes would go back to the shako's greasy

interior. 'I'm going to have the pretty lady, oh yes, Obadiah's going to have her!'

Hakeswill stalked in front of the twelve. 'You're going to wear red coats, now, not bloody green. You're going to carry muskets, not those toys!' He gestured at the twelve rifles that were stacked by the unlocked arms chest. He laughed. 'You're going to be real soldiers, like Sergeant Hakeswill, your friend, me.' He cackled. 'You hate me, don't you?' The face twitched involuntarily. 'I like that. Because I hate you!' He took his hat off, looked inside, and his voice became whining, obsequious. 'I hate them, I really do.' He looked up, his voice going back to normal. 'You think I'm mad?' He laughed. 'Not so I don't know.' He saw their eyes flicker to the left and turned. The bastard Sharpe was approaching. Limping. Hakeswill put his hat on and saluted. 'Lieutenant, sir.'

Sharpe returned the salute. 'Sergeant.' His voice was civil. 'Stand the men at ease.'

'But, sir, Lieutenant, sir . . .'

'At ease, Sergeant.'

Hakeswill twitched. He could not fight Sharpe through the formal hierarchy, only in the dark lanes of his hatred. 'Sir!' He turned to the Riflemen. 'Detail! Stand at ease!'

Sharpe looked at the Riflemen, his Riflemen, the men he had led from Corunna, and he saw the misery in their faces. They were being stripped of their pride along with their green jackets. Now they must take one more shock. He hated making speeches, he felt tongue-tied, inadequate. 'I've just come from the Colonel's tent and, well, I shall be leaving the Battalion. Today.' He saw the expressions change into something approaching despair. 'I wanted to be the one to tell you. Sergeant!'

Hakeswill, elated at the news, stepped forward, but saw that Sharpe was talking to Harper. Hakeswill stopped. He could sense a danger in the air, but he could not pin it down.

'Sir?' Harper's voice was tense.

'Pick up the green jackets. Bring them here.' Sharpe was talking calmly, almost casually, the only man who seemed unaware of the tension.

'Lieutenant, sir!'

Sharpe turned. 'Sergeant Hakeswill?'

'My orders are to take the jackets, sir.'

'Where, Sergeant?'

Hakeswill cackled. 'To the gunners, Lieutenant, sir. To be used as swabs.'

'I'll save you the trouble, Sergeant.' Sharpe's voice was almost friendly. He turned away and waited till Harper brought the jackets. 'Put them there.' He pointed at the ground next to him.

Harper bent down. He remembered Hakeswill's crazy words, spoken into his shako, and Harper was sure what they meant, and now he tried to warn Sharpe. 'He's after Teresa, sir. He knows where she is.' He muttered it, sure that Sharpe had heard the news, but the officer's face stayed calm and relaxed. Harper wondered if he had spoken too softly. 'Sir?'

'I heard you, Sergeant, and thank you. Rejoin the rank.' Sharpe still did not react, instead he smiled at the twelve men. 'We've been together for seven years, some of us, and I don't think this will be the finish of that.' Hope flickered into their faces. 'But if it is, then I want to thank you. You're good soldiers, good Riflemen, the best.' Now their faces showed some pleasure, but he did not look at them, nor at Hakeswill, but crossed to the arms chest and picked a rifle at random. He held it up. 'I'm sorry you're losing these. I make

you one promise. You'll get them back, as you'll get back your jackets.'

They smiled openly, Hakeswill cackled and then saw Sharpe's face. Sharpe was staring, in horror, at the lock of the rifle. He looked up at Hakeswill. 'Sergeant?'

'Lieutenant, sir?'

'Whose rifle is this?'

'Rifle, sir? Don't know, sir.' He twitched. He could feel a threat somewhere.

'It's loaded, Sergeant.'

'Loaded, sir? Can't be, sir.'

'You checked?'

Hakeswill hesitated. His power was preserved through meticulous attention to military detail, but in his eagerness to strip off the green jackets, he had not inspected the rifles. His mind sorted through the problem and he smiled. 'Not yet, Lieutenant, sir. But they're not in the chest yet, sir, Lieutenant, are they? I'll inspect them in a minute.' He twitched furiously, the blue eyes blinking as he tried, vainly, to control his face.

Sharpe smiled, still courteous. 'I'll save you the trouble, Sergeant.' He laid the first rifle down, carefully, and then picked up the others, one by one, and pointed each at Hakeswill's vast belly. He cocked each flint, pulled each trigger, and Hakeswill's face twitched each time. Sharpe's eyes did not leave the Sergeant's face, not even when he stooped to pick up another rifle, and he watched the spasm and saw the relief each time as the spark died in an empty pan. The Riflemen, humiliated by the Sergeant, grinned at the fear they saw in Hakeswill, but they were still nervous of him. He was the man who could not be killed and Sharpe knew that their nervousness had to be dispelled. He put the last rifle in the chest and, as carefully as he had put it down,

picked up the first. Hakeswill stared as Sharpe pulled back the flint, past the half cock, back till the sear clicked into place. The Sergeant licked his lips, twitched, and flicked his eyes up to Sharpe's face then back to the muzzle that was pointing at his belly.

Sharpe walked slowly towards Hakeswill. 'You can't be killed, is that right?' Hakeswill nodded, tried to smile, but the huge muzzle was coming towards him. Sharpe walked slowly. 'They tried to hang you, and you lived, is that right?' Hakeswill nodded again, his mouth a rictus. Sharpe was limping from the bullet wound in his thigh. 'Are you going to live for ever, Sergeant?' One of the Riflemen sniggered and Hakeswill darted a look to see which one, but Sharpe jerked the barrel up and the movement brought the eyes back. 'Are you going to live for ever?'

'Don't know, sir.'

'Not "Lieutenant, sir"? Lost your tongue, Hakeswill?'

'No, sir.'

Sharpe smiled. He was very close to the Sergeant and the rifle was pointed up beneath Hakeswill's chin. 'I think you're going to die, Sergeant. Shall I tell you why?'

The blue, child-like eyes flicked left and right as if searching for help. Hakeswill expected to be attacked by night, in the shadows, but never in bright daylight among hundreds of potential witnesses. Yet no one was taking any notice! The rifle jerked, touching his sweated skin. 'Sir!'

'Look at me, Sergeant. I'm telling you a secret.'

Hakeswill looked at Sharpe, their eyes level. 'Sir?'

The Riflemen watched and Sharpe spoke clearly for them. 'I think, Sergeant, that no one can kill you. Except.' He spoke slowly, as if to a child. 'Except,

Sergeant, someone whom you had tried to kill, and whom you failed to kill.' The fear was obvious on the sweating face, the yellow paling. 'Can you think of anyone like that, Sergeant?'

The face twitched, shook, and the rifle jerked up again into the chin. 'No, sir!'

'Good!' The stubby foresight of the Baker was cold on Hakeswill's skin. Sharpe dropped his voice so that only the Sergeant could hear him. 'You're a dead man, Obadiah. The magic's gone.' He suddenly shouted. 'Bang!'

Hakeswill leaped back, startled, let out a pathetic yelp like a whipped child, and stumbled on to the grass. Sharpe laughed at him, pointed the gun and pulled the trigger on to an empty, unloaded pan. Hakeswill sprawled on the grass, his face murderous, but Sharpe turned away from him to his grinning Riflemen. 'Shun!'

They snapped to attention. Sharpe spoke to them again, but this time his voice was crisp. 'Remember, I've made you a promise. You'll get your rifles back, your jackets back, and you'll get me back!' He did not know how he could do it, but he would. He turned back to the Sergeant and pointed at the seven-barrelled gun on Hakeswill's shoulder. 'Give me that!'

Hakeswill handed it over meekly, with its ammunition pouch, and Sharpe slung the gun on his own shoulder next to his rifle. He looked down at the Sergeant. 'I'm coming back, Sergeant. Remember that.' He scooped the jackets into an awkward bundle, put them under his arm, and limped away. He knew that Hakeswill would exact a revenge on the Riflemen, but he knew, too, that the Sergeant had been humiliated, shown to be vulnerable, and the Company, Sharpe's Company, needed to know that much.

It was a small victory, a petty victory even, but it was a start on the long fight back, a fight that he knew must end in the breach at Badajoz.

Part Four

Saturday, April 4th
to
Monday, April 6th
1812

CHAPTER 21

News came that the French, at last, were moving; not against Wellington at Badajoz, but towards the new Spanish garrison in Ciudad Rodrigo. The reports came from the Partisans and from the despatches they had captured, some still stained with the blood of enemy messengers, and told of disagreements among the French Generals, of delays in gathering their troops, and their difficulties in replacing the French siege artillery, all of which had been captured inside the northern fortress. The news spurred Wellington into greater speed; he wanted the siege of Badajoz done, and he could not be persuaded that the French chances of retaking Ciudad Rodrigo were remote. He did not trust the Spaniards in the town and wanted to march the army north to bolster his allies' resolve. Speed! Speed! Speed! For the six days after Easter he pounded the message at his Generals and staff officers. Give me Badajoz! For the six days the new batteries built in the ruins of the Picurina Fort had fired incessantly at the breaches, at first with small effect until, almost unexpectedly, the loosened stone had cascaded into the ditch and was followed by a dust-spewing avalanche of rubble from the wall's core. The sweating, powder-stained gun crews had cheered, while the infantry, guarding the batteries against another French sortie, stared at the

incipient breaches and wondered what welcome the French were preparing for the assault.

By night the French tried to repair the damage. The Picurina guns sprayed the two breaches with grapeshot, but still, each morning, the broken edges of the stone-work had been padded with thick bales of wool and so, each dawn, the gunners fired at the mattresses until, in an explosion of greasy fleeces, the padding fell away and the iron balls could start again on the wall proper; gouging at it, crumbling it, carving the double path into the city.

The dam still stood and the floodwaters still stretched south of the city, forcing any assault on the bastions to march obliquely against the walls instead of straight on. The northern batteries pounded at the dam's fort while the infantry dug their trenches forward, trying to take their spades and muskets to the very edge of the small fort, but the trenching was thrown back. Every gun on Badajoz's east wall, from the high kestrel-ridden castle, to the Trinidad bastion, opened up on the creeping trench till the workers were smashed and no one could live in the iron hail, and so the attempt was given up. The dam would stay, the approach would be oblique, and the engineers did not like it. 'Time, I want time!' Colonel Fletcher, wounded in the French foray, was out of bed. He pounded the map in front of him. 'He wants a bloody miracle!'

'I do.' The General had entered the room unheard and Fletcher twisted round, grimacing because the wound still hurt.

'My Lord! My apologies.' The Scottish growl sounded far from apologetic.

Wellington gestured the apology away, nodded at the men waiting for him, and sat down. Major Hogan knew the General was just forty-three, yet he looked older.

Perhaps they all looked older. The siege was wearing them down as it was wearing away the two bastions, and Hogan sighed because he knew that this meeting, on Saturday 4th April as he carefully noted at the top of his notebook page, would once more be a wrangle between the General and the Engineers. Wellington took out his own map, unrolled it, and weighted the corners with ink bottles. 'Good morning, gentlemen. Expenditure?'

The gunner Colonel pulled paper towards him. 'Yesterday, my Lord, one thousand one hundred and fourteen twenty-four-pounders, six hundred and three eighteen-pounders.' He gave the figures in a flat monotone. 'One gun burst, sir.'

'Burst?'

The Colonel turned the paper over. 'Twenty-four-pounder in Number Three, my Lord, high-shot half-way down the bore. We lost three men, six wounded.'

Wellington grunted. It was astonishing, Hogan always thought, how the General dominated a room by his presence. Perhaps it was the blue eyes that seemed so knowing, or the stillness of the face round the strong, hooked nose. Most of the officers in this room were older than the Viscount Wellington, yet all of them, with the possible exception of Fletcher, seemed in awe of him. The General wrote the figures on his small piece of paper, the pencil squeaking. He looked back to the gunner. 'Powder?'

'Plenty, sir. Eighty barrels arrived yesterday. We can keep firing for another month.'

'We'll bloody need to. Sorry, my Lord.' Fletcher was hatching marks on his map.

A trace of a smile flicked the corners of Wellington's mouth. 'Colonel?'

'My Lord?' Fletcher affected surprise. He looked up

from the map, but kept his pen poised as though he was being interrupted.

'I can see you're not prepared for the meeting.' Wellington gave a small nod to the Scotsman and turned to Hogan. 'Major? Any reports?'

Hogan turned his notebook back two pages. 'Two deserters, my Lord, both Germans, both from the Hesse-Darmstadt Regiment. They confirm that the Germans are garrisoning the castle.' Hogan raised his eyebrows. 'They say morale is high, my Lord.'

'Then why desert?'

'A brother of one, my Lord, is with the KGL.'

'Ah. You're sending them there?'

'Yes, sir.' The King's German Legion would welcome the recruits.

'Anything else?' Wellington liked to keep the morning conferences brisk.

Hogan nodded. 'They confirm, sir, that the French are devoid of roundshot, but claim plenty of canister and grape. We already knew that.' He hurried on, forestalling a complaint of repetition from the General. 'They also say the city is terrified of a massacre.'

'Then they should plead for a surrender.'

'The city, my Lord, is partly pro-French.' It was true. Spanish civilians had been seen on the walls, firing muskets at the trenches sapping forward towards the fort at the dam. 'They are hoping for our defeat.'

'But.' Wellington's voice was scornful. 'They hope to avoid reprisals if we win. Is that right?'

Hogan shrugged. 'Yes, sir.' It was, the Irishman thought, a vain hope. If Wellington had his way, and he would, the assault would be soon and the way into the city hard. If they did win through the breach, and Hogan acknowledged the possibility that they might not, then the troops would lose all vestiges of discipline.

It had always been so. Soldiers who were forced to fight through the terror of a narrow breach claimed the right to possess the fortress and all within it. The Irish remembered Drogheda and Wexford, the towns sacked by Cromwell and his English troops, and the stories were still told of the victors' atrocities. Stories of women and children herded into a church that was fired, the English celebrating while the Irish burned, and Hogan thought of Teresa and her child, Sharpe's child. His thoughts snapped back to the meeting as Wellington dictated a fast order to an aide-de-camp. The order forbade any looting inside the city, but it was given, Hogan thought, without much conviction. Fletcher listened to the order and then, once again, pounded the map with his fist.

'Bomb them.'

'Ah! Colonel Fletcher is with us.' Wellington turned to him.

Fletcher smiled. 'I say bomb them, my Lord. Smoke them out! They'll give up.'

'And how long, pray, before they give up?'

Fletcher shrugged. He knew it could take weeks for the squat howitzers to reduce enough of Badajoz to smoking rubble, to burn the food supplies and thus force a surrender. 'A month, my Lord?'

'Two, more like, perhaps three. And let me advert you, Colonel, to the notion, imperfectly understood though it may be within the walls, that the Spanish are our allies. If we indiscriminately bomb them with shells it is possible, you will grant me, that our allies will be displeased.'

Fletcher nodded. 'They'll not be too happy, my Lord, if your men rape everything that moves and steal everything that doesn't.'

'We will trust to our soldiers' good sense.' The words

were cynically said. 'And now, Colonel, perhaps you can tell us about the breaches. Are they practical?'

'No, sir, they are not.' Fletcher's Scottish accent was stronger again. 'I can tell you a good deal, sir, most of it new.' He turned the map round so that the General was looking at the two bastions from the point of view of an attacker. The Santa Maria was to the left, Trinidad to the right. Fletcher had marked the breaches. The Trinidad had lost half of its face, a gap nearly a hundred feet wide and the Engineer had pencilled in his estimate of the height reduction. Twenty-five feet. The flank of the Santa Maria facing the Trinidad was equally badly hit. 'The breaches, as you can see, my Lord, are now about twenty-five feet high. That's a hell of a climb! That's higher, if you'll forgive me for pointing it out, than the unbreached wall at Ciudad Rodrigo!' He leaned back as if he had made a scoring hit.

Wellington nodded. 'We are all aware, Colonel, that Badajoz is appreciably bigger than Ciudad Rodrigo. Pray continue.'

'My Lord.' Fletcher leaned forward again. 'Let me advert you to this.' He grinned as he used one of Wellington's favourite expressions. His broad finger settled on the ditch to the front of the Santa Maria. 'They've blocked the ditch here, and here.' The finger moved to the right of the Trinidad breach. 'They're boxing us in.' His voice was serious now. He could twist the General's tail from time to time, but only dared do it because he was a good Engineer, trusted by Wellington, and he saw it as his job to give his true point of view and not be a lickspittle. The finger tapped the ditch. 'It seems they've put carts in the ditch, upturned carts, and lengths of timber. You don't have to be a genius to work out that they plan to fire those obstacles. You can see what will happen, gentlemen. Our troops will

be in the ditch, trying to climb a bloody great ramp, and there'll be no escape from the grapeshot. They can't go left and right into the darkness to regroup. They'll be trapped, lit up, like rats in a bloody barrel.'

Wellington listened to the impassioned outburst. 'You're sure?'

'Aye, my Lord, and there's more.'

'Go on.'

The finger stayed to the right of the Trinidad breach. 'The French have dug another ditch here, in the bottom of the ditch, and flooded it. We'll be jumping into water, deep water, and it looks as if they're extending it. Round here.' The finger traced a line back in front of both breaches.

Wellington's eyes were on the map. 'So the longer we wait, the more difficult it becomes?'

Fletcher sighed, but conceded the point. 'Aye, there's that.'

Wellington raised his eyes to the Engineer. 'What do we gain by time?'

'I can lower the breaches.'

'By how much?'

'Ten feet.'

'How long?'

'A week.'

Wellington paused, then. 'You mean two weeks.'

'Aye, my Lord, perhaps.'

'We do not have two weeks. We do not have one week. We must take the city. It must be soon.' There was silence in the room. Outside the windows the guns hammered over the floodwaters. Wellington looked back to the map, reached over the table, and put a long finger on the huge space between the bastions. 'There's a ravelin there?'

'Aye, my Lord, and still being built.' The ravelin was

sketched on the map; a masonry wedge, diamond shaped, that would break up an attack. If the French had been given time to finish it, before the siege guns had started firing, it would have been like a new bastion, built in the ditch, outflanking all attacks. As it was it formed a vast, flat-topped obstacle, surrounded by the ditch, smack between the two breaches.

Wellington looked up to Fletcher. 'You seem very sure of this new information?'

'Aye, my Lord, I am. We had a laddie on the glacis last night. He did a good job.' The praise was grudging.

'Who?'

Fletcher jerked his head towards Hogan. 'One of Major Hogan's lads, sir.'

'Who, Major?'

Hogan stopped fidgeting with his snuffbox. 'Richard Sharpe, sir, you'll remember him?'

Wellington leaned back in his chair. 'Good Lord. Sharpe?' He smiled. 'What's he doing with you? I thought he had a company?'

'He did, my Lord. His gazette was refused.'

Wellington's face scowled. 'By God! They do not let me make a man Corporal in this damned army! So Sharpe was on the glacis last night?'

Hogan nodded. 'Yes, sir.'

'Where is he now?'

'Outside, sir. I thought you might want to speak to him.'

'Good Lord, yes.' Wellington's tone was dry. 'He's the only man in the army who's been to the top of the glacis. Fetch him in!'

There were Generals of Division, of Brigade, gunners, Engineers and staff officers and they all turned to stare at the tall, green-jacketed man. They had all heard of him, even the Generals newly arrived from England,

because this was the man who had captured a French Eagle and who looked as if he could do it again. He looked battered and hard, like the weapons that festooned him, and his limp and scars spoke of a soldier who fought grimly. Wellington smiled at him and looked round the table. 'Captain Sharpe has shared all my battles, gentlemen. Isn't that right, Sharpe? From Seringapatam to today?'

'Since Boxtel, sir.'

'Good God. I was a Lieutenant-Colonel.'

'And I a Private, sir.' The aides-de-camp, the young aristocrats that Wellington liked as his messengers, stared curiously at the scarred face. Not many men fought out of the ranks. Hogan watched the General. He was being genial to Sharpe, not because the Rifleman had once saved his life, but because he suspected that in Sharpe he had found an ally against the Engineers' caution. Hogan sighed inwardly. Wellington knew this man. The General looked round the room. 'A chair for Captain Sharpe?'

'Lieutenant Sharpe, sir.' Sharpe's words were almost a challenge, certainly bitter, but the General ignored them.

'Sit down, sit down. Now, tell us about the breaches.'

Sharpe told them, not awed by the company, but he added little to Fletcher's account. He had not been able to see clearly, the darkness was relieved only by a very occasional gun-flash from the city's walls, and much of his account was based on the sounds he had heard as he lay on the glacis lip and listened, not just to the French working parties, but to the British grapeshot smashing through the weeds and rattling on the walls. Wellington let him finish. It had been a concise statement. The General's eyes held Sharpe's. 'One question.'

'Sir?'

'Are the breaches practical?' Wellington's eyes were unreadable, cold like steel.

Sharpe's gaze was as hard, as unyielding. 'Yes.'

A murmur round the table. Wellington leaned back. Colonel Fletcher's voice rose above the noise. 'With respect, my Lord, I do not think it within Captain, Lieutenant Sharpe's competency to pronounce on a breach.'

'He's been there.'

Fletcher muttered something about sending a heathen to kirk and not making him a Christian. The quill in his hand bent almost double under the pressure of his fingers, he let it go and the split nib spattered ink across the two bastions. He thumped the pen down. 'It's too soon.'

Wellington pushed himself away from the table, stood up. 'One day, gentlemen, one day.' He looked round the table. No one challenged him. It was too soon, he knew that, but perhaps any day would be too soon to take on this fortress. Perhaps, as the French claimed, it was impregnable. 'Tomorrow, gentlemen, Sunday the fifth. We assault Badajoz.'

'Sir!' Sharpe spoke and the General, who had been expecting a protest from the Engineers, turned towards him. 'Sharpe?'

'One question, sir?' Sharpe could hardly believe that he was talking, let alone in such challenging tones and in such a company, but he might not get this chance again.

'Go on.'

'The Hope, sir. I would like to lead the Hope.'

Wellington's eyes were cold and glinting. 'Why?'

What was he to say? That it was a test? The supreme test, perhaps, of a soldier? Or that he wanted his

revenge on a system, a system represented by a pox-scarred clerk in Whitehall, that had made him superfluous, unwanted? He suddenly thought of Antonia, his daughter, of Teresa. He thought that he might never see Madrid, Paris, or know how the war would end, but the die was cast. He shrugged, looking for words, unsettled by the impenetrable eyes. 'I don't know, sir. I want it.' He sounded to himself like a petulant child. He could sense the eyes of the senior officers on him, curious eyes, looking at his shabby uniform, his old, irregular sword, and he damned them to hell. Their pride was buttressed by money.

Wellington's voice was softer. 'You want your Company?'

'Yes, sir.' He felt a fool, a shabby fool in a glittering setting, and he knew that all of them could see his broken pride.

Wellington nodded towards Colonel Fletcher. 'That Colonel will tell you, Sharpe, and pray God he is wrong, that on Monday morning we'll be handing Captaincies out with the rations.'

Fletcher said nothing. The room was silent, embarrassed by Sharpe's request. The Rifleman felt as if all his life, all that had been and all that might never be, was balanced on this silence.

Wellington smiled. 'God knows, Sharpe, that I think you are a rogue. A useful rogue and, thankfully, a rogue who is on my side.' He smiled again and Sharpe knew that the General was remembering the gory Indian bayonets reaching for him at Assaye, but that debt had long been paid. Wellington picked up his papers. 'I don't think I want you dead, Sharpe. The army would be, somehow, less interesting. Your request is denied.' He left the room.

Sharpe stood there, quite still as the other officers

filed out, and he thought how, in these past few miserable weeks, he had fixed all his hopes and ambitions on that one thing. His Captaincy, his Company, their jackets, rifles and trust; even, because he did not seriously believe he would be killed, the chance to reach the house with the two orange trees before the maniacal horde, before Hakeswill, and all had been fixed on the Hope, the Forlorn Hope. And it had been denied.

He should have felt disappointment, anger even, at the refusal, but he could not. Instead, flooding through him like pure water scouring a foul ditch, was relief; utter, blissful relief. He was ashamed of the feeling.

Hogan came back into the room and smiled up at him. 'There. You've asked, you got the right answer.'

'No.' Sharpe's face was stubborn. 'There's still time, sir, still time.' He did not know what he meant, or why he said it, except that on the morrow, in the first darkness of evening, he would somehow face that test. And win.

CHAPTER 22

Sergeant Obadiah Hakeswill was feeling contented. He sat by himself, church parade done, and stared into the depths of his shako. He spoke to his hat. 'Tonight, it is, tonight. I'll be a good boy, I won't let you down.' He cackled, showing his few rotting teeth, and looked round the Company. They were watching him, he knew, but would take care not to catch his eye. He looked back into the greasy depths of the hat. 'Scared, they are, of me. Oh yes. Scared of me. Be more scared tonight. A lot of them will die tonight.' He cackled again and raised his eyes fast so that he might catch a man staring at him. They were all studiously avoiding his eyes. 'You'll die tonight! Like little bloody pigs under the pole-axe!'

He would not die. He knew it, despite what Sharpe had said. He looked back into the shako. 'Bloody Sharpe! He's scared of me. He ran away! He can't kill me. No one can kill me!' He almost shouted the last words. They were true. He had been touched by death and he had survived. He reached up and scratched the livid, red scar. He had hung for an hour on the gallows, a scrap of a boy, and no one had pulled his feet so that his neck would snap. He did not remember much of the experience; the crowds, the other prisoners who had joked with him, but he would always be grateful to the sadistic bastard who had hung them the slow way, without a drop, so that the crowd would have a spectacle

to watch. They had cheered every spasmodic jerk and useless struggle until the executioner's assistants, grinning like actors who are pleasing their audience, came to hold the dangling ankles. They had looked at the crowd, asking their permission to pull, and teased the prisoners. They had not bothered with the twelve year-old Obadiah Hakeswill. He was cunning then as now and had hung still, even as the pain drifted him in and out of consciousness, so the crowd thought he was already dead. He had not known why he clung so tenaciously to life; it would have been faster and far less painful to be ankle-tugged to death, but then the rain had come. The clouds had split apart in a downpour that cleared the streets in minutes and no one could be bothered with the last small body. His uncle, furtive and frightened, had cut him down and hurried the limp body into an alleyway. He had slapped Obadiah's face. 'Listen, you bastard! Can you hear me?'

Obadiah must have said something, or moaned, because he remembered his uncle's face, peering close. 'You're alive. Understand? Little bastard! I don't know why I bothered, except your mother wanted me to. Can you hear me?'

'Yes.' His face was twitching and he could not stop it.

'You're to bugger off, understand? Bugger off. You can't go home, they'll get you again, you hear me?'

He had heard, and understood, and buggered off, and never saw his family again. Not that he missed them much. He had found the army, like so many hopeless men, and it had served him well. And he could not die; he had known it since he was alone in the alleyway, had tested it in battle, and he knew that he had cheated death.

He unsheathed his bayonet and wondered, for a

258

second, whether to give it to one of the Privates to sharpen. He would like to humiliate the big Irish bastard, but on the other hand he always liked to do the job himself when there was killing ahead. The assault would happen today; everyone knew it, though no announcement had been made, and there would be killing enough for everyone. He looked into the hat. 'You'll excuse me a moment? I'll talk again soon.'

He put the shako down and picked up his stone. It blurred in his hand, honing the bayonet's leading edge, but he did not look at the work. He stared instead at the Company, recognizing their fear and feeding from it. Hakeswill was content. He had broken the bastards until they fetched his food, washed his clothes, and changed the straw in his shelter. Two of them he had beaten into pulp, but now they were like puppy dogs, eager to please. He had won his major battles. Sharpe was out of the way, and Harper was broken down into a Private, a red-coated Private. The Captain was afraid of Hakeswill, so was Price and so were the Sergeants. Life could be, Hakeswill knew, a lot worse. He put a thumb on the blade, knew the edge could be sharper, and the stone started again on long, whispering strokes.

Private Clayton looked sideways at Hakeswill, laughed, and said something to his companion. Hakeswill saw the laugh, but pretended not to notice. He would take care of young Clayton, but after the siege, when he had time to think the problem through. Clayton had a pretty wife, the prettiest in the Battalion, and Hakeswill had his eye on Sally. She would have to wait until he had done with Teresa.

The thought of Sharpe's woman made him scowl. He was not certain why he wanted her so much, but he did. She had become an obsession that disturbed his sleep. He would take the bitch and kill her afterwards.

It was not because she had fought him, and won; others had done that. He remembered the woman in Dublin who had stuck a gutting-knife in his belly. She had got away and he had felt no resentment, but Teresa was different. Perhaps it was because she had shown no fear, and Hakeswill liked to see fear. He could remember the ones he had killed, the ones he had not needed to kill, right back to that prig of a vicar's daughter who had stripped for him as he held the adder close by her neck. Dorcas, that was her name, and her father had trumped up a sheep stealing charge that had nearly killed him. Hakeswill smiled to himself. He had burned down the vicar's tithe barn on his first night after the hanging. He thought again of Teresa, and the edge of his bayonet became sharper, and he knew that he wanted her very much. Not just for revenge, not just because she was Sharpe's woman, though that was important, but because he wanted her. She was so beautiful, so utterly beautiful, and he would take her, kill her, and the bastard Sharpe would lose her. The anticipation brought on his involuntary twitch.

He changed hands so that the bayonet was in his right hand and, wedging the stone between his knees, he spat on it and began on the point. It would be needle sharp when he had finished, so sharp that it would slide sweetly into a man's guts as if there was no skin to puncture on the way. Or a woman's! He cackled aloud at the thought, alarming the Company, and he thought of Teresa. Sharpe would know who had done it, but there was nothing he could do about it! Hakeswill could not be killed! He looked up at the Company. They wanted to kill him, he knew, but so had the men of a dozen other companies and all had tried. He could remember the musket balls going past him in battle, fired from behind, and once he had seen a man taking

deliberate aim. He stroked the bayonet, remembering his revenge, and then thought of the night ahead.

He had planned his assault carefully. The South Essex, with the rest of the Fourth Division, would be attacking the breached face of the Trinidad bastion, but Hakeswill would take care in the ditch. He would hang back, let others do the fighting, so that he was fresh when the cheers came from the top of the breach. Then, when the chaos started, he would cross the wall and go up into the dark streets that led to the Cathedral. He only needed two minutes' lead, which was all he was likely to get, but he knew, as he tested the perfectly prepared blade in his hands, that he would succeed. He always did succeed. He had been touched by death, released, and he felt in his soul that he had been inspired to succeed ever since. He looked up. 'Clayton!'

The Company froze and stared at Clayton. The young Private grinned, as if he was not worried. 'Sergeant?'

'Oil, get me oil.'

'Yes, Sergeant.'

Hakeswill cackled as the boy walked away. He would save him for after Badajoz, after the killing, for the time when he would have to pick up the other problems that he had deferred. There was the oilskin bundle that was buried beneath a boundary stone two miles down the Seville Road. Hakeswill had visited the spot last night, heaved the stone off the field embankment, and rummaged through the stolen goods. It was all safe and he had left most of it there because there would be no point in trying to sell anything in the next few days. Badajoz would be stuffed with loot, prices would drop to rock-bottom. It could all wait. He had taken only Sharpe's telescope, with its distinctive brass plate, which he planned to leave beside Teresa's body. He picked up his hat, stared down into the interior. 'Then he'll

be blamed, won't he? Or else that bastard Irishman!'

'Sergeant?'

The eyes rolled up. 'Private Clayton?'

'The oil, Sergeant.'

'Don't bloody stand there!' Hakeswill held up his bayonet. 'Oil it. And be careful! Don't spoil the edge.' He let Clayton walk away and then looked down into the hat. 'Nasty little boy! Perhaps he'll die tonight, and that will make things easier for us.'

Harper watched the twitching, malevolent face and wondered what was inside the shako. The whole Company wondered, but no one dared ask. It was Harper's opinion that there was nothing inside, that the whole performance was a contrived demonstration of madness to unsettle the Company. The Irishman sharpened his own bayonet, the unfamiliar musket bayonet that lacked the rifle blade's handle, and he made his own plans for the night. There were still no orders, but the army, with its strange, collective instinct, knew that the assault was planned and if, as seemed likely, the South Essex were ordered into the breach, Harper intended staying close to Hakeswill. If a chance came to kill the Sergeant, he would, or else he would try to make sure that Hakeswill did not slip alone into the city. Harper had decided not to volunteer for the Hope, not unless Hakeswill volunteered, and he thought that unlikely. Harper's job was to protect Teresa, as it was Sharpe's, the whole Company's, even Captain Robert Knowles's, who had visited his old Light Company and listened seriously as Harper told of Hakeswill's threat. Knowles had grinned, reassured Harper, but still the Irishman feared the consequences of the chaos in a breach. He leaned back and listened to the guns.

The gunners, with the same instinctive knowledge that the assault was imminent, served their guns with

extra effort as if each stone shard chipped from the breaches would save an infantryman's life. The smoke from the twelve batteries hung like a sea-fog above the still waters of the flooded stream, smoke so thick that the city could hardly be seen, and more smoke was pumped relentlessly from the huge guns. The cannon were like bucking monsters that hissed and steamed between each shot as the blackened gunners sponged and rammed, then heaved the beasts back on to target. The gunners could not see the breaches, but the wooden recoil platforms were marked with deep cuts and the officers and Sergeants lined the gun trails on the cuts, checked the elevation screw. With a flick of the glowing match the gun would bellow again, leap back, and a heavy iron ball would vanish in the fog with a sudden whorl of smoke that was followed by the grinding crash of impact.

Perhaps it was the tempo of the guns that made the men so certain that the assault was this Sunday night, or else the sight of newly made siege ladders in the Engineers' park. Two of the attacks, the one on the castle, and the one by the river, at the San Vincente bastion, would carry ladders to try a surprise escalade. It could not work, of course, the walls were too high. The battle would be lost or won in the breaches.

'Company!' Hakeswill's voice grated at them. 'On your feet! Hup, hup, hup!'

They scrambled to their feet, pulling jackets straight, and Major Collett was there with Captain Rymer. The Major waved the men down again. 'You can sit.'

This had to be the announcement, Harper thought, and he watched as Collett drew out a sheet of paper and unfolded it. There was a buzz of excitement in the Company, a shout for silence from Hakeswill, and Collett waited for quiet. He looked at them

belligerently. The assault, he said, would be soon, but they knew that, and they waited for orders. The Major paused and looked down at the piece of paper. 'This order has come, and I will read it to you. You will listen. "I advert the army's attention to the events pursuant of the capture of Ciudad Rodrigo."' Collett read in a flat, hard voice. He could not pronounce Ciudad with the soft 'C', so instead pronounced it 'Quidad'. '"The inhabitants of that town, citizens of Britain's ally, Spain, were offered every kind of insult and injury. There will be no repetition of that behaviour in Badajoz. Any attacks on civilian property will be swiftly and condignly punished by death, the apprehended perpetrators being hung at the place of their crime."' He folded the paper. 'You understand? Keep your thieving hands to yourself and your breeches buttoned. That's all.' He glared at them, turned on his heel, and marched away to the next company. The Light Company looked at each other, shrugged, and laughed at the message. Who would do the hanging? The provosts would not be far to the front in any fighting, it would be pitch dark in the streets, and a soldier deserved some loot for fighting through a breach. They were the ones who would do the fighting, and the dying, and who did not need a drop of drink after that? Not that they intended any harm to any civilians. The Spanish, most of whom in Badajoz were on the enemy's side, could choose for themselves how they welcomed the victors. They could leave their doors open and the drink on the table, or they could choose to be unfriendly, in which case? They grinned and went back to sharpening the seventeen-inch blades.

A few moments later a second rumour arrived, as strong as the first which had announced the assault, and this rumour, flashing through the camp, brought

relief and frustration. Everything was postponed. They had all been given another twenty-four hours to live.

'Where are we going?' someone shouted.

They laughed, forgetting Hakeswill's baleful presence. 'Badajoz!'

Tomorrow.

CHAPTER 23

Suddenly there was optimism. Hogan's face, so long lined with concern, crinkled at the eyes; there was an urgency in his speech, a new hope. Two loyal Spaniards had escaped from the city, climbing the wall by the river, and had safely reached the British lines. Hogan's finger stabbed down on to the familiar map. 'There, Richard, there. Tomorrow we'll destroy it!'

The finger was pointing towards the wall between the two breached bastions. The Spaniards said it was weak, that it had not been repaired properly after the previous sieges, and they swore that a few shots would bring the wall tumbling down. It would mean a third breach, a sudden breach, a gap that the French would have no time to fill with careful defences. Hogan's fist slammed on to the map. 'We've got them!'

'Tomorrow then.'

'Tomorrow!'

April 6th dawned with a clear sky, and a light so pure that, before the siege batteries opened fire, the city could be seen with every roof, church, tower, and bastion delicately etched. It was a spring morning, full of hope as green as the new plants, a hope put there by a third, surprise breach. The gunners made their minimal adjustment, the trails inching around on the platforms, and then the order was given. Smoke jetted, thunder echoed over the lake, the balls smashed at the

repaired masonry as the gunners slaved, dragged at their weapons, rammed, sponged, and rammed again, working with a knowledge of victory. To the south, clear of the smoke-fog on the lake, the Engineers peered at the unbroken stretch of wall. It jetted dust in a hazy cloud, started from the dry mortar by the cannon-strike, but it held all morning. The cannons hammered on, smiting the wall with shattering force until, early in the afternoon, the labour was rewarded.

The wall began to slide, not piece by piece as the bastions had given, but in one solid, spectacular chunk. Hogan jumped for the joy of it. 'It's going!'

Then the view was lost. Dust boiled up like smoke from an explosion, the sound rolled across the water, and the gun crews cheered themselves hoarse. The dust drifted slowly away and there, where once there had been a seemingly solid wall, was now a third, huge breach; as wide as the others, but fresh, undefended, and the orders were given. Tonight, gentlemen, tonight at dusk. Into the breaches and the gates of Spain would belong to Britain.

All afternoon, as clouds came from the east, the guns fired so that the French could not work in the breaches. The gunners worked willingly. Their job was done and this was the last day of effort, the twenty-second day of the siege, and tomorrow there would be no more heaving and sweating and no more enemy counter-battery fire. Badajoz would be theirs. The Engineers counted ladders and hay-bags, stacked the huge axes that the leading troops would take into the attack, and thought of the comfortable beds that waited in the city. Badajoz was theirs.

The orders, just twenty-seven paragraphs, were issued at last and the men listened in silence as their officers told them the news. Bayonets were polished again,

muskets checked, and they listened to the flat notes of the cathedral clock. First darkness and Badajoz was theirs.

Captain Robert Knowles, now part of the Third Division, stared up at the huge castle with its colony of kestrels. The Third Division, carrying the longest ladders, was to cross the stream and climb the castle rock. No one expected the attack to work, it was merely a diversion to keep troops pinned in the castle, but Knowles's men grinned at him and swore they would climb the wall. 'We'll show them, sir!' And they would try, he knew, and so would he, and he thought how splendid it would be if he could reach Teresa first, in the house with two orange trees, and hand her and the child safely to Sharpe. He looked again at the vast castle, on its high, steep rock, and he vowed he would fight as Sharpe fought. The devil with a fake attack! They would attack for real.

The Fifth Division, brought back across the river, would mount another escalade with ladders; this time against the north-east bastion, the San Vincente, which towered above the slow river. Like the castle attack, it was intended to pin down enemy troops, to stop reinforcements going to the south-east corner, for it was there, at the three breaches, that Wellington knew he must win his victory.

The breaches. The Fourth and Light Divisions would make the real attack; the assault on the three breaches and the men, waiting as the clouds spread over the sky, imagined the boiling of troops in the ditch, the fighting that was to come, but they would win. Badajoz would be taken. The guns fired on.

Sharpe found a cavalry armourer who put the huge sword against a treadled wheel and the sparks flowed from the edge. He had checked his rifle and loaded

268

the seven-barrelled gun. Even though his own orders forbade him to go into the ditch he wanted to be ready. He was a guide, the only man who had already walked to the lip of the glacis, and his task was to lead the Forlorn Hope of the Light Division to the brink of the ditch opposite the Santa Maria bastion. There they would leave him and go on to attack the bastion and the new breach while, off to the right, the South Essex and the Fourth Division marched on the Trinidad. Once Sharpe had taken the Forlorn Hope to the ditch, he was to return and guide other battalions up the slope, but he hoped, against hope, that he could find a way into the fight and over the wall to his child.

The bell tolled six, then the quarter, and on the half, the men lined up out of sight of the city. They carried no packs, just weapons and ammunition, and their Colonels inspected them, not to check on uniforms, but to grin at them and encourage them, because tonight the common man, the despised soldier, would write a page in history and that page had better be a British victory. Tension stretched as the sun sank, imagination making fears real, and the officers passed the rum rations down the ranks and listened to the old jokes. There was a sudden warmth in the army, a feeling of difficulties that would be shared, and the officers who came from the big houses felt close to their men. Imagination did not spare the rich, nor would the defenders, and tonight the rich and poor in the ditch would need each other. The wives made their farewells and hoped for a live husband on the morrow, and the children were silent, awed by the expectancy, while in the doctors' tents the instrument cases were opened and the scalpels honed. The guns fired on.

Seven o'clock. A half-hour only left and Sharpe and the other guides – all except the Rifleman were Engineers – joined their battalions. The Forlorn Hope of the Light Division was half composed of Riflemen, hoping for the laurel-wreath badge. They grinned at Sharpe and joked with him. They wanted the thing done and over in the way that a man facing the surgeon's knife hastened the fatal clock. They would move at half-past seven and by half-past nine the issue would be decided. Those that lived would be drunk by ten and the wine would be free. They waited, sitting on the ground with their rifles between their knees, and prayed the clock on. Let it be over, let it be over, and darkness came and the guns boomed on, and the orders had to come.

Half-past seven, and the orders still not given. There was a delay and no one knew why. The troops fidgeted, grew angry against unseen staff officers, cursed the bloody army and the bloody Generals because in the darkness the French would be swarming on the breaches, preparing traps for the British! The guns stopped firing, as they should have done, but there were still no orders and the men waited and imagined the French working on the new breach. Eight o'clock sounded, and then the half, and horses galloped in the darkness. Men shouted for information. There were still no orders, but rumoured explanations. The ladders had been lost. The hay-bags were missing and they cursed the Engineers, the lousy army, and the French worked on.

Nine o'clock, and murder was being prepared in the breaches. Delay it, Sharpe thought, let it be tomorrow! The attack should go in on the heels of the guns, in the minutes of darkness when there was a trace of light so that the battalions would not get lost on the glacis.

Still the time ticked away and still they waited and still the enemy were given precious minutes to work on the defences. Then there was a stir in the darkness. Orders, at last, and there would be no delay.

Go, go, go, go, go. The ranks moved with the clinking of metal and thumping of rifle and musket stocks. There was a sense of relief to be moving in the darkness, in the bleak, total darkness, and the six thousand five hundred men, English, Irish, Scottish, Welsh and Portuguese moved against the city. The guides ordered quiet and the orders went back, but they were moving at last and no one could silence the thousands of boots that scraped and scuffed by the road that led between the flood and the Pardaleras Fort. Far to the north, the Third Division filed over the bridge by the broken mill that spanned the Rivillas and the air was filled with the croaking of frogs and the fears of men. The city waited in darkness. Silence in Badajoz.

The Lieutenant who was leading the Forlorn Hope touched Sharpe's elbow. 'Are we too far to the left?'

They had lost all touch with the Fourth Division. It was dark, utterly dark, and there was no sound from the fort or from the city. Sharpe whispered back. 'We're all right.'

Still there was no firing, no sound from the city or from the Pardaleras that was now behind them. Silence. Sharpe wondered if the attack would be a surprise to the French. He wondered if perhaps the enemy had been fooled by the delay, perhaps the troops had relaxed, were waiting for another day and if the greatest gift the gods can give a soldier, surprise, had been given to the British. They were close now. The dim, dark shadow of the fortress blotted out half the sky. It was huge in the night, vast, unimaginably strong, and the slope of the glacis was beneath Sharpe's feet and he

paused as the sixty men of the Forlorn Hope aligned themselves and thrust their ladders and hay-bags to the front. The Lieutenant scraped his sword from the scabbard. 'Ready.'

There was firing from the right, far off, where the Third Division had been spotted. It sounded miles away, like someone else's battle, and it was difficult to believe that the sound had anything to do with the dark glacis leading to the fortress in front. Yet the sound would alert all the French sentries and Sharpe hurried up the slope, angling to his left, and still there was no sound from walls or bastions. He tried to make sense of the shadows, to recognize the shapes he had seen just three nights before, and his footsteps sounded loud on the grass and he could hear the panting of men behind him. Surely the French would hear! At any moment, he almost cringed at the reality of the imagination, the grapeshot would stab down from the walls. He saw the corner of a bastion, recognized the Santa Maria, and a relief went through him as he knew he had brought the Hope to the right place.

Sharpe turned to the Lieutenant. 'This is it.' He wished he was going with him, that he was leading the Hope, but it was not to be. The glory belonged to the Lieutenant who made no reply. Tonight he was a god, tonight he could do no wrong, because tonight he was leading a Forlorn Hope against the biggest citadel the British army had ever attacked. He turned to his men.

They went. Silent. The ladders scraped over the stone lip of the glacis, down into the ditch, and the men scrambled down, slithering on the rungs, falling on to the thrown hay-bags. It had begun.

Sharpe watched the walls. They were dark and silent. Behind him, at the foot of the glacis, he could hear the tramp of feet as the battalions approached and then,

ahead, he heard the Lieutenant shout at his men and the first scrambling of boots on the breach. It had started. Hell had come to Badajoz.

CHAPTER 24

In the cathedral that day the prayers had been unceasing, muttered, sometimes hysterical; the words had accompanied the beads as the women of Badajoz feared for the dead who would come to their streets that night. Just as the British army knew the assault was coming, so, too, did the defenders and inhabitants of Badajoz. A host of candles flickered before the saints as if the tiny flames could keep at bay the evil that surrounded the city and came pressing closer as the night gloom filled the cathedral.

Rafael Moreno, merchant, trickled powder into his pistols and hid them, loaded and primed, beneath the lid of his writing desk. He wished his wife were with him, but she had insisted on joining the nuns in the cathedral, foolish woman, and praying. Prayers would not deflect the soldiers, bullets might, but it was more likely they could be bribed by the cheap red wine he had put in his courtyard. Moreno shrugged. The most valuable possessions were hidden, well hidden, and his niece insisted she had friends among the British. He could hear Teresa upstairs, talking to her child, and doubtless she had the heathen rifle loaded and ready. He liked his niece, of course, but there were times when he thought that his brother Cesar's family were more than a little too wild. Downright irresponsible even. He poured himself wine. That child upstairs, improving in

health, God be praised, but a bastard! And in his house! Moreno sipped the wine. The neighbours did not know, he had seen to that. They thought she was a widow whose husband had died in last year's battles between the French and the disintegrating Spanish armies. He heard the clock in the cathedral tower begin wheezing as it wound itself up to strike the bell. Ten o'clock in Badajoz. He emptied his glass and called for a servant to refill it.

The bell sounded, and below, in the cathedral, beneath the vaulted ceiling and the gold ledges, below the huge, dark chandelier, and beneath the sad eyes of the Virgin, the women heard the crackle of muskets begin far away. They looked up, over the glow of the candles, at the Mother of God. Be with us now and in the hour of our need.

Sharpe heard the first toll of the hour, and then no more. As it sounded, so the first fireball rose from the battlements, arced its spark-path in the blackness, and then plummeted to the ditch. It was the first of a storm, the tight-packed balls flaming and falling as the carcasses were rolled on to the breach, and suddenly the breaches, the ditch, the ravelin, the obstacles, and the tiny figures of the Forlorn Hope were swamped in light, light poured from above, by flames that caught on the obstacles in the ditch, and the Hope began to climb as the fire was bright on their bayonets.

The battalions behind cheered. Silence was done. The front ranks reached the ditch and the ladders scraped over. Men hurled themselves after the hay-bags and scrambled down ladders, a flow of men in desperate haste to cross the ditch and climb the huge ramps of the breaches. They were cheering, urging themselves on, even as the first tongues of quicksilver flame raced

275

down the breaches of the Santa Maria and Trinidad.

Sharpe dropped as the mines exploded. Not one or two, but tons of powder packed in the ditch, on the lower slopes of the ramps, was ignited and exploded outwards, and the Forlorn Hope was gone. Taken in an instant, ground into fragments of wet horror, all dead, as the first files of the first battalions were hurled backwards by the flame and flying stone.

The French cheered. They lined the parapets, the bastions; and the guns that had been handled round to fire down into the ditch, guns which had been double shotted with canister, were unmasked. Muskets spat, were drowned by the cannon flames. The enemy cheered and shouted obscenities, and all the time the carcasses were thrown, lighting the targets, and the ditch was slopping with fire, a container of flames that would only be drowned in blood, and still the men went down the ladders and into the ditch.

The third breach was silent, the new breach. It lay between the bastions, a huge fresh scar that could lead into the city, but Sharpe saw the French had worked well. The ditch in front of the wall was huge, as wide as a parade ground, but filled with the squat, half-finished ravelin. The ravelin was twenty feet high, shaped like a diamond, and the only way to the new breach was to go round it. The way was blocked. Carts had been tipped over in the approach ditches, then covered with timbers, and the fireballs had lit the obstacles so that they flamed huge and fierce, and no attacker could get close. Only the breaches in the bastions, the Santa Maria and the Trinidad, could be approached, and those were dominated by the enemy guns. They fired again and again, the ammunition hoarded against this night, and still the British tried, and still they died yards from the breaches' base.

Sharpe went back down the glacis, into the shadows, and turned once to see the high, great walls of the battle lit by fire. Flames jetted from the embrasures, writhing smoke into the maelstrom below, and in the light of the fires he saw strange patterns at the top of the breaches. He stopped and stared, trying to make sense of the shapes glimpsed through the harrowing fire and smoke, and saw that the French had crowned each breach with *Chevaux de Frise*. Each one was a timber, thick as a battleship's main mast, and from each chained timber there sprang a thousand sabre blades; the blade barrier, thick as a porcupine's coat, to hook and tear any man who reached the summit. If any did.

He found the Colonel of his next battalion, standing with drawn sword, staring at the fire-edged glacis. The Colonel glared at Sharpe. 'What's happening?'

'Guns, sir. Come on.' Not that the Colonel needed to be told, or to be guided. The face of the Santa Maria bastion was a sheet of reflected flame and they marched towards it as, suddenly, the canister whistled down the slope and cut huge swathes through the Battalion. The men closed ranks, marched on, nearer the lip, and the gunners doused the glacis with bursting canister and the Colonel waved his sword. 'Come on!'

They ran, order disappearing, and hurled themselves at the ditch. Bodies littered the glacis, twitched by new blasts of shot, and still more men climbed the slope and poured into the vast fire bowl. Men jumped towards hay-bags and landed, instead, on the dead or wounded. The living pushed forward towards the breach, trying to claw their way to the shattered stone, and each time the French gunners, high on the terrifying walls, swatted them back so that the ditch floor was thick with blood. Sharpe watched, appalled. His orders were to go back to where the reserve waited, to guide more

men forward, but no man needed to be guided this night. He stayed.

Not one man had reached a breach. The ditch between the glacis and the ravelin was black with men, disorganized men, the mingling of the Fourth and Light Divisions. Some cowered there for safety, thinking the shadow of the ravelin would give them protection from the guns that scorched down at them. But there was no safety. The guns could reach every inch of the ditch, firing in scientific patterns, killing, killing, killing, but for the moment they fired only where the British moved, towards the breaches, and the spaces before the great, stone ramps were thickening with dead. The guns fired canister, tin cans that burst apart in the muzzle flame and scattered musket balls like giant duck-shot, while other guns were loaded with grapeshot, naval ammunition, that rattled against the ditch wall.

It was not just the guns. The defenders hurled anything that would kill from the ramparts. Stone lumps, the size of a man's head, crashed down into the ditch; gun-shells, their fuses cut to a quarter inch and lit by hand, fizzed down and sent red hot fragments scything on the ditch's floor, and even kegs of powder, fused and lit, were rolled down the breach slope. Sharpe watched one barrel, bouncing and tumbling, its fuse spinning madly red, finally leap into the ditch and explode in the face of a dozen Riflemen who were running for the Santa Maria breach. Only three lived, blinded and screaming, and one of them wandered, insensate with pain, into the burning timbers that blocked the path to the new breach. Sharpe fancied he could hear the man's dying screams bubble with the flames, but there were so many dying, and so much noise, that he could not be certain.

The noise of the living in the ditch was a growl and,

suddenly, it rose to a sound of fury and Sharpe looked right to see a wave of men, Riflemen and red-jackets, charging forward. He groaned. They had stormed their way up the ravelin's sloping face, desperate for victory, and the burgeoning attack spread out on the diamond's top flat surface and ran with levelled bayonets towards the new breach. The French were waiting. Guns that had not fired were touched with flame, the grapeshot ripped in from three sides and the attack died in a dancing horror as men were struck as by contrary iron winds. A few lived, ran on, and found that the ravelin led to another sheer drop, into another ditch before the breach and, as they hesitated, the French infantry dropped them with musket fire and there was nothing but bodies left on the ravelin's top, bodies that had fallen and left unrecognizable dark smears on the stone.

The guns were winning the night. The ditch was blocked by fire. Men could not go right or left because of the flaming timbers that jammed the main ditch on either side of the two bastions, just as the approaches to the third breach were blocked. The four fires, fed with fresh timber from the walls, defined where the British could go, a space that was terrible with gunfire. Yet still more men went over the edge, hurrying down the ladders as if there was some safety in the milling, scrambling horde that bulged at the edges as fresh groups charged towards a breach. The ditch was filling with men, hundreds and hundreds of men, shouting men, holding their bayonets above the crush, and the grapeshot would lick down and clear a space of the living and the space would be filled again as men trampled the dying. The guns would belch again, and again, and the metal scraps turned the ditch into a charnel house. Still they went forward, incoherently brave, trying to

reach an enemy they could not see or touch, and they died as they cursed and struggled forward.

They went in small groups and Sharpe, crouched on the glacis, watched as an officer or Sergeant led them forward. Mostly they died in the ditch, but some, at last, reached the breach and clambered upwards. A dozen men would go and, in seconds, there would be six, and three would reach the stone and begin to climb while the men on the glacis lip, next to Sharpe, knelt up and fired their muskets at the walls as if they could clear the path for the scrambling men. Sharpe wondered if the French were playing with them. Sometimes no gun would fire on the small, desperate groups, even though guns swept the approach to the breach, and he would watch them struggle, higher and higher until, casually almost, the enemy would pluck them off the stone, tumble them dead, and a new high-tide mark of blood was marked on the breach. Once a man even reached the *Chevaux de Frise*, he swept at the sabre blades with a musket, bellowing defiance, and then he was hit by an unseen French infantryman and he fell, twisting like a rag doll, down the slope and the French jeered him and poured fire down.

Sharpe went right, looking for the Fourth Division and the South Essex, but the ditch was a massive sink of death, of weird shadows cast by the fires, and he could make out no faces in the packed crowd that was filling the space between the ravelin and glacis. Men sheltered behind parapets made from the dead, others clumsily reloaded muskets and fired them uselessly at the towering stone that crushed them with fire. He ran for a minute, right on the edge of the glacis, stumbling on the uneven paving and hearing the canister above him, in front of him, yet he was untouched. Small groups of men were on the glacis lip, Light Companies

mostly, who rammed and fired, rammed and fired, hoping that their bullets might ricochet from an embrasure and kill a Frenchman. The canister flung them backwards, ragged down the slope, and beyond the bodies, in the darkness, more men waited for the orders that would send them running to the light, to the ditch, to the hundreds of dead. Sharpe had never seen so many dead.

He was still fifty yards from the Trinidad, but he could see that its breach was no better than the Santa Maria. The foot of the breach was smeared with bodies, its approaches bare of the living, though small groups of men dashed from the shadows of the ravelin and screamed defiance as they clawed at the stones and were blasted away. Bugles sounded to the right, the shouts of officers and Sergeants, and there was the South Essex! He saw them flowing up the glacis in close column and his Company, Rymer's Company, lined the ditch and fired their ineffectual muskets at the wall's height while the other men scrambled at the ladders, flung themselves on hay-bags, frantic in their haste. Men bunched at the ditch's edge, the guns hammered from the wall, their hot breath hard on the glacis, and Sharpe saw the Battalion shudder like a wounded thing, reform, smash itself under new impacts. But they were over, scrambling in the ditch and he saw Windham, his cocked hat gone, scything his sword towards the breach, and new guns fired until the sound of the city was like a weight of solid thunder.

They died in dozens, but still they went towards the breach, and more men came from the ditch, from other Regiments, and they tried, and pushed, and fought, and scrambled up the stone till it seemed they had to win for there was not enough shot in the world to kill so many men. The gunners rammed and fired, loaded

281

and fired, and the powder kegs banged down the slope, and the shells were thrown, fuses lit, so the dark explosions splintered the men, and they died and it was done. The dead choked the living, the breach had won. A few men, very few, still lived and struggled upwards, shredding their hands on the nailed boards laid down the upper slope, and Sharpe saw Leroy, sword in hand, cigar inevitably between his teeth, look up into the night, so slow, and then he fell, tumbling, fell, screaming into the ditch. A last man reached the sword blades, the very top, he clawed at them, blood on his hands, and then he shook, quivered, filled with a dozen bullets and the highest man, dead on the Trinidad, slid down, blood on stone, till he was caught.

The survivors were behind the ravelin, digging into the dead, and the French mocked them. 'Come to Badajoz, English.'

Sharpe had not been with them. He knelt, fired once at the wall, and watched the death of the Battalion; Collett, Jack Collett, neck severed by a roundshot, even Sterritt, poor, worried Sterritt, a hero now, killed in the ditch at Badajoz.

'Sir?' A voice curiously calm in the torment of sound. 'Sir?'

He looked up. Daniel Hagman, strange in red coat, stood over him. He stood up. 'Daniel?'

'You'd better come, sir.'

He went towards the Light Company, close to him now and still on the glacis, and he saw in the ditch where men had drowned in the deep water. The black humps of their bodies broke up the ripples in red and dark patterns. The guns were quieter now, saving their anger for the fools who would come from behind the ravelin. The breaches were empty of all but the dead. The huge fires roared, greedy for the lumber that was

tossed from the walls, and an army was dying between their flames.

'Sir?' Lieutenant Price, his eyes stark with the horror, ran to Sharpe. 'Sir?'

'What?'

'Your Company, sir.'

'Mine?'

Price pointed. Rymer was dead, a tiny wound, an insignificant wound, red on his pale forehead. He lay backwards on the slope, arms wide, staring at nothing, and Sharpe shuddered when he remembered how he had wanted this Company, and thus this man's death, and now it was given to him.

So easy. It was all done? Out of the horror, the pulverizing fire and iron that smothered the south-east corner of Badajoz, death had given Sharpe back what had once been his. He could stay on the glacis, firing at the night, safe from the carnage, a Captain again, the Company his, and men would account him a hero because he had lived through Badajoz.

A musket ball whirred past his head, making him jerk back, and there was Harper, the red jacket discarded, huge in a blood-stained shirt, and the Irish face was stone hard. 'What do we do, sir?'

Do? There was only one thing to do. A man did not go into a breach to fight for a company, not even a Captaincy. Sharpe looked over the ditch, over the scoured ravelin and there, untouched by blood, was the third breach, the new breach, the unattacked breach. A man went first into a breach for pride, nothing else, just pride. A poor reason, paltry even, but enough, perhaps, to win a city. He looked up at Harper. 'Sergeant. We're going to Badajoz.'

CHAPTER 25

Captain Robert Knowles crossed the bridge by the ruined mill and wondered at the calmness of the night. Beneath him the Rivillas stream whispered from the dam, ahead the huge castle blotted out the sky and, in the darkness, it seemed impossible that men could dare hope escalade the giant bastion. Wind rustled the new foliage in the trees that grew precariously on the steep hill that led up to the castle. Behind Knowles came his Company, carrying two ladders, and they paused with him at the foot of the slope, their excitement suppressed, and peered up at the looming walls. 'Bloody high!' A voice came from the rear rank.

'Quiet!'

The Engineer officer who was guiding the Battalion was nervous and Knowles became annoyed at the man's fidgeting. 'What's the matter?'

'We're too far over. We must go right.'

They could not go right. There were too many troops crowding at the hill's base, and it would cause chaos if the battalions tried to re-align themselves in the darkness. Knowles shook his head irritably. 'We can't. What's the problem?'

'That.' The Engineer pointed to his left. A huge shadow sprang from the dark rock, high over them, a shadow with a crenellated outline. The bastion of San

Pedro. Knowles's Colonel appeared beside him. 'What's the problem?'

Knowles pointed to the bastion, but the Colonel dismissed it. 'We must do what we can. Are you all right, Robert?'

'Yes, sir.'

The Colonel turned to the Light Company and raised his voice a little above a whisper. 'Enjoy yourselves, lads!'

There was a growling from the ranks. They had been told that this attack was merely a diversion, not intended to succeed, but then General Picton had damned Wellington's eyes and said that the Third Division did not make fake attacks. The Third Division would go all the way, or not at all, and the men were determined to prove Picton right. Knowles, for the first time, felt the seeds of doubt. They must climb a hundred feet of almost sheer rock, and then put ladders against a wall that looked forty feet high, and all the time under the guns of the defenders. He thrust the doubts away, trying, as he always did, to emulate Sharpe, but it was difficult, faced with the enormity of the castle, to feel confident. His worries were interrupted by hurrying footsteps and one of Picton's aides was calling for the Colonel.

'Here!'

'Go, sir! And the General wishes you God speed.'

'I'd rather he wished me a case of his claret.' The Colonel slapped Knowles's shoulder. 'Off you go.'

Knowles could not draw his sabre. He needed both hands to cling to the rock hill, to pull himself up while his feet found desperate footholds. His Captaincy was heavy on his shoulders. He hurried, wanting to stay ahead of his men because he knew Sharpe would lead,

and he imagined, as he climbed, the first heavy musket balls plummeting down to crush in the top of his skull. His men seemed to be so noisy! The ladders scraped on rock, on tree-trunks; the musket stocks banged on stone, the feet clattered pebbles loose, but still the castle was silent, the great shadow unrelieved by the gun flames. Knowles found himself thinking of Teresa, inside the city, and hoping, against all the evidence of the massive walls, that he could reach her first. He wanted to do something for Sharpe.

'Faster!' The shout was from one of his Sergeants, and Knowles, his thoughts elsewhere, snapped his head back and stared up. High above him, falling, falling, was the first carcass. The fire roared in the sky; it tumbled end over end, shedding sparks, and he watched, fascinated, as it plunged into a thorn tree that grew close by. The tree flared into flame and the first muskets banged from the castle wall. They seemed far away.

'Come on!'

More fireballs and carcasses fell from the ramparts; some lodged in the narrow space by the wall's foot, others fell in streaming shreds of fire down the rock slope and took men with them, screaming as the flames captured them, but Knowles climbed on and his men pressed behind. 'Faster! Faster!'

A cannon crashed out its load from the San Pedro bastion and canister whipped through the trees and crackled on stone. There was a cry behind him, a shout of despair, and he knew a man had gone, but there was no time to worry about casualties, just to scramble upwards, the going easier as they neared the top, and Knowles felt the excitement of battle that would carry him past fear and into action.

'Keep going!' The Colonel, surprisingly agile for his

years, overtook him and reached the space at the wall's base first. He leaned down and helped Knowles up. 'Get the ladders!'

The musket balls smacked down, but the shot was an awkward one for the defenders; they had to lean right over the battlements and shoot straight down, almost at random, into the flaring light at the bottom of the wall. The cannons were far more dangerous, shooting from the San Pedro and from a smaller bastion to Knowles's right, a bastion jutting from the castle wall. Canister scraped the wall, promising death to men on ladders, but that was a fear that had to be ignored.

'Here!' The first ladder loomed over the rock slope and Knowles ran to it, pulled it towards the wall, and more men were manhandling it, swinging it upwards, until it thumped against the battlements. The Colonel waved them on. 'Good lads! The first one over gets the best whore in Badajoz!'

They cheered and the Colonel dropped, felled by a bullet from above, but they hardly noticed. 'Me first! Me first!' Knowles pushed through, boyish in his excitement. He knew that Sharpe would lead, and so must he, and he scrambled up the rungs, wondering what a fool he was, but his legs pumped automatically and it occurred to him, with sudden horror, that he had not even drawn his sabre. He looked up, saw the arms of defenders pushing at the ladder and he began to fall sideways. He shouted a warning, let go, and thumped down into a press of men. Miraculously not a single bayonet touched him. He picked himself up.

'Are you hurt, sir?' A Sergeant looked worriedly at him.

'No! Get it up!' The ladder was not broken. Another canister splintered on the wall, the men swung the ladder again and this time Knowles was not near enough

to be first and he watched as his men began climbing. The first was shot from above, thrown clear by the second man, more pushed behind, and then the whole ladder with its human cargo disintegrated in splinters and flesh as a barrel-full of grapeshot, fired from the San Pedro bastion, found a full target. Stones were being hurled from the castle parapets that crashed into knots of men and bounced down the rock face. Suddenly Knowles's Company seemed to be halved in strength, he felt the frustrations of defeat and looked frantically for the second ladder. It had gone, back down the slope, and then there were voices shouting at him. 'Back! Back!' He recognized his Major's voice, saw the face, and he jumped into the shadows and left behind the broken ladders and bodies of the first attack beneath the triumphant shouts of the enemy.

'Any news from the castle?'

'No, my Lord.' The Generals fidgeted. In front of them the south-east corner of Badajoz flickered with bright fire. The two soaring bastions, scarred by the unconquered breaches, framed the flames, fed them, and the smoke boiled scarlet into the night. To the right, and seemingly far away, more fire glowed above the silhouetted castle and Wellington, cloaked and gloved, tugged nervously at his reins. 'Picton won't do it, y'know. He won't.'

An aide-de-camp leaned closer. 'My Lord?'

'Nothing. Nothing.' He was irritable, helpless. He knew what was happening in the great pit of fire ahead. His men were marching into it and could not get out the other side. He was appalled. The walls were three times bigger than Ciudad Rodrigo, the fight unimaginably worse, but he had to have the city. Kemmis, from the Fourth Division, pushed in by his side.

'My Lord?'

'General?'

'Do we reinforce, sir?' Kemmis was hatless, his face smeared with dirt as if he had been firing a musket himself. 'Do we send in more men?'

Wellington hated sieges. He could be patient when he had to be, when he was enticing the enemy into a trap, but a siege was not like that. Inevitably this moment had to come, when the troops had to be ordered into the one, small, deadly point, and there was no escaping it unless the enemy was simply starved into submission and there had been no time for that. He had to have this city.

Sharpe! For a second the General was tempted to damn Sharpe, who had assured him the breaches were practical. But Wellington suppressed the thought. The Rifleman had said what Wellington had wanted him to say and even if he had not, then Wellington would still have sent in the troops. Sharpe! If Wellington had one thousand Sharpes then the city might be his. He listened gloomily to the sounds of battle. The French cheers were loud and he knew they were beating him. He could withdraw now and leave the dead and wounded to be recovered under a flag of truce, or he could send in more men and hope to turn the battle. He had to have the city! Otherwise there could be no march on Spain this summer, no advance to the Pyrenees, and Napoleon would be given another year of power. 'Send them in!'

Feed the monster, he thought, that was grinding his army, his fine army, but the monster must be fed until it gave up. He could make up the shattered battalions, the reinforcements would come, but without Badajoz there was no victory. Damn the Engineers. There were miners in Britain, hundreds in Cornwall alone, but

none with the army, no Corps of Sappers who could have tunnelled under the bastions, packed the cavern with powder, and blown the French to kingdom come. He found himself wondering whether he should have slaughtered the garrison at Ciudad Rodrigo, whether he could have lined them up in tens and shot them, then left the bodies to rot in the town ditch so that any Frenchmen who chose to contest another breach could only expect the terrible vengeance of the English. He could not have ordered it, any more than he would order it here if they won this night. If.

He turned irritably towards his aides. His face was long and harsh-shadowed in the torchlight cast from Lord March's hand. 'Any news of the Fifth?'

The answering voice was low, anxious not to add to the bad news. 'They should be attacking now, my Lord, General Leith sends his apologies.'

'God damn his apologies. Why can't he be on time?' His horse shied, struck by a spent musket bullet, and the General soothed it. He could expect nothing of the escalades. Leith was late and the garrison at San Vincente would be warned, while Picton was hoping for the moon if he thought he could lay his long ladders against the castle wall. Victory, he knew, would have to be carved here, at the south-east corner, where flame and smoke churned over the ghastly ditch. Distantly, like a reminder of another world echoing in the depths of hell, the Cathedral bell tolled eleven, and Wellington looked up into the blackness and then back at the flames. 'One more hour, gentlemen, one more hour.' And then what, he wondered? Failure? Hell was no place for miracles.

On the walls the French gunners slackened their fire. They had drowned the ditch in death and now they listened to the screams and moans that came from

below. The attacks seemed to have stopped, so the gunners stretched, soaked their faces with water splashed from the buckets used to wet the sponges, and watched as fresh ammunition was brought up the ramp. They did not expect much more effort from the British. A few men had climbed the breaches, one was even impaled on the sabre blades, but it was a hopeless effort. Poor bastards! There was no joy any longer in shouting insults. A Sergeant, leather-skinned and hard, leaned on a gunwheel and flinched. 'Christ! I wish they'd stop screaming.'

A few men had lit surreptitious cigars that they hid from their officers by leaning deep into the gun embrasures. One man wriggled forward, past the acrid muzzle, until he could peer down into the ditch. The Sergeant called wearily to him. 'Come back! Those Rifle bastards will get you.'

The man stayed. He peered down, far down, at the writhing horror in the ditch. He pulled himself back. 'If they get in they'll bloody slaughter us!'

The Sergeant laughed. 'They won't get in, lad, not a chance. In two hours you'll be tucked in bed with that horrid thing you call a woman.'

'You're jealous, Sergeant.'

'Me? I'd rather go to bed with this.' The Sergeant slapped the barrel of his gun. The wreathed 'N', Napoleon's symbol, was searing hot. 'Now get back here, lad, put that bloody cigar out, and look smart. I might need you, God help me.'

A call from the observation point. 'Make ready!'

The Sergeant sighed and stood up. Another tiny group of idiot British were running towards the Santa Maria breach and his gun covered the approach. He watched them down the length of his glistening gun, saw them slip on blood, stumble on stone, and then

291

they were in his target zone. He stood to one side, touched the match to the powder-filled reed, and the green-jacketed men were beaten into fragments. It was so easy. The Sergeant bellowed orders for the reloading, listened to the hiss as the sponge seared down the bore, and was glad that he was at Badajoz this night. The French had begun to fear this Lord Wellington, to turn him into a bogey man to frighten their sleep, and it was pleasing to show that the English Lord could be beaten. The Sergeant grinned as the bulbous lumps of canvas-wrapped grapeshot were rammed into the cannon. This night Wellington would taste defeat, utter defeat, and the whole Empire would rejoice. This night belonged to France, only to France, and Britain's hopes were being buried where they belonged; in a ditch for the dead.

CHAPTER 26

'This way! This way!' They were going right, away from the San Pedro bastion, clawing a path on the hill's steep side until they had turned a corner and would receive some shelter from the grapeshot. The first attack had been horribly repulsed, but the Third Division would try again. They could hear the fury at the main breach, far away, and see on the sheeted floodwaters the dim reflections of the fires that were consuming the Light and Fourth Divisions. Knowles could feel a madness in the air, beating its dark wings against a city, bringing a night of insane death and crazy effort. 'Light Company! Light Company!'

'Here, sir.' An old Sergeant, steadying his Captain with a hand, and then a Lieutenant leading a dozen men. My God, Knowles thought, is this all that is left? But then he saw more men, tugging the cumbersome ladder. Another Sergeant grinned at him. 'Do we go again, sir?'

'Wait for the bugle.' He knew there was no point in making a scattered attack that could be picked off piecemeal by the defenders. The whole Division must go together.

Knowles suddenly felt good. There was an impression in his head, one that had been nagging him, and now he pinned it down. The musket fire had been light from the parapet. The grapeshot had confused him,

but now, thinking back to the chaos of the first attack, the shattering ladder, he remembered how few had been the musket flashes from the walls. The French must have left a skeleton garrison in the castle, and a confidence surged through him! They would do it. He grinned at his men, slapped their backs, and they were glad that he was confident. He was trying to think how Sharpe would do this. The danger was not the muskets, the danger was from the defenders toppling the long, rickety ladders. He ordered off a dozen men, under the Lieutenant, and told them they were not to try and climb the ladder. Instead they were to fire at the ladder's head, scour the parapet of its defenders, and only when the parapet was clear and he had led the men over the battlements were they to follow. 'Understand?'

They grinned and nodded, and he grinned back and drew the curved sabre from its scabbard.

The Sergeant laughed. 'I thought you were going to forget it again, sir.' The men laughed at him and he was glad of the darkness to cover his blush, but they were good men, his men, and he suddenly understood, as never before, the sense of loss that Sharpe had suffered. Knowles wondered how he was to climb the ladder and hold the sword, and knew he would have to put the blade between his teeth. He would drop it! He was nervous, but then, instead of bugles, there were shouts and the trampling of feet and the moment had come.

The survivors of the Third Division erupted from the darkness. The carcasses flowed down, and the cannon in the small castle bastion shredded the attack, but they were screaming defiance and the ladders swayed in the ungainly curves until they slammed against the castle wall.

'Up!' He jammed the blade between his teeth and

gripped the rungs. Musket balls came down and then he heard his own guns firing, the Lieutenant calling the orders, and he was climbing. The great, irregular granite blocks were going past his face, and he scrambled up, the fear a living thing beside him, and he concentrated on keeping the sabre between his teeth. His jaw ached. It was such a stupid thing to worry about because he was nearing the top and he wanted to laugh and he was afraid, so afraid, because the enemy would be waiting, and he felt his knuckles graze against the granite as the slope of the ladder took him close to the wall. He took the sabre from his mouth.

'Stop firing!' The Lieutenant stared up and held his breath.

Knowles had to use his fist, wrapped round the sabre handle, as a prop to help him up the last rungs. It was easier than climbing with the blade in his teeth. He suddenly felt foolish, as if someone might have laughed at him for climbing a ladder with a sabre in his mouth, and he wondered why the mind chose such irrelevant and stupid thoughts at such a moment. He could hear the guns, the screams, the crash of another ladder, and the man behind pushed at him, and the top was there! This was the moment of death and his fear harrowed him, but he pushed over the top and saw the bayonet come sawing towards him. He leaned to one side, tottering on the ladder, and swung his right arm for balance and, to his surprise, saw the sabre at the end of the arm cleave down into the enemy's head. A hand pushed him from behind, his feet were still pedalling at the rungs, but he had run out of ladder! He was falling forward on to the body of the dead man, and another enemy was coming, so he rolled and twisted and knew he was there. He was on the ramparts! There was a keening in his throat, that he did not hear, a

sound of insensate fear, and he thrust up with the sabre, into the man's groin, and the scream winged into the night and the blood pulsed on to Knowles's wrist, and the second man was with him.

They had done it! They had done it! The men were coming up the ladder, and he was filled with a joy that he did not know existed. He was on his feet, his blade bloodied to the hilt, and the enemy were running towards them, muskets outstretched, but the fear was conquered. There was something odd about the Frenchmen's uniforms. They were not blue and white. Knowles had a glimpse of red turnbacks and yellow facings, but then he was jumping forward, remembering that Sharpe always attacked, and the sabre twisted a bayonet aside, flicked up, and he had the man in the throat. 'Light Company! To me! Light Company!'

A musket volley shattered along the parapet, but he was still alive and more of his men were joining him. He heard the enemy shouting orders. German! These were Germans! If they were half as good as the more numerous Germans who fought for Wellington, but he would not feel fear, only victory. He led his men down the wall, bayonets out. The enemy were few and out-numbered, and every yard of wall that Knowles's men cleared was another yard where ladders could safely be climbed and the castle parapet filled with the red uniforms.

The Germans died hard. They defended each case-ment, each stairway, but they stood no chance. The castle had been denuded of troops, only a thin battalion left, but that battalion fought grimly. Each minute that they saved on the battlements was another minute for the central reserves to reach the castle, so they fought on, despising the odds, and screamed as they fell from

296

the parapets, chopped down by the redcoats, and fought till the wall was lost.

Knowles felt the joy of it. They had won the unbelievable victory. They had climbed a rock hill and a castle and they had won! He pounded his men on their backs, hugged them, laughed with them, forgave them all their crimes, because they had done it. It did not matter that the vast castle buildings would still have to be cleared, the dark, treacherous courtyards, because no one now could take this battlement from them. The British had won the city's highest point and from here they could fight downhill, into the streets, down to the main breach, and Knowles knew he would reach Teresa first and he would see, some time in the night, the gratitude on Sharpe's face. He had done it. They had done it. And for the first time that night, it was British cheers that startled the air in Badajoz.

The cheers could not be heard at the breaches. The castle was a long journey away, at least a mile's ride by the time a horseman had circled the floodwaters, and it would be minutes yet before the messenger would be despatched. Picton waited. He had heard the bell strike eleven as he saw his first, magnificent men cross the parapet, and he waited, listening to the sounds of battle, to know if they had won or were being chopped to pieces in the castle yards. He heard the cheers, stood up in his stirrups and roared his own, then turned to an aide-de-camp. 'Ride, man, ride!' He turned to another staff officer and clapped the man mightily on the back. 'We've proved him wrong! Damn his eyes! We did it!' He chuckled, anticipating Wellington's reaction when the news arrived at midnight.

Anger would take a man through a breach, sheer passion, but a small idea helped. It was not much of an idea, hopeless even, deserving the name Forlorn, but

it was all Sharpe had, and so he stared at the ravelin that stretched so invitingly towards the third, unsullied breach. There was no point in trying to outrace the grapeshot across its flat, diamond surface. Any man who tried was flicked hopelessly away, contemptuous meat to the gunners' fire. Yet the third breach was the newest, and the French had been given small time to entrap it, and Sharpe could see, through the sifting smoke, that the *Chevaux de Frise* on the new breach's summit was too short. There was a gap at the right hand side, a gap three men could pass abreast, and the only problem was reaching the gap. There was no approach in the ditch. The fires still seethed, white hot and violent, and the only path was across the ravelin. They must climb the ravelin, brave the top, and jump into the ditch, and it must be done at the ravelin's edge, close to the flames, where the diamond shape narrowed and the fatal journey was short.

He had no right to take the Company on the journey. This was a Forlorn Hope, born of despair and nurtured by pride, and it belonged to the volunteer, to the foolish. He knew he did not have to go himself, but he wanted no dead man's shoes. He had waited, letting the violence of the last attack spend itself in the ditch, and there was now a kind of truce before the breaches. As long as the British stayed quiet, harmless behind the ravelin, the gunners let them be. Only when men came into the firelight, towards the breaches, did the muzzles spout flame and the grapeshot crease the ditch floor. Back in the darkness, down the glacis, Sharpe could hear orders being called. Another attack was coming, the last reserves of the Division being fed into the ditch, and that was the moment, the hopeless moment, when the feeble idea, based only on the narrowing width of the ravelin, must be tried. He turned to his men and

drew the sword, the blade a great streak in the night, and the steel hissed as he swung it to the point at the firelight.

'I'm going there. There is one more attack, just one, and then it's all over. No one's touched that central breach, and that's where I'm going. Over the ravelin, down into the ditch, and I'll probably break my bloody legs because there are no ladders or hay-bags, but that's where I'm going.' The faces were pale, staring at him as they squatted on the slope. 'I'm going because the French are laughing at us, because they think they've beaten us, and I'm going to hammer those bastards into pulp for thinking that.' He had not known how much anger there was inside him. He was not a speechmaker, never had been, but the anger gave him words. 'I'm going to make those bastards wish they had never been born. They are going to die, and I can't ask you to come with me, because you don't have to come, but I'm going, and you can stay here and I won't blame you.' He stopped, out of words, unsure even of what he had said. The fires crackled behind him.

Patrick Harper stood up, stretched his huge arms and in one of them, catching the fires of death, was a vast axe, one of the many that had been issued to cut at the obstacles in the ditch. He stepped forward, over the dead, and turned to look at the Company. In the flamelight, hard by the terrible ditch, Patrick Harper was like a warrior sprung from a forgotten age. He grinned at the Company. 'Are you coming?'

There was nothing to make them go. Too often Sharpe had asked the impossible of them, and they had always given, but never in this horror, never like this, but they stood up, the pimps and the thieves, murderers and drunks, and they grinned at Sharpe and looked to their weapons. Harper looked down on his Captain. 'It

was a fine speech, sir, but mine was better. Would you be giving me that?' He pointed to the seven-barrelled gun.

Sharpe nodded, handed it over. 'It's loaded.'

Daniel Hagman, the poacher, took Sharpe's rifle. No man was a better shot. Lieutenant Price, nervously flexing his sabre, grinned at Sharpe. 'I think I'm mad, sir.'

'You can stay.'

'And let you get to the women first? I'll come.'

Roach and Peters, Jenkins and Clayton, Cresacre the wife-beater, all were there, and all felt the nervous exhilaration. This was a place fit to go mad in. Sharpe looked at them, counted them, loved them. 'Where's Hakeswill?'

'Buggered off, sir. Haven't seen him.' Peters, a huge man, spat on the glacis.

Below them the last battalion was climbing the slope, almost within the firelight, and Sharpe knew that the Company must attack at the same time. 'Ready?'

'Sir.'

A mile's ride away, unknown to the rest of the army, the Third Division was clearing the last of the castle yards. It had taken nearly an hour's hard fighting against the Germans and against the French who had pounded up from the central reserve in the Cathedral square. A mile in the other direction, equally unknown, Leith's Fifth Division had stormed the San Vincente. The ladders had split apart, the wood green, and the men had fallen into a spiked ditch, but other ladders were brought up, the muskets smashed at the battlements, and they had won a second impossible victory. Badajoz had fallen. The Fifth Division were in the city's streets, the Third possessed the castle, but the men in the ditch and on the dark glacis had no way of knowing. The news travelled faster inside the city. Rumours of

defeat raced like a plague through the narrow streets, up on to the Santa Maria and Trinidad bastions and the defenders looked fearfully behind them. The city was dark, the castle silhouette unchanged, and they shrugged and told each other it could not be true. But what if it was? Fear batted at them with grim wings.

'Make ready!'

By God! Another attack. The defenders turned from the city and looked over the walls. There, from the darkness, from the corpse-littered slope, another attack surged towards the ditch. More meat for the guns, and the fire flashed down the priming tubes, the smoke crashed out, and the mincer turned on.

Sharpe waited for the first gun, heard it, and started running. To Badajoz.

CHAPTER 27

The heights of the wall disappeared in smoke, the flames lancing through, and he jumped, the sword high, and the men in the ditch screamed at them. 'Down! Down!'

He had not counted on this. The ditch was crammed with the living, the dying, and the dead, and the living clawed at him. 'Get down! They'll kill us.'

He had sprawled down on bodies, but he scrambled up and heard his men thumping around him. There were small fortresses in the ditch, piled corpses, that soaked the grapeshot and sheltered men who themselves crouched on other corpses.

The bullets flickered into the ravelin's shadow, and the wounded pulled at him, and Sharpe swung the sword ahead of him, clearing a path. He screamed at them, 'Out the way!' The dead could not move, and he was wading in bodies, slipping on blood, and to his right, by the Trinidad, the gunners were shredding the last attack.

Hands clutched at Sharpe, tried to pull him down, and out of the darkness a bayonet was thrown at him. Behind him Harper was shouting, in his own tongue, rousing the Irish. A man reared up in front of Sharpe, clawed at him, and Sharpe hammered down with the sword hilt. Ahead was the ravelin's sloping face with the light bright above it and the guns were waiting.

Sharpe felt the temptation to sink into the rank stench in the ditch and let the night hide him. He swung the sword again, using the flat, and a man fell, and Sharpe's feet were on the slope and he climbed, not wanting to, fearing the oblivion, his body cringing from the death that ravaged the ravelin's top. He stopped.

There was a new sound in the ditch, a sound so mad that he had turned, the sword bright in his hand, and he looked unbelievingly behind him. The survivors of the South Essex, their yellow facings smeared with blood, were struggling towards him. They had seen their Light Company carve a path to the ravelin, and now they wanted to join the madness, but it was their voices that had stopped Sharpe.

'Sharpe! Sharpe! Sharpe!' They chanted it senselessly, a war cry, and men who did not know what it meant picked up the sound, and the ditch stirred, and the shout bellied into the night. 'Sharpe! Sharpe! Sharpe!'

'What are they saying, March?'

'It sounds like "sharp", my Lord.'

The General laughed because moments before he had wished for one thousand Sharpes, and now, perhaps, that rogue was giving him the city. His aides-de-camp, hearing the grim tone of the laughter, did not understand and did not like to ask.

The gunners, high on the wall, heard the chant and did not understand. They were massacring the newest attack on the Trinidad, hurling it back as they had hurled the others back, but then they saw the ravelin's top dark with men, and the men were shouting, and the whole ditch was moving that they had thought filled with corpses, and the corpses had come to life and were coming to them, for their revenge, and the dead were shouting. 'Sharpe! Sharpe! Sharpe!'

The madness was on Sharpe, the glory of it, the song of battle shrieking in his ears, so he did not hear the gunfire, or feel the blast of the shot, or know that, behind him, crossing the diamond, the men were falling, and the guns were tangling the air with death. He jumped. He had crossed the ravelin, running, the heat of the fire close on his right side, and the drop was huge. The new ditch was strangely empty, and he jumped, seeing a stone leap from a musket strike. The jump winded him, pitched him forward, but he was up and running.

'Sharpe! Sharpe! Sharpe!'

I will die here, he thought, in this empty ditch with the strange white bundles that stirred in the small breeze. He remembered the wool-padding that had protected the two breaches and wondered at a mind that could notice such irrelevant things at the point of a death.

'Sharpe! Sharpe! Sharpe!'

I will die here, he thought, just at the foot of the slope, and then he hated the bastards who would kill him and the anger drove him up, slipping on the rubble, unable to fight, only to climb, to carry the sword to the French flesh. There were men around him, screaming unintelligibly, and the air was thick with smoke, grapeshot, and flame. Harper was passing him, the huge axe held easily, and Sharpe, refusing to be second, drove his legs towards the dark sky beyond the row of shining blades.

'Sharpe! Sharpe! Sharpe!'

Private Cresacre was dying, his guts strung blue on his lap, his tears for himself and for his wife, who he would suddenly miss though he had beat her cruelly. And Sergeant Read, the Methodist, the quiet man who never swore, or drank, was blind, and could not cry

because the guns had taken his eyes. And past them, mad with lust, a battle madness, went the dark horde who followed Sharpe and tore their hands on the rough stone, going up the slope, up, where they had never dreamed to go, and some went back, torn by the guns, piling the new ditch as the other was piled, but the fine madness was on them.

'Sharpe! Sharpe! Sharpe!'

You save your breath for climbing, but shouting dulls the fear, and who needs breath when death waits at the summit? A bullet clanged on Sharpe's sword, jerking it in his hand, but it was whole, and the blades were near. He went to the right, his whole brain singing with the scream of death, and a stone moved beneath his left hand, throwing him, and a huge hand pushed at him, heaved him, and Sharpe grabbed at the thick chain that anchored the *Chevaux de Frise*. The top, death's peak.

'Sharpe! Sharpe! Sharpe!'

The French fired once more, the guns slamming backwards, and the new breach was taken, two vast men standing at its crest, untouched by fire, and the French ran with nowhere to run, and Harper screamed at the sky because he had done a great thing.

Sharpe leaped, downhill, into the city, and the sword was a live thing in his hand. A breach was taken, death cheated, and death wanted a payment. The sword chopped down on the blue uniforms, and he did not see men, just enemy, and he ran, slipping, falling, down the breach until the ground was firm beneath him and he was inside. Inside! Badajoz. And he snarled at the bastards, killed them, found a gun crew cowering by a wall and remembered the song of death, the leaping flames. The sword hacked at them, cut them, chopped them, and an axe was whirled at them, and the French

abandoned the new, low wall behind the breaches, because the night was lost.

A dark tide flowed over the breach, over the other breaches, a tide that made now no coherent sound. It was terrifying in its incoherence, the sound of the banshee, the keening of too much sorrow, too much death, and the madness turned to insensate rage, and they killed. They killed till their arms were tired, till they were soaked with blood, and there were not enough men to kill and they turned into the streets, a scrabbling, dark flood, up into Badajoz.

Harper leaped the wall built behind the breaches. A man cowered there, pleading, but the axe dropped and Harper's lips were drawn back around his teeth and he was sobbing an anger at the city. There were more men ahead, blue-uniformed, and he ran at them, the axe circling, and Sharpe was there, and they killed because so many were dead, so much blood, an army had nearly died, and these were the bastards who had jeered at it. Blood and more blood. An account to be balanced with a ditch full of blood. Badajoz.

Sharpe was crying. Venting an anger that had waited for this moment. He stood, the sword dark red, and he wanted more Frenchmen to come to his sword, and he stalked them, teeth bared, screaming at the night, and a body moved, a blue arm lifted, and the blade whirled, bit, was lifted again, and bit down once more, clean to the pavement.

A Frenchman, a mathematician conscripted as an artillery officer, who had counted forty separate attacks on the Trinidad and had repulsed them all, stood quiet in the shadows. He was still, quite still, waiting for this madness to pass, this blood lust, and he thought of his fiancée, far away, and prayed she would never see anything as horrid. He watched the Rifle officer and

306

prayed for himself that he would not be seen, but the face turned, the eyes hard-bright with tears, and the mathematician called out. 'No! Monsieur, no!' The sword took him, disembowelled him as Cresacre had been disembowelled, and Sharpe sobbed in rage as he ripped again and again, thrusting down at the gunner, ripping him, mutilating the bastard, and then the giant hands gripped him. 'Sir!' Harper shook him. 'Sir!'

'Christ!'

'Sir!' The hands pulled on Sharpe's shoulders, turning him.

'Christ.'

'Sir!' Harper slapped him. 'Sir.'

Sharpe leaned back against the wall, his head back, touching the stone. 'Oh Jesus. Oh God.' He was panting, the sword arm limp, and the pavement ahead was shredded with blood. He looked down at the artillery officer, torn into a grotesque death. 'Oh God. He was surrendering.'

'It doesn't matter.' Harper had recovered first, the axe shattered in a killing strike, and he had watched in awe as Sharpe had killed. Now he quieted Sharpe, soothed him, and watched the sense come back even as the madness climbed up the city streets.

Sharpe looked up, calm now, his voice bereft of all feeling. 'We did it.'

'Yes.'

Sharpe leaned his head back again, on to the wall, and his eyes closed. It was done, the breach. And to do it he had discovered that a man must banish fear as never before, and with that fear must go all other emotion except rage and anger; humanity must go, feeling, all must go except rage. Only that would conquer the unconquerable.

'Sir?' Harper plucked at Sharpe's elbow. No one else

could have done this, Harper thought, no one but Sharpe could have led men past death's peak.

'Sir?'

The eyes opened, the face came down, and Sharpe stared at the bodies. He had slaked his pride, carried it through a breach, and it was done. He looked at Patrick Harper. 'I wish I could play the flute.'

'Sir?'

'Patrick?'

'Teresa, sir. Teresa.'

God in heaven. Teresa.

CHAPTER 28

Hakeswill had not meant to go into the ditch, but, as soon as the South Essex made their attack and had left the Light Company to give covering fire from the glacis lip, he had seen that there was greater safety for him in the shadow of the ravelin. No chance, there, of an axe-blow in the dark from Harper, and so he had swung himself down a ladder, snarling at the frightened men, and then, in the chaos, had burrowed deep into the bodies in the shadowed ditch. He saw the attack go in, saw it fail, and he watched as Windham and Forrest tried to rouse other attacks, but Sergeant Hakeswill was snug and safe. Three bodies covered him, still warm in death, and he felt them shudder from time to time as the grape fragments struck home, but he was safe. At some time in the night a Lieutenant, a stranger to Hakeswill, tried to provoke him from his lair, screaming at the Sergeant to move and attack, but it was simple to grip the Lieutenant's ankle, trip him, and the bayonet slid so easily between the ribs and Hakeswill had a fourth body, surprise on its face, and he cackled as he slid expert hands over the pockets and pouches and counted his loot. Four gold coins, a silver locket and, best of all, an inlaid pistol that Hakeswill tugged from the Lieutenant's belt. The weapon was loaded, balanced to perfection, and he grinned as he thrust it into his jacket. Every little helped.

He had tied his shako with strings beneath his chin. He fumbled at the knot, tore it apart, and held the hat close before his face. 'We're safe now, safe.' His voice was ingratiating, plaintive. 'I promise you. Obadiah won't let you down.' Near to him, just beyond his parapet of corpses, a man sobbed and screamed and called for his mother. He was a long time dying. Hakeswill listened, his head cocked like an animal, and then he looked again into the hat. 'He wants his mother, he does.' Tears came to his eyes. 'His mother.' He looked up into the darkness, over the flames, and he howled at the sky.

There were periods of quietness in the ditch, periods when the death did not plunge downwards and when the mass of men, living and dead, crouched motionless beneath the high muzzles, and then, just when it seemed that the fight might be over, there would be a stir in the ditch. Men would try to rush the breaches, be restrained by other men, and the guns would fire again and the screaming would start again. Some men went mad, the agony too much, and one man thought the guns were the sound of God hawking and spitting and he knelt in the ditch and prayed until a lump of God's spittle took off his head, but Hakeswill was safe. He sat with his back to the ditch scarp, his front protected by the dead, and he talked into his hat. 'Not tonight. I can't do it tonight. The pretty lady will have to wait, yes she will.' He wheedled into the hat, and then listened to the fight with a professional's ear. He shook his head. 'Not tonight. Tonight we lose.'

He did not know how long he was in the ditch, or how long it took the dying to die, or how many times the lifeless flesh quivered around him as the canister pulverized the pile. Time was measured by sobs, by guns, by the passing of hopes, and it ended, unexpec-

tedly, with the great shout. 'Sharpe! Sharpe! Sharpe!' Hakeswill's face twitched over his parapet and watched as the living climbed from the spaces between the bodies and they were going away from him, over the ravelin, and to his right another attack clawed up the Trinidad.

'Sharpe! Sharpe! Sharpe!' The two men, he thought, must die, and he cackled at them, willing the canister to shred them, but they kept climbing and the shout went on. 'Sharpe! Sharpe! Sharpe!'

Hakeswill saw Sharpe slip almost at the top of the ramp and the Sergeant's heart leaped for joy; he was shot! But no, the bastard was pushed on by Harper, reached up for a chain, and there he stood, high on the central breach, lit by flames, and the Irishman was beside him, blades in their hands, and Hakeswill watched as they turned once to gesture a great triumph towards the British. Then they had gone, down to the city, and Hakeswill pushed the bodies aside, rammed his shako on his head, and kicked his way through the crowd that was flooding towards the Trinidad.

At the breach's head men swung the great axes, the chains split, and the *Chevaux de Frise* was heaved ahead of them and into a trench the defenders had dug on the rubble crest, and then the British were jumping the blades, shrieking murder, and sliding down the broken stones to the city's interior. They were berserk with rage. Hakeswill could feel it, the madness, and nothing would stop them this night. Even the wounded were pulling themselves up the breach ramps, some on their bellies, trying to reach the city and asking only for a chance to hurt as they had been hurt. They wanted drink, and women, and deaths, and more drink, and they remembered that Spaniards had fired at them from the city's walls and that made every living person in Badajoz an enemy. So they went, a dark, scrabbling

stream, over the breaches and up into the alleyways and streets, trampling the wounded in their rush, more coming, more, the breaches living with the mass of men scuttling into the city, spreading up into Badajoz, revenge.

Hakeswill went with them up a long street that led to a small plaza. He knew he was going in roughly the right direction, uphill and angling left, but he was trusting to instinct and luck. The plaza was already crowded with soldiers. Muskets sounded as door locks were blasted open, the first screams were coming from the city's women and some, not wanting to be trapped in their houses, tried to run higher up the hill. Hakeswill watched one caught. Her earrings were ripped from her and blood sprayed on her dress as that, too, was torn from her and she was naked, spinning between the soldiers who pushed her, laughed at her, and then leaped on her. Hakeswill skirted the group. It was not his business, and he guessed that the woman who had escaped would lead him to the cathedral. He followed.

Captain Robert Knowles, elated and tired, leaned briefly on the castle gateway. Hooves echoed in the streets. Philippon, the French General, with a handful of mounted men had ridden away, escaping, down to the bridge that would take them to refuge in the San Cristobal Fort. They had lost the huge fortress and, as they rode, they heard the dark business begin behind them. They whipped the horses, raked back with spurs, clattered on to the bridge and behind them, running, came the fleeing French infantry. Philippon's face was grief-stricken, not for the city, but for his failure. He had done all that could be done, far more than he had hoped, yet still he had lost. Wellington, damned Wellington, had won.

Knowles's men crowded into the gateway, jeering the departing enemy, and one of them seized a torch from its bracket. 'Permission to go, sir?' The flames lit the eager, hungry faces that watched Knowles. 'Go!'

They cheered, ran whooping into the streets and Knowles laughed for them, hefted his sabre, and followed. Teresa. He ran into the dark streets, the doors bolted, the ground-floor windows covered in intricate iron bars and he was soon lost, alone, in the tangle of streets. He stopped at a crossroads, listening to the screams up and down the hill, and then guessed that he should follow the street with the richest houses. A man pounded past him, uphill, and he saw the distinctive crossbelt of a French soldier. The man was armed, his long bayonet gleaming, but he did not stop, just kept running, his breath coming in rasping heaves. Knowles ran downhill, his boots echoing from the dark houses, and then the street stopped, opened into a big plaza and there, above him, was the cathedral.

There was panic in the plaza. The last French had gone, escaping north, but the people of Badajoz had not gone with them. Those that were not in their houses were here, struggling up the cathedral steps, crowding its doors, hoping for sanctuary. They ran past Knowles, barging into him, ignoring him, and he looked wildly around him. There were so many streets! And then he saw, dark behind the cathedral, a small alley with balconied houses and he ran, staring up at the buildings and then he stopped, turned, and he saw two trees, a recessed frontage, and he pounded on the closed door. 'Teresa! Teresa!'

Hakeswill had taken the right-hand street that led up from the small plaza and, sure enough, the women had run ahead of him to the Cathedral. He slowed to a walk,

chuckling to himself, and then he heard the shouts, very close, and his first instinct was that Sharpe had reached the house first.

'Teresa! Teresa!' That was not Sharpe's voice! An officer, by the sound of it, but not Sharpe, and Hakeswill flattened himself against the opposite wall and watched the dark shape pounding at the door. 'Teresa! It's me! Robert Knowles!'

A shutter opened on the first floor, seeping dim candlelight, and Hakeswill saw a woman's shape, slim and long-haired. It must be her! He felt the excitement inside him, shifting restlessly, uncoiling, and then she called down. 'Who's that?'

'Robert! Robert Knowles!'

'Robert?'

'Yes! Open up!'

'Where's Richard?'

'I don't know. I wasn't with him.' Knowles was standing back, staring up at the narrow balcony. The screams were coming nearer, the musket shots, and Teresa looked down the hill at the first flickerings of burning houses. 'Wait! I'll open up!' She banged the shutters close, latched them, and opposite, in deep shadow, Hakeswill grinned to himself. He could rush the door as she opened it, but the officer, he could see, was carrying a drawn sabre and he remembered that the bitch herself carried weapons. He looked up to the balcony. It was not high and, beneath it, the ground-floor window was barred with a lattice of black iron. He waited.

The front door opened, creaking on hinges, and he saw the girl silhouetted in the gap for the brief instant it took for Knowles to enter. The door shut and Hakeswill moved, surprisingly fast and soft for such a man, straight to the barred window that gave such easy

314

footholds, up till he could reach back to the balcony's base and then the strength was all in his arms. He paused briefly, his face suddenly twitching, but then the spasm passed and he pulled, the powerful arms making it easy, hand over hand till his feet caught on the balcony and he climbed over the rail. The shutter was wooden, gapped for the night air and he could see the empty room. He pushed at the shutter. It was locked, but he pushed again, increasing the pressure, and the wood creaked, bent, and then splintered inwards. He froze, but the noise of the city's sack was covering his own noise, and he moved again, into the room, and the bayonet whispered from the scabbard.

A cry: he turned, and there, in a wooden cot, was a baby. Sharpe's bastard. He cackled to himself, crossed the room and stared down. The child had cried in its sleep. He took off his hat and held the hat over the baby and talked to the hat. 'Do you see? There it is. Like I was once? Is that right, Mother? Like me.' The child moved and Hakeswill crooned. 'Sleepibubber, sleepibubber. You remember saying that, Mother, to your Obadiah?'

A footstep on the stairs, another, the creak of wood, and voices outside. He could hear the girl and the officer and he dropped the hat, on to the baby, and pulled the pistol from within his jacket. He was still, listening to her voice, the bayonet in his left hand, pistol in his right, and the baby cried again, in her sleep, and Teresa opened the door and spoke to it in gentle Spanish.

And stopped.

'Hello, missy!' The face twitched, yellow in the candlelight, the mouth grinning, black teeth showing on rotten gums, and the raw scar on the ungainly neck,

twitching with the head. Hakeswill laughed. 'Hello! Remember me?'

Teresa looked at her child and the bayonet was just above Antonia's cot and she gasped. Knowles pushed her aside, brought up the sabre, and the pistol flared, waking the child, and the bullet threw Knowles backward, backward through the door to fall with Hakeswill's cackle the last sound in his life.

Hakeswill kept the bayonet above the baby and pushed the pistol, still smoking, back into his jacket. The blue eyes turned to Teresa, her own gaze fixed on the bayonet, and he grinned at her. 'Didn't need him, missy, did we? Only takes two to do what we're going to do.' He cackled, a mad sound, but his eyes were level and his bayonet steady. 'Shut the door, missy.'

She swore at him, and he laughed. She was more beautiful than he remembered, the dark hair framing the fine face, and he bent down and put his right hand beneath the baby. It was crying. She moved towards it, but the bayonet flickered, and she stopped. Hakeswill picked the child up, bedclothes bundled, and he held it awkwardly in his right arm and his left was held out and bent back so that the needle-pointed bayonet was at the tiny, soft throat. 'I said shut the door.' His voice was low, very low, and he saw the fear on her face and his desire was heavy, so heavy.

She shut the door, slamming it on Knowles's dead feet, and Hakeswill nodded at it. 'Bolt it.' The bolt slammed home.

The hat was still in the cot and Hakeswill regretted it because he would like his mother, whose likeness was in the crown, to see this, but it could not be helped. He walked slowly towards Teresa, who backed away, back towards the bed where her rifle was laid,

and he grinned at her, twitched, and the triumph was in his voice. 'Just you and me, missy. Just you and Obadiah.'

CHAPTER 29

'Which way?'

'God knows!' Sharpe searched frantically for a main street. The central breach faced a tangle of alleys. He chose an opening at random and started running. 'This way!'

There were screams ahead, shots, and bodies lying in the alleyway. It was too dark to tell if the corpses were French or Spanish. The alley stank of blood, death, and the nightsoil thrown earlier from the upper windows, and the two men slipped in their haste. Light came from a cross-alley and Sharpe turned instinctively, still running, with a huge bloodied sword held like a lance.

A door opened ahead and spilt men into the alley, blocking it, and after them came wine barrels, huge tuns, that they hammered with their musket-butts until the staves burst and the wine cascaded on to the cobbles. The men dropped, put mouths to the gushing liquid, scooped at it, and Sharpe and Harper kicked them aside, pushed past, and came out into the small plaza. One house burned, throwing the light that had attracted them, and in the blaze they could see a medi-aeval depiction of hell. The people of Badajoz suffered the torments of red-jacketed devils. A naked woman wandered, sobbing and bloodied, in the plaza's centre. She was too hurt to feel any more, too abused to care,

and when new men, fresh from the breach, grabbed her and threw her down she made no protest, but sobbed on, and all around it was the same. Some women struggled, some had died, others had watched their children die, and around them the victors capered, half dressed, half drunk, lit by the fire and festooned with their loot.

Some of the devils fought, squabbling over women or wine, and Sharpe saw two Portuguese soldiers bayonet a British Sergeant, seize the woman beneath him, and drag her into a house. Her child, screaming hysterically, toddled after, but the door was slammed and the child left. Harper's face showed a terrible fury. He kicked the door, bursting it open, and plunged into the house. A shot was fired, splintering the lintel, and then the Portuguese came out, one after the other, thrown with a bone-crunching force and the Irishman picked up the child, handed it in, and shut the door as best he could. He shrugged at Sharpe. 'Others will get her.'

Which way? Two roads led uphill, the larger to the left, and Sharpe took it, pushing through the riot, the scenes from hell. Once, inexplicably, the pavement seemed to be running with silver coins that no one touched. One by one the doors were shot open, the houses ripped apart, a whole city at an army's mercy, and the army had little. A few men showed decency, protecting a woman or a family, but the decent men were too often shot down. Officers who tried to stop the carnage were shot, discipline was dead, the mob ruled Badajoz.

Screams deafened the two men, and they were thrown back on to a wall by a horde of women, stark naked, who, slobbering and spitting, had erupted from an unbarred door. A nun screamed at them from the

doorway, but more women came from inside and Sharpe knew a madhouse was emptying itself into the streets. There was no point in locking up the mad in Badajoz this night and there were whoops from behind and cheers as the soldiers charged up and into the lunatics. One pulled at the nun, while another leaped on to a huge, naked woman's back, gripped her wild, grey hair as reins, and all the soldiers tried to ride a lunatic.

'There, sir!' Harper pointed. Above them and ahead was the cathedral tower, its square, crenellated outline obvious in the sky, and from its arched openings the bells jangled a cacophony because drunken men were dangling on the ropes, signalling a victory.

They stopped at the street's end, in front of the cathedral, and to their left was a great plaza, the rape beneath its trees lit by a huge fire, and to their right a dark alley. Sharpe started towards it, but his arm was pulled, and he turned to see a girl, short and weeping, clinging to his sleeve. She had been roused from a house, chased, and her pursuers came after as she held on to the tall man whose face had looked untouched by the madness. '*Señor! Señor!*'

Her tormentors, in the white facings of the 43rd, reached for the girl and Sharpe swept the sword at them, cutting one man's arm, and he watched their bayonets drop for the attack and the girl was hampering him. He swung again, being forced back by British bayonets, but then Harper came between him and his attackers, the seven-barrelled gun whirled as a club, and they went back.

'This way!' Sharpe shouted and, with the girl still clinging to him, he pushed into the alley. Harper came behind, threatening the men of the 43rd with the giant gun until they gave up and went for easier spoils, and

then the Sergeant turned after Sharpe to find the alley was a dead end. Sharpe swore.

Harper seized the girl, who shrank away, but his touch was gentle and his voice urgent. '*Donde esta la Casa Moreno?*' It was the limit of his Spanish, and the girl shook her head. He tried again, letting his voice reassure her. 'Listen, Miss. *Casa Moreno. Comprendo? Donde esta la Casa Moreno?*'

She spoke in fast, excited Spanish, and pointed to the cathedral. Sharpe swore again in exasperation. 'She doesn't know. We'll go back.' He started forward, but Harper put out a hand.

'No, look!' There were steps leading to a side-door and the Irishman pushed Sharpe towards it. 'She means through the cathedral. It's a short cut!'

The girl stumbled on her dress, but Harper caught her and she clung to his hand as he pushed open the huge, studded door. Sharpe heard the Irishman draw in a breath.

The cathedral had been a refuge, a sanctuary, but no longer. Troops had invaded it, had chased the women, caught them, and now, under the myriad votive candles, the women were being raped. A nun, her habit ripped apart, was spreadeagled on the high altar while an Irishman of the 88th, down from the castle assault, tried vainly to climb up to her. He was too drunk. The girl gasped, began to scream, but Harper held her firm. '*Casa Moreno? Si?*'

She nodded, too appalled to speak, and led them across the great floor of the transept, between the altar and the transcoro, and round the huge chandelier that had been cut from its moorings and had crashed down on to the flagstones, crushing a Corporal from the 7th who still twitched under its weight. Dead lay on the floor while the wounded, sobbing in their misery, crawled

towards the obscuring shadows of the nave. Be with us now and in the hour of our need.

A priest, who had tried to stop the soldiers, lay by the north door and Sharpe and Harper stepped over the body, into the great plaza, and the girl pointed again, to her right, and they ran until she pulled Harper right again, into a dark alleyway seething with troops who beat at shut doors and, in their frustration, fired shots at upper, barred windows. Harper protected the girl, held her close, as they pushed through the men, Sharpe's sword their passport, and then the girl shouted at them, pointed, and Sharpe saw the dark shapes of two trees and knew he had arrived.

There were cheers from the doorway, a creaking, a great crash, and a mass of men in front of them melted away as they streamed into Moreno's courtyard. Barrels waited for them, thick barrels, full barrels, and the men fell on the wine, forgetting everything else, and in his counting house, praying next to his wife who had returned home at midnight, Rafael Moreno prayed and hoped he had provided enough wine for the soldiers and thick enough bolts for his counting house door.

Hakeswill cursed. He heard the commotion below, the crashing of the great doors, and he spat at Teresa. 'Hurry!'

A bullet splintered the shutter and buried itself in the ceiling and he turned, fearing Sharpe, but it was only a stray shot from the street. The baby was awkward in his arm, but it was his best threat and he did not want to kill it yet. The bayonet was still at Antonia's throat, her crying reduced to heaving, breathless sobs, and Hakeswill twitched the blade, ground his teeth as the twitching caught him, and bellowed again. 'Hurry!'

She was still dressed, damn her, and he wanted this business done! Two shoes off, that was all, and he

twitched the bayonet again, drawing a trickle of blood, and he saw her arms go up to the fastening of her dress. 'That's right, missy, don't want baby to die, do we?' He cackled, and the cackling became a racking cough, and Teresa watched the blade at her child's throat. She dared not attack him, dared not, and then the coughing stopped and the eyes opened again. Get on with it, missy. We've got time to make up, remember?'

Teresa slowly undid the knot at her throat, pretending to fumble with the material, and she saw the excitement in his face and then he began to swallow rapidly so that his Adam's apple pulled at the scar's tip. 'Hurry, missy, hurry!' Hakeswill could feel the excitement. She had humiliated him, this bitch, and now it was her turn. She would die, and so would her bastard, but he would have his enjoyment first and he began to work out in his head the problem of holding the baby while he took her, and then he knew she was taking her time. 'I'll slit its throat, missy, then yours. But if you want this little bastard to live, you'd better take them clothes off, and fast!'

The door bulged under Harper's boot, the crash spinning Hakeswill round, and then the bolt sheared, the door shook on its hinges, and Hakeswill held the bayonet vertically above Antonia's throat. 'Stop!'

Teresa had reached for the rifle. She froze. Harper was through the door and his momentum drove him on to the cot and then he, too, was utterly motionless as he sprawled, on all fours, and stared at the seventeen-inch bayonet. Sharpe, the girl behind him, stopped in the doorway and his sword, which had been reaching towards Hakeswill, was suspended in mid lunge so that its blood-thickened tip quivered in the room's centre.

Hakeswill laughed. 'Bit late, aren't you, Sharpy. They called you that, didn't they, Sharpy? Or Dick. Lucky

Sharpe. I remember. Clever little Sharpy, but it didn't stop you being flogged, did it?'

Sharpe looked to Harper, Teresa, then back to Hakeswill. He gestured slowly at Knowles's body. 'Did you do this?'

Hakeswill cackled and his shoulders heaved. 'Clever little bastard, aren't you, Sharpy? Of course I bloody did it. The little bastard came to protect your lady.' He sneered at Teresa. 'My lady, now.' Her dress was open at the neck and Hakeswill could see a slim gold cross against her brown skin. He wanted her, he wanted that skin beneath his hands, and he would have her! And kill her! And Sharpe could watch, because none of them would dare touch him while he still threatened the baby.

The girl behind Sharpe moaned and Hakeswill's head twitched towards the door. 'You got a whore there, Sharpy? You have! Bring her in!' The girl stepped over Knowles's body and into the room. She moved slowly, terrified of the yellow-skinned, belly-paunched man who held the heaving, sob-racked baby. She went to stand by Harper, her foot kicking Hakeswill's shako that had fallen from the upset cot. The hat rolled to a stop, upended, by Harper's hand. Hakeswill watched her. 'Very nice. Pretty little missy.' He cackled. 'You like the Irishman, do you, dearie?' She was shaking at the sight of him, and Hakeswill laughed. 'He's a pig. They all are, the bloody Irish, dirty great pigs. You're better off with me, missy.' The blue eyes went back to Sharpe. 'Shut the door, Sharpy. Gentle now.'

Sharpe shut the door, careful not to alarm the twitching man who held his baby. He could not see Antonia's face, just the great saw-backed bayonet that was above the bundle of bed-clothes. Hakeswill laughed at him. 'Very good. You can watch now, Sharpy.' He looked at

Harper, frozen grotesquely where he had tripped. 'And you, pig. You can watch. Stand up.'

Hakeswill was not sure how he would do this, but he would work something out because he knew that, as long as the child was in his power, then all these people were in it, too. He liked the new girl, Harper's girl by the look of it, and he could take her with him, out into the city, but he would have to kill Sharpe and Harper first because they knew he had killed Knowles. He shook his head. He would kill them because he hated them! He laughed, then saw that Harper had not moved. 'I told you to stand up, you Irish bastard! Stand!'

Harper stood up, his heart beating at the risk, and in his hands he held the shako. He had seen the picture in the crown and he had no real idea who it was, but he stood up, one hand holding the hat, the other reaching inside it. He saw Hakeswill's face show alarm. The bayonet quivered. 'Give it to me.' The voice had become whining. 'Give it to me!'

'Put the baby down.'

No one else moved. Teresa did not understand, nor did Sharpe, and Harper had only the vaguest idea; a hunch, a straw that was the only thing to clutch in this whirling madness. Hakeswill shook, his face jerking spasmodically. 'Give it to me!' He was sobbing. 'My Mammy! My Mammy! Give her to me!'

The Ulster voice was soft, growling deep from the massive chest. 'I have my nails on her eyes, Hakeswill, soft eyes, soft eyes, and I will claw them out, Hakeswill, claw them out, and your Mammy will scream.'

'No! No! No!' Hakeswill was swaying, crying, cringing. The baby was crying with him. The yellow face looked at Harper, the voice was pleading. 'Don't do it. Don't do it. Not to my Mammy.'

'I will, so I will, and I will, unless you put the baby

down, you put the baby down.' He spoke in a rhythm, as to a child, and Hakeswill swayed with the rhythm. The head went into violent twitches and, suddenly, the fear was gone and he looked at Harper.

'You think I'm a fool?'

'Mother's hurting.'

'No!' The madness was back, instantly, and Sharpe watched, appalled, as the great shambling man retreated into the insanity that had always seemed close. He was crouching now, knees below the baby, and rocking himself as he wept, though the bayonet was still above the child and Sharpe still dared not move.

'Your Mother's talking to me, Obadiah.' The Ulster voice turned Hakeswill's head back to Harper. He was holding the hat by his ear. 'She wants you to put the baby down, put the baby down, she wants you to help her, help her, because she likes her eyes. They're nice eyes, Obadiah, Mother's eyes.'

The Sergeant was breathing in short, fast gasps, and he nodded his head. 'I will, I will. Give me my Mother!'

'She's coming to you, so she is, but put the baby down, down, down.' Harper took one gentle step towards the Sergeant and held the hat out, not far enough, and Hakeswill's face was the face of a child who will do anything not to be whipped. He nodded eagerly, the tears coursing down his cheeks.

'I'm putting baby down, Mother, putting baby down. Obadiah never wanted to hurt baby.' And the great blade came up from the throat, the hat was inched nearer, and then Hakeswill, still crying and twitching, put the baby on the bed's coverlet and turned, bullet fast, to snatch at the hat.

'You bastard!' Harper pulled the hat back and threw a huge punch. Teresa snatched the child to safety, at the head of the bed, and then turned, the rifle in her

326

hands and she was clawing at the flint. Sharpe lunged with the sword, but Hakeswill was going back from the punch and the blade missed. Hakeswill had fallen, still without the hat, and he reached for it again. The rifle fired, the range less than a yard, but he was still going for the hat and Harper kicked him, sending him backwards, and Sharpe's second blow missed again.

'Stop him!' Harper threw the hat behind him and grabbed at Hakeswill. Teresa, not believing that she could have missed with the rifle bullet, swung the empty gun at the Sergeant and the barrel, scything through the air, knocked Harper's arm so that his snatch missed and all he could touch was Hakeswill's haversack. He gripped it, pulled at it, and Hakeswill bellowed at them, swung his own fist, pulled away so that the haversack straps broke and it was left in Harper's hand. Hakeswill looked for the hat. It was gone, beyond Sharpe and his sword, and Hakeswill gave a long, low moan because he had only found his Mother a few days before, and now she was gone. His Mother, the only person who had loved him, who had sent her brother to rescue him from the scaffold, and now he had lost her. He moaned again, slashing with the bayonet, and then jumped for the shattered window, splintered the remains of the shutter, and threw a leg over the balcony. Three people reached for him, but he swung the bayonet, raised his other leg, and jumped.

'Stop!' Harper's bellow was not at Hakeswill, but at Sharpe and Teresa who were blocking him. He pushed them aside, unslung the seven-barrelled gun that he had not fired in the breach, and put it to his shoulder. Hakeswill was sprawling in the roadway, scrambling to his feet, and it was a shot Harper could not miss. He felt his lips curl into a smile, he pulled the trigger, the gun smacked into his shoulder like a mule's kick, and

the window was blotted by smoke. 'Got the bastard!'

The cackle came from the road, the jeering cackle, and Harper fanned at the smoke, leaned from the balcony, and there, in the shadows, the lumpen figure was moving away, hatless and gross, the footsteps lost in the city's screaming. He was alive. Harper shook his head. 'You can't kill that bastard!'

'That's what he always says.' Sharpe dropped the sword, turned away, and Teresa was smiling at him, offering him the bundle, and he began crying, he did not know why, and he took his daughter into his arms and held her, kissed her, tasting the blood on her throat. She was his. A baby, a daughter, Antonia; crying, alive, and his.

EPILOGUE

They were married the next day by a priest who shook
with fear because the city was still being sacked and
there were flames over the rooftops and screams in the
streets. Sharpe's men, those who had come to the
house, tidied up the courtyard and threw out the
drunks. It seemed a strange place to be getting married.
Clayton, Peters and Gutteridge guarded the main gate
with loaded muskets, acrid smoke drifted into the court,
and Sharpe did not understand a word of the ceremony.
Harper and Hogan, their faces, in Sharpe's opinion,
stupidly happy, looked on. The Sergeant had whooped
with joy when Sharpe told him that he and Teresa would
marry; Harper had thumped Sharpe's back as if they
were the same rank, and claimed that he and Isabella
were very happy for them.

'Isabella?'

'The wee girl, sir.'

'She's still here?' Sharpe's back felt as if it had been
struck by a French four-pounder.

Harper blushed. 'I think she may want to stay on with
me, for a wee bit, you understand. That's if you don't
mind, sir.'

'Mind? Why should I mind? But how the hell do
you know? You don't speak Spanish, she doesn't speak
English.'

'A man can tell these things.' Harper said the words

mysteriously, as if Sharpe would not understand. Then he smiled. 'But I'm glad you're doing the right thing, sir, so I am.'

Sharpe had laughed. 'Who the hell are you to tell me what the right thing is?'

Harper shrugged. 'I'm the true faith, so I am. You'll have to bring the wee one up a Catholic.'

'I don't intend to bring the wee one up.'

'Aye, that's true. It's woman's work, sure enough.'

'I don't mean that.' He meant that Teresa would not stay with the army, nor he go to the hills, and so he would still be away from his child and his wife. Not for a while, but the time would come when she would leave, and he wondered if he was marrying only to give Antonia a name, her legitimacy, something he had never had himself. He was embarrassed by the ceremony, if a frightened priest standing among grinning soldiers constituted a ceremony, yet he felt a shy joy, was touched by pride because Teresa was beside him, and he supposed he loved her. Jane Gibbons was many miles and more impossibilities away. He listened to the words, felt awkward, and watched the happiness on Teresa's aunt's face.

Man and wife, father of a child, Captain of a company, and Sharpe looked up, past the trees, into the wide sky where the kestrels hung, and then Teresa plucked his elbow, spoke something in Spanish and he thought he knew what she had said. He looked down at her, at the slim beauty, the dark, strong eyes, and he felt a terrible fool because Harper was grinning, just as Hogan and the Company were grinning, and the girl, Isabella, was crying for happiness. Sharpe smiled at his wife. 'I love you.' He kissed her, remembering that first kiss, beneath the lances, and it had led here. He smiled

at the thought, because he was glad, and Teresa, happy that he was smiling, clutched his arm.

'I can kiss the bride, Richard?' Hogan beamed at them both, clasped Teresa, and planted a huge kiss on her that made Sharpe's men cheer. The aunt clapped them, spoke in quick-fire Spanish at Sharpe, and then brushed at the remains of dirt and blood on his uniform. Then Lieutenant Price insisted on kissing the bride, and the bride insisted on kissing Patrick Harper, and Sharpe tried to hide his happiness because he believed that to show an emotion, any emotion, was to expose a weakness.

'Here.' Hogan held up a cup of wine. 'With the compliments of the bride's uncle. Your health, Richard.'

'It's a funny way to get married.'

'They're all funny ways, whichever way you do it.' Hogan beckoned to the servant who was holding Antonia, made the girl hold the baby up and he trickled red wine into its mouth. 'There, my love. It's not every wee girl who gets to go to her parents' wedding.'

At least the child was well. The illness, whatever it was, had gone and the doctors, thanking God because they had done nothing, said it was a malady that went with growing. They had shrugged, pocketed their fee, and wondered why God spared the bastards.

They left the city that afternoon, an armed group that could defend itself against the violence that still ravaged Badajoz. The dead lay on the streets. They climbed out through the Santa Maria breach and the ditch was still full, thick with bodies, so thick that heat came from the hundreds and hundreds of dead. Some men searched in the carnage, looking for brothers, sons, or friends. Others stood at the ditch's edge and wept for an army, as Wellington had wept when he

stood on the glacis, and the great heap steamed in the April chill. Teresa, seeing the breaches for the first time, muttered in Spanish and Sharpe saw her eyes go up to the walls, to the silent guns, and he knew she was imagining their power.

Colonel Windham was on the glacis, staring down to where his friend Collett had died, and he turned as Sharpe and his party climbed the ladders from the ditch. 'Sharpe?'

'Sir?'

Windham saluted him, strangely formal amongst so much death. 'You're a brave man, Sharpe.'

Sharpe was embarrassed. He shrugged. 'Thank you. And you, sir. I saw the attack.' He stopped, out of words, and then remembered the portrait. He took it from inside his jacket and handed over the wrinkled, stained picture of the Colonel's wife. 'I thought you'd like this, sir.'

Windham looked at it, turned it over, back again, and then looked at Sharpe. 'How on earth did you find it?'

'It was in the hat, sir, of a man called Obadiah Hakeswill, who stole it. He also stole my telescope.' The glass had been in Hakeswill's haversack, and was now in Sharpe's. He jerked a head towards Harper, standing with Isabella. 'Sergeant Harper, sir, did not steal a thing.'

Windham nodded. The breeze tugged at the tassel on his hat. 'You've given him back his Sergeantcy?' The Colonel smiled in resignation.

'Yes, sir. And I'll give him his rifle and green jacket next. If you have no objection.'

'No, Sharpe. The Company is yours.' Windham smiled briefly at Sharpe, perhaps remembering the con-

versations about humility, then looked at Harper.
'Sergeant!'

'Sir?' Harper stepped forward, stood to attention.

'I owe you an apology.' Windham was obviously
embarrassed deeply by the need to speak so to a
Sergeant.

'No apology needed, sir!' Harper's face was straight,
his bearing formal. 'A striped back is very attractive to
the ladies, sir.'

'Blood and hounds!' Windham was relieved to be off
the hook. He nodded at Sharpe. 'Carry on, Captain
Sharpe.'

They walked back to the camp, leaving the stench of
the dead behind them, and the sounds of the city faded
as they walked. They passed the trenches and the bat-
teries, and Sharpe saw where a gunner had planted
spring flowers on a parapet. The weather was turning,
warming to a dry summer, and he knew that the army
would be marching soon, north and east, going into
the heart of Spain.

Badajoz was done.

That night, two miles down the Seville road, a twitching
figure scrabbled down beneath a field marker, mutter-
ing to himself, knowing he could not be killed, and
pulled out the oilcloth bundle of stolen goods. Hakes-
will was deserting. He knew he could not go back. There
was a witness to the death of Knowles, the portrait had
been in the Sergeant's hat, and he understood that
only a firing squad awaited him. He sniffed the night
air and was not worried. He would go somewhere and
find something, as he always did, and this was not the
first night that he had been utterly alone, homeless, and
his dark shape loped into the night, seeking mischief.

A man went into a breach for one thing only, pride, and Sharpe had been there. He had stood at the top of a breach, fear defeated, and gone down into a horror that tarnished victory as blood tarnished a sword. He lay awake and thought of streets running with wine, silver, madness and blood.

He had hoped for so much; for a Captaincy, for revenge on a clerk, for a company, for a woman he loved and a child he had never seen, and the hopes had been won at Badajoz. He lay in Leroy's tent, its owner in hospital with a terrible wound, the night was quiet, dark, silent for the first time in weeks, and a great victory had been won. The gates of Spain had been burst open. He looked at his woman, beautiful in the firelight that seeped through the canvas, and he marvelled that he was married. Then he looked at the child, dark hair and snub nosed, that slept between them and the love welled up, incomprehensible, uncontrollable. He kissed his daughter, Antonia, and in the flamelight she seemed terribly small and vulnerable. Yet she was alive, and his, his only relative by blood. She was his, to be protected as he must protect all those other souls who liked him, were proud of him, and proud to be in his ranks – Sharpe's Company.

HISTORICAL NOTE

On the morning of 7 April 1812, Philippon and the survivors of the city garrison surrendered in the Fort of San Cristobal, thus sealing one of the British Army's most famous victories; the storming of Badajoz.

The next day, around mid-day, Wellington ordered a gallows erected in the plaza by the Cathedral and, though there is no evidence that the gallows were used, the threat was sufficient to bring order to the city's streets. Thus ended one of the British Army's most notorious episodes; the sack of Badajoz.

I have tried, in this story, to offer some reasons why the sack was so pitiless. The rules of war condoned it, and the instincts of soldiers who had survived such a horrific fight demanded it. Those soldiers also suspected, with some justification, that the inhabitants of Badajoz were pro-French. None of this, perhaps, excuses their behaviour; many of the soldiers who ransacked the city had taken no part in the assault, but they were reason enough for the ordinary soldier on that climactic April night. Some historians suggest, diffidently, that Wellington allowed the sack, and let it continue beyond the first day, as a warning to other towns that harboured French garrisons. If true the warning did not work, as the British were to discover one year later at San Sebastian. The fight there was just as hard, and the sack afterwards just as horrific.

The sack of Badajoz was not without one famous love story. A Lieutenant of the 95th Rifles, Harry Smith, met and married a fourteen-year-old Spanish girl, Juana Maria de los Dolores de Leon, who was fleeing from the horror. She was not completely unscathed, her earrings had been torn bloodily from her lobes, but Lieutenant Smith found and protected her. Years later, after her husband had been knighted, a town was named after her in South Africa that was itself to see a famous siege; Ladysmith.

I have tried to be faithful to the events of the campaign. Thus, for instance, the guns sunk into the wall at Ciudad Rodrigo existed, and the story of the Nottinghamshire Battalion charging across the planks is true. Each battle described in the story happened, though the attack on the dam was not made at battalion strength, nor was it made as early in the siege. It happened on 2 April, under the command of Lieutenant Stanway of the Engineers who, like the unfortunate Fitchett, failed to take enough powder and so the explosion miscarried.

On the morning of 7 April, beneath the breaches, there was found a mass of bodies, still warm, and observers guessed their number at twelve or thirteen hundred dead. Wellington wept at the sight. Many historians have blamed him for attacking too soon, though, given the pressures on him, and his lack of a proper Engineering train, his decision is difficult to criticize. Hindsight is a great General. Badajoz was won by sheer bravery, bravery like that of Lieutenant Colonel Ridge of the 5th Fusiliers whose exploits I borrowed and gave to Captain Robert Knowles. Ridge died, shot at the end of the fight, and Napier gave him a famous epitaph: 'And no man died that night with greater

glory, yet many died, and there was much glory.'

The novel does not do justice to the Fifth Division whose attack on the San Vincente bastion, made late, was most responsible for the city's fall. There was no Forlorn Hope on the third, the central breach, and accounts of the night differ as to whether any man even reached that breach. The Light Division claimed that some of their dead were found on its slopes, but most survivors disagree, and so, with a novelist's freedom, I took the breach for Sharpe. There was one final attack on the breaches, which succeeded, but Wellington did not order it until he was certain that the Fifth Division were in the defenders' rear. Purists will also be offended that Sharpe attacked Ciudad Rodrigo with the Third Division, and Badajoz with the Fourth, but it is the fate of fictional soldiers to be always where the fight is thickest even when that means a cavalier disregard for the make-up of divisions. Some battalions were involved in both assaults, notably those of the Third and Light Divisions, so my sin is not too great.

I have tried to be exact, with the above exceptions, to the real events. The letters and diaries of the campaign are, as ever, a trove of information. Thus, for instance, the details in the book of the daily weather conditions are taken from the diaries and I feel a constant debt to those long-dead soldiers whose memories I plunder. One myth should be put to rest. Badajoz was not assaulted on Easter Sunday. 6 April was the second Monday after Easter in 1812, and no amount of imagination can change that fact.

The castle walls at Badajoz are unchanged, the only addition to the scenery is a road that passes at the foot of the castle hill. The breaches in the two bastions have been repaired and the giant ditch is now a municipal

garden. The glacis is entirely gone. The approaches to the breaches, like the San Miguel Hill, have been built over. The approach to the Trinidad is hidden by non-descript buildings, and that to the Santa Maria by a modern and remarkably ugly bull-ring. The area of the central breach is still a passage through the walls, the defences between the two bastions being largely destroyed, but it is possible to climb to the bastions' parapets and into the embrasures, and marvel at the courage of men who would attack such a place. Ciudad Rodrigo's defences are better preserved; the breach repairs are visible above the glacis, and the marks of British cannon balls are still chipped into the church tower. The Fort of San Cristobal, across the river from Badajoz, is in almost perfect repair. The South Essex could march in tomorrow and have it set up for defence within an hour. Best preserved of all are the defences of Elvas, just across the border, and all are worth visiting.

The memorial plaques in the Trinidad bastion (where the Madrid road enters Badajoz) recall the assault and sack of the city, but not that of 6 April 1812. They remember 14 August 1936, and some inhabitants still remember the massacre which followed the assault by Franco's troops. History has a sad way of repeating itself in Badajoz. It is not a pretty city; some people have described it as gloomy, as if the ghosts of too many battles stalk the streets, but I did not find it so. As in other places in Portugal and Spain, I met with much kindness and courtesy, and was given every help with my researches.

The last words in this book can be left with a man who became accustomed to having the last word: Wellington. Writing to the War Minister, and talking of his 5000 casualties, he said: 'The capture of Badajoz affords

as strong an instance of the gallantry of our troops as has ever been displayed. But I greatly hope that I shall never again be the instrument of putting them to such a test.'

AZINCOURT

THE LAST KINGDOM
THE PALE HORSEMAN
THE LORDS OF THE NORTH
SWORD SONG

The GRAIL QUEST Series
HARLEQUIN
VAGABOND
HERETIC

STONEHENGE: A NOVEL OF 2000 BC

The STARBUCK Chronicles
REBEL
COPPERHEAD
BATTLE FLAG
THE BLOODY GROUND

GALLOWS THIEF

By Bernard Cornwell and Susannah Kells
A CROWNING MERCY
FALLEN ANGELS

The WARLORD Chronicles
THE WINTER KING
THE ENEMY OF GOD
EXCALIBUR

Sharpe's Eagle

Bernard Cornwell

'Sharpe asked three things of his men. That they fought as he did with a ruthless professionalism. That they stole only from the enemy and the dead unless they were starving. And they never got drunk without his permission.'

Richard Sharpe is having a difficult war. Excluded from promotion because he is always on the battlefield, up against pompous, incompetent colonels, and worst, suddenly finding himself at the head of an inexperienced company who use all twenty five drill-book approved movements to load and fire their muskets.

A soldier like Sharpe can't be kept down though and his promotion to Captain, when it comes, makes a dangerous enemy in the upper ranks. As Sharpe approaches bloody battle in Talavera, he knows he is fighting for his own honour and that of his men.

A Sharpe Adventure

ISBN: 978 0 00 727624 0

Sharpe's Gold

Bernard Cornwell

'The stench was thick by the hermitage and buzzing with flies, and Sharpe paused by the steps. There was almost a reluctance to go inside, not just because of the bodies but because of what the hermitage might not contain. The gold.'

Fresh from battle and covered in glory, Sharpe and his regiment are called north by Wellington. On arrival though Sharpe is sent on a desperate mission – to go behind enemy lines and secure the gold so vital to the success of the war. Success means riches – not just for the army, but for Sharpe and his men.

The enemy he faces strikes terror in to the hearts of all around – a renegade guerrilla band whose leader has a particular loathing for Sharpe who has stolen his woman.

A Sharpe Adventure

ISBN: 978 0 00 727626 4

Sharpe's Sword

Bernard Cornwell

'This was his world now, this small saddle of land between the escarpment and the knoll, a tiny piece of grassland that was warm in the sun and pretty with flowers. There he would meet his enemy, and there he would win. Sharpe was going to war.'

Richard Sharpe is about to face his most violent enemy yet. Even though he is the veteran of many battles, Colonel Leroux is a man of such inventive cruelty, Sharpe must watch his back. Sent away from the battle fields where he thrives, Sharpe is charged with the safeguarding of Britain's skilful and valued spy, El Mirador.

Sharpe must face the minefield of aristocratic Spanish society with its politics and intrigues. His guide is La Marquesa, a lady of a certain reputation. Beset by secrets, and with no-one to trust, how will Sharpe survive this dangerous assignment?

A Sharpe Adventure

ISBN: 978 0 00 727627 1

Sharpe's Enemy

Bernard Cornwell

'Sharpe had once been told: 'A Soldier is a man who fights for people who cannot fight for themselves.' Behind Sharpe, in the Gateway of God, were women who could not fight for themselves. Sharpe would go back.'

The unstoppable Sharpe has been commissioned as a Major by order of King George, but with promotion comes deadly responsibility. Heading the newly formed Rocket Troop has its own challenges – the rockets are neither safe nor accurate. On top of this Sharpe must rescue a group of vulnerable innocents – women being held for the pleasure of a band of British deserters.

Their leader is Sharpe's bitter enemy, the malevolent Sergeant Hakeswill. Sharpe has *very* serious reasons for wanting Hakeswill to die a painful death, but he must put them aside and concentrate – the lives of thousands of Allied soldiers depend on it.

A Sharpe Adventure

ISBN: 978 0 00 727625 7

Sharpe's Honour

Bernard Cornwell

'Reluctantly, pain in his eyes, Pakenham looked at Sharpe. "Is there anything else you have to say?"
Sharpe looked back defiantly. "Permission to die in my Rifleman's jacket sir."
"Denied." Pakenham looked as if he wanted to add that Sharpe had disgraced his uniform, but the words would not come. "These proceedings are over." He stood, and Sharpe was led from the courtroom, his hands tied, condemned to the gallows.'

Burdened under the weight of grief and guilt for actions in the past, Sharpe must lead his men in to battle once more. Victory depends on the fragile relationship between England and Spain being maintained at all costs.

But this is war, and the French Intelligence officer, Pierre Ducos in an unholy alliance with the Spanish inquisitor, and his brother, the sinister Slaughterman, is determined to win for France by any method, and central to his plan is the death of Richard Sharpe. When the manipulative spy La Marquesa enters the fray, violence meets deadly intrigue and Sharpe finds himself a fugitive, hunted by foe and ally alike.

A Sharpe Adventure

ISBN: 978 0 00 729859 4

Sharpe's Regiment

Bernard Cornwell

'Going home? England? He did not want to go, but if the alternative was to watch a Battalion die that had earned its right to tramp down the roads of France, then he would go through hell itself. For his regiment and for its Colours that had flown through the cannon smoke of half a continent, he would go to England so that he could march into France. He would go home.'

Sharpe's men are at risk of being wiped out – not by the enemy but by bureaucrats in Whitehall. There is rumour of fresh recruits being collected in England and Sharpe must go home to find them.

Far from finding troops of brave and eager soldiers, Sharpe uncovers a nest of traitors, each determined in his way to destroy Sharpe's regiment. Not even the influence of the Prince Regent can protect Sharpe as he undertakes the most desperate gamble of his career.

A Sharpe Adventure

ISBN: 978 0 00 729865 X

Sharpe's Revenge

Bernard Cornwell

'Sharpe lost all sense of time. The fear was gone, as it always seemed to vanish once danger was present. Nairne's men, thinned out and bloodied, pushed forward into gun fire. Smoke thickened. Knots of men lay in blood where canister had struck. The wounded called for help, or vomited, or cried, or just lay softly to let death come.'

1814. There are rumours that Napoleon is dead, or has run away, but Sharpe has one last battle to fight before he can lay down his sword – it is the battle for Toulouse. Little does he know it will be one of the bloodiest conflicts of the war.

The battle is not the end of Sharpe's challenges – he is stabbed in the back by a whispering campaign branding him a thief and a liar. Sharpe must discover who has framed him, and conduct a revenge as ingenious as it is devastating.

A Sharpe Adventure

ISBN: 978 0 00 729853 2